W9-ASV-765

"EMMELINE
IS A BRILLIANT SUCCESS . . .
AUDACIOUS AND ENTHRALLING!"
—*Cosmopolitan* Magazine

"A DARK BOOK, POWERFUL, ENERGETIC AND SUSPENSEFUL."
—*Washington Post*

"MASTERFUL . . . A POIGNANT, TRAGIC LOVE STORY."
—*St. Louis Post Dispatch*

"A STUNNING, HAUNTING BOOK . . . ROSSNER HAS NEVER BEEN BETTER."
—*Library Journal*

"DEEPLY MOVING . . . HAUNTING . . . ROSSNER WRITES ALMOST AS IF SHE IS FATE."
—*Publishers Weekly*

"AUDACIOUSLY STUNNING . . . A GRAVE TALE OF LINGERING IMPACT."
—*Kirkus Reviews*

Books by Judith Rossner

Attachments
Emmeline
Looking for Mr. Goodbar

Published by POCKET BOOKS

Emmeline

Judith Rossner

PUBLISHED BY POCKET BOOKS NEW YORK

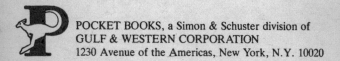

POCKET BOOKS, a Simon & Schuster division of
GULF & WESTERN CORPORATION
1230 Avenue of the Americas, New York, N.Y. 10020

Copyright © 1980 by Judith Rossner

Published by arrangement with Simon and Schuster
Library of Congress Catalog Card Number: 80-15553

All rights reserved, including the right to reproduce
this book or portions thereof in any form whatsoever.
For information address Simon and Schuster, 1230
Avenue of the Americas, New York, N.Y. 10020

ISBN: 0-671-81681-0

First Pocket Books printing September, 1981

10 9 8 7 6 5 4 3 2 1

POCKET and colophon are trademarks of Simon & Schuster.

Printed in the U.S.A.

Nettie Mitchell told me about Emmeline. Nettie is ninety-four years old and still lives in Fayette. She knew Emmeline when she herself was a child and Emmeline was an old woman.

FOR
MORDECAI PERSKY

Part One

THIS is the story of Emmeline Mosher, who, before her fourteenth birthday, was sent from her home on a farm in Maine to support her family by working in a cotton mill in Massachusetts. The year was 1839.

Fayette, where Emmeline lived, was then known for its fine dairy cattle, but Emmeline's parents had a small farm on a rocky hillside, and even in good times they had not prospered. This was a period in which business conditions were poor throughout Maine, and for three years Emmeline's father had been unable to find work to supplement the small yield from the farm. Then, the past season, a killing frost had come in June to destroy all their tender seedlings. Now it was only the third week of November, but from the look of their larder they might have been well into winter.

There were nine children, and they were hungry all the time. The three-year-old cried to nurse at his mother's breast when the one-and-a-half-year-old was in her arms, but Emmeline's mother didn't get enough food to provide milk for two children. In fact, since the death of her last baby, within hours of its birth, she seemed to have difficulty providing enough for one. Emmeline, the oldest child, would watch and think what a help it would be if only she could nurse them. At most tasks she and her mother worked together like

3

equals. Sarah Mosher was thirty-one years old; Emmeline was thirteen.

For some time now there had been a feeling among the older children and their parents that something would *have* to happen; there must be some change from the outside that would make it possible for them to go on. Sarah Mosher, always intensely devout, trusted that God in His own way and time would help them, but Henry Mosher had stopped going to church in recent weeks, saying that if God had no time to bother about him, then he had no time for God. When help finally came, it was difficult, at first, to find in it any sign of God's work.

Emmeline's aunt and uncle, Hannah and Abner Watkins, came to visit from their home in Lynn, Massachusetts, for the first time in many years. It was a painful visit for everyone. Not only were the Watkinses shocked at how little food there was, and at how badly matters were going in general, but Hannah, in particular, had a very critical air, her manner suggesting that if Henry Mosher's moral fiber had been stronger, there would not have been poor business conditions or late frosts in Maine. Emmeline's mother, still not recovered from five babies in four years, and the last born only to die within hours, seemed ashamed under her sister-in-law's scrutiny. And this, in turn, was an agony to Emmeline, who loved her mother perhaps even beyond a daughter's usual love, and never questioned her perfection.

Meals were the worst time, for they were trapped together around the long table that dominated the common room, staring at each other or at their plates, which always looked as though others had been there first and eaten their fill. Hannah talked constantly, her voice like the repeated banging of an unlatched door in a storm; just when you thought the storm had subsided, the banging began again.

When she was not expounding on the glories of Lynn, Massachusetts, of her home and her husband, Hannah talked a great deal about the city of Lowell, with its huge cotton mills and its benevolent system under which the millowners provided for the board and protection of their employees. It was because of this system that the mills had been able to attract such good help—fine, respectable girls, not unlike Emmeline— from the poverty-stricken farms of Maine and New Hampshire. It was in Lowell that Abner had earned the money to set up the shoemaking establishment he now operated in Lynn.

"There's girls in Lowell," Hannah said, "who've sent their brothers through school, or lifted the mortgage on their folks' farm—by theirselves. And they have a good time all the whilst they're doing it. Lowell's nothing like what you imagine."

Nobody had imagined anything about Lowell before Hannah began talking about it.

"There's hundreds of girls just like Emmeline," Hannah said. "Younger, some of 'em. Earning enough past room and board to send home two dollars a week."

A hush fell over the table, then. The children couldn't imagine that amount of money, and their parents hadn't seen it at one time in some years. For the first time Emmeline felt anxious in a way that seemed to be about herself, although she didn't yet know why.

"How does that sound, Emmeline?" Hannah asked.

Why had she been singled out?

"Now, Hannah," her father said in a low, troubled voice.

"Never mind, Henry," Hannah said. "You could lift your mortgage in a few years. And meanwhile you'd have food. Not that she'd have to stay so long, if she didn't come to like it."

It was then Emmeline understood for the first time that Hannah was trying to persuade her parents to send her to work in Lowell. She looked at her plate, waiting for her father to tell Hannah that it was out of the question, wishing for the hundredth time that the Watkinses had never come, expecting that her mother would remind Hannah of her tender age. (It was the first time she had ever felt young for her years.) She looked to her mother for reassurance; her mother started, then flushed.

They were thinking of doing it, then. Of sending her away from home. All life seemed to drain from her body, and she was filled with a feeling of dread so strong as to make it difficult to breathe, impossible to move or to speak.

"Just think how proud you'll be, Emmeline," Hannah said.

Emmeline looked at her father, who was toying with his food instead of eating it. On her mother's lap, William reached for the small piece of corn bread left on the plate the two shared. The other young ones were beginning to leave the table, but Andrew and Harriet, at eleven and ten old enough to have some idea of what was happening, waited to see if it was important. To Emmeline's right, at the head of the table, sat Luke and her father. Luke was pretending to look at his plate, but he was really watching her, his sorrowful gray eyes hidden under lowered lids. Luke was the closest to Emmeline in age, being just eleven months younger than she, and the closest in love and confidence as well.

Tears came to her own eyes for the first time, and she lowered her head so no one would see. Her throat ached with the effort to keep from crying.

Hannah was speaking of how much more interesting it was to work in a mill than to labor endlessly on a farm, though her father had told Emmeline that during her spinster years, Hannah had been just as certain that a farm in Fayette was the only decent place to live. It was when she was already thirty-four years old, and well "past the second mark," that Hannah had gone to

a church social in Livermore Falls and met Abner
Watkins. Abner was only twenty-eight, but he had been
away from Livermore for twelve years, having left his
home at the age of sixteen and gone to Lynn, where he
apprenticed himself to a master shoemaker. He had
stayed with this man for twelve years, but upon being
refused the hand of the youngest daughter of the family
had returned home, heartbroken. One week after he'd
met Hannah, they were married and on their way to a
new life, not in Lynn, but in Lowell. It was 1832, and
the great mills were in their heyday. Within days of
their arrival, Abner had secured a position in a mill
shop where leather parts and pieces were repaired, and
two years later he was overseer of that shop. In another
three years, he had saved enough to open his own shop
in Lynn. Now his wife championed Lynn and Lowell
and pitied those who were left in Fayette.

"Enough, Hannah," her father said. "I think we've
had 'bout enough for now."

"That's true," Hannah said. "She needs time to get
accustomed to the idea."

Had they decided, then? Emmeline was afraid to
look at her mother's face and find an answer sooner
than she could bear to. She set the plates in the
hot-water tub on the stove. There was no need to
scrape them anymore; there was never a crumb on any
of them. Her own plate, with the bits of food left when
she had become too upset to eat, was clean by the time
Rosanna handed it to her to put in the water.

Her father and the older boys went back to work in
the barn. Abner, a slight, uneasy man who was dwarfed
by his wife, trailed after them. Her mother sat down to
spin, and Hannah took up the toothed "cards" with
which they combed through the wool. Emmeline
brought the wool basket to the fire, meaning to pick it
over, but when Hannah sat down next to her, she
couldn't remain still. Getting her shawl from its hook,
she left the house before any of the younger children

would notice that she was going and want to come with
her.

It was the last week of November, a cold, gray day.
The light snow that had already fallen had left only an
icy frosting on the earth. Soon the real snows would
come. Emmeline had prayed that the Watkinses would
leave before snow prevented the coaches from coming
through. Now she couldn't pray for their departure
because she might be going with them.

She walked along the rocky ledge on which the house
was set, then down the slope to the road. Leaning
against a tree, she looked up at the house and its
surroundings, seeing them in a new way, full of an
intense, despairing love.

The house had been white when she was little, but
now the paint had worn off and the boards were gray
and shabby. There was a good barn, though it was
separate from the house, having been built by her
grandfather when that was the style. Around the house
was a ring of great old maples, ashes and hemlocks that
appeared to have been planted to frame it, the reality
being that the house had been set down in their midst.

At the highest point on the ledge stood the largest
maple, its roots writhing along the top of the earth to
reach more solid ground. Emmeline pictured herself
swinging with Luke from the long, heavy rope he had
thrown over the lowest branch. Sometimes the rope
swung so widely that they went out past the ledge, to
the other side of the road, and she screamed, clutching
him for what she thought was her life. She saw her
father and Luke attaching buckets to that maple and
the others, and herself going to inspect the partly filled
buckets, letting the sugar water touch her fingers so she
would have reason to lick them. If the buckets were
nearly full and it rained, everyone ran around collect-
ing them, emptying them into the big pot where the sap
would cook down to syrup. She saw Luke and herself
and the little ones, sitting in front of the fire on a rainy

day, wrapped in quilts while their clothing dried on the hearth. She saw them roasting dried corn until it burst; she saw them listening for raindrops on the roof from the attic, where all of them, except the two youngest, slept. She thought of the sudden precious moments of silence, when the younger children had gone to bed and Luke and her father were out, perhaps visiting with neighbors, and the fire ceased to crackle. As though in natural concert, she and her mother would set down their handwork and stare into the dying fire without speaking.

But this thought broke through the dam that had checked her feelings, and a terrible panic arose within her as, for the first time, she let herself feel the possibility of losing her mother. She turned away from the house and ran across the road to the pond.

It was the most beautiful pond in Fayette, with its thick fringe of trees broken only in two places. There was the path were they entered to bathe and swim in the summer, and to fish during much of the year. And then, on the far side, there was a larger opening where the sawmill stood close to the shore.

Not far from Emmeline was the huge rock on which they all left their clothes when they bathed, and on which she had spent endless hours with the younger children, pretending to have been shipwrecked—on Mica Island. It was a wondrous rock, a slab of granite perhaps five feet wide and three feet high, and about six feet at its longest point. The granite was filled with thousands of pebbles and chunks of quartz and millions of fragments of mica, many of which were still large enough to be pried from the granite and peeled away, layer by layer, until the last wispy film sat on the tip of a finger, ready to be blown into the wind.

She began walking the crusty edge of the pond, away from the house. The sky was darkening and the air was taking on the feel of snow. The pond was so still as to make it difficult to believe one might ever penetrate its

surface, impossible to think that there was life moving
under that surface even now. She shivered, and
wrapped her shawl more tightly around her. She knew
that she would be chilled to the bone before long, but
almost welcomed an outside misery that would match
what she felt inside.

She walked on, barely bothering to push aside the
briers and brambles that blocked her way and stuck in
the loose weave of her homespun. Near the mill, she
turned into the woods, just in case there were men
working. When she was well past the mill, she returned
to the banks of the pond, but stayed within the first ring
of trees wherever she could, so she wouldn't be seen,
although there was no one to see her. Certainly not at
this part of the pond, where there wasn't a single home.
She felt lost, although she knew that she was not. Her
fingers and toes grew numb with the cold. If she
stopped walking her body would begin to shake.

She had no sense of how much time had passed.
Suddenly she saw a picture of her parents, standing
over her frozen body, having searched the woods all
night to tell her they wouldn't let her go to Lowell. She
saw her mother's face after the death of the last infant,
who had lived so few hours that they hadn't even
named him; the exhaustion and the anguish had been
more than Emmeline, watching her, could bear.

She wanted to rest, but couldn't allow herself to do
so. She felt that if she stopped, when she stood up again
she would be in a strange place. Snow was falling
lightly; she didn't know when it had begun.

Finally she came to a part of the pond where she was
sure she'd never been before. Trees grew close together
clear to the bank, so that there was no natural path, and
she had to thread her way among them in the snow,
which was falling heavily now. At one point her foot
slipped into the pond, and the icy water immediately
found its way through her boot and stocking to her
skin.

If she got sick, she wouldn't be able to go to Lowell.

Perhaps she would even die, and then how would Hannah feel about her meddling? How would her parents feel? Her mother? No, that was too awful to think about. Again she saw her mother's face, this time after the death of the baby Samuel. Of the three deaths, Samuel's had been the worst, because he was already seven months old—more than an infant. A placid, sunny-faced baby who made them all smile when he smiled. He had been taken in the middle of the night without any warning at all, no one even suspecting that he was ill, so that her mother awakened in the morning to find him stiff in the bed between herself and her husband. Emmeline saw her family gathered around the grave in the woods on a spring day so beautiful that the younger children couldn't stay still through the brief ceremony, but kept darting off after butterflies and giggling at sounds they barely remembered from the year before. Hours later she'd returned to fetch her mother, who was asleep in the grass near the fresh mound of dirt.

"Not yet, Emmy," her mother had said when Emmeline tried to lead her away. "Part of me's still down there."

The sky was dark now, except for the dim light from the stars and the snow's reflection. Her entire body ached, but the mica rock wasn't far away. Past the rock, up on the ledge on the other side of the road, she could see a flickering light from the hearth fire in one window of the house. She began running and didn't stop until she reached the rock. Mica Island. Then, without bothering to pick out the twigs and thorns that had stuck in her dress and shawl, she climbed onto the slippery, snow-covered rock and fell into a deep sleep.

When she awakened, only a few flakes of snow were falling and the sky was clear. She knew that it must be the same night, although she felt as if she had slept for days. She was lying on her side. She felt something in her clenched hand and opened it; as she was awakening, her fingers had pried loose a large chunk of mica at which she and the others had worked for weeks while the weather was still warm. Now the precious, magical stuff was free and lay in the palm of her hand. It occurred to her that someone seeing the mica from above might think it a simple substance, yet underneath its top layer lay hundreds of others waiting to be found.

Trust in the Lord with all thine heart;
and lean not unto thine own understanding.

The words of the proverb entered her mind and she lay on the rock without moving, knowing that she was both cold and wet, not minding either. She and her mother had prayed to God for help, but when He had sent it, she had been frightened. It seemed to her now that she had been not only selfish, but blind, as well.

Fear thou not; for I am with thee: be not dismayed;
for I am thy God: I will strengthen thee; yea, I will
help thee; yea, I will uphold thee with the right hand
of my righteousness.

She looked at the sky, feeling God's presence in each flake of snow, in every tree, in the chunk of mica in her hand, and she felt for the first time that she would be able to go if they sent her.

I will strengthen thee; yea, I will help thee.

The fear might come back, but she would be able to live with it. She would be frightened, but she would not be alone.

E<small>MMELINE</small> awakened in the attic with a sense of dread whose cause she did not immediately know. The room looked strange. The other children were asleep on the two large mattresses on the floor that served them all as beds; she barely knew their names. She stared at the sloping roof, at the rafters, at the sky beyond the small window, and wished for snow—only then remembering the reason for her wish. This was the morning her father would bring her and the Watkinses to Hallowell, where they would meet the coach in which they would ride to Portland. From Portland, Hannah and Abner would go on to Lynn, while Emmeline, if all went according to plan, would change over to one of the big wagons sent out by the mills to bring new girls to Lowell.

She sat up, then looked down at Luke, sleeping on one side of her, and Harriet on the other. Beyond Harriet lay Andrew, then Abraham, then Rosanna and Rebekah. During their first night in Fayette, Hannah and Abner had squeezed in at the end of the second mattress, but they hadn't slept well, and so a mattress had been improvised for them out of straw and quilts on the floor of the downstairs room, at the opposite end from her parents' bed. Everyone looked peaceful now, even Harriet, who had been in a barely concealed rage for the three days since it had been established that Emmeline was going to Lowell.

There was a small amount of homespun in the house that had been intended for Harriet, whose own dress was quite threadbare; this was her second year in it, and Emmeline had worn it for two years before that. With Hannah's help, Emmeline had made herself a second dress out of this material, for Hannah had said there was no question but that Emmeline must have a change of clothing for Lowell. Until the night before, Harriet had treated Emmeline's journey as though it were a poorly disguised plot to get her cloth.

Harriet was the fourth child in the family, but only the second girl, having been born after Luke and Andrew. Of all the children, it was Harriet only who quarreled constantly with Emmeline. It was Harriet who, the year before when she was nine, had responded to some request of Emmeline's by hissing, "You're not my mother!" with such vehemence that Emmeline had stopped short, as though she'd been struck by a heavy object.

Somewhere in the back of her mind Emmeline had assumed that Harriet would be relieved by her departure, so that she'd been astonished, upon climbing the ladder to the attic the night before, to find Harriet in a state of wild agitation over the fact that she was leaving. As Emmeline reached the mattress, Harriet had thrown her arms about her, sobbing, "Emmy, Emmy, don't go to Lowell! I'm afraid for what'll happen to you in Lowell!"

"There's nothing to be afraid of in Lowell," Emmeline said, steeling herself lest Harriet set off her own fears. "It's not terrible. Just different."

But Harriet sobbed more than ever, so Emmeline held her for a while, stroking her hair, promising that she would write when she reached the city and describe it to them in detail. Eventually Harriet calmed down and moved to the edge of the mattress, so that Emmeline could be between her and Luke—a simple act she was usually unwilling to perform. Later, Emmeline could hear her breathing regularly.

She knelt, facing the attic window, and said her prayers; often, if Luke had forgotten to do this, he would join her when she began. Now, though, he lay stiff and unhappy on the mattress. When she lay down, she could see in the small amount of light coming through the attic window that his eyes were open, and when she touched his face she felt tears.

"It won't be for long, Luke," she promised. "Don't cry."

"Not crying," he said.

Now, in the morning, Emmeline didn't want to awaken Luke, or any of them. She was hoping to have a little time alone with her mother. Carefully she crawled from the mattress and made her way down the ladder. The fire had been started and her mother sat near it, nursing William. Everyone else was still sleeping. Her mother smiled at her wearily.

"Did you sleep, Emmy? I didn't close my eyes, worrying."

"Don't Mama," Emmeline said. "I'm not scared."

She hung the new dress on one of the nails in the hearth so it would be warm when she put it on. The chunk of mica nestled in one of its pockets.

At one end of the long table was the wooden box Luke had fashioned to hold her belongings. (Andrew had made her a wooden comb of her own.) The box was about one foot high and two feet wide, made of smooth pine boards. Luke was always a fastidious workman, and he had taken particular care that every rough spot was sanded and that the lid closed properly.

"Your father don't want you to go," her mother said. "Not even now. If you don't want to."

She felt a surge of love for her father; if only he would wake up and come to sit with them. How long was it since they'd been able to sit together, just the three of them, by the fire, without Hannah's voice grating at them, or some other interruption?

She slipped into the new dress and got the wooden

comb Andrew had given her. William had finished feeding. She took him from her mother and sat with him on the floor in front of the rocking chair, holding him while her mother separated her braids, then ran the comb lovingly through her hair. Hannah had suggested that her hair would be easier to care for if some of it were clipped off, and they had stared at her in silence. Emmeline's hair had never been cut and fell to well below her waist, light brown, full of gold and red lights in the summer, but darker and silkier in the wintertime. Harriet regularly announced that she was going to let her hair grow "all the way" too, but then in the hot weather it would irritate her and she would ask to have it cut back some. Harriet didn't have the patience to care for her own hair, and most days their mother was too busy. On this morning, though, Sarah ran the comb through Emmeline's hair slowly, then carefully formed each braid. Before she had tied the second braid, Emmeline had fallen into a peaceful state that was close to sleep, and she was therefore doubly startled when suddenly the room began to fill with people. Hannah and Abner were awake and standing when she opened her eyes, and then her father appeared, and soon Luke and the others began trooping down from the attic.

Thus Emmeline's last hours in Fayette were spent not in quiet seclusion with her parents, but in the middle of the morning's activities. Before she knew it, her father had hitched the wagon and brought it around to the road.

As though in a trance, she put on her shawl and tied the box with the precious piece of rope her father had found for her. She kissed each of the family goodbye, not letting herself cling too long to anyone. Hannah and Abner climbed onto the seat next to her father, and she squeezed in next to them, but then, once there, she couldn't bear to go without leaning down to embrace her mother once more. Sarah pressed the Bible into her hands.

"Oh, no, Mama," she said. "I can't."

"You'll bring it back," her mother said. "You're the only one reads it anyway."

Sarah had been taken from school in her second year, when her own mother died and she was needed to help with the two younger children. Reading had always been a chore for her, and she had argued for Emmeline to remain in school every year until the last one, when it had no longer been possible for her to manage even an occasional week without her daughter.

As Emmeline sat undecided as to whether it was all right for her to accept the Bible, the wagon began moving.

Past the Wrights' and then, a little ways down the road, the Wilsons', where the old barn had caved in under the weight of the previous winter's snow. The Wilsons' geese honked wildly as the wagon passed, clustering first in one spot close to the house, then in another. Emmeline noticed every detail, but from an unnatural distance, as though she had already left Fayette and were looking back through the wrong end of a spyglass. She had never traveled farther than to Livermore Falls, and that was just a few miles in another direction. She felt ill, though she hadn't touched her breakfast.

Past the general store and Judkins' Tavern, at the Corners, then onto the Hallowell Road. At one time the mills had sent their own wagons throughout Maine and New Hampshire to recruit girls, but they didn't need to do that anymore. Now the wagons went to Nashua and Portland, and girls who couldn't reach those towns on their own had no easy way to get to Lowell.

She didn't speak to her father or look over at him during the long ride. There was a wall around her which she needed if she were not going to make a display of her feelings. When they all stood on the front porch of the store in Hallowell, and Hannah told Henry Mosher that he needn't wait for them to board the coach, Emmeline felt only relief, for she was sure the wall would become stronger in his absence.

"You go along, Henry," Hannah said. "It's close to noon already. Emmeline will be fine—won't you, Emmeline?"

"I *am* fine, Papa." Her voice trembled but didn't break. "I'll send a letter from Lowell when I'm able."

He looked from her to the Watkinses, then back to her. He embraced her. Then he turned and left them without another word.

Abner went to the tavern across the road, while Hannah and Emmeline entered the store, sitting down on kegs near the stove. This store was considerably larger than the one in Fayette, and there were several people in it. A corner in the front served as the post office and was set off by a wooden counter with bars above it. In a corner in the back, a boy of about Emmeline's age was grinding corn. On the other side of the stove, in the window light, a woman was sewing a boot upper to its sole. There were only three kinds of fabric in the store at Fayette Corners, but here there was a larger selection—including a cotton with a floral print. After a while the woman asked if they would like tea.

"No, thank you," Hannah said firmly. Hannah, so talkative in the midst of her family, had drawn into herself among the strangers in the store. Emmeline wanted tea very much at this moment, but didn't know how to say this to her aunt.

The woman now seemed eager to engage them in conversation, but the effect of her eagerness was to make Hannah exclude her more carefully than before. Turning to Emmeline, she began speaking, in a low but intense voice, of all those Lowell glories not already covered in their conversations at home.

But every word Hannah uttered had the opposite effect from what was intended. When she promised that Emmeline would make friends in the new city, Emmeline remembered that she had never been able to talk to other girls as easily as she could to her mother. When Hannah told her about the number of books in the circulating library, Emmeline thought of the year before, when the schoolteacher had lent her *The Pioneers* by James Fenimore Cooper, and she had read aloud from it to the family each night, everyone enthralled and then a bit guilty that the Bible could not hold them in the same grip as Mr. Cooper did. When Hannah mentioned that she had written on a piece of paper the name of a friend from her own Lowell days with whom she hoped Emmeline would be able to board, Emmeline saw her own home, and the hearth, and her mother singing to one of the babies. She thought it must be one of the babies who'd died, but no matter how she strained to see its face, she couldn't tell which of them it was.

Suddenly there was a clattering of hooves, and a clanging and squeaking of wooden wheels. The coach had arrived. She ran to the window, and her heart skipped a beat with excitement, for it wasn't at all the simple covered wagon she had expected. It was freshly painted in a deep but bright green, with red and yellow trim, and it was drawn by two horses which, though not great beauties, put to shame her father's tired mares.

"Now, what do you think of that, Emmeline?" Hannah asked with obvious satisfaction.

There was a flurry of activity in the store; although no one else was getting on the coach, the storekeeper had several parcels and a small bag of mail to be put on it. Abner came out of the tavern and crossed the road, and three other men came out to stand on the tavern porch and observe. The coachman fetched water for

the horses. Hannah had unbent to the extent of telling
the woman who was making shoes that she was taking
her niece to Portland, and so on. Her mother had said
that Hannah meant no harm with her brusque ways,
but only wanted to help them, and Emmeline needed to
believe that now.

The inside of the coach was an immediate disappointment, for while it would take hours to know the extent
of their discomfort, the walls were rough, unpainted
pine boards, as though the person who had painstak-
ingly decorated the outside had been called away
before he could finish the job. And there were only
three narrow benches to sit on.

The first of these was occupied by three people who
never turned to greet them—or, indeed, to speak to
each other—during the entire journey. They were an
elderly couple and a woman of somewhat fewer years
who might have been their daughter but was, as
Emmeline later learned, the woman's younger sister.
They had lost the farm near Augusta on which they'd
lived all their lives, and were going to Lowell to find
work. Emmeline and the Watkinses sat on the back
bench; the middle one remained unoccupied until they
reached Lewiston, where there were four new passengers.

These were a young girl and three small children who
called her Mama, though she looked only a year or two
older than Emmeline. The two older children sat on the
bench, and she held the baby on her lap. For a long
time they were silent. But then the children lost their
fear, and as they did, they became restless and irritable.
The baby cried steadily, while one of the older children
asked, "When will we get to Lowell, Mama? When will
we get to Lowell?" at regular intervals, as though it
were the refrain of some sad song. Emmeline didn't
know which of them to pity most, and was astonished to
see that Hannah and Abner, on her left and right, slept

or looked out of their small windows, failing to notice the misery just a foot away from them.

"D'you think I could help her?" she finally whispered to Hannah.

"You don't know who they might be, Emmeline," Hannah said, very firmly, as though this were an answer to the question.

Emmeline opened her Bible, but couldn't make out the words in the shaky, jostling coach and closed it again. Then she shut her eyes, thinking that perhaps she would sleep for a while. But as soon as her eyes were closed her mind went to her mattress at home, so she opened them again. At that moment the carriage hit a large bump in the road, and one of the children, having turned to face Emmeline, pitched forward into her lap, then fell back down to the floor, where she was wedged between Emmeline's legs and the middle bench. The mother, instead of helping the child, began to yell at her, and the child set up a piteous wailing.

"I'm sorry, Miss," the mother said, twisting around so that she too was now facing Emmeline. "She didn't know what she was doing." Her speech was strange, and Emmeline had great difficulty making out her words.

"'Course not," Emmeline said. "Can I pick her up?"

The little girl stopped screaming and looked up at Emmeline, the mere promise of comfort enough to soothe her. Like her mother, she had large brown eyes and a darker complexion than Emmeline had ever seen. She came into Emmeline's arms without hesitation and rested against Emmeline's bosom as though it were the only one she had ever known. The mother, less easily comforted, leaned against the side of the coach, tears rolling down her cheeks, while the oldest child, a boy of perhaps five, looked out the window, sometimes standing to see better and each time being warned by his mother that he would fall and hurt someone. Emmeline recognized now that she was hearing a dialect and began to hunt for familiar words in the stream. On its mother's lap, the baby fretted in such a way as to suggest that there was nothing in the world bothering it except its mother's misery.

"They're young to make a journey," Emmeline said hesitantly.

This brought forth a fresh stream of tears, now mixed with words, among which Emmeline began to discern familiar sounds, then phrases, and finally whole sentences.

The girl's husband, who was old, or very old, or simply considerably older than she, had fought in the War of 1812. His wife had died. He had children by that wife, all of whom had gone somewhere, perhaps West. He was in his fifty-second year by the time this young woman met him in Montpelier, Vermont, to which her family had emigrated from Montreal when her father was still alive. She was fifteen and had no thought of marrying. Her mother was a widow with twelve children. They'd never known other than the worst poverty, and had always required help from others. Word had reached her of the factories going up in the south—in Manchester and Lowell. It had been her intention, before she met Waters, or Walters, or Wooters, to be a factory girl. She would have been happy, she knew, never to marry, but simply to work in a mill and buy pretty clothes and have candy every day. Then Walters had passed through Montpelier, and before she knew what was happening, he had married her, though she'd been certain it was her mother he was courting, and taken her across New Hampshire and Maine and down to Hallowell, to look for relatives whom he thought he had there, but whom they never found. He gave her three babies in five years, and then the urge took him to follow his sons West. A fresh outburst accompanied this last revelation, but now Emmeline was almost grateful for the tears; her own cheeks were burning with this confession. She had never heard its like before. When her own mother was carrying a child, it was never mentioned in the household, except indirectly. She glanced at her aunt; Hannah's eyes were closed.

After a while a new mood seemed to take hold of Florina, as she now told Emmeline she planned to call herself in Lowell. She said that she was determined to make a new life for herself. She was twenty-one years old, too young for her life to be over. She would get a job, and perhaps even one for Bernard, her oldest, as well. He was five; perhaps he could be a doffer. He was quick for his age, and that was a job done by children, or so she'd been told by a girl in Hallowell who'd come back from the mills. Hannah's eyes were still closed, but her face seemed to be set tighter than before. Emmeline looked at the curly-haired baby who slept on Florina's lap, and the little girl in her own, and did not dare to ask what would happen to them while their mother was at the mill. As though she had read the thought, however, Florina announced that in Lowell she would find a boardinghouse where the woman would take care of her children as well.

"Do they have such boardinghouses in Lowell?" Emmeline asked.

"They have everything you want in Lowell," Florina said, so fiercely that there was no mistaking one word, dialect or no. "Nellie Palmer stayed two years in Lowell," she went on in the same tone, as though she would carry on the argument with herself if Emmeline were unwilling to pursue it, "and come home with four dresses, two bonnets, a shawl, and lace for her wedding dress. And she was sending home money all the while!"

The little girl, whose name was Margaret, grew heavy on Emmeline's lap, and the bench became increasingly uncomfortable. Florina seemed to have finally talked herself into a kind of sleep. When Emmeline stirred, the child clung to her as though for her life. When they finally stopped at a tavern for the night, Margaret would not leave her, and after much crying Emmeline consented to have the child in her bed, though Hannah said she was being foolish and refused to speak a word to Florina.

They had had a good dinner with a roast—the first meat Emmeline had eaten in some time. The seven adults and three children from the coach had sat at a huge table with the couple who owned the tavern, as well as three men who had come only for the meal and were pressing on to Portland that night. Immediately afterward, they were ushered up to the one large "guest room" in the house. In a room about forty feet long, five beds were lined up neatly against one wall, with spaces of about two feet in between. At the foot of each bed was a chair. No effort at decoration had been made, but the room was neat and clean, as Hannah remarked, and quickly they divided the beds among themselves.

Florina took the farthest bed with her two older children; next there were Emmeline and Margaret; and then Hannah and Abner, whispering to each other until late in the night. On the fourth bed, the elderly sisters and the husband tossed and turned, but never spoke. Every bit of information about themselves that they could spare had been delivered at dinner; now their energy must be conserved for Lowell. On the fifth and last bed, the coach driver snored at great volume and with even greater irregularity, so that each time Emmeline had once more adjusted to the notion that she was not only away from home but on a bed raised several feet off the floor, she was awakened by a new thunderclap from that corner. Still, with warm little Margaret nestled against her, she eventually slept.

But the second day was considerably worse than the first. Those places which had become sore and bruised hadn't recovered during the night, so that within a short time Emmeline was in greater discomfort than she'd been at the previous day's end. Then too, Margaret's devotion began to tire her, for it came to

seem less the simple affection of a needy child than the
pathetic devotion of a dumb pet. Though Margaret
clearly understood Emmeline's words, she never
spoke. Her response to any movement of Emmeline's,
or to the suggestion that Emmeline might like her to
stand for a moment so she could shift her limbs, was to
cling more tightly.

"Are you all right, Emmeline?" Hannah asked.

"Only a bit cramped," Emmeline said.

"You can give her back to her mother, you know."
Hannah didn't trouble to whisper.

"Perhaps just for a while."

Margaret clutched at her frantically.

"She doesn't want to go," Emmeline whispered.

"You can't help that," Hannah replied.

But Emmeline couldn't tell that to the sleeping
Florina, and Margaret did not loosen her grip.

Finally, Hannah said in a loud voice, "You'll have to
take your child now, Miss. My niece can't hold her
anymore."

Florina, her voice tearful from the moment her eyes
opened, launched into a lengthy apology, saying she
hadn't meant to burden Emmeline, it was only that the
two had seemed to take to each other. Then she turned
to the child, anger in her voice.

"Come back here, now, and stop bothering the nice
ladies."

Margaret did not appear to hear her mother, but
when Hannah leaned over and said, "You must go now,
child," Margaret scrambled to her mother without
looking at Emmeline.

Tears welled in Emmeline's eyes for the first time that
day.

"Listen to me, Emmeline," Hannah said in a low
voice. "In Lowell there's lots of people . . . you'll
see. . . . There's lots of people in a city want you to do
something for them, and you don't even know who they
might be."

"What will happen to her?" Emmeline whispered.

"To them? They don't have people in Lowell. All she wants is to work."

"Her work's at home. How's she going to work, with three babies to take care of?"

Emmeline explained Florina's plan.

"She'll be on the streets in a week," Hannah said grimly. "There's no five-year-olds in the mills, and there's no boarding for children. Ain't that so, Abner?"

"What's that?" As usual, he appeared to have been summoned from a distant place.

"Have you seen a five-year-old in the mills?"

"Five? No, I can't say's I have."

"What's the youngest?"

"Well," Abner said slowly, "the doffer's the youngest, of course, and I don't think there's a doffer under ten or twelve."

A quiet settled over the coach's interior. Emmeline wondered if Florina had heard Abner's words, and decided that she would not be the one to repeat them. It wasn't as though Florina still had a choice; they were already close to Portland.

Country gave way to city. Gray sky was matched by monstrous gray stone buildings, some larger than the largest sawmill in Fayette. The horses' hooves made an incredible clatter as they came down on some sort of road that sounded like stone.

Gradually, fear crowded out the aches and pains of travel. Emmeline's lungs constricted so that it became difficult to breathe. She yawned continuously. In comparison with the battle she was waging to get a deep breath, nothing outside seemed real.

The coach drew to a halt. After a moment, someone opened the door. Ahead of her, blocking out the sky, was still another gray stone building. Between the building and the coach were the black stones on which she'd heard the horses' hooves pounding. She couldn't see the sky. People walked by. They looked quite different from the people she knew, though she could not have said why, beyond the fact that their clothing was better.

Emmeline was the closest to the door, once Florina and her children were out. The coachman gave her his hand and she stood, but then her knees buckled, everything went black, and she tumbled toward him.

When she regained consciousness, she was lying on the stones of the road, but something soft had been placed under her head. She opened her eyes. Hannah was leaning over her; she couldn't see Abner, but there were other people standing around, watching her curiously. Hannah kept telling them to move back so she could get air, but Emmeline was no longer having difficulty breathing. She was simply without the strength to move. Two women walked away from the space at her feet and she saw, for the first time, the large canvas-covered wagon which had loomed behind them all along, almost blocking the road. A coachman sat on the front bench, holding the reins. As Emmeline watched, a girl climbed up onto the wagon, receiving her box from someone on the road, and disappeared behind the coachman into what appeared to be an enormous black hole.

Emmeline tried to sit up, but she didn't yet have the strength. The remaining people around her drifted away, and now she could see that a gentleman stood on the road near the front of the wagon, talking to one of a few waiting girls. Some held boxes not unlike Emmeline's own, but one girl had a small, elegant brass-bound trunk. As the man talked with a girl, he wrote in a large black journal cradled in his arm.

Suddenly Emmeline realized that one of the waiting girls was Florina. She had left her children at the side of the road. Margaret sat Indian fashion, holding the baby on her lap; the boy stood close by, his thumb in his mouth. Florina never glanced at them; it was as though she hoped the man would think they weren't hers.

Hannah helped Emmeline to a sitting position. The man nodded, and the girl he'd been talking to climbed onto the wagon. After one more girl had passed the man, Florina came forward and began speaking. He wrote something in his book. But at that moment the little boy detached himself from his sisters and ran to his mother, pulling at her skirts to be noticed. The man looked at the little boy, then over to the other children, then back to Florina, who never stopped talking to him—apparently still hoping to distract his attention from them. But he shook his head. Then Florina grew frantic and seemed about to kneel down before him.

"Next!" he called.

The remaining girl came forward. Florina was still pleading, but he ignored her. She pointed in Emmeline's direction, as though something about Hannah or Emmeline could save her, but when he continued to ignore her, she shook off the little boy and ran to Emmeline, throwing herself down on the stones beside her.

"Please help me," she said tearfully. "Please."

Emmeline was about to ask what she could do when Hannah interrupted.

"We can't help you, Miss," Hannah said. "You've gotten yourself into this and you'll have to get yourself out."

Florina's jaw grew slack and her eyes glazed over. Emmeline wanted, at the very least, to offer sympathy, but she could not help and was afraid to anger Hannah. Margaret was coming toward them without the baby, who lay on the stones at the side of the road, crying convulsively. The little girl had left the poor thing with its brother, and the boy, in turn, had put it down on the road.

"*Your* work now, Emmeline, is to get yourself fixed up to talk to that gentleman," Hannah said. "And yours," she said to Florina, "is to attend to that baby. You had better let my niece do what she needs to do and attend to your own family."

Florina trudged off, weeping bitterly. Hannah helped Emmeline to her feet, then brushed off her dress and shawl and pushed the hair back from her forehead.

"No time to do more than that," Hannah muttered. "There's only one girl left before you."

Suddenly Emmeline was frantic for herself, and all thoughts of Florina had vanished.

"What will he ask me? What will I say?"

"Just tell him whatever he asks," Hannah said. "You're fourteen. That's not a lie," she added very firmly, as though she could in this manner make up for the fact that it was. "You're only a few months away, so it's not a lie."

Emmeline walked slowly toward the wagon. She was convinced that she would be rejected, if not because the gentleman suspected her true age, then because she'd been caught in a lie, and if not because she'd lied, then because she had been seen fainting on the road and they would not believe she was in good health. For the first time she became concerned that if she were not accepted, she would have no way to make up to the Watkinses for their generosity in paying her coach fare. However, the man greeted her kindly and simply asked her name.

"Emmeline Mosher."

"And how old are you, Emmeline?" He was entering her name in his book. She thought that he looked just a little bit like her father.

"Fourteen." She crossed her fingers in the folds of her skirt.

"And where are you from?"

"Fayette."

"Fayette. Is that Maine, now?"

"Yes, sir." It had never occurred to her that there was anyone who didn't know precisely where Fayette was.

"Are you in good health, Emmeline?"

"Oh, yes, sir. I've never been sick a day in my life."

"And what do you have with you?"

"Just my box. My aunt has it. There."

"All right, Emmeline. Why don't you fetch your box and take your leave of your aunt."

It had happened so quickly that she was nonplussed. She was sure the other girls had talked with him for longer. He hadn't even asked her why she wanted to work in Lowell! Slowly she returned to Hannah. She was dizzy, as though she might faint again, but she held herself stiff against the possibility. Hannah and Abner were beaming at her. She couldn't remember having seen Abner smile before. Only now, when she was leaving and he could be certain of not being burdened with her, could he be friendly.

"You have our address," Hannah said, handing Emmeline her box. "Here." She tucked a piece of paper into Emmeline's hand. "This is the name of my friend who runs a boardinghouse for the Appleton Corporation. Once you get to Lowell, ask if you can't board with her. She'll take good care of you."

Emmeline nodded. She was dazed. They kissed her goodbye, and then, almost before she knew it, her box was up with the driver and she was being helped onto the wagon.

UNDER the canvas the light was dim. Girls whispered among themselves. There were thirty of them, perhaps more. They filled the wagon, but comfortably, with enough room left so that they could lie down to sleep if they wished.

There was a shouted warning from outside that the wagon was about to move. Emmeline dropped to the floor, brushing against the girl closest to her, who didn't appear to notice. There was some shifting around as the wagon jerked to a start. Groups began to form, or perhaps there had been groups all along. Perhaps all the other girls knew each other. Certainly they must be older and more experienced than she, or at least have a better idea of what was going to happen to them.

She felt that the girl whose skirts touched hers was looking at her, but she didn't yet dare to look back. She took the piece of mica from her pocket and in the dim light began to peel away its top layer, but then she thought that she had better preserve it for Lowell, so she put it back in her pocket and clasped her hands in her lap.

The girl coughed softly. Emmeline looked at her, but the girl's eyes slipped away from her own. Emmeline felt her cheeks grow warm with the rebuff. But when the girl coughed again, and Emmeline failed to take notice, the girl whispered something.

"Did you speak?" Emmeline asked.

"I said that I felt the chill," the girl whispered.

Emmeline saw now that she was not arrogant or indifferent but only frightened, like herself. In addition to her shawl, Emmeline was wearing a long scarf Hannah had given her, and she offered it to the girl.

"Oh, no, I couldn't," the girl said.

Emmeline prevailed upon her, saying, truthfully, that she was quite warm herself, and the girl finally took it, with thanks so profuse as to set off a whole new fit of coughing. The continuous hacking quality of the cough made Emmeline uneasy, for she hadn't known an adult to sound that way, only young children who were quite ill. The girl's name was Opal and she was twenty years old, though her frailness made her seem younger. She was from a town that wasn't far from Portland, but was small, like Fayette. Emmeline told Opal about the boardinghouse owned by her aunt's friend, and it was agreed that Opal would try to get a place there as well.

It was late the following night when they finally approached Lowell. In the morning, Emmeline had given Mr. Barker, the gentleman with the notebook, the name of her aunt's friend. He told her that there were no openings just now in the Appleton mills, but then, seeing her distress, had promised to place her and Opal together in a good boardinghouse.

Opal was asleep now, her head resting in Emmeline's lap. Emmeline herself had awakened some time earlier and was sitting fully alert, her senses straining for changes outside the wagon. Most of the girls were sleeping, but here and there someone stirred, and then the girl against whom she rested would move, and then a sigh, barely audible, would pass through the wagon, as though the sleeping bodies were slender trees in the forest, bent by a wind that promised far worse weather ahead.

Somewhere a noise grew that fortified this impression, for it was more like thunder rolling in steadily, though from a great distance, than anything else. Yet it was not thunder, nor was it the thunderous roll of the wagon wheels to which she had long since become accustomed. It was a steady noise which grew louder as they moved on.

The others were awakening and sitting up, rubbing their eyes, looking at their neighbors. They whispered to each other, but Opal slept, though by now the noise was so loud that one couldn't hear the sound of another's voice unless it was directly in the ear. Emmeline found Opal's hand and held it tightly.

Louder and louder.

"Water. It's water." Under the horses' hooves, the quality of the road changed as the noise reached its peak. They had been on dirt; now the hooves pounded on wood. "It's a waterfall!" The phrase was chain-whispered through the wagon as the girl closest to the back opening found the courage to look out.

They were passing over the bridge at Pawtucket Falls, though none of them had ever seen a waterfall of its dimension and it hadn't occurred to any of them that this was what she was hearing. The road changed again and slowly the noise of the Falls died down.

They were in Lowell, having crossed over the Merrimack River, within whose nearly V-shaped curve the city nestled. It was the Merrimack's waters, tumbling down the Falls and through the various locks into the canals, that provided most of the power to run the waterwheels in the basements of the Lowell mills. There were other rivers, but the Merrimack dwarfed them, its average width being six hundred feet while the next largest, the Concord, averaged two hundred.

After a while the wagon slowed. The sound of the road changed once more; now they were riding along brick streets. Opal slept on, but excitement was gathering among the other girls. Some were doing their hair and fixing their shawls. One girl stretched and uttered the kind of great loud yawn one never allowed oneself except at home, and everyone giggled nervously. The wagon slowed further and then stopped. There was a moment of absolute silence when they all looked at each other but didn't dare to move. Opal was still asleep.

There were sounds at the front of the wagon; then the flaps were parted and Mr. Barker came in, holding a kerosene lamp, hunching over to stand under the canvas. At each stop he would call four or five names, and those girls were to come forward with their baggage.

"Buttrick . . . Seabrook . . . Skinner . . . Breed."

The girls made their way over the others to the front, one smiling bravely, the others visibly frightened. Emmeline hoped that when her turn came her fear wouldn't show. The flap was closed and the wagon jerked forward again. After a short time the procedure was repeated. On the third stop, she and Opal were called. With some difficulty, she shook Opal awake.

"Where are we?" the other girl asked.

"In Lowell," Emmeline whispered. "Come with me." The others who had been called were already outside. "Quickly," she said. "Are you all right?"

"Yes," Opal said. "I was just sleeping."

Emmeline helped the other girl to her feet; then they took their boxes and made their way down from the wagon.

THEY were standing on brick. The moon cast enough light so that Emmeline could almost see its true color. In front of them was what appeared to be one extremely long three-story brick house and was actually a row of connected houses. At the end of the row there was a space, and then, at a right angle to the row of homes, another brick building which was six stories high and more massive in appearance. This was one of the two mills of the Summer Corporation. Past the coach and across the brick road was yet another row of houses. It appeared to be a world made entirely of brick.

The door of the house directly in front of them flew open to reveal a creature unlike anyone Emmeline had ever seen. Enormous in both height and girth, she had a wild mane of black-and-gray hair that billowed out from her head, then fell down over her shoulders and bosom. She wore a dress that appeared to be made entirely of patchwork quilts, and around her shoulders was a red-and-purple-plaid shawl; Emmeline had never seen such brilliant colors in cloth.

The woman held up her lamp and peered at the girls. Emmeline trembled. She had shiny black eyes that appeared to be going right through each girl, and bright red cheeks, and her chin was almost pointed; the effect was of a witch.

"And what troubles have you brought me this time, Barker?"

The voice was extraordinarily loud, with a harsh timbre that cut into the dim night, and there was a thick brogue which at first made her almost as difficult as Florina to understand.

"No trouble at all, Mrs. Bass," Mr. Barker said mildly. "I have four fine girls here for you."

"Ah, you always say that. Let me see. Bring them closer."

Emmeline stepped forward with the others, only half aware that Opal was hanging back in the rear.

"Closer," Mrs. Bass said. She was looking directly at Emmeline now.

"Name?"

"Emmeline Mosher."

"Now, there's one for the first row, eh, Barker?" Mrs. Bass said, winking—something Emmeline had never seen a woman do before.

Mr. Barker smiled. "She had a family note for Mrs. Thornton. But the Appleton hasn't an opening."

"You'll be glad of it, too, child," Mrs. Bass said. "The food Old Biddy Thornton serves . . . sometimes I think she must chain the girls to the beds at night to make them stay!"

Emmeline was so absorbed in the attempt to understand Mrs. Bass, so diverted by the sounds of those words she could discern—by the way child became *choild* and sometimes, *sometoimes;* by the endless trilling of every r—that at first the outrageous nature of the remark did not even strike her. She turned to Mr. Barker for help in responding, but he was already introducing Mamie Warren and Eliza Prescott, two girls who had been together on the wagon and spoken only to each other the whole time.

Opal coughed softly.

"Who was that?" Mrs. Bass demanded loudly, as though she had detected a criminal act.

When Opal failed to speak, the other two girls turned to look at her. Head down, she came forward.

"How long have you had that cough, child?" Mrs. Bass asked.

"I think I took a chill on the wagon," Opal said in a voice so low that Mrs. Bass made her repeat the words.

"Are you telling me, now," Mrs. Bass demanded, "that you never coughed before you got on that wagon?"

It had been put in such a way that Opal could not answer, and she began coughing in earnest.

"Go home and get tended to, child," Mrs. Bass said. "I cannot have a sick girl here."

Emmeline watched with tears in her eyes as Opal protested that she was not really ill, but Mr. Barker comforted her, telling her that he would find her another good place. Mrs. Bass muttered something in Gaelic, then told the other girls to follow her into the house. Emmeline was the last to enter, because she stood watching Opal return to the wagon with Mr. Barker, nearly sick with feeling, not only for Opal but for herself, over the loss of Opal.

First Florina, and now Opal. It was her first lesson in city life, it occurred to her as she finally mounted the stairs to Mrs. Bass's: she would be discarded if she had difficulties that became apparent to the people around her.

They followed Mrs. Bass through the central hall-way, which was lighted by two gas lamps held in beautiful lanthorns. The house was quiet, which did not prevent Mrs. Bass from speaking in the same tone as she had used outside.

"I've kept a good supper for you, girrrls," Mrs. Bass said—except that she said soooperrrr, so that until they found themselves in a room with three long tables, one of which was still set at one end and laden with food, Emmeline was unable to identify what it was that she had kept for them. "In spite of the hour. They get here later with each trip, and that's the truth of it, but I know how it feels to be hungry."

The truth was that Emmeline had eaten more good food in the past few days than she had seen in months before that. Yet she ate ravenously with the other girls—flapjacks that were barely warm, but still good with jam; fruitcake; tea with milk and honey; and then, when she felt as though she might burst but the others were still eating, a thick slice of bread smeared heavily with butter.

Mrs. Bass was smiling at her with satisfaction.

"I set the best table on any corporation," she said. "Anyone will tell you that. I feed you better than your own mother ever did."

Resentment stirred within Emmeline. What did this woman know about her mother? It was not possible to argue, and yet Mrs. Bass's saying this served to increase the fear and mistrust that Emmeline had felt since that first moment when she had seen the woman ferret out and reject Opal.

"Come," Mrs. Bass said, "collect your boxes and I'll take you up to the long attic."

They followed her through the hallway and up the stairs. At the first landing, she stopped to catch her breath, turning to Emmeline.

"How old are you, Emmeline?" she asked suddenly, her voice again making no allowance for the hour.

"Fourteen," Emmeline said. "Nearly."

She laughed. "You're half asleep, child. Do you want help with your box?"

"No. Thank you."

Emmeline was confused rather than grateful for her kindness. Mamie and Eliza were just behind them on the steps; now they and the rest of the world would know her age—a possible disability, to set her apart from the others. She couldn't possibly accept help, though she had never climbed an entire flight of stairs before, and it was difficult to cary her box and manage her skirts so that she wouldn't trip on them.

Finally they reached the third floor. They were in a long, narrow room that would have been quite large had not a steeply sloping roof cut off a good deal of standing space. Three large beds lined the long wall opposite. When Mrs. Bass held up her lamp, Emmeline could see that two girls were sleeping in the closest one, while there was only a single form in the next. At the far end of the room, where there was a window, stood an empty bed. Mrs. Bass said that Mamie and Eliza should share that one, since they were already acquainted, and that Emmeline should get into the bed where there was now a single shape.

Whispering and giggling, without a question or a moment's hesitation, Mamie and Eliza moved toward their bed and opened their boxes to find their nightgowns. Emmeline had a nightgown too. It was Hannah's, and much too large for her, but Hannah had said she must have it.

"Hilda's a sensible girl," Mrs. Bass said. Her voice had lowered to something approaching normal speaking tones. "You'll be all right with her." Then she turned and went down the stairs, taking the lamp with her.

Emmeline watched until the light disappeared and her eyes became accustomed to the darkness. There were three dormer windows in the sloping roof, and a reasonable amount of light came in through them. She was inclined to put on her nightgown over her dress, which she didn't feel she could take off, but she was fearful of being noticed and laughed at. She sat on the edge of the bed for a while and then, leaving the nightgown in the box, took off her boots and crawled under the covers, curling up as well as she could without touching the other body. The bed was, or seemed to be, even higher off the floor than the tavern beds had been, which was frightening. What if she should fall? She moved in just a bit toward the other girl. Hilda. Once, like all the babies, Emmeline had slept between her parents in their bed, but in her memory there was only the mattress on the floor in the attic.

She had forgotten to say her prayers. She got out of bed again and knelt on the floor.

> *The Lord is my shepherd; I shall not want.*
> *He maketh me to lie down in green pastures:*
> *　he leadeth me beside the still waters.*
> *He restoreth my soul. . . .*

She recited the entire psalm, and yet when she was finished, it felt wrong—as though she had left out some vital portion. She recited it again in her mind, but if she'd lost a line, she couldn't find it. If only the moonlight had been a little brighter, she could have found the lines in the Bible. But it would be futile to try. Besides, the more she thought about it, the more it seemed that the problem lay outside those words.

My God, my God, why hast thou forsaken me?

No. Why had that come into her mind? It was foolish; it wasn't He who had moved. She returned to bed, covering herself and then looking up at the night sky through the dormer window. *That* was it—it wasn't God had forsaken her, but that she did not feel as though He could *see* her in Lowell. It was the knowledge that He would be with her that had enabled her to leave Fayette; yet now she felt—and her knowledge that this was wrong, for He was everywhere, did not change the feeling—that she had left God in Fayette with her family!

Her mind returned to Mrs. Bass. In the dining room she had read to the girls from a series of posted regulations, the first of which was that they must all go to church on the Sabbath. It seemed strange that any regulation should be necessary; if church had been open at this hour, she would have been relieved and happy to go. In church, with a pastor standing before her, she would certainly come to feel God's presence again.

She realized that she had lost track of the days of the week, and tried now to remember which one it was so that she would know how long she had to wait until Sunday. Today had been Thursday . . . or was it Friday? No. Well, she could wait—as long as she knew Sunday would come. But meanwhile . . . if only she could talk to the girl in the bed with her. Hilda. If only they could be friends, what a difference it would make! If they were friends, then when they got into bed at night it would be very much as though she were back in Fayette with Luke and the others.

The thought of Luke undid her, though, and she began to cry—not loudly, but in a way that she could not control. At first she was concerned that she would disturb Hilda, but finally, when she saw that the other girl never stirred, she gave in to the tears as though she were letting herself float on the pond, and eventually, in a kind of damp but gentle misery, she fell asleep.

In her sleep, she covered her ears. A set of bells jangled so loudly and hideously that it was as though someone had taken the church bells from the belfry and set them in her ears. A rooster began crowing, but there was something horribly wrong with that noise too. Her eyes opened. She had no idea where she was. Next to her, on the bed, a figure was flapping its arms as though they were wings, and crowing like a rooster.

She was in Lowell. But what was happening to her?

"I smell the country!" the mock rooster crowed. "I smell the country!"

"I'm sorry!" Emmeline cried, bolting upright. But she couldn't say any more because she didn't know any reason she should actually be apologizing. "I came very late last night, and—"

"I *hear* the country!" shrieked the same demented voice. Emmeline now realized that this was the girl whose bed she had shared. "What are you saying, Country? I can't understand a word of it!"

Emmeline didn't understand why not. She understood the other girl, although she could hear that their speech was different.

"Oh, Lord," a voice groaned from the next bed. "Isn't it bad enough that we have to endure the bells in the morning? Do we have to live through the rooster once more as well?"

"Yes, Hilda," said another, softer voice. "Why don't you be a dear and light the lamp and leave us in peace for a few minutes?"

In a moment Hilda had leaped over Emmeline and gone to the wall, where she lighted an oil lamp that was fastened into a lanthorn there.

"All right, Country," she said then. "Let's have a look at you."

"You mustn't let Hilda frighten you," the first of the other girls said. "D'y'know the expression, its bark is worse than its bite? That was first said of our friend Hilda when she found a new girl in her bed in the morning."

Emmeline noticed that at the other end of the room, Mamie and Eliza had awakened and were watching from their bed.

"Name?" Hilda inquired.

"Emmeline Mosher."

"Moshah? Moshah?" Hilda repeated, exaggerating the accent which Emmeline herself could not yet hear. "Emmeline Moshah from whayahh? Maine, no doubt. The wilds of Maine."

"Fayette."

"Where you come, no doubt, from poor but worthy stock who happen to have fallen upon hard ti—"

"That's enough," Emmeline snapped, surprising herself far more than the others, for she was still trembling with fear. "I won't let you attack my parents!"

There was a pause. Emmeline could feel them all watching her.

"How old are you, Emmeline?" Hilda asked suddenly.

"Fourteen," Emmeline said, her cheeks burning. "Almost."

"Oh, dear Lord, I've been heckling a child." Hilda threw up her hands and looked at the ceiling.

"I'm not a child."

"Of course you're not," the first of the other two girls

said. "Listen, Emmeline, I'm Abbey and this is Lydia. You mustn't be frightened of the way we talk. We'll help you. I know how terrible it is at first. I remember."

Emmeline smiled at her in gratitude, but she was still trembling.

"We've been here for eight months," Abbey said, "but we're still in the long attic because we don't want to be separated, and the openings downstairs have only come one at a time."

"While I," said Hilda, "have been up here for three years and shall be here forevermore."

"Why is that?" Emmeline asked, because that seemed to be what was wanted.

"Because I choose it," Hilda said. "Because whenever there's any vacancy at all, it's up here, so that I most often get to have my own bed. And because I am as far away as possible from the Great Wide-mouthed Bass."

Lydia and Abbey giggled nervously.

"Hush, Hilda," Abbey said. "She could be coming up right at this moment."

"Miss Abbey's function in this room," Hilda said airily, "is to protect me—and others—from myself. For nine months of each year, in any event. It's a wonder I survive the other three without her supervision."

"What our Hilda does the rest of the year," Abbey said, a mixture of pride and hostility in her voice, "is to teach school in Keene."

Emmeline was not only impressed but confused, for she found herself now in the position of having talked back to a schoolmistress.

"Ah, she's blushing," Lydia said softly. "She needs time to get used to us rowdy city girls, don't you, Emmeline?"

Emmeline could not speak. The others noticed that Mamie and Eliza were listening and began to speak to them as well.

"Everyone teases," Abbey announced. "Not just Hilda. Everyone will tease you about your accent, until you begin to sound like Lowell. And your dress. And you'll have to get a bonnet. You probably came with just an old shawl for your head—isn't that so?"

Emmeline nodded, embarrassed, although Mamie and Eliza were nodding too.

"It's getting late," Lydia said, and she and Abbey became one whirl of activity. Mamie and Eliza got out of bed and began to dress more slowly.

"Will I be the youngest?" Emmeline asked Hilda, who did not seem to be in such a great rush as the others.

"In this house, certainly," Hilda said. "Not in the entire mill. There are some your age—fourteen, fifteen—though not many. Then there are a few who are younger—doffers, mostly. That's not hard work, and they let children do it, if the family's already boarding on the Corporation."

Hilda's manner had changed. She was much more like a schoolmistress now, and the edge was gone from her voice.

"You'll be able to find better work than that," Hilda said, knotting her hair into a bun. She was almost ready to go. The three Lowell girls wore neat black dresses with white collars—a world apart from her own dress, or Mamie's and Eliza's, but as much like one another as the gingerbread figures Pastor Evans' wife cut for her Christmas tea. "You sound as if you've had some school."

"Every year until last," Emmeline told her, not without pride. She was about to add that her mother had insisted upon her schooling, but saw that the three girls, each of whom had appeared to be at a different stage of readiness, were now magically ready to go downstairs at the same instant. She watched in a panic as Abbey, then Lydia, and finally Hilda went to the stairs.

"When will I see you again?" she couldn't help but call, for being left with Mamie and Eliza was almost worse than being left alone.

Hilda turned. "We'll be back for breakfast."

"When will that be?"

"Two hours from now. At seven." Hilda paused and came back into the room, responding to the fear in Emmeline's face.

"I'm sorry," Emmeline said. "I don't want you to be late on my account."

"It doesn't really matter," Hilda told her. "We're supposed to be there at five, but I work in the cloth room, and I happen to know that there won't be any cloth ready for me to count if I arrive early this morning."

"Is that a good place to be?" Emmeline asked, thinking that perhaps she could find work there.

"You can earn more elsewhere, but it's the most comfortable. I have a great deal of choice now, but you most likely won't have any choice at all. Did the Bass give a hint of where she'd take you?"

"She said I was for the first row," Emmeline offered hesitantly.

"Oh. . . ." Hilda was irritated. "She's such an old . . . That just means that you're pretty, Emmeline. It doesn't have anything to do with which room you're in."

Emmeline blushed, humiliated by her own indiscretion. She thought she had better get dressed, but feared that any movement would make Hilda go away sooner. She felt the other girls watching, and prayed that they hadn't heard.

"I'd better go now," Hilda said. "Do you want me to fix your hair so that it's not so country?"

"No, thank you," Emmeline said. She was afraid that if she were mistaken for a Lowell girl, more would be expected of her.

"All right, then," Hilda said. "Remember to tie your boxes securely when you leave, all of you. The Bass is a great snoop. I'll see you at breakfast."

And then she was gone. A moment later, Mamie and Eliza disappeared. Emmeline looked around, thinking that she should get up and change her dress and do her hair. But she couldn't move. It was as though she had never been to sleep at all. She looked longingly at the pillow; if she could only set down her head and fall asleep, she would make the mill vanish from her life.

But then reality forced itself upon her in the form of the first sounds of machinery starting up in the mill. Suddenly she was fully awake. The noises grew louder. She went to the far window but could see nothing except the opposite tenements. With each moment the noises grew louder and she grew more incredulous, for the mill was a good distance from the house, or so it had seemed at night, and none of the room's windows even faced toward it. She prepared herself and went downstairs, seeing and hearing no one until she reached the ground floor and walked back toward the kitchen, whence Mrs. Bass's voice shrilled easily over the sounds from the mill.

A bit of daylight was beginning to come into the dining room, where the long tables were already set for breakfast. Hesitantly she made her way into the kitchen. Mrs. Bass was at the enormous stove, tossing flapjacks and talking in a rapid, apparently endless stream to Mamie and Eliza, who were eyeing the food with considerably greater interest than they were listening to her words. Mamie and Eliza had done each other's hair into an approximation of the Lowell bun, and while they still did not resemble the city girls, they looked even more like each other, with their identical parts through identical brown hair, than they had before.

"Where've you been, child?" Mrs. Bass interrupted herself to ask when Emmeline appeared at the door, but then, without waiting for a reply, she returned to her narrative.

"There's no sense in getting any of you into the carding room, if we can help it, with the cotton flying around . . ." (She said *floi-in,* so that it took a moment to understand what she meant.) ". . . getting into your hair, your eyes . . ." *(Ois.)* ". . . and the Good Lorrrd only knows. . . . I'll take you two to the weaving room first—that's where they need the girls now, and there's other weaving rooms beside Maguire's. . . . I don't like to put my girls in Maguire's, but we'll have to see . . . and we'll try you at drawing in, Emmeline." *(Emmeloin.)* "It's pleasant enough, and after a bit it'll pay you as well as most of them." She looked up and saw Emmeline's eyes on the flapjacks. "You pooorrr child, why didn't you tell me you was starrrved?" And she handed Emmeline a hot flapjack, giving some to Mamie and Eliza as well. "You could use some more flesh on you, child. How old did you say you was? Fourteen? So young to be here without anyone! How many are there at home besides you?"

"Eight," Emmeline said. "And my mother and my father."

Mrs. Bass paused and looked up at her. "And you're going to feed all of them, are you?"

"I must," Emmeline said.

Suddenly another set of loud bells went off. This was the seven-o'clock signal to stop work at the mill and return to the boardinghouse for breakfast. Within a short time, girls began to enter the dining room—such a great crowd of them that in spite of the number of places she'd seen set at the table, Emmeline was astonished.

She could also see now that her anxiety over being mistaken too soon for a Lowell girl was ill founded. Even Mamie and Eliza, in their new hairdos, were in no such danger. The dining room was in full light now, and as the mill girls streamed in, with their slick, neat hairdos, their dark, carefully pressed dresses almost invariably set off by starched white collars, Emmeline knew in despair that she could never be one of them. She did not differentiate among them, nor did it occur to her that virtually all of them had once felt as she did now, and that many, beneath their uniform attractiveness, were still far from contented. They seemed a happy, world-wise group, too closely knit to ever stretch to admit her. They filled the room quickly, sat down in their seats so surely that they might have been assigned—except for the occasional brief squabble over possession of a particular chair—and proceeded to eat hugely and well, without, it seemed, ever interrupting their conversations. Emmeline felt lucky to find a seat beside Hilda.

"Did the Bass say where she would bring you?"

"She did, but I couldn't follow what she said." Emmeline looked nervously around her, but Mrs. Bass was at the table farthest from them, supervising, directing, talking, and all the while putting food into her own mouth, though she remained standing.

Abbey laughed. "Did she not tell you about the cotton floi-in' in your ois the whole toim?"

"You're going to get the new girl into trouble as well as yourself, if you don't speak in a lower voice," Hilda said.

Across the table, Mamie and Eliza huddled together, looking, for all their new hairdos, little better than Emmeline, except for the fact that there were two of them, which made a great difference in her mind.

Very soon, breakfast time was over, and the girls were bustling out of the dining room, getting their shawls from the hooks in the hallway, and filing out of the house, usually in couples. It had seemed like five minutes, but it had been half an hour. Only Mamie and Eliza and Emmeline were left. Mrs. Bass said that they must go now to the mill. When Emmeline told her that she'd left her shawl upstairs, Mrs. Bass said that she would take the other two first and then come back for Emmeline. She didn't mind at all.

Emmeline ran upstairs to fetch her shawl, then came down to what appeared to be an empty house. She didn't know what to do with herself and finally decided to wait for Mrs. Bass on the front steps. But as she passed through the hallway, she was arrested by two sights. The first was of the great keeping room—the large, comfortable parlor, full of upholstered chairs and with several tables scattered around as well. The second, on the opposite side of the hallway, was a room which at first she could only see in part, for the door had been left ajar. It was unlike any room Emmeline had ever seen, and, indeed, unlike any other room in the boardinghouse, having the effect of being an extension of Mrs. Bass's own person, and being in fact the room where she (once along with her young children) lived. The walls were covered with a fantastic patchwork of intricate designs on various pieces of wallpaper (which Emmeline had never seen or even heard of). Some of the designs were of historical scenes—a general handing a treaty to an Indian chief whose horse stood next to him, and so on—while others were floral. They were pasted next to and over each other without apparent regard for size or color. The effect of the walls was overwhelming, even had Emmeline not, at the same time, been seeing her first velvet divan and a huge bed with a brass headboard. Near the divan was a framed glass mirror which was by far the largest one she'd ever seen. She was overwhelmed by the desire to see her reflection, but could not do so withou actually entering the room. The floor was covered in much the same manner as the walls— that is, with odd bits of floral woolen carpeting that had been patched with bits of other carpets of various colors. There were plants growing in tubs on a chest of drawers. There had been plants in the kitchen as well; it was the first time Emmeline had seen them inside a home.

She stood in the doorway, torn between duty and desire. She was fairly certain that she was alone in the house, but she didn't know when Mrs. Bass would return. She wanted to see herself in that large, clear looking glass, but knew that she should not enter this room without permission. There was no mirror in her own home, though several families in Fayette had them. It was a year or so since she had seen a good reflection of herself, and now she'd been told that she was pretty. At home they had never spoken of appearance. In the town, some girls were known to be liked by the boys for being pretty, but at home she had only her mother to compare herself to, and her mother's beauty was so great, in Emmeline's eyes, as to make her feel ugly—or at least dim—by comparison.

Tiptoeing, her heart beating furiously, she moved into the room, but then froze. There were footsteps behind her. She turned. In the doorway stood a girl she had noticed at breakfast because the girl had been holding a compress to her forehead and not speaking to any of the others. She was tall, slender and extremely pale.

"I'm sorry," Emmeline stammered. "I'm not—I didn't—"

"It's all right," the girl said. "It's not really all right to be in Mrs. Bass's room, but everyone wants to look in the mirror."

Emmeline couldn't speak or move. She felt for the first time in her life what it was like to be one of those children called to the front of the schoolroom over some misdeed.

"Mrs. Bass lets each of us look before church on Sunday," the girl continued, "unless she's angry for some reason." She winced and again raised the compress to her forehead.

"Are you ill?" Emmeline was finally able to ask, in a voice that she didn't recognize.

"I have a nervous affliction," the girl said.

"I'm sorry." She didn't know the meaning of the words, which had the sound of some dreadful disease, and could only wonder how the girl had passed Mrs. Bass's scrutiny if she was ill.

The girl watched Emmeline as though she were trying to make up her mind about something. Then she said, "My name is Mary Steadman."

"Emmeline Mosher."

"Look," Mary Steadman said, the compress still above her eyes. "Look, if you want to. I'll keep watch for you."

Too embarrassed to say thank you, but unable to resist the lure of the looking glass, Emmeline turned and virtually crept up on it. When she was finally in front of it, her eyes were closed—as though she would thus prevent *it* from seeing *her*. Finally she opened them—and immediately closed them again. Before her she had seen a creature so pathetic, so ugly, so *country* that she couldn't bear to believe it was herself. She opened her eyes; the creature was still there. The carefully sewn homespun dress now appeared dirty and irregular in color, misshapen in form. The hair was childish and unkempt, the stance more that of a colt than of a proper young woman. She was mortified! How could she have believed for a moment that she was growing into a pretty woman? The people who had suggested it must have been mad. Or perhaps they had been trying to comfort her. She ran from the room— past Mary Steadman, through the hallway, and out the front door.

Only the utter strangeness of the world that greeted her prevented her from going farther.

First of all, the mill noises increased tenfold at the moment she opened the door to them, and were now so loud that it was difficult to believe she wasn't right in their midst, rather than several hundred yards away. There were the brick buildings and the brick road she remembered from the night before. The very sky and the air had a different feeling than they had in Fayette. A strong wind carried massive clouds across the sun, changing the day from gray to sunny, then back again, with a suddenness that had the effect of being in step with the noises from the mill.

A woman stood on each of the two front landings of the tenements directly across the road. They chatted as they shook their mops over the rails. They looked ordinary and comfortable in a way that Mrs. Bass did not, and Emmeline half-hoped that one of them would speak to her. Then she remembered the girl in the mirror, the girl she must bring with her now to seek employment.

She must at least compose herself—conceal that girl as well as she could. She ran her fingers through her hair, wrapped her shawl more neatly around her. She ran a hand over her face with the almost-conscious intention of smoothing the lines of horror she had seen there. She practiced looking at the ladies across the road without any expression on her face, but was strangely uncertain of the effect.

Once in a while, a small coach, usually drawn by just one horse, rolled by. The coaches were painted a shiny black, rather than the bright colors of the one that had brought her from Hallowell to Portland, and yet they were somehow more elegant. In one of the coaches she saw a fine-looking lady and two children with beautiful curly hair. Her mind followed them as the coach rolled up the road, turned off before the mill, and disappeared. She thought they might be royalty, though she could not have assigned them a country or devised any reason for royalty to be in Lowell.

After a while, a tiny figure emerged from the small brick building in front of the mill which Emmeline would later learn was the countinghouse. As the figure moved closer, she recognized Mrs. Bass's bright shawl. There was no one with her, which meant that Mamie and Eliza had already been employed. Emmeline mustn't disgrace herself by being the first to fail. She decided to meet Mrs. Bass halfway up the road, but in her eagerness she misjudged the steps that led down to it, and instead of descending in a ladylike fashion, she walked into the air and tumbled down in a heap.

"Are you all right, dear?" a woman's voice called from across the road.

And then Mrs. Bass's shrill, breathless voice—"She's all right! I'll take care of the child!"

Emmeline pulled herself to her feet.

"There, now." Mrs. Bass was beside her. "You haven't hurt yourself, have you, Emmeline?"

Emmeline shook her head, though she ached all over. Her dress was covered with dust, which Mrs. Bass helped to brush off. When she had the semblance of neatness again, they began walking toward the mill.

With each step the noises from the mill grew louder, and Mrs. Bass shouted louder to be heard.

She would take Emmeline to the carding room first. The carding itself was done by men, and that was filthy work, with the cotton and "pepper trash" flying around, getting in your eyes, sticking in your hair and your clothing. But in another part of the room were the drawing frames, where fibers were laid in one direction and drawn together from cleaned sheets into rope. It was less dirty here, it was pleasant, easy work, and she would rather see an innocent young girl like Emmeline here than in the weaving rooms, where she might end up with a bounder like Maguire. To be sure, drawing in did not pay so well as weaving, but this didn't matter for the first couple of months anyway, when she would be paid as a spare hand. All spare hands were paid fifty-five cents a week over their room and board, and the pay went up to a dollar in two or three months if their work was satisfactory. Later they were paid according to their specific tasks and the amount of work they produced.

They were in the shadow of the mill. It was a while since she had been able to make out any of Mrs. Bass's words. The noise was unimaginable; it filled her lungs and her eyes as well as her ears, and her stomach had a strange feeling that was somewhere between hunger and nausea. Sometimes Mrs. Bass had to shove her gently because, without thinking, she had ceased to move.

Three men stood talking outside the small brick building in front of the mill which was the countinghouse. One of them nodded at Mrs. Bass, but the others ignored her. For a moment Emmeline thought she recognized the gentleman from the wagon, but it was only that he, that all of them, looked more like each other than any of them looked like the people at home. Across the face of the big mill building, in granite letters, was the name SUMMER CORPORATION.

There was a cry of "Watch it!" and within inches of her a large cart full of uncleaned cotton rolled by on tracks she hadn't previously noticed. Two men pushed the cart, which moved easily on the iron tracks through an open door, into the darkness of the mill. Over to their right, the tracks extended around the side of the building, which was on the bank of the river. Mrs. Bass took firm hold of her hand and pulled her into the mill.

Only then did she feel the full brunt of the noise. From a distance it had been a thunderous roll. As they'd come closer, the sounds within the thunder had become differentiated; there was no steady roll, but instead an unending series of horrendous bangings and clackings and squeakings. She put her hands over her ears. Tears came to her eyes and spilled down her cheeks, and the feeling in her stomach became more intense, closer to nausea. She was afraid of losing her breakfast. The floor trembled beneath her with the force of the vibrating heavy machinery. The only power-driven machinery she had ever seen was the water-powered wheel at the gristmill. Here she saw people switching on and off machines but had no sense of what made them erupt with power, so that the power seemed magical and then all the more ominous. Against the evidence of her blurred eyes, she felt that everyone in the room was about to die.

Cotton filled the air, for this was the room where it was cleaned and combed through, or carded. She stood fairly close to a set of carding machines whose metal teeth whirred ominously. She couldn't stop the tears from coming. Her face felt as though it were already covered with a thin layer of cotton wisps. If only they would stop the noise for one moment so she could get accustomed to the rest of it! The aisles between the machinery were not wide, and she was terrified that she might get caught on the teeth of one of the machines. Her heart beat at a fearful pace.

Mrs. Bass pulled the hand from her left ear and shouted directly into it that she must not get caught in one of "the monsters," which of course intensified her fears. For one moment her legs appeared to be paralyzed. She didn't fall, but she couldn't move them, either. Finally Mrs. Bass took her arm and half-pulled, half-pushed her toward the windows at the back of the room.

The daylight was bright here, and there was less cotton flying. A tall man in a black suit was examining one of the machines—a drawing frame—and speaking to its operator, who appeared to be able to hear him, though Emmeline did not understand how. A row of these frames stood at the window in full light. A girl attended each frame, though most of the other machines in that enormous room were attended by men. As a matter of course, they shouted at each other when they had to speak.

"Do you have need of a spare hand, Mr. Baxter?" Mrs. Bass shouted, pulling Emmeline's hand from her ear. "I have a fine young girl here for you."

Mr. Baxter eyed her in a grave but not unpleasant manner.

"I can use her," Emmeline thought she heard him shout back. "But it's the weaving rooms where they really need girls this week."

"I've just brought them two!" Mrs. Bass shouted triumphantly.

"All right, then," Mr. Baxter said. He was still shouting too, but you could not tell it from looking at him. "We'll try her."

All Emmeline heard was "try," which had an

ominous sound to it. What would become of her were she to fail at this "try"? On the other hand, how could she survive this noise if she remained?

Mrs. Bass disappeared from her side, but she barely noticed. Mr. Baxter led her to his desk, where he entered into a notebook her name, birthplace, and so on. She felt others' eyes upon her, but did not look away from Mr. Baxter. She was becoming just slightly accustomed to the noise, so that while it did not grow less fierce, her eyes stopped tearing and she lost the immediate fear that she wouldn't be able to keep down her breakfast.

Someone came over to speak to Mr. Baxter, and as she waited, she looked at her surroundings with unblurred eyes for the first time. The variety of "monsthers" would have bewildered her even had she been familiar with machinery. In that one room, in addition to the drawing frames, were the gins, whose saw-toothed wheels loosened the seeds and "pepper trash" from the cotton, and the whippers and willows, which beat it into a lighter state; from there it would be sent to the pickers, from whom it would return wound on cylinders. Then there were the four different machines involved in the carding process itself. After being carded, the sheets of clean cotton would come to the drawing frames to be pulled through so that the fibers lay in one direction, at which point they would be drawn together into a loose rope. Lastly, there were the two separate machines that would twist this loose rope into a tighter "roving" and stretch it into the form in which it would go to the spinning room. Once it was thread, it would be "dressed," or sized with steaming starch, wherever necessary. Finally, in the weaving rooms, it would be strung onto the looms and woven into cloth.

Mr. Baxter took her arm. She started. He had been trying to direct her to a drawing frame and she hadn't heard him.

"Your wages will be fifty-five cents a week above board while you're learning," he shouted. "You'll receive them on the Saturday before the thirtieth of each month."

At this moment neither the date nor the money had any significance to her. It was impossible to imagine herself here a month from now. Furthermore, she didn't know the day's date, nor was she particularly accustomed to knowing it. She was only vaguely certain that it was the first week of December.

Mr. Baxter brought her to the first drawing frame and introduced her to the operator, Sophie Hopkins, a small, bright-eyed young woman whose hair was braided in a coronet around her head, but who appeared, in every other way, to be stamped from that same mold that had produced all the competent, self-assured young women Emmeline had seen during the morning.

"Sophie's a good teacher," Mr. Baxter shouted.

Sophie's manner was noncommittal. There was a look about her that suggested she might be mischievous at another time, but now she was all business. She was one of those select few girls who could perform any task in the mill and who, if she had been a man, would have long since graduated to loom fixer and eventually, in all likelihood, to overseer. As it was, she worked as a dresser, the highest paid of the girls' jobs, for as many weeks as she could tolerate the fumes in the dressing room. Then she transferred to the drawing frames or wherever else she was needed.

Sophie demonstrated. At one end of the machine stood a large cylinder wound round by a wide sheet of cotton. As the sheet unwound from the cylinder, she guided it onto the conveyor belt which drew it onto the frame, making sure that it was straight at the front end, then moving briefly to the back end to determine that the rope produced by the frame wasn't jamming in the machine. In itself, it did not appear to be difficult work.

Yet when Sophie finished the demonstration, and said
that she would stand behind while Emmeline followed
a sheet through the frame, Emmeline's mind abruptly
stopped functioning.

The machine, which moments before had been a
mass of wood with various leather straps and iron
pieces attached to it, now seemed like a real monster
which might, in fact, devour her. She was afraid to
approach it, much less to imitate Sophie. In fact, for a
moment she couldn't remember a word of what Sophie
had said, or any part of what the other girl had done.
She simply stared in horror at the machine.

"Don't be afraid," Sophie shouted in her ear. "I'm
right here beside you."

And then a miracle occurred. Sophie's words repeated themselves several times over in Emmeline's
mind, except that the voice they were spoken in was not
Sophie's shout, but the sweet, soft voice of her mother.

Don't be afraid, Emmy, her mother said. *I'm right
here beside you.*

Emmeline could feel her as though it were she in
Sophie's form standing beside her, encouraging her,
reminding her of how she would be helping them all by
sending money to Fayette. And feeling her mother
there next to her, she started the machine and began
feeding the cotton straight into it, then walked around
it to attend to the soft rope as it fell into the barrel at
the other end. She didn't stop until the entire cylinder
had been emptied into the machine, and then she
pressed the switch and turned to Sophie. She had no
idea how long she had been at her task, and she might
have been in Fayette for all the noise she had been
aware of while she was working. Her heart was beating
as though she had just raced Luke to the Corners,
though certainly she'd had no concern with speed as
she worked. She was shaking.

"Very good," Sophie said with an approving smile.
"You'll do very well in the mill, Emmeline."

But her mother's praise, whispered afterward into her ear, was even more extravagant.

She spent what remained of the morning with Sophie, and by the end of it they were attending two drawing frames between them. The din continued, and her ears had begun to ring steadily with it, but somehow she tolerated both the ringing and the outside noise, though she never became remotely comfortable. Her arms began to ache, and her feet grew hot and tired. But she'd lost her fear because of the knowledge that she could summon her mother when she needed to.

After a while, she began to steal glances at the room around her. Once she met the eyes of a young man who was operating one of the huge carders, with its many-toothed rolling cylinders. He smiled, but she pretended not to notice. Another time, a man came to pick up the barrel full of rope and leave her an empty one. He welcomed her to the Corporation and asked where she was boarding. She pretended not to hear him. She wasn't at all pleased. She thought him forward, and only wished that someone would tell him her age so he would understand that she was too young for such attentions.

At half-past noon a loud bell went off, and the machines in the carding room came to a halt, almost at the same instant. She looked at Sophie.

"Press your switch," Sophie said. "Time for dinner."

She heard Sophie's voice as though a substantial amount of cotton had been wadded into her ears. She shook her head, but the feeling remained. Everyone was going toward the door now, some silent, most chattering gaily, but all moving quickly because the half hour they were allotted for their midday meal included the time it took them to walk to the boardinghouse and back.

Mrs. Bass's was Number 10; Sophie was in Number 39, in another row. Emmeline was disappointed, but comforted herself with the thought of seeing Sophie that afternoon. Before her, three girls walked arm in arm. They wore identical gray-and-yellow plaid shawls and those bonnets which were virtually a trademark of the Lowell girls. They looked beautiful to Emmeline in their fashionable camaraderie. How she longed to be one of them! But at the moment that she admitted this longing to herself, she vowed that she would never buy herself a single article of clothing until her family was no longer in need.

The hallway hooks were already full of shawls and bonnets. Some girls had begun eating. There was an empty seat beside Hilda again, and gratefully Emmeline went to it, not daring to ask if perhaps Hilda had saved it for her. The smell of a delicious roast and potatoes made her realize how hungry she was—and thirsty, as well. The cottony feeling had invaded her throat as well as her ears, and she took a glass of milk and drank every drop before helping herself to food.

"And how did you do this morning, Miss Emmeline of Fayette?" Hilda asked in that special mocking tone of hers.

"All right, I think," Emmeline said. "They put me at a drawing frame."

"Have you seen the other new girls?" Abbey asked from the other side of the table.

Emmeline was about to tell her that she knew only that they'd been taken in the weaving room when a sudden quiet fell upon the table, and then the room. Emmeline looked up. Mamie and Eliza had appeared at the dining-room entrance, a picture of desolation. Eliza's head rested on the shoulder of her friend, who was supporting her. She was crying. Mamie led her to the two empty seats at the end of the table. Emmeline observed them from beneath her lids. Mamie filled both their plates, but neither showed any sign of touching her food. The girl next to Mamie whispered a question whose answer was whispered around the table until it came to Emmeline: Her nerves had prevented Eliza from tying the simplest knots at the loom, or even threading a shuttle. Her hands had simply refused to work for her. The overseer had been kind and patient and had been willing to give her another chance to try in the afternoon, but Eliza had decided she could not go back there, and now she would learn whether simpler work could be found for her elsewhere in the mill. You could see that only the need to comfort her friend kept Mamie from crying too, for she knew that if Eliza could not find work she was capable of doing, they would be separated. Tears welled in Emmeline's eyes as she thought of how they must be feeling. She stared at her plate; the food no longer looked appealing.

"What will become of her if she cannot work on another machine?" she whispered to Hilda.

"It will depend on how hopeless she is," Hilda said coolly. "If she's really bad, she'll be put on a list and no one will employ her."

"But—"

"But eat your food," Hilda said. "It happens with some regularity."

Emmeline dared not question her further, but she couldn't eat, either. Everyone had become subdued when Mamie and Eliza appeared, but now the chatter and the banging of plates and silver were louder than they'd been before. Emmeline thought of Florina and Opal, and how the Lowell world had closed over them—like a bubbling stream that disguised a deep and dark current pulling in the opposite direction. You would not have known that something bad was happening without looking at Mamie and Eliza. Where would they go if they couldn't get by here? Where were Florina and Opal? Perhaps Opal, at least, had managed to find a place in Lowell.

"It's awful, isn't it?" the girl on the other side of her whispered.

Emmeline looked at her. It was someone she hadn't

noticed before, yet the girl had a bright face with lively eyes, and there was a beautiful red ribbon braided through her hair knot.

"My name is Fanny Bartlett," the girl said. "I know yours is Emmeline, because I heard Hilda say it."

Emmeline smiled. Fanny Bartlett was the first girl she'd met in Lowell who seemed really eager to be friendly. She glanced at Hilda, who was ignoring both of them.

"You must try not to think about it," Fanny advised in a low voice, "or you won't be able to eat, and if you don't eat now, you'll be fearfully hungry through the afternoon."

She had the rapid, assured speech of someone who had been in Lowell for a considerable time. Emmeline picked at the food, as much to oblige Fanny as because she'd regained interest in it.

"You must tell yourself that she likely comes from a good home, and for all we know she will be just as happy to go back there. Otherwise, you will always be in tears over some poor soul."

Fanny asked Emmeline's age and was the first person who did not seem to find it reason for either amusement or condescension; she said that she had had a friend on the Boott Corporation, where she worked before coming here, who was even younger than Emmeline. Fanny herself was eighteen and came from Springfield, Massachusetts. She had worked in Lawrence for more than a year before coming to Lowell the previous year.

Suddenly the bell rang. Emmeline looked at her nearly full plate in dismay; she'd only begun to regain her appetite.

Fanny laughed. "Put the meat in the bread and hold it in the folds of your skirt," she whispered. "It's against the rules, but you'll be in trouble if you don't eat something. Do you want to walk back with me?"

Emmeline readily assented, then turned to Hilda, who she felt was watching her.

"Do you know that's against the rules?" Hilda asked.

"Yes," she said, "but Fanny—"

"Never mind," Hilda said, standing. "I just wanted to know if you knew."

She began to walk away, but Emmeline was concerned that Hilda was annoyed with her.

"Will you walk with us, Hilda?" she asked.

"I don't walk with Miss Bartlett," Hilda said stiffly, and joined some other girls who were leaving the room.

Emmeline stared after her in astonishment. Fanny was also standing now, waiting. Emmeline couldn't tell if Fanny had heard Hilda and had no idea herself what to make of the words. Because it was the easiest thing to do, she finally dismissed them from her mind, telling herself that she would question Hilda in the evening. Then she joined Fanny and the others heading back toward the mill. The small stream of girls from each house joined the other streams to form a great river of female figures moving up the brick road. This time she didn't cover her ears against the noise, because Fanny was diverting her with stories and questions during the entire walk. It was only when they reached the countinghouse that she realized that somewhere along the way, she had dropped the bread and meat.

The first operatives were already at their machines, and the noise was at full volume. Fanny saw someone she wanted to talk to and disappeared from Emmeline's side, saying that she would see her at supper. The noise grew worse by the moment. How foolish to have hoped that she was already accustomed to it! Just outside the big doors she stepped aside for a moment to gird herself, then, resisting the temptation to put her hands over her ears as she had in the morning, when she was a new girl fresh from the country, she entered the carding room with the last of the returning operatives.

Sophie was already at the drawing frame, but as Emmeline went to join her, Mr. Baxter beckoned her to him and told her that she was to be sent up to one of the weaving rooms to learn to loom. She must not, he said quickly when he saw her expression, take this for a bad sign, but for a good one. They were sending Sophie up to one weaving room and her to the other because she had proved herself such a ready learner. There was more thread on the warp beams in both weaving rooms than there were weavers to handle it.

So absorbed was she in what would await her in the weaving room that it did not enter her mind, until she passed a damp-eyed Eliza on the steps, that it might be Eliza she was replacing. Emmeline greeted the other girl, but Eliza did not appear to notice Emmeline passing within inches of her, much less to hear the greeting. Another girl was accompanying Eliza down to the carding room, although Emmeline had been sent on her own and told to ask for Mr. Maguire.

She pushed open a heavy door and found herself in the first of the two weaving rooms. In appearance as well as in feeling, it differed vastly from the carding room, which was much, much larger and held so many different kinds of machines. The noise, if still great, was less overwhelming. There were only two rows of large looms—twenty in all—which, in spite of the differences in size and construction from theirs at home, were immediately recognizable to her. The overseer was letting out filling to an operative, so that his back was to Emmeline. Some girls attended one loom; others went back and forth between two. At the far end of the room, Emmeline saw Mamie working with another girl; Mamie looked up and caught her eye, then quickly looked down again. After a while, the overseer turned and saw her. This was Mr. Maguire.

Something about the way he looked struck her immediately, but she didn't know what it was. His hair was black and glossy and curled down over his forehead and his ears. His color was high, his cheekbones were prominent, and he had a rather large, jutting jaw. His eyes were small and black, shiny and humorous.

"Well, now, who have we here? Is this the new girl who learns so quickly?" His voice was deep and musical, but the speech was Mrs. Bass's! As a matter of fact, to her eyes they might well have been brother and sister, which was, she now realized in confusion, what had struck her right away when she saw him. "If you're to be my angel of mercy," Mr. Maguire continued, "then you must tell me your name."

"Emmeline Mosher."

"Come along, then, Emmeline." He was regarding her with a combination of amusement and seriousness. She could barely look at him, for she was remembering Mrs. Bass's dire warnings. "I'll give you to Corinne," he said. "She's good with the new girls."

Corinne was large and robust in appearance, but shy in manner, with a voice that was virtually inaudible over the din of the looms. Emmeline watched carefully as the other girl demonstrated the threading of the shuttle, and she was able to master that step, as well as the actual weaving of the filling threads into the warp threads that were strung onto the loom, with relative ease. For all the differences in the size of the equipment and the texture of the cloth, it was not so different from the weaving of homespun she had done in Fayette. But tying the knots when the threads broke was considerably more difficult. She eventually mastered the filling knots, but each warp knot she had to tie was an agony. Warp threads were not only starched before they were brought to the weaving room, but were also strung so tightly on the loom as to make it almost impossible to get the grip that was necessary to tie them. Many times, as the thread broke between her fingers or slipped out of them, she was close to tears, and only saved herself by thinking, *Remember carefully so that you can write to Mama.*

She had begun the afternoon with a reasonable optimism. The dull aches and little pains that had plagued her before midday seemed to have disappeared as she left the carding room. But they returned quickly when she resumed work, and their intensity rapidly increased. A band of pain now ran from one arm across her back, up to her neck, and then down into the other arm. Her feet swelled further in her shoes and burned as though she were standing on hot bricks. At home she frequently moved around to relieve the monotony of spinning and weaving. Here there was no such opportunity. Furthermore, she was hungry. Her stomach was a small child crying out within her. It seemed after a while that she had never been so hungry in Fayette, even when food was scarcest. She thought with longing of the bread and meat she had dropped on the road.

A dial at the top of the loom measured the amount of cloth woven on it. Corinne would be paid by the amount of work she produced, and Emmeline felt doubly anxious because she was concerned that her slowness would cost the other girl wages. This anxiety, in turn, made her clumsy. Her eyes grew bleary and her temples throbbed. It seemed that she had been in the weaving room for days.

Surely it was time to go back for supper. There was a clock on the wall opposite Mr. Maguire's desk, but she couldn't see its face from her loom. When Corinne told her she might "take a little rest," she walked over to the clock. It was not quite three in the afternoon! She stared at it, first in disbelief, then in horror. It was impossible that she had been in the weaving room for only two hours! At that moment, as she tried to determine whether she hadn't made some error in reading the time, she was convinced that she would not be able to last another four hours in the weaving room no matter how she tried. She felt tempted to run immediately and spare herself the humiliation of being found inadequate later.

"The first day is the worst," said a voice behind her. A deep and soothing voice that carried a brogue like Mrs. Bass's.

"Thank you," she stammered. "I know I—" but the words trailed off as she turned to him, for she had no idea how to finish the sentence.

"You're doing very well, Emmeline," he said. Then, "Do they have anything else they call you?"

She smiled, because only he and Mrs. Bass pronounced it *Emmeloin*.

"I mean," he said, "do you have a shorter name?"

"My father calls me Emmy," she said. "My brothers and sisters say Emmy too. Or Em." Luke was the one who called her Em. She thought of Luke and her father for the first time that day, wondering what they were doing right now and whether they were waiting to hear from her.

"Ah, that's better. Now, Emmy, the girls always believe they shall not survive the first day. Try not to think about it at all—that's the best way. Do as well as you're able, and think as little as you're able."

Was this the man whom Mrs. Bass thought unkind? It seemed impossible. Emmeline would have gone back to the loom in any event, for she had little choice, but it was his words which gave her hope that she might withstand the ordeal of that first day.

But, indeed, as the day wore on, the ordeal grew worse. Her feet by now had swelled so much that her toes were numb, and her neck and shoulders ached so badly that each time she raised one arm she was sure it would be the last time. She was becoming accustomed to the noise, but only in the sense that it had begun to feel as though it arose from within her head instead of attacking it from the outside. While the throbbing in her temples seemed a direct result of the workings of some powerful engine controlled by the Summer Corporation. Tears hovered inside her bleary eyes, but did not fall because there was no single sharp pain or harsh word to release them.

She was now tending the loom by herself. Over the incessant whirring and clatter of the machines, the girls talked among themselves, but Emmeline was only vaguely aware of their conversation. Mr. Maguire came by frequently to look over her shoulder and tell her that she was doing very well for the first day. He was seldom still. He himself supplied the filling thread to the operatives, all the while engaging in pleasant conversation with them. It was beyond Emmeline's imagination that this was the man from whom Mrs. Bass thought she required protection.

The darkness deepened. Mr. Maguire circled the room, lighting the oil lamps on the walls. Pain and exhaustion pervaded Emmeline's body, finally erasing even random thoughts from her mind. The world around her ceased to exist. At seven o'clock, when the bells rang, she didn't immediately understand what they were. She stood motionless in the midst of threading a shuttle, and didn't move until Corinne came to show her how she must leave her loom at the end of the day. Then her knees buckled beneath her—as though, finally relieved of her labors, she would not be given the strength to walk away.

"One of the new girls can't bear to leave," someone said. "She loves the weaving room so much she wants to stay over her time the first day!"

A few girls laughed, but one said that Emmeline was too green and miserable to be teased.

Emmeline heard them as though through bales of cotton.

Mamie walked by between two other girls without so much as a glance at Emmeline. Corinne asked which house Emmeline was boarding in, and Emmeline told her.

"I'm in Thirty-four—Mrs. Johnson's," Corinne said. "Oh, well, then, see you tomorrow." And she moved ahead of Emmeline to join her friends.

Mr. Maguire was making the rounds of the room, checking each loom.

"The girls start the first day wondering if the mill shall have them," he said, "and finish wondering if they shall have the mill."

She smiled. She didn't know whether to leave or stay. He had a wistful look which would become familiar to her; at the end of the day he always looked as though he were dreaming of the faraway place he'd come from.

"I *must* stay in Lowell," she said.

"Of course, of course. You *shall* stay. And you shall do beautifully. And you shall even find it easy, after the first few days."

She was silent. She couldn't believe that.

"Who's boarding you?" he called over his shoulder. He had finished checking the looms and was putting out the lights in the lamps.

"Mrs. Bass."

He said nothing. She began to move toward the door.

"Can you read?" he asked.

"Oh, yes."

"Do you know about the library?"

"I know that there is one."

He began to tell her how to find it and what it would cost her to join, but then he turned and saw her expression—and laughed at himself.

"Here the poor girl can barely stand on her two feet," he said, "and I'm telling her how to walk to the library!"

She didn't know whether to move on.

"If you wait until I . . ." he began, then changed his mind. "No, you'll get down fine," he said, almost as though to himself. "I've more to do here. You run on to the house and have yourself some food and a good night's sleep."

She thanked him and said good night. Her mouth and throat were dry, but her hunger was gone, and food had no appeal. She was one of the last of the girls to straggle into the house, and would have gone directly upstairs to bed had not Mrs. Bass seen her from the entrance to the dining room.

"There you are, child," she said. "Where are the other new girls?"

"I don't know, Ma'am."

"Well, come in, then. Come and get some food in you."

Emmeline followed her into the dining room, not looking for anyone, only wanting to sit down. There were two empty seats, and Mrs. Bass sat beside her—pouring her a glass of milk, which she drank immediately, filling Emmeline's plate with food, in which Emmeline could not take an interest. She couldn't even smell it.

"And how did you find drawing in?" Mrs. Bass asked.

"They put me in the weaving room this afternoon," Emmeline said. Her eyes were closing.

"Which weaving room?"

"Mr. Maguire's."

Mrs. Bass muttered something in Gaelic. Emmeline's eyes opened. The woman's face had darkened like the sky before a storm. Although Emmeline didn't understand Mrs. Bass's feelings, she was shaken by them—as though she herself were a shallow-rooted sapling that would have to weather the storm.

"Listen to me, Emmeline . . ." She uttered the name in that way in which only one other person had ever pronounced it. "You must keep away from Maguire. He's dangerous."

"Dangerous?" She was awake now. "I don't understand."

"You must take my word for it," she said. "He's hurt girls like you. A girl was turned off the Corporation on his account. A girl who looked . . . The first time I saw you I thought of her."

"What must I do?" Emmeline asked, frightened in spite of herself.

"You must keep away from him. There's nothing for it, if they've put you in the weaving room. But you must never so much as walk outside of it with him. Now eat your supper." She stood and began moving around the room, talking to the other girls.

Emmeline looked at the food on her plate, but it

might have been cotton for all its appeal. She ate a bit of the sweet bread, picking around the fruit and nuts in it, their chewy texture more than she could manage. There were pickles and relishes on the table, and she found herself reaching for a pickle, which had the virtue of a smell she could discern. Its sourness was pleasant to her tongue. She drank some more milk.

After the meal, some girls left the room hastily, while others lingered to talk. Fanny Bartlett stopped to ask how Emmeline had fared; Emmeline had forgotten her existence until that moment. Emmeline told her that she had managed. Fanny said she supposed, it being Emmeline's first day, that Emmeline would not care to take a walk with her along Merrimack Street. Emmeline told her, without humor, that she was not certain she would be able to walk up the stairs to her bed.

"Fanny wants the new girl to come on one of her walks," the girl beside Emmeline whispered audibly to her companion as Fanny left the room.

There was a stifled giggle, and then something else was said about Fanny and her walks, but Emmeline was too tired to try to make sense of it. She gathered herself for the move upstairs as though she were preparing for a long journey, and when she finally reached her bed she fell asleep on it without taking off her clothes or getting under the covers or moving over to make room for Hilda. Five minutes later, or so it seemed, the morning bells were going off in her ears. She couldn't believe that the night had passed. How was it possible that her body ached more than it had when she'd gone to bed, that she was as tired as though she had worked through the night instead of sleeping? She stared at the others as though they were part of a bad dream she'd been having before she awakened, though she could no longer remember what had happened in the dream.

The second day was better than the first only in that she was less fearful. Not only did Mr. Maguire continue to encourage her in a way that made it clear that she was not in danger of being turned off the Corporation, but when she was in his kindly presence she forgot entirely Mrs. Bass's dire warnings—as though they had been about someone else. The knots came more easily than they had the day before, so that she didn't get scared each time she saw a break in the thread. At the end of the day, Corinne told her that she was rapidly becoming an "old hand."

On Sunday she slept soundly through the church bells and the breakfast hour, though Hilda and Abbey told her later that they'd tried to rouse her. When she finally awakened, she was alone in the long attic and had no idea of the time. It was a gray day.

She dressed and went downstairs, to find that the other girls had returned from church and were in the dining room. Mrs. Bass made it clear that while she might be excused this first Sunday, she must attend church regularly.

In the afternoon there was a light snow. For the first time, she sat in the great keeping room with the other girls, who were talking, reading, mending, and writing letters. She had been in Lowell for a week; certainly it was time for her to be writing home. Yet she could not bear the thought. It wasn't only because she was afraid of sounding unhappy. At the mill she thought often of her mother, sometimes even pretending that they were together and her mother was listening as she herself explained the functions of the various machinery and the customs of the city. At the big, impersonal mill, this picture provided her with the support she required to carry on, but in the more homelike atmosphere of Mrs. Bass's, thoughts of her mother threatened to dissolve her will and turn her into a helpless child. She was conscious of her age all the time and knew the other girls were too, for she had heard one whisper to another that Emmeline was not yet fourteen—in a manner that suggested this was a serious defect in character. She tried to make up for her age by acting cool and self-sufficient when she was in a group, but aside from the effect that this pose had on some of the other girls, the very pretense made her feel less independent than ever. She could not even read her Bible yet, for the memories that it evoked were so powerful that she feared they would shatter her precarious balance; what would happen if, lying in bed or sitting in a comfortable chair in the keeping room, she were to directly address her mother in writing?

So she didn't write home that first Sunday, but for the first time sat in the great keeping room and listened. The conversation—the gossip, the jokes, the serious information—was overwhelming to her, as it was to girls much older than she when they were new to the city. Not only was the talk faster and cleverer than any she had ever heard, but in its quantity, and in the intimacy of its subjects, it often left her head spinning. In her second week, as her body became habituated to the work and she found herself able to stay awake for a while after supper, she was learning, it sometimes seemed, more than she ought to know about more people than she had ever known to exist.

If she sat down in Mamie's vicinity, Mamie moved or turned her back on Emmeline, who finally realized that the other girl was angry with her for replacing her friend in the weaving room, although apparently Abbey and one or two others had told her that the fault was not Emmeline's. Eliza had found a place in one of the Tremont mills, and it was understood that if she did well there, Mamie would join her at the end of the month. There was talk of other girls who had failed to find a place, or had been turned off the Corporation for lateness or other poor behavior. Occasionally girls were sent home with consumption, but that never happened in Mrs. Bass's because of her rigor in screening newcomers. It was in hearing the talk about this dreaded disease that Emmeline came to understand, for the first time, why Opal had been sent away just for coughing.

There were dark hints about Fanny, who was not liked by the other girls. She was considered "loose," a word whose meaning was foreign to Emmeline in this context. There was speculation that Fanny took walks only in order to speak with men from the mills along the way, and not because she couldn't sit still for long enough to read a book, as she claimed. Emmeline didn't question Hilda further about Fanny, as she'd meant to, because Fanny was her only friend and it would have seemed disloyal. No one else had made the barest overture to her. In the keeping room, she listened to the conversation with her eyes cast down, unsure that the girls should be saying the things they said, but quite sure that she should not be so eager to hear every word.

Abbey had a beau who was liked by all the other girls except Lydia, who thought him not nearly good enough for her friend. Any man coming to call on one of the girls (acceptable if Mrs. Bass granted permission the previous day) had to speak to that girl among the others in the keeping room and was subject to considerable teasing during the visit, as well as a certain amount of mockery afterward. A rather disreputable-looking man who sauntered into the keeping room and eyed the girls in a way they did not like was Mrs. Bass's son, who worked in a low capacity in one of the Lawrence mills. He had a wife whom Mrs. Bass would not allow into her house, and indeed she always took her son to the back room, where he would be away from the girls. Mrs. Bass also had a daughter named Victoria, "the apple of her eye," who had married very well and lived the life of a real lady in Boston. The girls' feelings about Mrs. Bass varied from mistrustful affection to outright (if well-concealed) fear and dislike, but none of these feelings prevented them from finding in her an object of perpetual interest. They passed on bits of information about her as though they were sweets from the tray of one of the peddlers who were forbidden admission to Mrs. Bass's, though they invaded most of the other boardinghouses regularly.

It was as the wife, then the widow, of Jacob Bass, a Yankee and an engineer, that Mrs. Bass had achieved her comfortable social position. The Irish had not yet come to America in substantial numbers, and of those few who had made their way to Lowell, only she and Stephen Maguire had risen past low forms of labor. Jacob Bass was a strange and brilliant man who had been instrumental in devising and building much of the original mill machinery. He was said to have treated his helpers with greater kindness than any other Lowell employer, until he suspected them of wrongdoing, at which time he turned upon them—without question, and with such vehemence as to make all around him fearful. He never laid off his employees in poor times, as others did, yet he docked them severely if they were so much as two minutes late for work. He disappeared for days at a time, as often in winter as in summer, and was said to have hidden in a cave outside Lowell, looking at a nearby waterfall, not eating, simply thinking of new machines. He had ended his own life, hanging himself in the barn of his home on the outskirts of Lowell. He had left his widow with two young children, a mortgage, and not a penny to her name, but with enough friends in high places so that she was able to secure the management of one of the boarding-houses.

It was one of the worst-kept secrets of Lowell that Molly Bass and Stephen Maguire were cousins, and that Mrs. Bass could not stand the sight of Stephen but was devoted to his wife. Mrs. Maguire was the former Ivory Stone, whose father, Elijah Stone, was agent of the Summer Corporation, a man who was said to profess great devotion to the Lord and not only demand that devotion in others, but insist upon controlling their manner of displaying it. Ivory was the favored of his two daughters, and his hatred of Stephen Maguire was so great that it was visible to the most casual observer seeing them briefly together at the mill.

Stephen Maguire had come to Lowell in 1822 in a band of Irish laborers working on the expansion of the Pawtucket Canal, as well as the construction of the other canals which would bring water for power to the mills. When that work was finished, he had labored at the construction of the mill buildings themselves. He was virtually unique among those early Irishmen, however, in that he had later found employment within the mill itself—in the iron shop of the Summer Corporation, where he caught the eye of Jacob Bass. Stephen had a genius with machinery and quickly became Bass's valued assistant. It was on a trip to the Irish shantytown called the Acre, where Stephen lived, that Jacob had met his future wife, Stephen's cousin, Molly.

There had always been antagonism between Stephen and Molly and it didn't abate now, but the two men remained good working friends, and when the mill opened, Stephen was made overseer and first mechanic of the iron shop. It was during this period that he met and courted Ivory Stone over the furious opposition of her father. It was said that Elijah Stone had eventually consented to the marriage only because Ivory threatened that if he did not, she would marry Stephen in the Catholic church and go to live with him on the Acre. Stone then gave his consent on the condition that they live with him in his home. And there Stephen and Ivory still lived, along with their four children, Mr. Stone, a widower, and Mr. Stone's maiden sister.

In the ensuing years Stephen Maguire had performed every man's task in the mill and then been overseer of each room in turn, because his father-in-law insisted that he must know every aspect of the Corporation in order to advance through it. From what Emmeline could make out between the lines of the keeping-room conversation, it appeared that Mr. Maguire was more

liked than admired among the girls, something in his
familiarity with them, his eagerness to talk, even to
entertain them with stories and jests, keeping them
from looking up to him as they did to some of the
overseers. But Ivory Maguire was universally admired.

Stephen Maguire had once told someone that his
wife had an eye for injustice so keen that she could see
one when it reached Lawrence and be waiting for it
with a stick at the Pawtucket Bridge before it could get
into Lowell. The remark had been received without
irony and repeated among the girls as a pithy way of
describing what they knew to be true: Mrs. Maguire
was a woman of conscience. Along with Philomena
Whitehead, the wife of another overseer, she had been
instrumental in starting the library and in initiating the
series of Lyceum lectures that brought speakers like
Mr. Emerson and Mr. Graham to Lowell; she was
involved not only in the city's cultural activities, but in
its physical and spiritual welfare too, being active in the
Episcopal Church and in a committee that sought to
open a public hospital to benefit the mill employees.
She was also said to have a strong sense of the injustice
that kept women illiterate while the men in their
families, sometimes with less ability, were sent off for
an education. Her very clothing and demeanor inspired
confidence, for in spite of her wealth she insisted upon
dressing always in the simple black "uniform" of the
mill girls, and never wore jewelry or rouge, though it
was coming into fashion among the others in her circle.
Lastly, Ivory Maguire was said to have acted with great
dignity during the fuss over Lucy Shorter, the girl who
had been dismissed "on Mr. Maguire's account" three
years earlier, making it a point to appear with her
husband in places where she might not otherwise have
been, meeting him often at night with her carriage,
making her devotion to him clear in a way that it had
not been to most observers before. Mrs. Maguire held
a Christmas tea each year for those among the mill girls
whom she considered her "friends," but it was some-

how clear that her friendliness, as opposed to her charity, was confined to such occasions.

Near the end of her second week in Lowell, Emmeline borrowed pen and paper from Hilda and finally wrote to her mother. She said that the work was hard but she was managing well; that the girls were nice; that at the end of December she would be sending her first wages. When she had finished, she stared at the letter in disbelief. How many times that week had she said to herself, *I must put this in my letter to Mama?* The letter contained six lines, in the last of which she said that she hoped all was well at home and sent her love to her brothers and sisters. What had seemed important at the moment when it occurred was now lost in the tide of events. Besides, to relate any one incident would have required such an abundance of explanatory detail that the very thought of writing it exhausted her. Furthermore, with all the explanations in the world her mother would not be able to imagine Lowell, and this, if she let herself think about it, was frightening to her. She had never had a thought or an experience that she couldn't share with her mother, and the sense that she could never fully convey Lowell gave her a feeling of isolation over and beyond the simple longing for home.

She looked forward to attending church again, for she had never lost that sense that God could not find her in Lowell and she wanted to tell Him where she was. She said her prayers faithfully each night but had no conviction that she was heard, and once in a while she found herself searching the sky, as though here she could find no closer sign of His presence. Surely being in church would change that.

On her second Sunday in Lowell she attended the First Freewill Baptist Church with Fanny, who had once been a Methodist but said that she would just as

lief go to Baptist church with Emmeline. Fanny lent her
a bonnet. Fanny loved fine clothes and had no obligations at home, so that she had a larger wardrobe than
many of the other girls. She had offered to lend
Emmeline a shawl as well, which Emmeline could not
let herself accept. But she had already seen that
without a bonnet one announced oneself as just fresh
from the country.

The long walk to the church was the first she had
taken beyond the mill and was difficult for her, since
her feet had swelled almost a full size and the boot
leather pressed against her sore toes. But it was a clear,
sunny day, and there were many diversions along the
way. The church was on Merrimack Street, and to
reach it they had to pass a series of elegant shops with
windows full of goods—clothing, jewelry, and even
upholstered furniture—the like of which Emmeline had
never seen. Then, the streets themselves teemed with
elegant people walking to church in fine woolen coats
and suits. Many women wore coats cut so well they
might have been dresses, but for their heavy fabric.
And then, of course, there were the bonnets.

Several times along the way they were greeted by
young men Fanny knew. No amount of gossip could
have prevented Emmeline from admiring the other
girl's ease in talking with them. Fanny chatted lightly
about her work, introduced Emmeline as her friend,
discussed one or another person who had left the mills.
Fanny had been at the Boott Corporation before
coming to the Summer mill and knew an astonishing
number of people. Alone with Emmeline after each
encounter, she spoke lightly but never cruelly of the
men they had met. One was handsome, another good
at his work; still another was a wonderful dancer but
unsteady in his habits. Fanny set great store by a man's
appearance; she herself wasn't really pretty, though she
looked fine to Emmeline, with her stylish clothes and
vivacious air.

If only, Emmeline thought, she could have one

friend who was as warm as Fanny and was as wise as Hilda. If only Hilda had offered herself as a friend. Hilda had no one close "pal" among the other girls but was respected by all of them. Fanny had only a slight connection—and that one negative—to the others, so that to be her friend did not mean to become a part of Lowell. Emmeline had left her old home but did not have a new one, nor anyone to replace the members of her family she had lost in the move—although Mr. Maguire sometimes seemed more like a kindly relative than an employer. Once she had dreamed he was driving her father's wagon past the sawmill on the far side of the pond.

On the corner before them was a huge granite fortress of a building. The doors were open and people mounted the steps, but it had not yet occurred to Emmeline that this was the church.

"Well," Fanny said, looking up at the clear blue sky as though she would not see it again for weeks, "here we are."

Emmeline looked up with a start and saw the cross, also of stone, "It doesn't look like a church," she said.

Fanny laughed so heartily that several people on the steps turned to stare at her disapprovingly.

The interior of the church was not only huge, but beautiful in an extremely forbidding way. The pulpit, the pews, even the stone floor were polished to a high sheen, and the windows, which from the outside had been a dull, mottled glass, now glowed with color.

In the front of the center aisle, the minister stood talking with a distinguished-looking couple. He himself was tall and angular, with thinning black hair and a mouth that occasionally signaled a smile without actually smiling. Fanny had nothing to say about the Reverend Richards, nor did she know the other members of the congregation. The girls here all worked on other corporations. Indeed, Fanny whispered, this was why she was willing to come here. In the Episcopal church, if your eye wandered for a moment during the service, someone was sure to say over Sunday dinner that your mind had been everywhere but in church that morning.

The first rows were taken on both sides of the aisle by people of the sort she had seen talking to the minister, the balance being about two-thirds mill girls and another third mill families, often with children, looking respectable but somewhat poorer than the girls. Some of the women wore dresses and shawls like her own, and they had a raw country look to them—like the girl she had seen that first day in Mrs. Bass's mirror. (She had not taken a chance on looking into it this morning.)

Soon Reverend Richards mounted to the pulpit and began to speak. His voice, while clear, had a thin, tight quality, and his speech was the speech of the Boston gentry, as close to an Englishman's accents as any Emmeline would ever hear. Repressing her disappointment, she tried to concentrate on his words.

He took his text from Proverbs, a passage that was relatively unfamiliar to her:

*My son, attend unto my wisdom, and bow thine ear to
    my understanding;*
*That thou mayest regard discretion, and that thy lips
    may keep knowledge.*
*For the lips of a strange woman drop as an
    honeycomb, and her mouth is smoother than oil;*
*But her end is bitter as wormwood, sharp as a
    two-edged sword.*
Her feet go down to death; her steps take hold on hell.
*Lest thou shouldest ponder the path of life, her ways
    are moveable, that thou canst not know them.*
*Hear me now therefore, O ye children, and depart not
    from the words of my mouth.*

Her mind wandered. If she did not understand the words, they had an ominous quality, and Reverend

Richards' voice did nothing to make them gentler. Beside her, Fanny fidgeted in her seat so visibly that Emmeline feared she would call attention to both of them. Still, Emmeline began to understand why church was required in Lowell, in the entire service, as it continued, there was neither warmth nor comfort, only a sense that here was one more place to be on guard.

They were among the first to leave. With Fanny, she ran down the steps a little more quickly than she should have.

They walked home a different way than they had come, detouring so that they passed two rows of unfamiliar boardinghouses. Most of the people they passed on this road were men, and Fanny told Emmeline that this was who boarded on this row—some in houses with their families, others alone, like the girls. As they reached the end of the row, a man called to Fanny from one of the windows, and she waved to him.

"Hold on, Fanny," he called through the window. "Like to talk to you a minute!"

"That's Billy Borden," Fanny said. "He was in the carding room at Boott with me." She giggled. "They used to call him Billy Boredom because when he was at one place for a week, he would ask for a transfer to do something else. He must still be on the Boott, though; these are Boott houses." She fussed with her bonnet and shawl.

Emmeline stood indecisively, not knowing whether Fanny wanted her to remain while she talked with her friend.

"Should I go back to Mrs. Bass's?" It was difficult to simply stand there, with men passing on the street, looking at them, as they passed, in a way that boys at home did not. There was a girl in Fayette, Annie Kemp, who liked Luke, and Emmeline had noticed that when she was in the vicinity, Luke looked at the ground all the time.

"If you like," Fanny said. "I'll see you in the dining

room." She pointed Emmeline back toward Merrimack Street.

Emmeline went on her way, but close to the point where she was to turn off Merrimack, she met up with Hilda and Abbey and Lydia, who were returning from St. Anne's Episcopal Church. Walking just in back of them were three other girls from Mrs. Bass's whom Emmeline didn't yet know.

"Aha!" said one of them, not bothering to keep her voice low. "Who goes to church with Miss Fanny Bartlett comes home alone!"

Emmeline was startled and did not know what to say.

"Leave Emmeline alone," Abbey said over her shoulder. "She doesn't know what you're talking about."

"Well," Hilda said, "it's best she learn, if she doesn't know already." She turned to Emmeline. "How did you walk back? Along the Boott row?"

Emmeline nodded. The girls in back of her tittered. Emmeline was full of curiosity, yet did not want to hear anything bad said of Fanny.

"And in Fanny's bonnet!" one of them exclaimed, giggling.

Emmeline felt her cheeks flush—more in anger than in shame, at that moment.

"Let's not be nasty," Hilda said.

"Miss Hilda, the schoolmarm, as ever," someone sighed.

But Hilda took Emmeline's arm and moved with her quickly, so that they were some yards ahead of the others. They turned another corner and they were almost back at Mrs. Bass's.

"What is it that's wrong with Fanny's bonnet?" Emmeline asked.

"It's not her bonnet," Hilda said. "It's her behavior. She has an easy way with men. She talks to anyone who talks to her."

So it was that very air of Fanny's which Emmeline

had admired that had gotten her into trouble. Emmeline didn't know what was expected of her. She would return Fanny's bonnet when she saw her, but beyond that . . .

"Must I do something?" she asked Hilda.

"That's up to you, Emmeline," Hilda said. "You're very young to risk acquiring a poor reputation."

Emmeline was frightened. If she was too young to risk her reputation, she was surely also too young to make her way through Lowell without a friend.

"She has been very friendly to me," Emmeline ventured.

"The girls who don't have friends always take up the new girls," Hilda said.

That was even worse, for it suggested that she must be the more careful of people as they were the more friendly to her.

"How will I find a friend, then?" Emmeline asked, hoping, of course, that Hilda would offer herself. Hilda would be more than a friend; she would be a guide, an older sister such as Emmeline herself had been to those of the girls at home who wanted her to be. With Hilda she would be safe from making the terrible mistakes that would doom her in Lowell.

But what Hilda said was "You must be patient, Emmeline. How long have you been here? Is it a week? Two? After a while you will find an affinity with some of the others. Girls your own age, or perhaps a little older. Don't try to make everything happen at once. That's what Fanny does."

Fanny was impatient to have friends. Fanny was friendly to new girls and to men, talking to both in the same jolly way. It was difficult to see the harm in that, but what Hilda was telling her was important. She must avoid Fanny, not because Fanny was bad, but because . . . but at that moment, as they stood in front of Mrs. Bass's, Fanny approached from the other direction, bobbing in and out amongst the groups of walking girls, moving faster than any of them. Emmeline started guiltily; there she was, the same warm girl who had befriended her. Then she grew confused, for Hilda was watching her. As Fanny came up to her, she took off the bonnet and handed it to Fanny. Fanny looked at Hilda and back to Emmeline. Then she took the bonnet from Emmeline and mounted the front steps without a word. It was unbearable.

"Fanny!" Emmeline called, "Thank you for lending me your bonnet!"

Fanny turned to her with a smile of such sweetness as to make Emmeline feel relieved that she'd spoken, anxious to reassure her further.

"Are you going to be in the keeping room until dinner?"

Fanny hesitated, then said that she thought not. She seemed to be avoiding looking at Hilda. She wasn't hungry anyway, she said. She thought she might just go upstairs and sleep right through Sunday dinner.

Hilda did not bother to modify her expression of disapproval.

"Can I not be polite to her?" Emmeline asked anxiously.

Hilda shrugged. "You are playing with fire, Emmeline. The girls will tolerate your country ways for a while, and your clothes. But if you lose your reputation, I fear there will be no way to gain it back." She walked up the stairs and into the house.

Now Emmeline was badly frightened. She wanted Hilda to explain how she could lose her reputation without doing anything wrong. She called after Hilda some words to the effect that she would be careful, but she had no idea of how she would go about being careful, aside from by not being friendly to Fanny. Her head ached terribly; she felt that she couldn't face either Fanny or Hilda. She tried to think of what her mother would advise in this circumstance. Surely she would want Emmeline to be kind. And yet her mother had never gone against the rules of either the Church or the townspeople, and Emmeline could not imagine her doing it here.

She ate her dinner in a mood of fearful abstraction, barely noticing when questions or comments were put to her. Afterward, she went directly up to her room and slept away the afternoon.

But Emmeline was spared the necessity of dealing with the question of Fanny Bartlett, for that very week Fanny was turned off the Corporation, having been found, during working hours, in a place "where she did not belong." For several days no one spoke of anything else.

It had happened in the morning, and Fanny was gone by the time they returned to Mrs. Bass's for their midday meal. The most prevalent account was that she had been found with one of her beaux in the machine shop, where there was no reason for any female to be, and had been discharged on the spot. The man had left with her. In one account, the man had been given the opportunity to stay, but had left with Fanny for the West. In another, they had both been discharged and had then thrown in their lots together. (It was later discovered that the man had neither left nor been discharged, but was still there in the machine shop, working on as though he had never heard of Fanny Bartlett.)

After a few days, Fanny disappeared from the conversation almost as completely as she had from the boardinghouse. But Emmeline dreamed of Fanny at night and could not forget her during the day. She dreamed that Fanny threw herself down on the cobblestones to ask for help. Unable to help in the dreams, Emmeline woke up each morning feeling not only the loss of her friend, but the guilt of the dream Emmeline who had stood by while her friend was cast out from Lowell. Only when she got to the mill did those feelings fade—to be replaced by a milder, but still guilty, sense that she was bad to have experienced even a bit of relief when she heard that Fanny was gone.

With Fanny's departure, Abbey and Lydia could share the sceond-floor bed they had been waiting for. They moved downstairs, and Emmeline went into the bed they had occuped. There was a new girl in the room. She had arrived on the day Fanny left and been placed in the bed with Mamie. She was Dovey Winton from New Hampshire, who seemed to Emmeline to be even more country in manner than she herself had been when she arrived. Dovey was extremely shy and spoke to no one but Mamie, who was, in turn, visibly happier than she had been since losing Eliza. Mamie stopped saying that if Eliza did well in the Tremont mill, she herself would move at the end of the month. Indeed, the only sign that there had ever been an Eliza whom Emmeline had replaced in the weaving room was that Mamie still refused to speak to Emmeline.

Hilda was content to have the bed to herself again, and it was understood that Emmeline would be the first to have a partner when a new girl arrived. But as winter deepened, the big wagons were no longer going out to recruit girls, and this meant that there were virtually no arrivals. In the meantime, Emmeline was alone in bed at night, for the first time in her life bereft of the simple comfort of a warm body beside her.

During her first night alone she didn't sleep at all, and in the ones that followed, rest was fitful. She was flooded by homesickness in a way that intense fear and exhaustion had prevented during her first days in Lowell. With paper and ink given her by Mrs. Bass, she wrote long letters to her mother which she did not mail, for they were full of details of her life and observations about Lowell which would have been incomprehensible or frightening to her mother. That this was true made Emmeline feel more distant from her than ever.

Christmas was coming. In the worst of their bad times in Fayette, Christmas had been a joyous day. They hung apples with cloves stuck in them near the fire, and the house filled with their spicy aroma. At church they heard the story of Christ's birth with as much pleasure and wonder as though it had been previously unfamiliar to them. After church the entire congregation was invited to Pastor Evans' home, where Mrs. Evans served warm cider and seedcakes. Where there were bad feelings between parishioners, they pretended to like each other so that the day would not be spoiled, and often forgot that they hadn't recently been friends.

In one of her unsent letters to her mother, Emmeline wrote that she could not imagine Reverend Richards in any home, so cold and austere a person did he appear to be. (It did not occur to her at this time to take the actual step of changing to the other Baptist church. How could she explain such a change to either pastor?) If only she could be at home for that one day! Then she might return to Lowell with her strength renewed. As it was, she was growing less rather than more competent at her work.

She was virtually ill with loneliness and could eat very little at each meal. Mrs. Bass asked if she was troubled, but she denied it. She had noticed that to be one of Mrs. Bass's favorites was to incur a certain amount of teasing from the other girls, and she wanted desperately to please them. As she walked home from church on Sunday, a man from the carding room spoke to her very nicely, but she didn't dare respond, thinking of Fanny and not even knowing whose view she might be in right now.

Her loom threads broke more often, and she was having greater difficulty than before in knotting them. Mr. Maguire was watching her and she was sure he was displeased. When, three days before Christmas, he asked her to speak with him at the end of the day, she was sick with fear, thinking that she was about to be turned off the Corporation. It seemed to her, as she waited for their conference, that the only thing worse than spending Christmas among strangers in Lowell would be to return to Fayette in disgrace.

But instead of berating her for her poor performance, Mr. Maguire asked, in the kindest tone imaginable, "What is it that's troubling you, Emmeline?"

Tears came to her eyes.

"Please give me another chance, Mr. Maguire," she begged, as though he had threatened to send her away at that moment. "My family has to have my wages! If only I can get some sleep, I know my work will be better!"

"Well, that's all I meant, Emmeline," he said. "You look as if you haven't slept since you got here. I'm concerned for you." He placed his hand on her shoulder in a gesture exactly like her father's when he was having a serious talk with one of the children. But she had not been touched by another person in many days, and the simple gesture released the tears she had been holding back for so long.

"Do you want to tell me?" he asked when he had allowed her to cry for a while.

But she couldn't speak because she was still crying.

"Maybe it's just that you're lonely," he said. "Christmas is coming on now, and you're away from your family. How old are you, Emmeline?"

"I'll be fourteen in March."

"Oh, my goodness," he said, "not yet fourteen. You know, I was thirteen when I left Cork and went to Manchester. Have you ever heard of Manchester, England?"

She said that she had not. Her tears were subsiding as she grew interested in what he was saying.

"If you have complaints about Lowell, Emmeline, always keep it in your mind that fate might have taken

you to Manchester, England, instead, and that would
have been a hundred times worse. Everything is worse.
The city is much bigger and much uglier; the work is
more tedious; the pay is much poorer; the workers are
treated like slaves. A person stands on his feet all day in
the mills and does the same tiny task over and over
without so much as a minute's break. And the hours are
longer. It's a monstrous place, run by monsters. A
Lowell girl cannot conceive of conditions in Manchester."

As he spoke his speech had become faster and his
brogue thicker, so that by the time he said, "a
monstherous place, run by monsthers," he sounded
exactly like Mrs. Bass. He caught himself and laughed,
but when the laughter passed, he had a funny expression, or rather a combination of expressions. She
thought to herself that she had never seen a person
whose face showed so many meanings within a short
time, or even at the *same* time.

"I know," he said, "that Manchester, England, is
uppermost in your mind just now."

She smiled shyly. He had such a loveliness to him,
quite unlike any of the men she had known in Fayette.
If it was her father's hand she had felt on her shoulder,
it was her mother's understanding that she felt from
him now. How glad she was that he was not one of the
young men it was dangerous to speak with! She was
safe with him, for he was older, much older than she,
married, and a father. Someday, perhaps, she would
find the nerve to tell Mrs. Bass how wrong she had been
about Mr. Maguire.

"In the meanwhile," he said, "do you have a place to
spend the Christmas holiday?"

She said that Mrs. Bass made a Christmas dinner, but
other than that . . .

"Well," he said, "Mrs. Maguire has some of the
older girls in for tea Christmas afternoon. I want you to
come and meet her, and talk with the others. It'll do
you good."

She was so grateful as to be speechless. Not only would he bear with her incompetence, but in one moment he had taken away the burden of her barren Christmas!

In the next three days she thought of little other than the Maguires' tea. If she still slept poorly, her wakefulness was due to anticipation, rather than despair. Instead of going to bed after dinner, she remained in the keeping room, listening to the gossip of the other girls, hoping for some clue as to whether any of them had been invited. He had asked her not to mention the tea because it was only possible to invite a few of the girls and he and Mrs. Maguire did not wish to offend the others. She was fairly certain that Hilda would be invited, for Hilda had referred more than once to having been in their home, but Hilda gave no sign, and Emmeline had given Mr. Maguire her word. He had given her a slip of paper with the directions for walking to the house. She kept the paper in her dress pocket, taking it out to reread it a dozen times each day. She knew the directions by heart, but she still kept looking at the paper.

On Christmas Eve, convinced that the night and the next morning would never pass, she slipped away from the cheerful group of girls singing carols in the great keeping room, took her shawl from its hook in the hallway, and slipped out of the house.

It was a clear, cold night. While she never felt as close to the sky in Lowell as she had in Fayette, the moon and the stars appeared to be brighter than usual. She walked to Merrimack Street and then north toward the Merrimack River. She didn't precisely have a destination, but in her mind were the directions for reaching the Maguire home. North to the end of Merrimack Street; left onto Pawtucket. The house was on the corner of Pawtucket and School streets, just before you got to the Falls.

It was colder at this end of Merrimack, for there were few buildings to stop the wind. In a few days she would have her first wages. Hilda had told her she must buy a warmer shawl, but it was out of the question for her to do so. Every penny must go to Fayette, where there was not even money for food. With a full stomach she could get through the winter without warmer clothes. She would simply have to avoid taking walks, other than the brief one to and from the mill, once the weather became too cold to bear.

There was the river. She could hear, but not see, the Falls. She remembered the night a few weeks ago when she had heard them without knowing what they were. Then it had been the loudest and most frightening noise she had ever heard; now, after a few weeks in the mill, it was soothing.

The river curved away from her, and suddenly she could see as well as hear the Falls. For all their noise, she could not have imagined that they would be so large, or so beautiful. They were thirty feet high and perhaps three times as wide, and the force of the water pouring down over them, shining white under the moon, was overwhelming. She moved across Pawtucket Street to be closer to them, then quickly ran back to the far side, feeling too close for comfort.

The roads were paved out here, though the walks were not. The homes stood on plots of land some of which were as large as the Mosher farm. There was barely enough light to read the street signs, but as she drew almost abreast of the Falls, she thought she must be at the right place. It was the only corner house, a huge stone mansion, made of the same gray stone as the Lowell Baptist Church. There was a fence around the front yard, though the back appeared to be unfenced and wild. The woody stems of bramble roses, their unplucked hips black and dry in the winter cold, rested along the fence. Two lighted lamps stood on tall posts, like sentinels, on either side of the ground near the front entrance, shedding light on the landing and on the name sign on the lawn: STONE. Briefly she wondered if she had reached the wrong house after all. Then she remembered that Elijah Stone was Mrs. Maguire's father.

Lights flickered in windows of both the upper and lower stories, lending the house a magical quality. Drapes framed the windows but were not drawn across them. Once or twice figures moved past the windows, seeming almost to glide in the flickering light. The gate of the picket fence was not latched, and she wanted desperately to walk in and peek through the windows, but knew she must not. She hung back for some time, trying to tear herself away. She had no idea of the time except that they had finished supper before seven thirty, and she'd left shortly thereafter. The curfew bells rang at nine, and the doors were locked for the night at ten throughout the mill houses.

She was just setting her mind firmly to leaving when she heard music coming from the house. She stopped, almost as though it had commanded her, and strained to hear better. She did not recognize the instrument it was being played upon—a piano, which she'd seen pictured in a book but never heard—but the lovely sounds came toward her through the windows of the big house.

Without thinking, she opened the gate and walked up the path. Circumventing the lighted area, she walked to the window where she had sensed the greatest activity. The music grew clearer and lovelier all the time. She was beyond stopping herself. She crept around the bushes, holding her breath. Standing on her toes, she could see most of the room; its richness and elegance set it apart from any room she had ever seen.

Satin drapes framed the windows. The carpet was woven in a cabbage-rose design on a green background. Above the mahogany wainscoting was a delicate wallpaper that looked like tapestry. Richly upholstered chairs and divans were scattered throughout the room; near them were tables and small chests on which were set astral lamps. One chest she could see quite well was lacquered in black and inlaid with mother-of-pearl. In the largest chair, at the focal center of the room, an imposing man in his fifties sat reading. At a tapestry frame, a woman, also of an older generation, was embroidering. On a divan, another woman, whose face Emmeline couldn't see, lay with a hand pressed to her forehead. Then there was the piano. On its bench sat a slender woman in a black dress, her fair hair in a braided crown. Her back was very straight and barely moved as she played. Her fingers were long and slim. Emmeline wanted to see her face but couldn't. Even more, she wanted to magically enter that home and sit beside the woman on the bench, closing her eyes and letting the music flood her soul. She closed her eyes; she could almost feel the room around her. When she opened her eyes, Mr. Maguire had entered the room.

There was something quite different about him, though she could not have said what it was. He was wearing a loosely fitted jacket and pants, but it was not so much his clothing as his manner. He appeared to be restless still, but in a different, less jolly way than he was in the weaving room, where he usually had a mischievous, anticipatory look, as though whatever he said next, or wherever he went, he might be having a really good time.

He walked to the piano and rested his hand on his wife's shoulder, then bent over and kissed the top of her head; she did not appear to notice. He walked over to the divan where the other woman lay, reading now, and appeared to be addressing some words to her. Perhaps she replied; he smiled. He called over to the elderly man, who looked up briefly and then went back to his book without any change of expression.

Suddenly Mr. Maguire came toward the window. She crouched down behind the shrubs, her heart beating so violently that she was sure it would give her away. When she finally dared to raise her head again, he was gone, but she remained motionless for a while, lest he be in a spot where he would see her if she moved.

As Emmeline walked home, she was so absorbed in her memories of the world behind the window that she failed to notice that she was virtually alone on the streets, except for an occasional man or group of men, or to be concerned about the time. When she reached Mrs. Bass's, she found the door locked, and only then realized that she was late. Surely it wasn't ten o'clock; then she would be locked out for the night! She knocked; there was no response. She grew frightened, feeling that she was already being punished for what she had done. She banged on the door and shouted Mrs. Bass's name so loudly that Mrs. Bass heard her from behind the closed door of her own room and came to the door.

Emmeline was trembling.

"Emmeline!" she exclaimed. "Where have you been, child?"

"I took a walk and got confused by the streets," Emmeline said. It was the first deliberate lie she had told in her life.

"You pooorrrr thing," Mrs. Bass purred, bringing Emmeline into the house and under her plaid shawl at the same moment. "Don't you know better than that?"

"I didn't mean to be late," Emmeline said as Mrs. Bass locked the door behind them.

"No, of course you didn't. Come, child, come into the kitchen and I'll give you a cup of good, hot tea."

Good, hot taaay. Emmeline felt all the more guilty then in benefiting from her lie.

Mrs. Bass led her into the kitchen, put up a kettle of water on the wood stove, and made Emmeline sit at the table while she set out fruitcake and tea.

"You mustn't just take it into your head to walk

around the city at night," Mrs. Bass said. "It's dangerous. There are bad men in the city. You're not in Maine anymore, child."

"I was looking for the country." Another lie, and yet not such a clear-cut one. (In truth, she was afraid of the Fayette woods at night, while the brick and mortar of Lowell barely changed from one time of day to the next.)

"It's your home you're wanting," Mrs. Bass said. "And your mother. Christmas is the worst time to be far from home, isn't it, now? But I make a good dinner for the girls, Emmeline, and I was even thinking to have a tea in the afternoon. And I'll surely—"

"Oh, thank you," Emmeline said quickly. "I've been invited to tea at the Maguires'."

There was a moment of silence while Emmeline worried that she had broken her promise by telling Mrs. Bass, even if Mrs. Bass was not one of the girls. Yet there was nothing she could have done. Mrs. Bass stood up suddenly and began clearing the table, though neither of them had finished her tea. She was muttering under her breath. Emmeline waited. She was tired now, but she didn't dare to move.

"You are privileged to be invited to Ivory Stone's house," Mrs. Bass said abruptly. "You must go, of course." Almost as though Emmeline had asked for her advice on the matter. "But you must watch yourself carefully."

Emmeline was fascinated by the struggle that appeared to be going on within her, not to speak of the possibility that she would now hear something interesting. Something that would explain to her the great gap between what she herself saw in Mr. Maguire and what Mrs. Bass said of him.

"What I have never understood," Mrs. Bass went on, almost as though speaking to herself, "is how such a girl as Ivory Stone could have allowed herself to . . ." She trailed off, but then suddenly noticed Emmeline's presence again. "Off to bed with you, Emmeline.

Only . . . If Maguire tries to get you off alone with him somewheres, don't go. Do you understand me, now?"

Emmeline nodded, though she didn't, nor did she see why Mr. Maguire would try to do that. She thanked Mrs. Bass for her kindness and went upstairs, trying to be quiet so that no one would notice her slipping in. But Hilda looked up from her book when Emmeline entered.

"I was walking by myself," Emmeline said. "I forgot the time."

"What did the Bass say?" Hilda asked.

"She said I mustn't walk at night. But she was kind."

"Of course," Emmeline heard Mamie say to Dovey, as though Emmeline were the only girl Mrs. Bass had ever been kind to.

"And will you continue to take walks at night?" Hilda asked—amused, but also curious.

"No," Emmeline said. "I'll try not to. But sometimes I miss Fayette so . . ."

"Well," Hilda said, "there's no chance of your reaching Fayette when you set out from Mrs. Bass's."

Mamie and Dovey made no secret of their amusement at this remark.

In her dreams that night, Lowell did not exist. She was looking in the window of the Moose Hill Baptist Church. Mrs. Maguire was playing the organ. It was all right for Emmeline to be there, even though Mrs. Maguire was unaware of her presence.

"Am I correct in assuming that you're going to Mrs. Maguire's tea?" Hilda asked her on Christmas morning in her usual matter-of-fact way. The other girls had gone down to breakfast and the two of them were alone in the long attic.

"Oh, yes," Emmeline said happily. "How did you know?"

She shrugged. "Mamie says he's partial to you."

"That's not fair," Emmeline said heatedly, as though accused of some crime. "He's nice to all the girls!"

Hilda smiled in a way that made Emmeline feel that for once, she'd given the correct answer.

"Never mind," Hilda said, "I'll show you the way, if you like."

At breakfast, all the girls were determinedly full of Christmas, as though to make up for the fact that they were far from home. Those who lived close enough to Lowell to go home had taken leave. While it was unfair to be even a little angry with them, the remaining girls pretended that they had never existed, and closed ranks. Everyone was cheerful, and Mamie actually addressed a few words to Emmeline at Christmas dinner, before remembering that Emmeline was her enemy. Even the atmosphere in church warmed a bit, as they sang Christmas hymns after the service.

Emmeline's excitement mounted as the day went on. At dinner she could barely enjoy the roast for fear of dripping gravy on her dress, and after dinner she braided her hair and coiled it into a bun with greater care than she had ever taken. Then she was still so anxious as she waited for Hilda, who insisted upon finishing a letter before they left, that she couldn't keep herself from talking as Hilda wrote. Finally, Hilda said she had never known Emmeline for such a chatterbox, an expression Emmeline had never heard before and found enchanting. Still, she forced herself to keep silent while Hilda completed her letter, and then together they slipped down the stairs and out of the house.

It had been snowing and there was a light crust on the walks. There had been little snow that winter, and it made her momentarily homesick to see it, but then she pushed all thoughts of Fayette from her mind. Abruptly, as much to help her forget home as because she was curious at that moment, she asked, "Hilda, is it true, as Mrs. Bass says, that a girl was turned off the Corporation on Mr. Maguire's account?"

"No, it's not true," Hilda said promptly. "And you'd do best not to listen to such nonsense."

Emmeline hesitated. "It never happened, then?"

"Lucy Shorter was a terrible flirt. She couldn't take her eyes from the men from the moment she arrived in Lowell."

"Was she like Fanny?"

"Worse. Fanny wasn't a bad girl, really. She knew how to behave; she just didn't have the self-control to make herself do it. She got silly as soon as a man spoke to her. But Lucy went after them. I was in the weaving room with her for a while. We couldn't believe the way she passed herself in front of his eyes all the time, dancing across the weaving room, calling his attention to every new ribbon or brooch. And she was a pretty girl, too. Cheap, but pretty. There's barely a man alive who won't take advantage of that kind of girl."

So Mr. Maguire had "taken advantage" of Lucy Shorter, but he was not responsible, because whatever he had done, any man would do the same. They were crossing Austin Street and soon they would turn onto Pawtucket. Emmeline wanted to ask Hilda how long it would take her to understand the Lowell rules, but she was afraid Hilda would take this to mean that she did not intend to follow them immediately. She wanted to know how Mr. Maguire had taken advantage of Lucy Shorter, but she feared being marked as an idiot, or a child, or both, if she asked.

She finally settled upon "Is Mr. Maguire a good man?" She remembered having heard an occasional fragment of conversation in Fayette about one lamentable deed or another. Often the question of whether the deed was eventually accepted seemed to depend less upon its nature than upon the goodness of the person who had committed it. The same act, performed by two different people, might be quite differently judged.

"He *wants* to be good," Hilda said, "and that is about the most that you can ask of a man."

Emmeline stole another look at Hilda, because she wanted to see if humor was intended. Hilda was not smiling.

"Don't you think Lucy Shorter wanted to be good?" Emmeline could not refrain from asking.

"What I think," Hilda replied, "is that you should be more interested in the Pawtucket Falls than in Lucy Shorter. And that I am very glad we are almost there, because I have never in my life heard so many questions outside of a schoolroom."

Emmeline feigned astonishment at the Falls, feeling guilty all over again. There was an aggressive strain in Mrs. Bass which made it seem almost natural to protect oneself by lying, or at least concealing, but Hilda was another sort of person. When Hilda pointed out the house, Emmeline commented upon its size and palatial aspect, and when they reached the yard, she pretended to be surprised that the name on the sign was STONE.

"It's Elijah Stone's house," Hilda said in her usual matter-of-fact tone. "Why wouldn't his name be on the sign?"

The woman who came to the door was tall and elegant. She wore a violet silk dress which was simply cut and yet more beautiful than any dress Emmeline had ever seen. Emmeline was stricken anew at the thought of the homespun under her shawl. Surely she would be the only girl present in such a dress.

The woman greeted Hilda by name, and Hilda introduced Emmeline in turn. She was Mr. Stone's sister, Priscilla Stone, whom Emmeline had seen at her tapestry frame the night before.

"Won't you come in?" Miss Stone said. "Many of the girls are already here." Her voice was soft and musical; her speech, like that of the Reverend Richards as well as the rest of her family, that of the educated Boston gentry. It sounded softer and pleasanter in this house, particularly when used by Priscilla Stone or by Ivory's younger sister, Patience, whom Emmeline had seen on the divan the night before with her hand pressed to her forehead, and who spent most of this afternoon in the same position.

Miss Priscilla Stone led them into the house. Gas lamps in sconces lighted the central hall, although it was only the middle of the afternoon and it would have been possible to see without them. Miss Stone handed their shawls to a maid and then led them into the room Emmeline had seen from the window. Now it was full of people.

Near the window outside which she had concealed herself the night before, Mr. Maguire stood talking to a small group of girls. They wore black silk. Every female in the room wore black silk or something better, and many wore beautiful collars and jewelry. Emmeline closed her eyes for a moment as though to free her mind from the knowledge of her homespun dress.

One voice rode above the others in the room. She opened her eyes. The man she had seen through the window, the man who must be Elijah Stone, sat in the same thronelike armchair he'd been in the night before, holding sway in the midst of the largest group of girls in the room. He had straight brown hair only mildly touched by gray; rough, ruddy skin; a nervous and yet powerful manner. Phrases like "Lowell and I looked at . . . Then we left for London, Lowell and Boott and I . . ." and other such unimaginable fragments reached her ears from time to time as Miss Stone continued to introduce her and Hilda to the other guests. Hilda knew some of them and exchanged a few words with each.

Again on the piano bench, but facing into the room now, talking to someone who sat beside her, was the woman who'd been playing the piano. She wore a simple black dress, unadorned by jewelry, and her blond hair was drawn into a tight bun, as it had been the night before. Her face, or so it seemed to Emmeline, was surprisingly "country"—it was a good, strong

face, quite angular and full of lines of care; not the face
of a woman who lived in luxury and pampered herself.
It was difficult for Emmeline to look away from her, but
they had reached the window and Mr. Maguire.

"Ah, there you are, Emmeline," he said immediately. "Come with me, then; I want you to meet Mrs.
Maguire."

He led her to the piano bench.

"I cannot bear to go to the mill anymore," Mrs.
Maguire was saying to a couple who now shared the
bench with her. She had a thin, high voice such as one
would expect to hear from a little girl, startling to
Emmeline in being so inconsistent with her strong
appearance. "When I see the cotton coming off the
carts, I can think only of the poor slaves who harvested
it." She began to tell the couple of her experience in
going with her father on a trip to one of the great
plantations, where she had been appalled by the
conditions under which the slaves lived and worked.

At her feet, two beautifully dressed little girls played
with elegant European dolls. (There were two Maguire
boys as well, but they were upstairs with a nursemaid.)
The voice of Elijah Stone punctuated the thin, high
words of his daughter.

"Ivory," Mr. Maguire finally broke in . . . *(Oivory*—
he would tell Emmeline weeks later that Ivory's father
flinched every time he uttered his wife's name.)" . . .
this is Emmeline Mosher, of whom I've spoken to
you."

"I'm very glad to meet you, Emmeline," Mrs.
Maguire said, warmly but without smiling. "I have
heard very good things about you from Mr. Maguire."

Emmeline felt her cheeks flush with embarrassment
and pleasure. She didn't know what to do with herself—with her foolish dress; with her hands, which
wanted to flutter all about, arranging and concealing
her, rubbing her eyes. Then she could feel Mr. Maguire
being amused by her discomfort, which, of course, only
served to increase it. She had seen him, with his gentle

humor, settle disputes that would otherwise have
become serious. Only that week he had spoken with
two girls who were arguing over the responsibility for a
series of broken warp threads. He had listened gravely
to both their stories, then said that indeed, he thought
this argument so serious that no matter how much they
liked each other, no matter how easy it would be to fix
those threads, they should probably end their friendship by thrashing it out on the floor. The girls had gone
back to work with their arms around each other,
lauging.

Now he was viewing Emmeline with that same
humor. Was Mrs. Maguire laughing at her as well? She
thought not. It was unlikely, in fact, that Mrs. Maguire
laughed at anyone. Emmeline found herself wondering
how old Mrs. Maguire was. In spite of the lines of care,
she looked considerably younger than Emmeline's own
mother; yet Mrs. Maguire had four children of her
own.

If only her mother could be here with her now, sitting
on the piano bench, talking with her. But her own
mother was in Fayette, cold and tired and hungry, with
no idea that rooms such as this existed—whether they
had made Ivory Maguire contented or not.

The tea was more elegant than any at Mrs. Bass's,
though the food itself was less lavish and less tasty. At
the head of the table, Mr. Stone easily dominated the
assemblage of thirty or so people. He frightened
Emmeline more than any man she had ever known,
perhaps mostly because of his fearsome reputation. His
speech and manners were fine, like his home, yet there
was a roughness to him, a kind of pointed vitality which
at once fed on those around him and was directed at
them. His words were those of a philanthropist. When
he spoke of the early mill days, of himself and Lowell
and Appleton and the others, there was a strong
implication that they had set out on a venture to utilize
poor farmlands while bringing a number of poverty-
stricken girls to a place where they could earn a living

while their characters were protected. Yet he was said
to have been the first to cut back wages three years
earlier, when labor became plentiful for the first time.
And the conditions on the Summer Corporation, from
the beginning, were said to have been the harshest of
any. Even as a host he had certain mannerisms that
made one wonder if he did not conceal others even
worse.

Aside from Mr. Maguire and himself, there was only
one other man in the room, an engineer named
Cooper, who had come with his wife—the couple with
whom Mrs. Maguire had been speaking earlier. Mr.
Stone, who was attentive to each female as she spoke,
failed to notice on the rare occasion when Mr. Cooper
had something to say. But what was even more striking
was that when Stephen Maguire ventured a word to
anyone beyond his immediate table partners, Mr.
Stone immediately broke in loudly with some anecdote
or inquiry for the table at large. Eventually, Emmeline
realized that the other girls were also embarrassed by
this rudeness, and were lowering their eyes when he did
this. Yet none of the women in his family seemed to
take any notice. At the foot of the table, three seats
away from Emmeline, Mrs. Maguire was telling Mrs.
Cooper that she had not slept well at night since her trip
through the South.

When they rose from the table, Emmeline wasn't
certain what was to happen next. She knew only that
she didn't want the day to end. They all gathered
around the piano, and for a while they sang carols while
Mrs. Maguire played, but Emmeline couldn't enjoy
herself, for she felt the afternoon drawing to a close,
and her contentment was edged with sadness.

Both Mr. Stone and Mr. Maguire had vanished,
though she had the impression that they had left the
room at different times and by different doors. She had
a vision in which Mrs. Maguire whispered that she
hoped Emmeline would stay when the others left. This,
of course, Mrs. Maguire did not do, but she did speak

to each of the girls in turn as they prepared to leave. She told Emmeline that she knew how difficult it was, at her age, to be so far from home, and that if she should ever be in need of help she was to come to them. Emmeline was so grateful, she felt she would melt into the floor, and simply stood staring at Mrs. Maguire; but then Hilda was pulling her away, saying that it was time to get back to Mrs. Bass's. It was the first time she had ever heard Hilda refer to that lady by her proper name.

"You didn't call Mrs. Bass by any of her funny names," she pointed out to Hilda when they had walked for a while in silence. It was snowing, and Lowell had a thick white cover over it now. The snowy fog shrouded the falls, though they could be heard as clearly as ever. Beyond them, she could see the bridge that spanned the Merrimack.

"Ivory considers her a friend," Hilda said.

"But how can that be, Hilda, when she and Mr. Maguire—"

"The wonder," Hilda said irritably, "is that you're able to keep your questions to yourself at the mill and at Ivory's, so that in all of Lowell, only I know what a pest you can be!"

Emmeline was stung. Tears came to her eyes, and she was grateful for the snow that made it difficult for them to see each other. The night air seemed colder than it usually did during snow, perhaps because of the warmth they had just left, or perhaps just because it was cold near the river. She thought of Fayette, and wondered if the joy of Christmas Day had been muted by her absence. She saw her mother sitting alone by the fire, and hoped that she was thinking of her. In less than a week she would be sending home her first month's wages. She wished she could see her mother's expression when she opened the envelope.

As they drew abreast of the bridge, a man was walking from it, in their direction, with his head down.

He wore no outer clothing. His hands were clasped behind his back, and his air was dejected. Emmeline was fairly certain that it was Mr. Maguire.

She looked at Hilda. Hilda had seen him too, but pretended that she hadn't. Emmeline's heart went out to him. She wondered if in spite of his good life he wasn't very lonely, and if he might not want to talk to them if he knew they were there. But Hilda began to walk more rapidly, as though to discourage Emmeline from mentioning the possibility. Emmeline had to struggle just to keep step with her until they reached the boardinghouse, where she could not eat supper because she was still full of the food she had eaten at the Maguires' tea. And she could not sleep for the pieces of the puzzle that was the Maguire-Stone family dancing around in her head.

Mʀ. Maguire visibly enjoyed the elevated mood in the weaving room on the day when the girls were to receive their wages. He laughed and joked and pretended, when he heard girls talking about what they would do with their money, to have forgotten what day it was. Then, when Emmeline told him that it was her first wages, he pretended to seriously believe that she had been in the weaving room for years.

"Are you going to buy your Lowell bonnet, then, Emmeline?" he asked when she insisted happily that it was her first payday.

She shook her head but couldn't look at him. "I don't really want one," she lied.

In the long line to the countinghouse, she could scarcely contain herself. The girls around her chattered excitedly about what they would do with their wages, but she kept to herself, thinking they would only make fun of her if she said she would send all her money home. One girl, flushed high with excitement, took a small notebook from her dress pocket and announced to the world that as of this day she would have been in Lowell almost three years and have exactly five hundred dollars in the Lowell Institution for Savings. Emmeline could not help but stare at the girl, for although she'd heard tales of such funds being amassed, she had never known for certain that she was looking at the possessor of such a sum.

Still, when the paymaster finally handed her the Railroad Bank notes totaling two dollars and twenty cents (board having already been deducted), she stared at them as though she had never heard of a greater amount, and had to be asked, finally, to move from the desk so the next girl could have her turn.

Once she had prepared the money for posting to Fayette, the excitement remained with her. Yet she could not bear to be in the keeping room after supper, as the other excited girls discussed what they would buy with their money. So she took a walk, at first intending simply to stroll along Merrimack Street.

It was a clear, not very cold evening. The snow from the Christmas fall was gone from the road, though there were still banks at the curbs and in the front yards of the houses. Once or twice she stopped to stare into the dark windows of the shops on Merrimack Street, but she was too happy about sending money home to mind what she couldn't have, and in a remarkably short time she had walked the length of Merrimack Street; taken a quick look at the Pawtucket Falls; returned home to Mrs. Bass's, a distance of about thirteen city blocks each way; and fallen into a deep sleep.

But the euphoria inspired by her first wages could not last, and as December passed into January, she felt more lonely than ever. No new girl had replaced Hilda as her bed partner, and Hilda, who at her best had a charm without warmth, withdrew from her further. Hilda was in a bad mood in general and seemed irritated with Emmeline in particular—as though Emmeline's failure to adapt happily to the Lowell regime were a reflection on her own managerial abilities.

In truth, January was the worst time of year for many of the girls, with no holiday to look forward to and spring still too far away to be imagined. In Fayette, where winters had been so long and difficult, it was

February and March that were the hardest months to get through. But when Emmeline thought of Fayette now, it was not as a place where she had ever been deeply miserable.

In the second week of January she had a letter from home, written by Harriet, obviously at her mother's behest. Considering that Harriet was not yet eleven years old, it was a kind of double-edged masterpiece, at once conveying their mother's gratitude for the money and requesting that Emmeline write to Harriet about the wonderful time she was having in Lowell, about her new friends and all her beautiful clothes. Emmeline tore up the letter, then struggled for the rest of the day to push it from her mind. *Her new friends and her beautiful clothes.* The injustice rankled so that she couldn't sit still. In the great keeping room, after supper, the conversation went by her as though her chair were vacant. She thought of the time when Harriet had screamed, "You're not my mother!" after Emmeline had asked her to do some small task. She thought of numerous other times when Harriet had seemed to almost willfully misunderstand her intentions or desires. What was strange was that none of it had ever bothered her until now. Harriet was three years younger than she. Harriet was a child.

Now Harriet was in Fayette at their mother's side while Emmeline was alone in Lowell, unable to glance at her mother's calm face for reassurance that Harriet's tirades were childish nonsense, that squalls passed, that life would get better.

If only there were one person in Lowell in whom she could confide! Mrs. Maguire had said she might come by if she needed help; but how could Emmeline knock at the door of the Stone house to complain about her sister and pour out her loneliness—when it was evil to feel that way about your sister, and she lived in a house with forty other girls? Just that day Mr. Maguire had asked her if she was feeling poorly again, but she hadn't known how to reply. She didn't want him to think she was complaining, and she was afraid to talk to him at length because the other girls might think she was courting his favor. Or perhaps they would think she was complaining about *them*.

Finally she took a walk, a habit of which she had been trying to cure herself. She walked through the Summer Corporation blocks until she came to the quadrangle around which the Appleton buildings had been erected. It was a lovely little park and would be more so, in the warm weather, when the snow was gone and the grass became green. Was it possible that she would still be in Lowell when spring came?

"Caught you!"

She wheeled around, thinking it was Mr. Maguire, but it was the man who had spoken to her in the carding room on that first day. With his bright red cheeks and woolen cap, he looked more like a boy than a man, and she stared at him, wondering which he really was, thinking that if he were a boy, it might be all right to talk to him. He was grinning with pleasure at having surprised her. She wondered where he had come from and whether he might be lonely too. He didn't look it. His face was rough, but not unkind; it was a country face, like the ones she saw all the time in Fayette. What would be the harm in throwing a few snowballs with him, in laughing and teasing as she laughed with Luke and Andrew?

Then a picture of Fanny Bartlett came before her eyes, and without a word, she ran away from him, never stopping until she reached Mrs. Bass's.

It was Sunday before she again gave in to the temptation to walk at night. Mrs. Bass had gone visiting, and the girls in the keeping room were admitting an occasional peddler. Emmeline had held herself away from the goings-on, pretending to be engrossed in her Bible, as one strange-looking person, who might almost have been an old woman in old man's clothes, showed a box of ribbons, another a tray with a bit of everything on it—combs, two or three brooches, some pieces of lace. Then another man, very old and bent over, and with a patch on one eye, came in with an assortment of sweets on an open tray. It was the sweets peddlers who most angered Mrs. Bass, who said that her girls were well fed and had no need of such unwholesome stuff. Her disapproval lent the sweets an extra appeal, so that now there was a great deal of giggling, and two or three girls were standing around the tray, deciding on what to buy. Hilda sat reading in a corner, an expression of mild disapproval on her face. Mamie and Dovey had joined the laughing girls around the tray, and the poor old man was just beginning to look around him for an escape. Slowly he edged toward the door, silently offering the tray, as he moved, to the girls clustered around the fringes of the room. But as he passed Emmeline, Mamie looked over at them.

"Oh, don't bother about *her*," Mamie called out. "She won't even buy herself a decent bonnet!"

Emmeline was stunned. In point of fact, everyone was shocked by Mamie's cruelty, but Emmeline did not wait to see that; she could only feel that they were looking at her. She ran from the room, snatching her shawl from the hook, barely stopping to make sure it was the right one. Then she opened the door and ran from the house.

She heard someone call her name, but it was beyond her to stop, or to face any of them. She could think only of escape. She would never go back to Mrs. Bass's.

It was a damp and bitterly cold night. In recent days she had taken to leaving her nightgown under her dress during the day, her shawl being inadequate even for the brief walk to and from the mill. Now the wind cut through all her layers of clothing as though it were mocking her.

There were a few inches of fresh snow on the road. Near the end of the row that was closest to the mill, several laughing girls were throwing snowballs at each other, hiding behind fences, squealing happily when they hit someone else or were hit themselves. It didn't occur to her that she might join in without an invitation; that this was not a close-knit band from one house, but, rather, girls who'd fallen together because they were restless, or homesick, or simply too energetic to sit indoors even after a day at the mill. Now particularly, with Mamie's remark a fresh wound in her feelings, she felt an insuperable barrier between herself and the others. She couldn't even bear to walk past them, but turned in the other direction, toward Merrimack Street, then walked once more in the direction of Pawtucket Falls.

Where could she go, if not back to Mrs. Bass's? Perhaps she would go on another corporation, and in that way vanish from the sight of Mamie and her friends. Eliza was presumably still in Lowell, yet she was never seen nor heard of at Mrs. Bass's or in the mill. Emmeline felt slightly cheered at the prospect of thus putting an end to her misery; but no sooner had she begun to calculate how she might effect such a change than she realized it was impossible for her to make it, for she would then be cut off from her one continuing source of comfort, Mr. Maguire. She could not dare to hope that she would see him again if she left his employ, much less that she would be invited to his home. That hope, however foolish it was, helped her to go to the mill each morning.

In church that day, two girls sitting next to her had been discussing a girl turned off the Boott Corporation because she was "forever staring out the window." But in the weaving room it was Mr. Maguire who was most likely to call to one girl or another—or all of them—to come to the window to witness a sharp change in the weather, or some particularly interesting cluster of clouds.

Mr. Maguire was the only person from whom she could be sure of some kind word each day. Not that anyone else (Mamie excepted) was bad to her; it was more that she had the sense that if she disappeared from the boardinghouse, no one would know the difference. In Fayette she had been so important that her mother hadn't thought she could manage without her.

She was almost running as she turned onto Pawtucket Street. There was the bridge over the River, and just beyond it, the Falls. The snow was melting in her boots, and her toes were numb. Her skirts were caked with snow, and her shawl helped so little against the wind that it seemed she might throw it away and feel no colder. If there had been any other place in Lowell for her to go, she might not have continued on toward the Falls. But even the churches would be closed at this hour.

A man was standing on the bridge, his back to her, looking toward the Falls. She thought immediately that it was Mr. Maguire, and then she thought that it was only because she wanted it to be that she had convinced herself that it was.

But as she drew closer, she could see that it was, indeed, Mr. Maguire. He was wearing a heavy white sweater, quite different from any garment she'd ever seen, and holding a jacket over his shoulder as though it were too warm to wear both. She had to restrain herself from running toward him. He was coming off the bridge now, down to the road, but she couldn't tell if he had seen her. If she continued walking as she was, they would walk directly into each other—unless he turned toward his home. She was shaking with the cold and with the fear that he would do that. She looked at the snowy road beneath her cold, wet feet and prayed that he wouldn't. When she looked up again, he was standing a couple of yards away and looking directly at her.

"Hello, Mr. Maguire," she said.

"Oh, then, it's you, Emmeline," he said.

She waited.

"What are you doing way out here?" he asked.

"Walking."

He laughed. "Well, of course you're walking. And freezing as well, by the look of you."

Because she was standing still, her body's shaking had become more pronounced, and she could barely keep her teeth from chattering. He put his jacket around her shoulders. She looked up at him gratefully, but as she did so, his expression changed—as though he had seen something in her face that he couldn't bear.

"Why don't you get yourself something warmer to wear?" he asked, but his voice was harsh, so different from the way it usually sounded that if her eyes had been closed, she wouldn't have known that it was he.

"I can't," she said. "I'm only here to send money home."

"Then stay indoors, for the love of God!"

She stared at him in horror. She had made him angry—the only person in Lowell who had seemed to care if she lived or died.

"How shall you help your family if you catch your death of cold in Lowell?"

But Lowell had slipped out from beneath her feet, and she was falling. She turned away from him, reeling, and began to run, the jacket slipping from her shoulders. He caught up with her almost instantly, for she was dizzy and couldn't even see where she was going.

"Emmeline!" He grabbed her arm to stop her. "Emmeline, what have I done? I'm sorry! Good Lord, I didn't mean to . . ."

She began to cry, standing in the snow, trying to get away without really wanting to. He picked up his jacket and put it around her again, tenderly this time, and his arm remained around her, warming her, supporting her at the same time. After a while, he took his arm away; she pulled the jacket more snugly around her.

"What I was trying to tell you, Emmeline, was that

you'd be better off with your friends in the boarding-house than you are talking to me out here in the cold."

"I don't have any friends at the boardinghouse," she said.

"How is that?" he asked. "A lovely girl like your-self?"

"I don't know," she said. She was still uncomfort-able, but the dizziness had passed and she could see again. "The other girls don't like me."

"That's not possible," he said. "Perhaps they don't know you yet. How long is it that you've been here, Emmeline?"

Emmeline. When he said her name, she felt as though she had never heard it before, because his deep, lilting voice changed it from a simple name into a word with many meanings.

"Six weeks." She could have sworn that he knew to the day.

"Are *you* friendly to *them?*" he asked.

"I don't know," she said again. "They're all older than I am."

And I would gladly dispense with the friendship of all of them to have moments like this with you!

"How old are you, Emmeline? Fifteen? Sixteen?"

"Fourteen." She crossed her fingers because her birthday was still two months away.

He was silent for a moment. Then he said, "Come, I'll walk you back to the boardinghouse."

"I can't go back there," she said. "One of the girls was making fun of my clothing. I can't go back."

"Do you think," he asked after a while, "that if we walk for a while, and talk a bit, that it might get better, and then you'll be able to go back? After all, you can't let one nasty girl keep you from home forever."

"It's not my home," she said, but already it had occurred to her that if she had a little more time with him, she might be able to face the girls at the boardinghouse. It seemed to her now that the voice that had called her name as she was running away had not been unsympathetic.

"Of course not," he said. "If it was your home, you wouldn't be wandering about Lowell like a lost soul."

She looked at him, because something in the way he said it made her wonder if he meant to be speaking of himself as well. Almost as though to ward off such a question, he laughed and told her that he'd had quite enough roaming himself, and was almost ready to go home. They began walking—away from the Stone house, toward Merrimack Street.

"I was younger than you are when I left Cork and went to Manchester," he said after a while. "Do you know about Manchester?"

"You told me once," she said.

"I stayed there for three years," he said. "When I was sixteen I left my mother . . . and my brothers . . . in Manchester and shipped out to Boston. I stayed in Boston for a year. Boston is better than Manchester in most ways—a better city, more kinds of work; but it was still . . . the Irish were treated like dirt there too. Lowell's the same, of course—every place is the same—but Ireland; only I didn't know that until later. At the end of winter, when I'd been there a year, I hired out to a contractor named Comiskey who was getting together a crew to work on the Canal. The Pawtucket, that is. It was more than twenty years old by that time, but it was small and shallow, and the locks were all in poor repair. It was nothing that would serve for the mills they were planning to put up. Lowell was country then, you know."

She was astonished; she could not imagine Lowell's ever having been different from what it was now.

"We walked up here from Charleston," he went on, almost as though talking to himself, now. "Twenty of us and Comiskey. Boott met us at the old locks with a couple of his men. They gave us each a set of tools and a box lunch. Those were the last things they ever gave us. It hadn't occurred to them that we'd need a place to sleep at the end of the day. If we'd been pigs, they'd have known we needed sties, but we were only Irishmen." He was silent for a while, as affected by the memory as she was by her first hearing of it. "Do you know the Acre, Emmeline? The Paddy Camp lands? No, of course you don't. Well, someday I'd like to . . . No. It doesn't matter. . . . It was April and there was still snow on the ground. We had to throw up shacks with such lumber as we could get. The first night we slept on top of trees we chopped down and laid side by side. One of the men got frostbite and lost half his toes."

She became aware of her own feet again. She was so accustomed by now to their hurting all the time that it was easy to forget them. Even in the morning it was difficult to pull on her boots.

"It wasn't just that they didn't think," Mr. Maguire said. They were approaching the corner of Merrimack Street. "They *meant* for us to be miserable so that we'd move on as soon as the work was done. They had no place for us in their permanent scheme; they only wanted to deal with fresh young Yankee girls like yourself." He laughed suddenly. "And indeed, who can blame them? Wouldn't I rather talk to you than to any of them?"

There was an embarrassed silence. She wondered if "them" included any of the people with whom he lived. She thought of the man who sat at the head of his dining table; she had heard nothing that would exclude Elijah Stone from the company of "them."

"Do we have to go this way?" she asked as they turned the corner into Merrimack Street.

He laughed. "If you don't turn off, you'll touch water sooner or later . . . in any direction."

"Really?"

"Indeed."

"I didn't know that."

"You're almost entirely surrounded by water here," he said, with obvious relish. "It's the next best thing to being on the ocean. Look here, Emmeline. . . ." He bent over and in the snow, with one finger, traced the curving Merrimack for several yards, showing her how the city nestled within its curve. Then he traced the Concord River around its eastern side and the Meadowbrook to the south. "Then there're the canals. There's the Pawtucket in back of us . . . here . . . and then there's the Hamilton . . . and the Eastern, and the Merrimack." He laughed with pleasure as he saw her staring at his snow map, entranced. "Of the canals, the only one that was here when I came to Lowell in 1822 was the Merrimack."

"Eighteen twenty-two!" She was startled because it seemed such an impossibly long time ago.

He smiled at her sadly. "You weren't born yet. Come. Let's head on back to Molly's."

Molly's. By now she could bear the thought of returning to Mrs. Bass's. But not yet!

"They thought they'd be finished with us by 'twenty-three," he said. "Unfortunately, there was still man's work to be done. And when that was finished, there was more. They kept waiting to be done with us, and they never were, though only a couple of us were able to . . . find employment inside the castle walls."

They were walking again—much too quickly. If only she could get him so interested in what he was telling her that he would forget to walk!

"Where is your family now?" she asked, thinking how lonely he must be in the midst of all these strangers. Then she remembered his wife and children, and wanted to explain what she'd meant, but he knew.

"My mother is here," he said. "My brothers . . ." He was having an argument with himself again. "My mother cleans one of the weaving rooms on the Appleton," he said suddenly. "She can't do any other work than that, and she won't stay home and take money from me. She's sixty-four years old and hasn't missed a day's labor since I brought her here and got

her into the mill in 1832. She thinks the Lowells and the
Appletons are saints."

There was a tiny old Irishwoman in the weaving
room who scrubbed and cleaned. She was bent over
with work and age, but eternally sweet-tempered. She
seemed to speak no English at all but not to require it
either. In this weather she wore several capes on top of
one another, a red one always being on top, and took
them off, one at a time, as she worked. The girls were
kind to her but made funny remarks about her talking
to herself in Gaelic and about her capes when Mr.
Maguire was not listening. Emmeline was particularly
glad now that she had never done this, because this old
lady might be very like Mr. Maguire's mother.

"And your brothers? Do you have only brothers?"

"Eight. There were ten of us, but one was killed in
the war with the Yankees."

"War?"

"War . . . feud . . . No, it was war, that's what it
was, in the old days. We were like a bleeding sore in
their midst when we didn't disappear, but stayed on,
and had families, and priests, and lived in those
miserable shacks, and built more of them. They wanted
in the worst way to have done with us. But they needed
us. So they fought us all the time instead of booting us
out altogether. My brother . . . he was the best of the
lot. The youngest."

It felt strange to hear him confess openly to prefer-
ring one of his brothers to the others. She thought of
Harriet and was silent.

He began singing a ditty whose words she could only
catch now and then: ". . . Ri-toot, ri-noot . . . And
then these farmers so cute, they gave all their lands and
timber to Boott, Ri-toot, ri-noot . . ."

They had reached the beginning of her row; it was
deserted.

"What of the others?" she asked.

He shrugged. "Two are in Boston; one went West.

Two're in Lowell, and Patrick . . . A good-for-nothing. You don't want to . . . Listen to me, Emmeline. It's late. I don't see another soul on the streets. You have to go in now."

"I don't care," she said vehemently.

"I don't want to hear that again," he told her, taking hold of her shoulders. "You *shall* care. You *shall* be a good girl. And work steadily in the mill. And send money home. And keep at it until . . ." He released her. "I'm going to leave you now. I want you to sleep soundly and come in ready to work beautifully in the morning. I'm going to take you off spare hand's wages—not for any reason but that you deserve it. When you've got your wits about you, you do as well as girls who've been at it a year. Your wages this month will be at a dollar per week, and soon you'll go on to piecework and earn more."

"Oh, thank you, Mr. Maguire!" she said. "I don't—"

"Never mind. I expect you to earn the wages, Emmeline. Good night." And he turned abruptly and walked away from her—without his jacket.

"Mr. Maguire!"

He returned to take it, somewhat sheepishly, from her outstretched hand.

"Thank you!" she called after him, but he didn't turn around again.

She watched until he rounded the corner and disappeared from sight. She felt like a different person. With his energy, with his lilting words, with his beautiful deep voice that had the quality of a stream—rushing from sunshine to dark, mysterious caves and then out into daylight again—he had breathed new life into her. When she walked into Mrs. Bass's she was not without apprehension, but she felt a solidity to her own existence that came from what he had given her.

They gave all their lands and timber to Boott.

She was singing, but checked herself because it

would not do for her to appear to be happy when she was past curfew and soaked to the bone.

A single lamp had been left lighted in the hallway. The keeping room was dark. Mrs. Bass appeared at the door to her room.

"Where've you been, child?" she asked. "You're late."

"I'm sorry," Emmeline said. "I was walking." She was beginning to shiver.

"Hilda says that one of the girls was mean to you and you ran away. Is that the truth of it?"

"Yes." She looked at the floor.

"Come in here and speak to me," Mrs. Bass said. "You're dripping water all over the floor. Look at you."

Emmeline followed Mrs. Bass into the room, where she obeyed instructions to take off her clothes in front of the fire, and was given a quilt to wrap around herself. Mrs. Bass then stuffed her wet boots with rags, saying that Emmeline must leave them in front of the fire so they'd be dry in the morning. Emmeline thanked her repeatedly, while wanting only to go up to her own bed and get under the cover and remember every word that Mr. Maguire had said to her. For the first time she could think with pleasure of not having to share the bed.

"Who was it hurt your feelings?" Mrs. Bass asked her. "What did she say?"

"I can't tell," Emmeline said—not out of loyalty to Mamie, but because it seemed that if Hilda hadn't mentioned Mamie's name, there might be some good reason. Too, there was something in Mrs. Bass's very eagerness to know that made her want to hold back. For all Mrs. Bass's constantly reiterated distaste for gossip, Emmeline had seen her hovering outside the keeping room sometimes in the evening, her ears so finely tuned to the conversation that she exploded with rage if someone spoke to her. Now, failing to elicit the

information about Mamie, Mrs. Bass turned, as though
by chance, to the Maguires' Christmas tea. Was not
Ivory Maguire one of the finest women Emmeline had
ever met, and so on? It was only when Emmeline had
satisfied her on this score that she was permitted to go
upstairs.

She was exhausted. She wanted to thank Hilda, but
Hilda gave no sign of being awake as Emmeline passed
her bed. Mamie and Dovey had been whispering but
became silent as she entered the room. She had to press
her lips firmly together as a reminder not to hum the
one line of the Kirk Boott ditty she could remember.

She was wide awake. She searched her mind for a
psalm to recite, but Mr. Maguire's stories kept crowd-
ing out the words of all but the most familiar prayer:

> *The Lord is my shepherd; I shall not want.*
> *He maketh me to lie down in green pastures:*
> *He leadeth me beside the still waters.*
> *He restoreth my soul. . . .*

But the pastures in her mind, as she drifted into
sleep, were the pastures outside of Lowell which she
had heard of but never seen. And the waters were not
still, but foamed and danced down steep falls, then
moved inexorably toward the waterwheels in the basements of the Lowell mills.

I⊤ was in her mind, as she entered the weaving room the next morning, that she must give no sign of her conversation with Mr. Maguire. While she was certain that meeting him had been an accident, she knew that many of the girls would not believe this. One or two girls who had been in the keeping room the night before had greeted her with a new warmth today. If Mamie's cruelty had disposed them kindly toward her, she didn't want to undermine that kindliness now.

So she was thoroughly disconcerted when Mr. Maguire, within hearing of Corinne and at least two of the other girls, and within sight of everyone in the room, held out to her a thickly fringed black wool shawl and said that his wife had sent it upon hearing that one of the girls was without a warm garment against the January cold.

The wool was as soft as the freshly whipped cotton in the carding room, and its weight was impressive. She was at once proud, grateful, and embarrassed. How could she thank Mrs. Maguire enough? How could she ever thank her?

"Oh, thank you!" she finally managed to say. "Please thank Mrs. Maguire for me! She's so kind!"

It was not even worn, though he claimed that it had been. Was this what rich people's clothing looked like when they had *finished* with it?

Then, suddenly, she became aware that the other girls were watching her. Why had he done this when the other girls could see? It did not occur to her, until she was on her way back to Mrs. Bass's, the new shawl warm around her shoulders, that he could not have presented it in any other way. She couldn't have appeared in such a garment without explanations.

Mrs. Bass gave her paper and ink for a note to Mrs. Maguire, as well as various unsolicited suggestions for its contents. Emmeline wrote to Mrs. Maguire that she was so grateful that she did not see how her feelings could be conveyed in a letter. And secretly hoped for a reply that would invite her to convey her gratitude in person at the Maguire home.

"That woman is a saint," Mrs. Bass said over and over. "She's the closest to a saint that I've seen in this country."

But sometimes it seemed to Emmeline that the shawl had set her off further than ever from the girls in the weaving room, and that those at Mrs. Bass's who'd been about to be friendly had changed their minds. Not that she would have given up her shawl for any or all of them. With it she could walk comfortably not only to and from the mill, but through the cold night air. (She did make it a point to return well before curfew.) Still, it didn't seem reasonable that she should not be able to have a warm shawl *and* friends.

She did not see Mr. Maguire again during her walks, although she could no longer pretend to herself that she was not looking for him. Nor did he speak to her at any length in the weaving room, unless she was in a group of girls. Perhaps he was concerned that she would be resented if he appeared to favor her beyond having given her the shawl. Not only did his caution, if that was what it was, fail to have the desired effect, it made her more desperate to have a real conversation with him and to be noticed again by Mrs. Maguire.

One night she said to Hilda, "It seems that some of the girls are angry with me—for having Mrs. Maguire's shawl. Corinne used to speak with me and she doesn't anymore. I don't know if Mamie has turned her against me, or if . . . They act as though it were *he* who had given me the shawl, rather than Mrs. Maguire."

"Then they don't know Ivory Maguire," Hilda said. "Or her husband. He would never do such a thing without asking her. And Ivory . . . she would give you the coat she was wearing, if she thought you needed it more than she."

That was reassuring, except that she thought she saw some new stiffness in Hilda's manner as well.

"Then they shouldn't be angry with me," she said tentatively.

"They're jealous," Hilda said.

"But they all have shawls," Emmeline protested. "Some even have coats. What are they jealous of?"

"It's a mark of favor."

"But why?"

"Because if he didn't like you, he wouldn't have thought to tell his wife that you needed a shawl."

"But you said she would give it to anyone who needed it!" Was she angrier with Hilda or with the facts of life Hilda was setting forth for her?—if indeed Hilda's description was accurate.

"That is correct," Hilda said. There was more than a hint of sarcasm in her expression, which made it even more difficult to accept the dry words. Hilda, for all her independence, had no difficulty living within the rules, spoken or unspoken. "Ivory would give you a coat, if she knew you needed it, no matter who you were. But if you were not young and very pretty, she would not have known that you needed it, because Mr. Maguire would not have noticed."

"But that's not fair!" Emmeline protested, loudly

enough for the other girls in the keeping room to stop what they were doing for a moment and look at her.

"The truth isn't fair," Hilda said. "It's just the truth."

"But I don't even think I'm pretty!"

Hilda put down her book and gave Emmeline a long, level look.

"Then it is time for you to learn that you are," she said. "And guide yourself accordingly."

But what had Emmeline done that she would not have done if she'd thought of herself as pretty? She had not been accused of being flirtatious, like Fanny Bartlett. She knew that there were girls who would be critical of her forwardness in even dreaming of being invited to the Maguires', but this criticism did not seem to her to be justified, since she had already been invited for tea. Furthermore, it had nothing to do with whether she was pretty.

Hilda had picked up her book again; her face was closed. The conversation was finished. Emmeline would have liked to take a walk, but was suddenly concerned that Hilda would see this as an act of defiance. Perhaps walking at night was one of the ways in which she had "guided" herself incorrectly.

Tomorrow was Sunday, a day she dreaded now more than the other six. Tomorrow Hilda would go to St. Anne's Episcopal Church with Abbey and Lydia and many others, and Emmeline would go to the Baptist church alone. Aside from church and meals, there would be nothing at all to occupy her. On Sundays the lack of activity combined with her isolation to make her doubly miserable. And on Sundays she did not so much as see Mr. Maguire's face. If something terrible were to happen to her on a Sunday, he would not hear of it for a full day.

This Sunday, however, something was different. The morning chill when they got out of bed was a little less formidable than usual. There was an atmosphere at the

breakfast table that might have been accounted for by
the fact that it was Sunday but somehow seemed to be
more than that. There was an air of expectation in the
house. Then, when they stepped outside to go to
church, there was no mistaking it—even in the midst of
the city: it was the week of the January thaw, that magical week when spring always appeared to have come
sooner than it properly should, if not sooner than one
wished.

In Fayette, if the thaw continued for more than three
days, green shoots would begin to push up through the
snow, only to die when the cold returned from wherever it had been hiding. For as long as the thaw lasted,
Emmeline would be urging her mother to come out and
feel the air, which, in the middle of the day, was
considerably warmer outside than in the house. But to
her mother, the winter cold was a hungry enemy
waiting outside the front door to devour them; she
could never believe that it had really vanished to a
point where it would be pleasurable to go outdoors.
Only church and vital errands were not put off until
spring.

In Lowell, there were few early signs of the thaw
beyond the warmth in the air and the packed snow just
beginning to turn to slush under their feet. Girls came
out of the boardinghouses, stopped, looked around
them and smiled, and those already on the streets
walked at a more leisurely pace than usual, and looked
less curled into themselves.

Through the services, Emmeline's mind was on
Fayette, with only occasional detours as she tried to
figure out how she could ever describe to Mr. Maguire
without sounding irreverent the difference between
Pastor Evans in Fayette and Pastor Richards in Lowell.
After church, the country beckoned to her.

It was even warmer now, and all of Lowell seemed to
be strolling along Merrimack Street. Everyone looked
happy, and she appeared to be the only person out on
the streets alone. Common sense told her that she

should go back to the house for midday dinner and
leave her warm shawl there, but she wasn't hungry and
this wasn't a day for common sense. Almost before she
knew it, she was walking toward the bridge and the
Falls. Mr. Maguire had told her that if she walked over
the Merrimack bridge she would soon be in the
country, and if she would be even happier to be
intercepted by the Maguires than she would be to reach
the country, the latter certainly had its appeal.

There were few people on foot as she neared the end
of Merrimack Street. Once a carriage passed and she
looked up eagerly when she heard the sound of children
laughing, but it was an unfamiliar family; a young boy
and a slightly older girl leaned almost halfway out the
window, relishing the warm air. She stepped sideways
too late to avert having her skirt splattered with the
slush churned up by the carriage wheels. If only the
road leading from the bridge out into the country were
not too deep in slush and snow for her to walk! She was
on Pawtucket Street already. If only the Maguires'
carriage would pass and Mrs. Maguire would invite her
to Sunday dinner! Later she could take the children for
a walk into the country. She was tempted to walk
across School Street instead of turning right toward the
bridge, but she stopped herself. She could not let them
see her like that, a pathetic orphan, waiting to be taken
in.

The Falls were ahead of her; she had never seen them
look more impressive. Chunks of ice were breaking up
under the sun and crashing down in the heavy white
water. Here and there, whole tree branches, a brown
leaf still clinging to one or another limb, slid down the
Falls, then continued downriver to the mills.

She walked up onto the bridge, leaning against the
railing, relieving her aching feet a bit by standing on
one and then the other, watching the river debris reach
the Falls and drop down. She did not allow herself to
look toward the Maguire home. It was true, she told

herself sternly, that what she had really wanted was to take a walk in the country.

On the other side of the bridge, the road continued through snow-covered pastureland. She could make out the road because the snow had been packed down by hooves and wheels and was darker, as it melted, than the snow on the ground. Here and there was a bare elm or maple tree, but it was mainly open field, that would be covered with grass, come spring. Her father could have had a cattle farm equal to any in Fayette had he had rich open fields like these. Or he could level the occasional slope and have land fit to grow anything.

Slowly she walked across the rest of the bridge and down onto the road. The slush was just deep enough so that her skirts touched it, but she was more concerned about her shawl, which was so thick that she couldn't knot it, but had to toss one end over her shoulder. Finally, since she was warm anyway, she took it off, folded it lengthwise several times, then put it over her shoulder, where she could hold it with one hand while she managed her skirts with the other.

It was slower going than she had thought it would be. On the far horizon, she saw what appeared to be a large cluster of trees, and this was her intended destination, but after walking for just a few minutes, she was no longer certain that she would reach it. Her boots and the hem of her skirt were soaked through, and the trees looked as far away as they had before. She turned to see how far from the bridge she had come. A rider on a horse was coming over the bridge; she moved to the edge of the road to avoid being splattered before she realized that it was Mr. Maguire. He slowed down as he approached, and then stopped alongside her.

"Now where do you think you're going, Miss Emmeline?" He managed to sound both stern and playful.

"Into the country," she said.

"Now, that's what I told myself when I saw you from

the window. She thinks she's going out into the country."

"You told me it was out here."

"And was I lying?" With his stick, he gestured around them. There was not a house in sight; it was the first time since she had come to Lowell that this was true.

She smiled. "No. Of course not. Though it's not quite so country as Fayette."

"How's that?" he asked.

"Perhaps it's just that there's more forest in Fayette, and less open field."

"Aye," he said. "There's forest here, but it's not dense, and you have to go out a ways to find it. Here it's pastureland." He gestured again with his stick, this time back toward the town. "Twenty years ago it was *all* pastureland."

She was silent. The sun was directly overhead now, and it was difficult to look up at him, yet she did not wish to look away.

"Come on up here," he said suddenly. "I'll show you forest, Emmeline."

He leaned over to help her up, and without hesitation she gave him the shawl, then let him pull her up so that she sat sidesaddle in front of him. She had never ridden on a saddle before. He put his arms around her so that he was holding the reins with both hands, and told her to grasp the saddle horn. Then he signaled and the horse began moving slowly along the road.

"I come from a beautiful place too, y'know," he said suddenly.

She did not know what he expected of her in the way of response. So often she had the feeling that there was a constant conversation in his mind, and his words to her were only the parts of that conversation he happened to say aloud.

"Do you?"

"Indeed. A seaport on the southern coast of Ireland. Clonakilty. In Cork. There's very few of us from there in this country. Clonakilty." He repeated it lovingly, as though he hadn't heard it aloud in a while. "D'y'know of Cork, Emmeline?"

She told him she did not. Could she tell him that she didn't know of Ireland? That she wasn't absolutely certain she had ever heard the name of that country, or the word Irish, before she came to Lowell and people spoke of him and of Mrs. Bass?

"It's more beautiful than you can imagine," he said. "Have you seen the ocean, then? Probably not, if you lived inland. The ocean in America isn't half as beautiful, anyway. Nor is the grass as green or the sky as blue." He laughed. "Now tell me you don't believe that."

But she had accepted the words as a simple statement of fact, and felt sad at what he had lost.

"They think you've come out of some slum and you're lucky to be here," he said, suddenly fierce. "But Lowell's the slum to me." And then, some minutes later, "Of course, I'm not being fair, now. It's Manchester that's the slum such as you never want to see. The English don't know how to do a thing decently if they want to. The Americans only want for some other Yankees to do it for. They forget everything they know when it comes to dealing with *us*."

Us. They. Again she wondered if They included Mr. Stone, and how Mr. Maguire could consider himself other than a Yankee when he had lived in America for so long, and become part of an important Lowell family.

"Is your family still at church?" she asked, when he seemed to have withdrawn into silence.

"Church?" he asked absently. "Oh, you mean . . . it's Sunday . . . No. They've all gone off to Boston . . . and left me here working because there's no one to take my place in the weaving room."

"How cruel!" she said indignantly, without stopping to consider the correctness of her remark. "They should have waited until you could go with them!"

"Well, now, I wanted you to say that, you know, else I wouldn't have told you, but it's not true. Certainly Mrs. Maguire isn't cruel. She's one of the finest women on the face of the earth. A wonderful woman."

"Of course," she said, her cheeks reddening with embarrassment. "I didn't mean . . . She was very good to me; I didn't mean to . . . I only meant they should have waited until—"

"Yes, yes, of course. But Mr. Stone had to go now to attend to some business, and Mrs. Maguire gets restless in Lowell. She can't find enough books here, and she's a great reader. She's an extremely intelligent woman, Emmeline, and Lowell doesn't have what she requires for her mind." This had a rote quality, as if it were part of another one of his discussions with himself.

"I don't mean to criticize Mrs. Maguire at all," she repeated.

He brought the horse to a stop. She turned in the saddle to look at him, but his face was so close to hers that she felt herself blush more furiously than before.

"Such a lovely girl," he said. "How long will you stay in Lowell to comfort me when I'm left behind? Not too long, I think. You have to help out your family and then go home and find yourself a nice young man to marry."

"I don't want to marry!" she protested heatedly, although it had never for a moment occurred to her that she might not.

"Just as well," he said. "There's not a young man in Fayette good enough for you. I know that already."

She was dumbfounded by this turn in the conversation, and had no idea what he would say or do next. Her face was still turned toward him, but they were so close she couldn't meet his eyes anymore.

"D'you know what you look like just now, Emmeline? D'y'know what your face is like? D'y'know that your lovely face melts and runs every which way according to what I'm saying?"

He did not wait for an answer, but suddenly hit the horse hard with his stick and shouted at it—a whole string of Gaelic words. The horse jerked into a gallop, which did not slow again until Lowell and its mills were lost behind them. The farther they got from the town, the more the road twisted, and the more sharply the horse veered around the curves. The first few times she was afraid of falling, but each time Mr. Maguire's arms pressed around her more tightly, so that eventually she became accustomed to tilting sideways, and knew that she was safe.

Finally they approached a heavily wooded place where the road disappeared between thick stands of hemlock and pine. Stephen Maguire slowed the horse to a near-walk as they entered the forest. Here the snow had barely melted, for the trees hung over the road which threaded its way between them. There was an extraordinary stillness; there didn't seem to be so much as a bird in there with them. There was no breeze.

After a while they reached a clearing. Open land sloped up on their right, to a rocky hillside. The rocks were clear, though still glimmering with the moisture of the melted snow. He halted the horse and handed her the reins, then dismounted and held out his hands to her. Leaving her shawl in front of the saddle, she handed him the reins and then slipped down into his arms. She looked up at him, waiting to see what they would do next.

"What are you doing to me, Emmeline?" he murmured.

"Doing?" she asked, troubled. "I'm not doing *anything.*"

"Is that what you think?" He released her, but she didn't move. Any step she took might be wrong—although if he was angry at her for doing something, his anger was not very convincing.

"I didn't mean to be critical of Mrs. Maguire," she said, tears welling in her eyes at the thought. "She's a fine lady, and she's been so good to me, giving me the shawl, inviting me . . . I would never do anything to hurt her!"

"You wouldn't, eh?" he said, looking at her in a way that was frightening even before she heard his words. "All right, then, I'll tell you what to do in that event, Miss Emmeline. Turn around and get on my horse and ride it back to the bridge and leave it tied up there. And go back to Molly Bass's. Don't worry about me; I'll get back."

She stared at him in pain and disbelief, the tears splashing down her cheeks now. Then she turned and ran, not for the horse, but simply for the road. She had no intention of riding his horse. She did not mean, at that moment, ever to go back to Lowell. She intended to walk in the opposite direction until she dropped, and then to lie still until she was dead. She struck out in that direction, but in a moment he had caught up with her. He grabbed her arm from behind, but she shrugged him off and kept running. He came around in front to block her; she looked around wildly. She needed to get away. She needed to never see him again. Even more, she needed to never be *seen* by him. She had a sense of humiliation infinitely keener than any that had ever been awakened by her country accent or poor clothes.

"Please," she said. "Please let me go!"

But he grabbed her arms and held her firmly.

"You said I should go," she pleaded with him, "and I want to." The anger was dissolving into a kind of hopeless despair.

"Don't you see, Emmeline," he asked, his voice as soft now as the river in the darkest part of the cave, "I was trying to make you go because I cannot?"

She was about to ask why he *should*, why either of them should, when he bent down and kissed her forehead. She looked up at him and he kissed her eyes. She opened her mouth to tell him that he had been like a father to her, and he kissed her lips. She swayed, as though she had been leaning on a support and it had been pulled away. He wrapped his arms around her and held her more tightly.

"Oh, my God," he said, "you're so lovely! Oh, my God!"

He kissed her cheeks, her chin, her eyes again, or rather her lids, for her eyes were closed. Her head was swimming. From some remote place, someone said that she should do as he had told her to after all, that she must get on his horse and go without him. But the voice spoke with the knowledge that it would not be heeded. She could not have obeyed if she wanted to. He would have to say it to her again, and she would have to know that he really meant it. She had no will of her own. They stood pressed together, he kissing the top of her head, until he decided that they should move, and then he took her hand and walked with her to the top of the rocky hillside, where there was one very large rock. He took off his jacket and spread it on the rock. She watched his every move. His figure stood out against the sun and the sky with a startling clarity: the blackness of his hair seemed the blackest blackness she had ever seen; the rosiness of his cheeks, the whiteness of the sweater that had been hidden by his jacket; the glossy brown leather of his boots were all more vivid than any colors she had seen outside of her dreams.

She sat down on his jacket and he sat beside her, careless of the fact that he was sitting on the damp rock. He took her hand, twisting to look at her, but he didn't speak for a long time, nor did she. She was knowing a most perfect contentment—without thought, without *room* for thought—of either the past or the future. The silence was perfect.

He began to hum. The sound of his voice brought tears to her eyes for the second time that day.

"What is it?" he asked.

She shook her head. "I love to hear you."

He began singing the song with its words, in Gaelic, and though she couldn't understand them, she felt that they were very romantic, and that in some way they were about her.

"Would you like to know the words of that song?" he asked her when he had finished. "It's the lament of an old sailor, forced to spend his life on the seas. 'It's all very well for ye to tell me to go back to land,' he says to his cronies. 'But ye know full well, the minute I step onto it, some lass will take hold of me and pull me down deeper than the ocean. So I'll just stay on my ship and take my chances, thanks all the same to ye.'"

She smiled. "Poor old soul."

"Indeed." He began singing another song, but then interrupted himself to ask whether she had had lunch. "No," she said, "but . . ." She didn't want him to think she needed food because she was afraid he would send her back to the boardinghouse for it.

He laughed. "But what? But what? You don't need food, then; you can get by on my songs? Come on, now." And laughing, he pulled her to her feet and led her back to the horse.

He never stopped talking on the way back to town. If it had been anyone else she might have been exhausted by the sheer flow of words, but from him they were so many more songs, lullabies to soothe her, driving out other concerns. Any sight or sound might remind him of something he wanted to say, or even of another song. Two brilliant blue jays sitting on a birch branch reminded him of a bird with a long name she couldn't catch, which he'd never seen in America, and which had a beautiful song, which he whistled for her. He detoured to show her a small group of abandoned log cabins, and when she commented on their size, which made her Fayette home seem palatial, he told her that he was going to take her to the Acre, to Paddy Lands, where he had lived during his first years in Lowell.

"It wasn't like these," she said.

"Far worse," he told her.

"No," she said with great certainty. "That's not possible."

He laughed. "You'll see."

They were riding back toward the town. Her heart quickened each time he mentioned something they would do together, for it was her sole fear now, a fear that had crowded into her mind as she listened to his songs and stories, felt his lips on the back of her neck and his arms around her, that she would never know a day like this again. Ivory Maguire no longer existed in clear focus. Somewhere there was a nameless group of people who would not want her to be here with Mr. Maguire. When she remembered how jealous Mamie and some of the other girls had been *without cause,* she shuddered to think of what they would say if they were to see her now. Or rather, she watched from a distance as a girl who looked like her shuddered; she herself was too happy to be affected by such remote possibilities. What right had they to condemn her, anyway? How much comfort had they given her? If she had been capable of any feeling but contentment now, she might have been angry with them for driving her to Mr. Maguire. As it was, she simply shoved them into that group called They, from which certain facts had to be concealed. What she did not yet see was that suddenly They comprised a very large group. In fact, there was no one in Lowell, aside from Mr. Maguire, from whom she did not have a secret.

There was Lowell on the horizon. She had never seen it this way before, the developed part, within the curve of the Merrimack, rising above the fields on this side of the river. What Boott and the others had wanted to do, Stephen Maguire explained, was to create an island, just south of the Falls, on which the mills would stand. They would be fed by power from the canal just south of them, whose water would then re-enter the river farther downstream. The elevation of the land south of the Falls had made this impossible. The original canal had been built around the high lands, and in widening it, they had followed the same path. Obviously, the canals could not be higher than the river that fed them. It was this fact which had led to the intricate canal system that threaded through the entire city to the various mills.

Before she'd known Stephen Maguire, Lowell had been merely a series of places—the mill, the boarding-house, the shops on Merrimack Street. Now it was one large and real place with various parts. A unity.

But this unity came from *his* mind, lay in *his* vision, and would collapse without him.

She was trembling.

"Put on your shawl."

"I'm not cold."

"Do it anyway." He slowed the horse, and she took the shawl and somehow managed to get it around her shoulders. "Now draw it over your head, like a hood."

She did as he asked, saying nothing, but suddenly feeling miserable. She didn't have the actual sense of doing something wrong, except at moments when she felt that *he* did.

"Now make yourself as small as you can, little Emmeline. So that if anyone should happen to see us, I can try to pass you for a child. Or a sack of potatoes." He muttered something else she couldn't hear through the hood. Then suddenly he set the horse at a brisk trot and they were pounding over the bridge onto what must have been Pawtucket Street, though she couldn't see, for her head was not only covered by the shawl, but was buried against his chest. When the horse stopped, she had no idea where they were, and was astonished to find that they were in the barn behind his home, which she could see through the open doors. She could have sworn that they had traveled much farther from the bridge.

He laughed. "Ah, now, you really do look as if you've just got off the boat!" He helped her down from the horse and grabbed her hand, pulling her toward the back of the house. But then at the back porch he stopped abruptly, listening.

"There's not a soul here," he assured her, but he barely seemed to believe it himself. He drew her to the kitchen window; they looked in together. There was a fire in the hearth. Tiptoeing, they went along the porch to the other window; it was the parlor. Empty, it was more thoroughly dominated by Ivory Maguire's piano. For the first time she noticed a portrait of Elijah Stone and his sister that hung over it. She looked at Stephen Maguire and was momentarily transfixed, for he too was staring at the room, at the portrait, as though he were a stranger to both.

"How long have you lived here?" she whispered.

"Since Ivory married me," he whispered back. "Thirteen years." He looked at Emmeline. "She wanted to live in her father's house."

Emmeline was silent.

"And the Lord knows"—suddenly he was speaking with his full voice again— "nothing else made any sense. He was newly a widower, he'd just built this great house, and there was just him and his sister and Patience. And the servants. In the Old Country we never thought of having a new home if there was half a space in the old one." He took her hand and led her into the house, through the pantry, to the kitchen. He'd had fires going in both the hearth and the cookstove. Drawings of some kind—blueprints—were scattered over the table, and there were bread and cheese as well, and a big empty mug, the remnants of his last meal.

He laughed. "This is my room," he said. "This is where I live when the family's gone."

This was where he was contented even when the family was there. She remembered seeing him, through the window, wandering around the parlor like a lost soul. If in previous times he had seemed fatherly to her, now he reminded her of one of her brothers in need of comfort, and she felt more like a mother than a daughter to him. This thought made her blush, and she looked at the drawings on the table so he wouldn't notice.

"That is my house," he said. "Or I should say, the house of my dreams. It's powered by water from the Falls, Emmeline, just like the mills. How does that strike you?"

But it only confused her, for she didn't see why anyone would need power in a house.

"You have central heat indoors—do you know what that is? Instead of huddling by a fireplace in the cold, you have a whole room that gets warm, and it all begins . . ." He shuffled around among the papers, finally finding what he was looking for. "Here, you see—here's the outside." It was a sketch of a very simple cottage with a pitched roof. He had drawn in the trees around it, and the brook. "Did you ever see the little brook that runs along the road outside the river, just east of—no, of course you haven't. I'll have to bring you to it. Anyways . . . my house is in-between the brook and the river." He laughed. "That's as close as I can get to the ocean in Lowell. I can't believe you've never seen the ocean. What of the time when you came through Newburyport on the wagon? Did you not see it then?"

"It was night," she said. "I was sleeping."

"That's terrible," he said. "In the spring . . . I'd love to take you to Nahant, Emmeline. In the summer we go to the Nahant Hotel. Or at any rate, Mrs. Maguire and her family spend summers there with the children, and I visit when I'm able. It's a great palace of a place, right up over the ocean. You wake up in the morning with the waves in your ears. God, how I'd love to see you running along the . . ." He broke off abruptly and turned away from her and from the sketches, pacing the kitchen for a while, then returning to her.

"Listen to me, Emmeline. You must never listen to me when I talk like that to you. Don't ever believe me. I'm dreaming. This is probably the last day we'll have together like this. Do you hear me? It was a combination of circumstances—you walking, me seeing you . . . I don't know that it was just circumstance, but it shan't happen again. I mustn't ruin my family, and you mustn't ruin your reputation. You're a lovely girl. Gossip travels in a mill faster than salmon swim downstream in spring. I've seen girls ruined because they weren't careful to—"

"I can take care of myself," she interrupted, steadying her voice as much as she could. She needed to stop him from what he was saying. His words contained as much meaning as if he had pulled her onto a raft from a river where she was drowning, only to suggest that she jump back into the water because she was in poor company. "You needn't see me any more or less than you care to," she said. "But I can lie." Was this herself speaking, who had so recently prided herself on her truthfulness? "I have a reputation already for taking walks by myself. I don't have a friend at Mrs. Bass's. I'll tell everyone that I got lost in the woods outside Lowell today. It won't matter. No one cares about me. Mrs. Bass doesn't want me to be in trouble, or to talk with you, but that isn't because she really cares about me."

He smiled. "You know that she hates me."

"She's told me many times to stay away from you. She said it even before I was put in the weaving room."

"The old witch," he said. "Not that she's wrong. Don't you want to know why she said that?" But he had given up, and didn't really want to tell her.

Emmeline shook her head. "There is nothing bad that I would believe about you," she said. "I don't believe that you would ever hurt anyone."

"What if I hurt someone without intending to?"

"Then you're not to blame," she said quickly. Hilda had said that he tried to be good and that this was the most one could ask of a man.

But she didn't really want to think about Hilda now; there was something wrong with the way she was using Hilda's words, and she didn't want to know what it was.

Her boots and stockings were soaked, and her skirt was dripping onto the wooden floor. She leaned over to wring out her skirt. When she looked up, Mr. Maguire was regarding her in a way that made her feel happy and ill at ease at the same time.

"Take off your shoes," he said. "I'll put them on the cookstove."

She hesitated, without knowing why.

"Only if you want to," he said. "Maybe I'd best just give you some food and send you on your way. Let me see. . . ." While he was preparing the food, she took off her boots, anxious for him to forget the idea of her leaving. He brought plates from the cupboard—not the china plates from the Christmas tea, which were from Europe and very beautiful, but simple white ones. He brought out bread and cheese, and apples in a big bowl. He asked if she wanted some tea, and then he asked if she minded his having a bit of liquor.

"No, surely not," she said. It was funny for him to ask, even funnier to think she might mind. Liquor was associated with lightness and gaiety in her mind; on the rare occasion when her father had some, he became playful and talkative. Her mother would not touch it, but Emmeline herself loved the smell and had wondered what magic it contained to change her father so.

"Why are you smiling?" he asked as he poured some into a mug.

"I was thinking about my father. He becomes jolly and talks a great deal when he has rum."

He laughed. "Well, of course, I'm not in any danger of talking too much, since this isn't rum but malt liquor."

She blushed; she had been thinking of how gay and talkative he was without it. He pulled over another of the drawings and began to explain the machinery to her, but she couldn't concentrate on his words; the more precious they became, the harder it was to listen instead of worrying about the day when she wouldn't hear them any longer.

He looked up. "Why do you blush like that?" he asked angrily. "Do you know what you do to me when you blush like that?"

She held her breath and waited; she was beginning to learn that his attacks, if that was what they were, would be followed by some display of affection, while his praise was likely to end in some verbal push that sent her reeling. She must try to remain calm through both.

He had forgotten to make her tea. He offered her a sip of his liquor. He had a mischievous look, as though he knew she would refuse and then he would tease her. Without hesitation, she took the mug from him and drank from it—nearly choking, because she had not expected the strong taste, or the fieriness as it went from her throat to her lungs to her stomach.

"Well, what do you think, Miss Emmeline?" he asked gravely.

She giggled. "It's very warm."

He was watching her. Did she feel strange from the liquor, or simply from the idea of having had it?

"No more for you," he said.

"Just one more sip?" she pleaded, not knowing why she was doing it. "Nothing will happen to me."

He gave it to her.

"No more. I can't let you get intoxicated."

"Intoxicated." A new word. "Oh, no. I won't get that. May I have a glass of water please?" He brought it to her and she sipped at it. Suddenly she was uneasy. She thought she heard voices somewhere in the house. He finished the liquor in his mug without a sign that it affected him in any way, and poured some more.

"Is anyone here?" she asked.

"I think not," he said.

"Are you certain?"

"Would you like to look and see?"

"All right." She rose to her feet, but uneasily, for she was not at all sure that if there was someone in the house, she ought to be looking. Still holding his refilled mug, he took her hand and led her into the dining room, then the parlor. Everything was still and perfect. There were the servants' rooms behind the kitchen, which he offered to show her, though neither could possibly be home; they were a couple who had gone off to Lawrence, where their daughter was being married. The other servants did not live in. In fact, unless it was one of their spirits Emmeline had heard, he doubted that the voice had come from downstairs.

"Do you think it was upstairs, then?" she asked, puzzled. It had sounded too close. It was a woman's voice, soft and tired; she had almost but not quite heard the words.

"Well, now, let's see. . . ."

He led her through the central hallway, with its highly polished floor and elegant staircase, up to the second story. Here, at the meeting of the two hallways which ran the width and depth of the house, she was overwhelmed once again by its size and beauty. There were at least a dozen doors; some were open, others closed. The walls were lined with a paper which differed in design and color from the one in the parlor yet produced the same effect. Here too, the floors were polished as she had never seen wood polished before. At the end of the left hall, under a south window, an ebony table inlaid with mother-of-pearl glistened in the sunlight like a massive jewel, and the floor beneath it shone almost as brightly.

She was frightened. Her heart was beating wildly. She wanted to leave without looking in any of the rooms.

"Please, let's go down," she whispered.

"What if there's someone here?" he whispered back.

"Do you think there is?"

"Surely not, or we wouldn't be here."

"Then why are we whispering?"

"All right!" he boomed out loudly.

She burst into tears. Contritely, he drew her to him.

"Emmeline, Emmeline, do you think for a moment that I would have brought you here if . . .

ohhhhh . . ." He raised the mug to her lips and told her
to take just a small sip. The tears were subsiding, but
the fear did not leave with them. And beyond the fear
was an enormous fatigue—as though she had in fact
been walking through the Lowell woods all morning,
instead of riding on his horse. Her body seemed to have
taken on great weight, and she couldn't move, yet her
heart continued its wild beating. Did he feel it against
him? Did he know that he was supporting her? That if
his arm were to come out from around her she would
fall? Did he understand that were she at this moment to
discover that someone was there with them, she would
still be unable to run—unless, perhaps, he ordered her
to? And that the knowledge that this was true turned a
simple fear into an awesome terror?

"Come," he whispered in her ear. "You need to sit
down for a bit." He took her hand and led her to the
south hallway, where, at the first door, she stopped
short, enthralled by the extraordinary beauty of the
room she was seeing.

Crimson satin drapes framed the windows; a rug of
subdued floral pattern covered much of the floor. On
the high, narrow bed, with its gleaming mahogany
headboard, was a white coverlet of some fluffy material
Emmeline had never seen before, as she had never seen
or heard of satin before coming to Lowell. On a small
stand stood a china washbasin with a pitcher; on a
high-backed gray velvet chair a book lay open, face
down, as though the reader had been called away and
would return at any moment.

"This is Priscilla's room. She's gone with the rest of
them."

The first room she had wanted to absorb from the
door; the next she wanted to enter. This was his
daughters' room. (The boys were in the west hallway
with Patience, who did not mind their noisiness. Elijah
Stone had the north hall to himself.) Each girl had a
bright quilt on her bed—patchwork of the sort they
made in Fayette, except that the fabric looked as

though it had never been used before. The floor was painted brick red, and there were flowers painted over the red. But it was less the decoration of the room that overwhelmed her than the toys, for she had never seen toys before, other than the two dolls at the Christmas tea. There were several dolls, and there was a wooden rocking horse. On a table stood brightly painted music boxes. But above all, there was a dollhouse so large that its roof touched the sill of the windows under which it stood, and so long that if Emmeline were to lie down next to it, she might not hide its length. It was fully furnished. She moved toward it, barely noting that Mr. Maguire had let go of her hand and had remained at the door. In front of the dollhouse she sank to her knees—and gasped, barely believing her eyes; the first room she saw was a miniature of this one in which she was kneeling, right down to a tiny dollhouse. She shivered with delight. Next to it was a less accurate but still close replica of Miss Priscilla's room, the tiny pieces of crimson satin standing out in the miniature room as they had in the real one. Slowly her eyes went past the girls' room, to the next one. There were no bright colors here. Two high and narrow beds were separated by a table piled high with tiny books and other objects too small to discern. A highboy appeared to be so perfectly real that if she opened one of the drawers she would find it full of tiny clothes. Near the window there was also a chaise, but this one was covered with some dark, serviceable fabric.

"Come, Emmeline."

"Oh, but can I just see—"

"What is it?" he asked impatiently. "What is it that you have to see?"

She turned to him. "Are you angry with me?"

"No. I'm not angry with you."

"It's so beautiful," she said. "I have never seen anything like it."

He was silent.

"Are these two their favorite rooms?" she asked.

There was no answer. She twisted around to see him, and he wasn't there. In a panic, she scrambled to her feet and ran out of the room, looking down each of the hallways.

"Mr. Maguire!" she called. "Where are you, Mr. Maguire?"

"I'm in here."

But she couldn't tell which room his voice had come from. Slowly she walked toward the last room in the south hallway. There were the two high beds and the dark chaise—and the books on the table. He was looking out the window and did not turn when she came to the door. She waited.

"You can come in," he said without turning.

But something prevented her. If the house was pervaded by the spirit of the Stone family, this room was his and Mrs. Maguire's. The beds were so high that each had a stool for climbing onto the mattress. She was tired again, and a little dizzy. She had lost the excitement of the dollhouse because for some reason he had disapproved of her pleasure in it. She would like nothing more than to lie down and rest for a while, but she could not lie down in this room on one of those beds. She leaned against the doorframe and closed her eyes. When she opened them, he was looking at her.

"What is it? I told you to come in."

But she couldn't take the first step, nor could she raise her head from its rest. Finally he came to get her, holding out his hand for her to take. When he saw that she could not even do that, he put his arms around her, then lifted her from the floor and carried her into the room. He moved toward one of the beds, but when he saw that she was crying, he brought her to the chaise instead, and did not begin to make love to her until he had smoothed her hair and held her for a while, drawing over her a black-and-white lap robe that someone had left folded at the foot of the chaise.

When she awakened the sun had gone down, but there was still light in the room. She was lying on her side, facing Stephen Maguire. He was still asleep. She was no longer tired, but she was uneasy. She did not understand precisely what had happened between them, though she knew that it was wrong because he had taken off some of her clothes. She had been uncomfortable—even briefly in pain— but none of that had mattered when measured against his holding her, his kissing her, his speaking to her affectionately as he had during almost the whole time. She had been frightened until after he'd finished, he'd made it clear to her that he was contented. Even now the guilty feelings wouldn't matter, if he seemed happy when he awakened.

After a while, his eyes opened.

"Hello, sweet child," he said sleepily.

"I'm not a child," she told him. But it was all right; he wasn't angry with her.

"No," he said, "if you were a child, we wouldn't have to worry about getting you home, would we? I could ride you to the door and not worry about being seen, because no one would have a word to say if they did see you."

"It's very early. I don't see why they'd talk." But she knew it was true.

"Because that's all the girls have to do in their time off, aside from spending their money and taking novels from the library."

"I hate them," she said fiercely.

"Oh, no, you mustn't say that, Emmeline. It's not becoming to you. A lot of them are lovely girls. Almost all of them. You'd be better off being their friend than mine."

"They don't want to be my friends," she said resentfully. "They have no interest in me." Why hadn't he believed her before? She wouldn't have minded so much except that he was talking about sending her back to them.

"I'm sure that isn't so. Anyway, it's neither here nor there at this moment. I have to get you back to them, safe and sound . . . and unseen."

"There's still daylight," she pointed out.

"Yes, sweetheart," he said, and her heart jumped with gladness that he should call her that, "there's still daylight. And we won't bring you home in the daylight." She allowed herself to lean back on the chaise. "But as soon as it grows dark . . . How are you feeling?"

"All right." She felt as though she'd had a full night's sleep for the first time since she'd left home, but she was afraid to tell him so for fear that he would make her walk home immediately.

"Are you certain?" He was guilty and anxious.

She smiled.

"Emmeline, do you understand that Mrs. Maguire will be home at the end of this week, and that I cannot see you like this when she returns?"

"Will I see you tomorrow, then?"

"Oh, dear God, yes, of course. . . . Well, perhaps, if we can . . . No. No, Emmeline. Now listen to me. You mustn't do this. You're going to hurt yourself. You can't be running out of the boardinghouse every night, I tell you. You'll be let go. Turned off the corporation in disgrace! Think of your mother, if you can't think of yourself!"

But her mother was too far away; she could only think of him.

"Tuesday, then?" she beseeched. She never felt her pride endangered in pleading with him, though she could not even hint at her loneliness to the other girls.

"Maybe," he said, and then, seeing her expression, "Probably. If all goes well. If there's no suspicion. If there are no questions and you don't show anything in the weaving room." He leaned over and kissed her. "Do you think I don't want to be with you all the time, lovely Emmeline? Do you think if I had my way I wouldn't move you in here to stay with me this week? This month? Forever?"

How could she keep her head, hearing these words? How could it matter that he was sending her home? He had a life to risk, while she had nothing that she could recognize as a life in Lowell, outside of him. She wasn't even certain that Emmeline Mosher existed in this place. If something unfortunate should befall Mrs. Maguire—which of course she did not want and would pray against—but if something were to happen, and Mr. Maguire were to become free to go to Fayette with her to meet her family, then she would slip into her real self again. But here, even with him, she was another Emmeline.

Now she was kissing him with abandon, throwing off the lap robe, running about the room, telling him that she loved him; that she was hungry; that she didn't want to go back to Mrs. Bass's, ever. Then, seeing his expression, she became frightened, though not nearly so frightened as she should have been, and stopped in her tracks.

"I know that I have to go back," she said. "I don't mind. It's all right now. I won't even mind being there." Because she could think about him. "I will go, and I will stay in as much as you want me to, and I won't say a word, or show anything by my behavior. I don't want to be sent away, and I don't want Mrs. Maguire to be angry with me. I understand that we won't be together like this when she comes home." But some time Mrs. Maguire would go away again. In the summer she would go to Nahant, and there might be other trips to Boston. "I don't mind, as long as I can see you at the mill." See him and hear his voice. Not to do either of those was unthinkable; the idea made panic arise within her. She didn't need to be with him in this way, but she needed to look at his face and hear his beautiful voice. "I'm ready to go, whenever you want me to."

He had relaxed considerably as she spoke. Now he came to her and kissed her.

"We'll have a bite of supper, and then perhaps I'll ride you as far as the Acre. I want you to see the Acre. From there it's only a short walk to Molly's."

It was getting dark. They sat near the cookstove, to be warm while they ate. He drank malt liquor, but offered her none now. It did not seem to have any effect on him; he simply talked on and on, anything that came into his head. One thing led into another, often by a route that was invisible to her. He went to the pantry and failed to find something he was looking for, muttered something she couldn't distinguish, then said that Mrs. Maguire was too occupied with problems of the mind to get the servants to keep the pantry in order. Mrs. Maguire was a remarkably intelligent woman, as fit as he to run a mill, that was the truth. It was the great regret of her life that in her own youth there had been no colleges for women to attend, and it had been a source of mixed pain and satisfaction to her when Mt. Holyoke Seminary had opened a few years earlier. He had urged her to attend, as a matter of fact, but she had claimed she would feel foolish, the only old woman among a bunch of girls. In his opinion, *this* was foolish, for she was only thirty-one years old at the time and this hardly made her an old woman. He himself intended to live to a hundred, and didn't see why it should be difficult to do so (he laughed), if only he could stay out of fights. He had a dream, actually, which he had never told anyone . . . well, he had told Ivory once in a light sort of way, and she had thought it such nonsense that he hadn't told her that it was more than a dream to him. It was that once their children were grown and married, he and Ivory should sell this house and go as far West as it was possible to go. He would follow Lewis and Clark's trail along the Missouri—did she know about Lewis and Clark? Well, no matter. Then he would push on even farther. He had seen only one ocean, for all his travels. He longed to see the Pacific. He had heard from other sailors that the Pacific was an entirely different color from the Atlantic. Wouldn't she love to see that? Maybe if Ivory wouldn't come with him, he'd take Emmeline. But by that time she would be married and have children of her own, so what was he speaking of? (*But I won't marry; I'll wait and go with you,* she would have said if he had asked. *I'll wait for you as long as I have to!*) She mustn't look so serious, he said. That was the difference between a foolish young girl like Emmeline and a sensible woman like his wife—Ivory knew when he was being ridiculous! Of course, some of her notions of what was ridiculous . . .

He wanted to go to the South one day, too. Just once he wanted to be in a place where it was warm *all year round*. He wanted to see cotton growing in the field. Sometimes he would watch the bales being unloaded from the railroad cars and wonder what it was like at the other end—in Alabama, and in Mississippi. Ivory could think only of the injustice of slavery when he talked about the Southern states, and he was no less against slavery than she, but there were other things than slavery to think about, and indeed there were times when it seemed to him that there was more than one kind of slave. There were times when he was rushing through the snow to work from sunup to sundown, a supposedly free man, when he told himself that he might just as well be a slave working in the hot sun, without even a shirt on, and then jumping into some fresh water afterward for a swim. There were places where you could swim in January! Did Emmeline know this?

He was all wrong, of course. He knew from Ivory what the slaves' lives were really like. Ivory had a sense of injustice so strong that she could not enjoy any of life's pleasures for worrying about the people who were deprived of them. Ivory was a member of Mr. Garrison's American Anti-Slavery Society, in Boston. If it were up to her, they would have become an active link in the new "Underground Railroad." It was the bitterest source of dissension in their family—between Ivory and her father, that was—that although their home in Boston stood empty but for the servants during most of each year, Mr. Stone would not allow fugitive slaves to be sheltered there. Mr. Stone saw nothing wrong in slavery, as you could tell if you'd ever . . . He wasn't a bad man, really; he just had his ideas. . . . They were all that way. They really failed to comprehend that humanity extended itself past the boundaries of the Anglo-Saxon race. The only one of them he'd ever known who was an exception to this was Jacob Bass, who could have become one of the great lords of Lowell, but had chosen to live a humbler life. Of course, this didn't explain why Jacob had chosen to marry a witch who'd have burned at the stake if she'd happened to have been born two hundred years earlier. Poor Jacob. Stephen Maguire missed Jacob more than he'd ever missed his own father when the old man died. It was due to Jacob—and not to his marriage, in case Emmeline had wondered—that Stephen had crossed the barrier from being another bloody Irishman (forgive him) to having a responsible job in the mill shop. No one else would have given him a chance, no matter how good he was.

It was because of Stephen's friendship with Jacob that Jacob had happened to meet, and later marry, only the Lord knew why, Stephen's cousin Molly Slattery. Nor had Stephen said anything to discourage this union, though he knew things about his cousin that would surely have . . . he would tell Emmeline something that he had never told . . . no, he shouldn't . . . he would tell her something no one in all of Lowell knew, except his mother and himself: Molly Slattery had a bastard child in Dublin. Not only that, she'd tried . . . no, never mind. That was enough. (It was more than enough for Emmeline, who hadn't even the time to try to guess what he was talking about.) Surely this knowledge would have made Jacob Bass push Molly out of his mind forever, but Stephen had never told because he didn't want to hurt Molly or anybody. Molly had rewarded him for this silence by moving heaven and hearth to prevent his marriage to Ivory Stone, spewing up, with equal abandon, tales true and untrue of Stephen's past; taking it upon herself, at one point, *to warn Elijah Stone* about the danger that threatened his daughter. Fortunately, Molly's manner and appearance had filled Ivory's father with such revulsion as to make him wonder, for the first time, if he had not been too hard on Stephen. Her brogue was thicker than Stephen's, for one thing, and Mr. Stone had a way of not hearing the most intelligent remark for the Irish brogue around it. Stephen often saw ideas of his own considered months or years after he'd proposed them, when Elijah Stone heard them from a colleague with Yankee speech he could listen to. Furthermore, Molly was what Mr. Stone, with fear and determination, pronounced an hysterical woman, perhaps the most dangerous category of human, and not to be allowed inside his home. Yet Jacob had loved his wife as much as a man could love a woman, and Jacob was the most wonderful . . .

In 1824 Stephen and Jacob had come down the Merrimack from Nashua on a raft, with lumber for the Summer Corporation waterwheels. It was a trip Jacob had made before and spoken of to Stephen. Stephen had been so excited by the idea that Jacob had consented to make the trip again, though by this time there was no need for him to choose his own lumber; Stephen could have done it for him. That raft trip was the only adventure Stephen had ever had that was better than his expectations; not a moment of it had been less than exciting or beautiful. Now, with the

railroad coming down from Nashua, it was hard for
Emmeline to appreciate . . . though of course that line
was itself a mixed blessing. Perhaps half a dozen hotels
had gone out of business in the past year, now that the
commercial travelers and others could press up to
New Hampshire without stopping to eat and tend to
their horses. Did Emmeline know that fine building on Merrimack, near Cabot, that had been
vacant since . . . But talking of present-day Lowell
streets had reminded him of their need to be on their
way.

"Come," he said abruptly, draining his mug. "We
must go now."

He seemed to be almost waiting for her to resist.
Instead, she decided to show him by her movements
that she was ready to go and would not be difficult. She
got on her boots and was through the pantry and out on
the porch before he had even found his sweater, and he
ran after her into the night, laughing.

"Whoa! What's gotten into you, Emmeline? Hold
on—I haven't even got on my sweater!"

She ran toward the barn. The mushy top surface
was turning back to ice, but she never lost her foot-
ing. She was trying to scramble up onto the horse
when he caught up and grabbed her, spinning her
around.

"Are you trying to get away from me?" he demanded, but he was still laughing.

She smiled up at him, falsely demure—coquettish,
really, for the first time in her life.

"I was only trying to get back to Mrs. Bass's as
quickly as you said I must."

"Ah, Emmeline," he murmured, his expression
softening, his whole manner changing so rapidly that
for a moment she was frightened again. "You're trying
to destroy me."

Only when he led her to the hay pile and spread out a
horse blanket for her did she understand that what she

had done was make it impossible for him to want to take her home, just then.

He was very nervous during the ride home. He decided that they would see the Acre another night, on foot. They were too visible on the horse. He started to go one way, then changed the route so that they went way out of their path, along the Pawtucket Canal, onto Dutton Street, curving around to Mrs. Bass's from the back end of Lowell, or what seemed to her to be such. It wasn't lighted, as the central section was, and most of the houses were poor. They passed a small stone building, no uglier than many others, and he told her that it was the jail and that the Acre was just on its other side. At one point he insisted that she get some more mud on her boots, which had dried, and let her skirts go through the snow again, to lend credence to her story that she had been lost in the woods. He rumpled her hair and gave her a stick, telling her to say she had picked it up in the woods.

She was sure that her greatest problem was that she must appear to be tired and miserable, while in truth she was suffused with a powerful sense of well-being. She did not mind that she had to lie to protect him and had no sense of being in danger herself. There had been nothing to protect in her life until now, and in the future she would be very careful. If the girls there should dislike her, she must remember that she did not need them so badly as she once had, for now she had Stephen Maguire.

It had been half-past six when they left his home. Everyone would be in the dining room when she arrived. She wasn't hungry, but she knew that she must pretend to be. She kept twisting around to fill up her eyes with him again before he left her, but he always told her to turn back. He left her at the point on Dutton Street where the mill houses began. She walked, or rather half-walked and half-ran, to Mrs. Bass's. Only when she opened the front door and heard the talk and laughter in the dining room did she realize that she was trembling.

She placed her shawl on its hook and walked slowly to the dining room entrance. Mrs. Bass stood at the far table, facing her, serving one of the girls from a platter. When she saw Emmeline she let out a shriek, so that everyone in the dining room stopped what they were doing. Mrs. Bass set down the platter.

"Emmeline!" Mrs. Bass called. "What on earth has happened to you?"

Suddenly, blessedly, Emmeline burst into uncontrollable tears.

"I was lost in the woods," she sobbed—astonished herself at how genuinely miserable she was, when she had been so thoroughly happy only moments before. "I wanted to take a walk in the country," she sobbed, as Mrs. Bass came toward her. "I was missing Fayette. I wanted to see the forest." As she spoke the tears came more heavily, so that she could barely speak. Mrs. Bass led her to a vacant seat.

"You pooorrrr thing," she said. "You must be staaarrrrved. We missed you at dinner, but we never thought . . . You poooorrrr thing." She heaped vast quantities of food on Emmeline's plate. "I'm going to speak with you later, child, about your wandering ways, but not now. You need a good meal and some rest."

Finally Emmeline stopped crying.

"I *am* very tired." Now it was true.

Mrs. Bass admonished her once more to eat, and then went to her own place.

Emmeline looked around her. She was sitting between two groups of girls, one from the first floor, the other from the second. She felt them to be curious but not unsympathetic.

"You must have been frightened half to death," the one called Dora said.

"After it began to get dark, I was," Emmeline said. "Until then . . . the truth is that it was very beautiful."

Dora smiled.

"I longed for space and trees," Emmeline continued. "Have you never missed those in Lowell?"

"Of course," Dora said. "My home is on the Kennebec."

"My father's fished in the Kennebec," Emmeline cried out with delight. "It's not very far from Fayette, at all!"

"When the spring comes," Dora said, "I always request a transfer if I'm placed where I can't see the river."

"How long have you been in Lowell?" Emmeline asked.

"Two years. Next year will be my last." Dora raised her eyes toward heaven, then caught herself. "It's not so bad as that, really. Not in the winter, anyway."

"It was very warm today," Emmeline said. "I think that may be why I thought to go."

One of Dora's friends asked where she had gone.

"Over the bridge at the Falls, to begin with."

"Pawtucket? That would be the beginning and the end of it for me!" the girl exclaimed.

"You're just lazy, Susan," Dora said, but Emmeline laughed.

"Don't you sometimes feel you'd walk forever just to get away from the brick?" someone else asked.

"I hate brick," Emmeline agreed, surprised by her own vehemence.

"Well, now, where did you go when you got over the bridge?"

"I just followed the road. It must be a coach road, though I didn't see any carriages or horses today." She barely heard her own lie. "It was so warm that I carried my shawl. I saw a lot of birds. I'm not certain that I've seen a bird since I came to Lowell. I saw blue jays, and a lot of sparrows, and some swallows." At one point in the woods as they rode home she had thought that she heard the low coo of mourning doves, but she hadn't been able to catch a glimpse of them.

"And so you just stayed on that one road?"

"There was a forest. I followed the road through it." She became confused as she realized she could not have gotten lost if she'd followed the road. "But then on the way back, I thought I saw a shorter path. That was when I got lost. I think I was walking away from Lowell, instead of toward it."

"You're very brave," Susan declared. "I would have sat down in the middle of the road and cried until someone found me."

"But I couldn't find the road!"

They all laughed, Emmeline along with them. She felt very good. She had come back thinking only of how she could stay out of trouble, and instead of facing hostility, she found herself part of a friendly group. She didn't realize that she herself was being more friendly; she only saw the difference in the others' treatment of her.

She felt Mrs. Bass's eyes upon her from the next table, and realized that she had barely touched her food. Now she dug into it as though she were famished, pretending to be oblivious to all else. Susan and the others were going to take a walk after dinner, since it was still quite balmy outside. Susan said that she didn't suppose Emmeline would join them on this particular night. Emmeline, thinking only that she dared not, said that she hoped they would ask her again.

She felt vaguely ill, but every time she stopped eating she felt Mrs. Bass's eyes upon her and forced herself to take a few more bites. She could not guess when she might safely say she'd had enough. After the other girls had gone, Mrs. Bass came and sat next to her, delivering herself of a tract on the various hazards of Lowell life, but Emmeline could barely listen. She felt ill.

"What is it?" Mrs. Bass asked.

Emmeline shook her head, but that made her feel worse.

"Are you all right, child?"

"I need to go out," Emmeline whispered.

Mrs. Bass stood and helped her out toward the back, and would have gone with her all the way to the yard, but Emmeline asked her not to. She could not bear to have the woman's eyes upon her. When she returned to the house, Mrs. Bass was waiting in the pantry. Emmeline could not look at her.

"I'm all right now," she said. "I think I ate too quickly." Refusing Mrs. Bass's offer of help, she went upstairs to her room.

Hilda was sitting on her bed, writing a letter. She appeared not to notice when Emmeline entered the room. Emmeline yawned. She was nearly overwhelmed by exhaustion now, but otherwise feeling fine. If only Hilda would give some acknowledgment of her ordeal so that Emmeline could know she believed it! But when the other girl saw that Emmeline was preparing for bed, she gathered her papers and left the room.

For a while, Emmeline engaged in an imaginary conversation with Hilda in which Hilda asked whether anything was wrong and she was able to convince her that there was not. But she felt too tired, and too happy, to dwell on this problem for very long. Nor did she remember her prayers; she was too full of Stephen Maguire to think of God. She tried to imagine what it would be like to live in the Maguire house. In her mind she picked up and played with the dolls she had seen. She could remember the clothing on each one clearly. When she closed her eyes, she could picture each room of the house as easily as if she were still in it. When she drifted into sleep she dreamed first that she was sitting in front of the dollhouse, telling a nighttime story to all the children. They were seated around her in a circle on the braided rug in the little girls' room. Then something went wrong. Mr. Maguire was calling to her that she must come out of the room. He couldn't come in

because it was too small. With great reluctance, she
came out, carrying something she needed to give him.
Perhaps it was the book she had been reading from; she
couldn't be sure because it was wrapped in a quilt or
some piece of cloth she had brought from Fayette. But
when she reached the doorway and tried to give it to
him, he had vanished, and suddenly she realized that it
was not the big house she was in, but only the
dollhouse. She was in despair because now she would
never be able to find him.

On Wednesday night she would meet Mr. Maguire on Suffolk Street, near the Acre. She had promised him that she would stay in with the other girls on Monday and Tuesday nights. And she had promised without even knowing that she would suddenly make several friends!

The balmy weather continued. On Monday night she went with Susan and Dora and the two other girls in their group, Esther and Mina, to the circulating library, which she had not yet seen. Nor had she seen a pale imitation of it. There were, in fact, more books here than she had seen in her lifetime—hundreds of them! How was it possible that Ivory Maguire could not find enough here to occupy her mind? The other girls were so pleased by her excitement that Dora insisted upon taking out a volume for her—Mr. Irving's *Tales of a Traveller*—since she herself didn't have the twenty-five cents required to join the library.

She was overflowing with good feelings, to which there was an anxious edge because the reason for them had to be concealed. In the weaving room, it was difficult for her not to stare at Stephen Maguire, something he had specifically warned her against. She was not to avoid him so thoroughly as to create suspicion by the opposite extreme, but she should know now, if she did not already know it, that the way you felt about someone showed in your face as you looked

at him, or her . . . particularly if you were a lovely
young girl named Emmeline Mosher. So it was best not
to look at him at all, for once she looked, it would be
both dangerous and difficult to stop. She was almost
grateful, for the first time, for the noise of the
machines, which kept her from hearing his voice.
Although he did not know it, hearing him had as
powerful an effect on her as seeing him.

On Tuesday night she sat in the keeping room and
tried to concentrate, but found it increasingly difficult.
Wednesday night was drawing closer. Once Susan
laughed and said that Emmeline must be thinking of
home, for she seemed to be a hundred miles away from
Lowell.

Mrs. Bass, who had to awaken earlier than the girls
and spend her day cooking and cleaning, often went to
her room a short while after dinner. On Wednesday
night, as soon as Emmeline was sure Mrs. Bass had
retired, she slipped out without telling any of her
friends. He had made her memorize the directions,
because he was afraid she would leave a piece of paper
where it might be found. There was a bright moon.
Instead of walking up to Merrimack Street and then
north toward his home and the river, she was to walk
southeast, through the most densely populated mill
area, and continue until she reached the canal on
Dutton Street.

So far, so good. There was the canal, its water
glistening under the occasional streetlight. She was to
stay with the canal and not walk on Suffolk, part of
which bordered the Acre. She saw no one else on
Dutton as she crossed the bridge where the Suffolk and
Merrimack canals met and continued past the machine
shops. There was the jail, where she had been in-
structed to wait for him. She was to speak with no one,
and if anyone bothered her, she was to knock on the
jail door or call out. The jailer was an old friend of
Stephen's, and he would help her. The jail itself was a

small gray stone box, not so different from many other Lowell buildings, except, of course, for the bars on the windows.

Stephen Maguire wasn't there yet, but she'd half-expected to wait for him. Three mornings out of four he dashed into the weaving room when most of the girls were already at their looms, and he was sure to do some funny little thing in his haste to start the day—not think to take off his cap, or have difficulty in finding the book where he recorded the times of their arrivals and departures.

There were no buildings of more than one story out here, and the wind cut across the open ground and the canals. There was a chill in the air that had been absent since the thaw began on Sunday. She gathered her shawl more tightly around her and walked a few paces up Fletcher, thinking he would come from that direction, but there was no one in sight. A short way up, on the other side of Fletcher, was a collection of ramshackle huts that were much too small to be homes, but not sturdy enough to be commercial buildings either. She walked closer to them, less out of curiosity than from the desire to keep moving. A decrepit wooden fence surrounded the buildings, of which there were quite a few—far more than she'd realized at first—but it wasn't a fence that would keep in (or out) anything that didn't want to be kept. As she drew closer, she saw two goats grazing—or at any rate, sniffing the hard ground between the two end shacks. She smelled chickens, and realized that she was no longer accustomed to farm smells. A man approached her from the other side of the fence, and suddenly she remembered Mr. Maguire's warning. She was about to turn and run toward the jail when she saw that it was he.

"I told you not to come here by yourself," he said sternly.

"Is this the Acre, then?"

He sighed. "Yes, Emmeline, this is the Acre. I don't suppose you had any way of knowing that. The jail had to be right across the road from the Acre so that they could get Irishmen into it easily. A Yankee has to work ten times as hard as an Irishman to get to jail."

She waited.

"Come in through the fence, then," he said after a moment. And then, when she was through and standing upright again, "Turn around."

She turned. She was standing at the door to one of the wretched little huts she'd tried to identify.

"That is not the house where I lived."

She laughed. "No, of course not."

"It's the house of one of my cousins. A cousin who didn't marry Jacob Bass. Or Ivory Stone."

"Are you telling me the truth?"

"I never lie to you. No, wait a minute. I might lie to you. If I tell you I don't love Mrs. Maguire, I'm lying to you. Or if I tell you she's not a wonderful woman. Understand?"

"Yes." She understood the words, if not why he was saying them to her.

"Then why are you here?"

"You told me to be."

"My family will be home soon. Perhaps tomorrow."

"You said they would come on Sunday."

"Perhaps. I don't know for certain. They could come sooner."

She watched his face. He was testing her, daring her to run back to Mrs. Bass's now. But *he* was the one who had wanted her to see the Acre! He was the one who . . .

"Mr. Maguire," she said, all of her effort concentrated on keeping her voice steady, "when I was on the bridge the other day, I had it in my mind to go for a walk in the country."

"Fourteen years old," he said after a while, "and already so much iron in you." He smiled. "All right, then. You're not going to allow me to pretend that a fourteen-year-old is seducing me against my will."

"I'm not seducing you at all." She didn't even know what the word meant.

"Is that what you think?" he asked, still smiling.

"And I don't believe you," she said, emboldened by her success. "I don't believe you would be living here. It was because of Mr. Bass that you were earning good wages, you told me so. You would have gone to a decent home no matter what. I don't believe you would have remained here."

"All right," he said. "All right, my love."

My love! She stared at him, wondering what would come next.

He took her hand and led her carefully along the icy, winding path that curved around the various hovels. They sidestepped honking geese and sleeping pigs and chickens and, once, a horse that stood directly in their path, its head considerably higher than the shack near which it was tethered. Voices could be heard from behind some walls. The barnyard smell was strong enough now in the middle of winter to give her a good idea of what it must be like when the warm weather came.

In a few minutes they were close to the other end of the Acre. Looking between the last shanties she could see the back of Cross Street with its ordinary, neat-looking houses. From the Acre, they looked like mansions.

"This is my brother Liam's," Stephen Maguire said at a shack that was a little better than the others. It was raised off the ground by a layer of stone, and the tarred paper covering the boards was nailed down in straight rows at regular intervals. Most of the others appeared to have been thrown up in a random fashion.

"Your brother lives here now," Emmeline repeated, as though to convince herself.

"Indeed. My brother and his wife and his seven children."

She gasped.

"He has regular employment at the Powder Works," Stephen continued, obviously relishing her reaction. "He might be able to get a house on the outside. He doesn't try. They don't try, any of them. I'm the only one."

"Perhaps they're comfortable," she said, thinking that she was warmer and better fed at Mrs. Bass's than she'd been in Fayette, but she would always be in Fayette if she had her choice.

"Of course they're comfortable," he snapped. "That's what's wrong. That they're comfortable in this slum!"

"Why is it wrong?" she asked earnestly.

"Aaaaaagggghhhhhh . . ."

He led her to the door of one of the last shacks and opened it without knocking. On the wall facing them, a fire burned in a stone fireplace so large and so handsome as to compete with the one in the parlor of the mansion where Stephen Maguire lived. He and his brothers had built it for their mother, who had stopped them when they had then tried to improve the building around it. At one side of the fireplace sat an old man who smoked a pipe. He looked directly at Stephen but gave no sign of recognition. Emmeline's attention was arrested by the sight of a much younger man, shuffling past the open doorway without appearing to notice her and Stephen. He was examining something in one of his hands. Stephen pushed her gently into the room and closed the door behind them.

In the part that had been hidden by the open door there stood a table with chairs. At the side of the table closest to the fireplace sat a tiny old woman who was Stephen's mother. She was sewing. Stephen had bought her a lamp once and she had insisted that he take it away with him, for it might fall and make a fire. The larder was on that table, as well as the dishes, both clean and just used. It was difficult to see how people could eat at it, yet there was no other place where they might do so. The other side of the room was a jumble of mattresses and dark quilts. In its entirety, the room measured perhaps seven feet by ten or twelve.

Stephen went to his mother and kissed her.

"I've brought a nice young girl from the mill to meet you, Mrs. Maguire," he said.

The old lady had absorbed his presence without taking note of it—as though he were there all the time—but hearing that there was a stranger present, she turned from the fire, rose to her feet, and came toward Emmeline, uttering a long string of words which appeared to be apologies, though Emmeline could not understand a word, for half were in Gaelic and the other half so heavily accented that it was impossible to differentiate between them.

"Miss Emmeline," Stephen said, "this is my mother."

They had the same eyes, the same high cheekbones, the same thin yet shapely mouth. The old woman's hair was gray, almost as long as Emmeline's and plaited in two braids that peeked out from the bottom of her purple shawl. She smiled at Emmeline; with the exception of two in front, all her teeth appeared to be gone.

Mrs. Maguire said something to her.

"She's offering you tea," Stephen said. "You must take it. She'll keep offering it until you do."

"Thank you," Emmeline said, smiling nervously. She glanced at the younger man, who was still examining the object in his hands.

"That charming fellow," Stephen said, "is my brother Michael. You may speak to him or not, as you wish. It's a matter of complete indifference to him."

Michael looked at her with dull eyes. Stephen might have brought another piece of furniture into the room.

"How old is he?" Emmeline whispered, as Mrs. Maguire poured water from the big kettle hanging on the fire to a small one on the table.

Stephen shrugged. "About thirty. I don't recall precisely. It hardly matters."

She looked toward the old man at the fireplace. Stephen had told her that his father had been dead when he left Ireland.

He laughed. "Do you want to see if it's moved yet?"

"Who is he?" she whispered, though he was speaking in a normal voice.

"It's a potato," Stephen said. "Do you know how the girls at the mill take up plants in the fall and bring them to winter in the weaving room? Well, there you have a potato my mother roots indoors each winter and sets out again in the spring. One potato wasn't enough for her to take care of; she had to acquire another."

She was troubled at his talking this way, even if the old man didn't understand. In Fayette, there were people who were no less strange than these, but no one would ever have suggested they should not be cared for . . . or said anything in their presence that would have hurt them if they *had* been able to understand. She smiled at the old man to show that she felt nothing but kindness toward him, and thought she saw him incline his head just slightly toward her.

Stephen was already seated at the table, buttering a piece of bread, out of which he took huge bites in a way he had not done when he ate at the Stone house; looking in the covered crocks on the table to see if there was something he wanted; getting up to dip his fingers in one of the pots hanging over the fire, then cursing because the piece of meat he picked out of it burned his fingers.

Still, for all the cursing, for all the sarcasm, he looked more comfortable than she had ever seen him, smiling as he watched his mother, in her bright shawl, pouring tea; looking at the fireplace he had built with such care.

When they took their leave, there was a stream of what were apparently apologies from his mother.

"Why was she apologizing?" Emmeline asked when they were outside again.

"Because you're one of the judges," he said.

"What does that mean?"

"You're a Yankee. The Yankees are our judges."
As usual, he was teasing and serious at the same
time.

"But I don't judge them! Or anyone!"

"Of course you do," he said. "You have eyes, and
ears, and a brain. Of course you do."

She was silent, angry with him but not wanting to
show it. They had too little time together to ever waste
any of it on being angry.

"You want to go home now, don't you?" he said.

He had wanted her to stop adoring him so, and it had
worked, for now. Still, she couldn't want to give up the
rest of the evening which might be the last she would
have with him for a while.

"I knew how you'd feel when you saw this place," he
said.

"It's not the place!" she burst out in spite of herself.
"I've never seen you be unkind before!"

"That's because you've never seen me at home," he
replied—and only realized what he had said when it
was out. "Well, shall I take you back now?"

"If you like."

"It's almost nine. You can't be in late again—you
know that, don't you?"

"Yes."

"Emmeline," he said, without moving, "what am I
going to do about you?"

"What do you mean?" she asked. "There's nothing
you have to do."

"They could all come home tomorrow."

"I'll just continue to do what I have to do."

"You haven't told any of your friends?"

"Of course not." She felt humiliated by the question—as though he were accusing her of wanting their
secret known. She began walking back toward where
she'd come in.

"Wait a bit," he said, coming after her, taking her
hand. "I've just had an idea." He guided her back to

the shanty he had said was his brother's. In the rear was a covered shed with sides and a door, which he opened. In the darkness, chickens clucked, and some larger animal moved—a goat, probably.

"Since you love my ancestral grounds, Miss Emmeline," he whispered, "we'll just linger on them a few minutes longer."

He led her to a pile of hay in the corner, up against the house, hissing softly to warn any animals that might be there. On the other side of the wall, people were talking—arguing. A baby was crying. It occurred to her that she had not heard a baby cry since she'd left Fayette, and that very thought made *her* want to cry, but she bit her lip to prevent herself. In the hay, he held her close and kissed her, making love to her with his body while warning her off with his words, telling her how careful they must continue to be, even when they were not seeing each other outside the mill.

That would be all right, for a while. If she could look at him, if she could hear his voice, then she could easily remain in Lowell and work. She no longer thought constantly of the day when she could go home. She thought of the day in the summer when Ivory Maguire would take her children to the Nahant Hotel. The baby was still crying on the other side of the wall as they rested. Its sounds made it impossible for her to forget the time, as she usually did. She was anxious to be finished with their parting tonight. She didn't want to think too much about what it would be like when she could not touch him.

She said she thought she'd best go back now, and he told her how delighted he was with her growing sense of responsibility. Around the corner from Mrs. Bass's, he kissed her and walked away without a word. But then on Saturday, as he passed her loom, he slipped a note into her hand. The note said that his family and the servants would return late on Sunday after all. She should come to his home on Sunday morning, unless someone she knew accompanied her to church, in

which event she should sit through the service and then
find a way to escape.

By Sunday, winter had returned with a vengeance,
but she was too preoccupied to notice. She was happy
that she would be with him one more time; frightened
because now it was surely the last time; angry because
if he had known yesterday that his family was coming
on Sunday, then he must have known all along. She
couldn't understand why he should lie to her. She
couldn't understand that part of him that always
needed to be able to escape, even though he so clearly
had the only power between them, and she asked him
for so little.

She walked part of the way to the Congregational
church with Susan's group, but her manner was abstracted, and Susan asked whether something was
wrong. She said no, that she was simply missing her
family, and then she got still angrier, though she wasn't
sure at whom, because she had become so accustomed
to lying. After today, she wouldn't need to lie for a
while, but she would always have to be careful. He kept
reminding her of that.

She ran the last part of the distance to his home,
knocked at the door, waited for him to respond, and
thought when he didn't that she should have gone
around to the back. She walked around the house and
peered through the kitchen window. He was sitting in
the same chair as before, his head on the table. He was
sound asleep. At the sight of him, whatever anger she
had felt vanished.

She knocked at the window, but he didn't stir. She
tried the door. It was open, and she walked in. He
heard her and wheeled around as he awakened, looking
as though he expected to be attacked. When he saw
her, he laughed.

"Ah, it's you," he said. "You scared me half to
death."

He sounded less than happy to see her. He was nervous.

"How did you learn that they wouldn't be home until tonight?" she asked.

"They always come Sunday night."

"Then why didn't you tell me—"

"Don't ask me any questions. Please, Emmeline."

She took off her shawl, but the fire had gone out in the stove and the room was cold, so she wrapped it around herself again.

"Do you have no sense of what it costs me to see you?" he asked angrily. "Do you not understand that you have no right to be here? Do you not understand why each time I swear it will be the last?"

"No," she said, squeezing the edges of her shawl, working desperately not to cry. "I don't understand. I don't feel as though I'm doing harm to anyone, most particularly to you. You have saved my life, Mr. Maguire. I cannot bear to harm you. I would rather leave now. . . ."

"'You have saved my life, Mr. Maguire,'" he repeated after her, wonderingly. "Emmeline, Emmeline, you have no sense that . . ."

She waited.

"What was that?"

"I don't know. I didn't hear anything."

"At the front of the house. Wait here." He left, but was back a moment later. "It's nothing. Come. Let's go upstairs; we'll make a fire up there."

But he didn't relax, once they were upstairs. He pulled her past the little girls' room as though the very fact of her standing there would tell them, when they came home, that something was amiss. He made a fire in his bedroom, then looked out the window, then muttered that he was an idiot to look out the window in the front of the house, when the carriage would be just as likely to come down Pawtucket and turn in at the back, to the barn.

"Why look at all," she asked, "if they come at night?"

"You can never be certain," he told her. "Once they drove the horses because they felt a storm coming, and they arrived before the sun had gone down."

It wasn't close to noon yet. She stood with her back to the fire.

"Sit over there," he said, pointing to the brass bed. "Sit up against the head poles. I want to look at you."

She obeyed, although the poles felt uncomfortable against her back.

He smiled. "Now I have you in a cage. And whenever I want you, I'll take you out, and when I've done with you, I'll set you back in."

She stared at him, not understanding that it was the brass poles that had put a cage into his mind.

His expression softened again. Once, when that funny thing had happened to his face, she herself had gone soft and liquid inside. Now her stomach grew taut with the knowledge that soon he would turn angry again. It occurred to her briefly that it was just as well that she would be seeing him only in the mill. Better to do without the extreme happiness if it was always to be followed by pain. But a moment later, when he came to the bed and touched her face as though he had never seen it before, this thought was lost in a flood of truer feelings.

How could she bear to be without him for months at a time? Not only did she love his stories, his very presence, but there were so many things about herself that she had never told anyone, but knew he would understand! She wanted him to know her family as though he had lived in Fayette. He'd had so much to tell her about *him*self that she'd had very little chance, until now, to tell him about *her*self! He didn't even know about Luke, or her mother! He didn't understand how difficult it was for her, sometimes, to be nice to Harriet! She had never told him the actual circumstances under which she'd left Fayette, or about the trip, or about Florina! Thinking of how much she needed to tell him, she clutched tightly at his arms. He pulled away.

"What are you doing?" he asked, as though she'd been trying to hurt him.

She sat up. She was frantic. It was as though she'd awakened from a bad dream in which everything she needed was being taken away, only to find that her very bed was not under her. She scrambled to the other side of the bed because she was afraid that she would pull at him again and make him angry. She must not pull at him. She must show him that she would not be a burden to him.

"What's wrong?" he asked.

"Nothing," she said. "I was thinking about Fayette. I was thinking that perhaps this summer I would find a way to visit my mother."

"Come back here."

"I think I ought to get back."

It worked, as it always did. He pulled her back to him and forgot about himself and his family and the time. As she forgot who she was, and where they were, until the church bells chimed noon.

"Get dressed quickly," he said; "else you'll be late for Sunday dinner."

She was serene. She felt him watching her as she dressed; for the first time she made no effort to conceal herself from him. She was not concerned about being late, but she didn't really mind leaving, either. He had told her that he could not do without her, and she believed him. He had told her that his life was cold and stale. He had told her that there was not a day of his life in America that he hadn't dreamed of going West to look for gold, but that this week he had forgotten the West, and gold.

She yawned. She would have dinner and then spend the afternoon with Susan and Dora. Perhaps she would rest briefly after dinner, and then they would all take a walk together. If she didn't have time now, perhaps later she would be able to look in the windows of the shops on Merrimack Street. She could pretend that she was about to buy herself a bonnet when she got her January wages. Perhaps by next winter the situation at home would be so much improved that she would occasionally be able to buy some little thing for herself.

He asked if she wanted him to walk with her part of the way home.

"No," she said. "You'd best not. I will really be fine by myself."

He tried to hold her back when she left, but she smiled and said that he knew that it was necessary for her to go. At the back door, he held her tightly for a long time, telling her that they would find ways to be together.

Her mood, as she walked back to the boardinghouse, was quite extraordinarily good.

SHE had never been more excited and happy than she was the day she received her second month's wages and posted them to Fayette. Eight dollars! By the following Christmas she would have sent home ninety-six dollars, even if her wages didn't increase during that time! Mrs. Bass came to sit by her while she was writing the letter that would accompany the notes, and when questioned by Mrs. Bass, Emmeline gave in to the temptation to admit that her work had been so good that Mr. Maguire had taken her off spare hand's wages. Mrs. Bass told Emmeline she was pleased in a way that suggested there was no way that this could have been a simple and just act on Mr. Maguire's part.

But Emmeline was not going to be bothered for long about Mrs. Bass. Not only had she remained friendly with Susan and Dora and their group, but a new girl had arrived, and for the first time since leaving Hilda's bed, Emmeline had a partner in her own.

The girl, whose name was Verna, lived just the other side of Chelmsford, in country that was still farmland, and her brother had brought her to Lowell on his horse. Verna was sixteen years old and shy, but eager to be friendly. Mrs. Bass brought her to Mr. Whitehead, who accepted her readily. There was an opening in the weaving room and Emmeline had been tempted to suggest that Verna come in there, but then it occurred to her that it might be just as well if Verna did not even know Mr. Maguire. Occasionally, Emmeline had the desire to share him with someone. If Verna did not know him, it might be possible to talk about him in some disguised form—as though he were in Fayette, for example.

Mr. Maguire seldom spoke to her in the weaving room, unless she was in a group of girls. Occasionally she looked at him from beneath lowered lids. Once or twice she found him staring at her with a concentration so deep that at first he failed to notice that she saw him. When he did, he would start and look away, and she would be sure that he was angry with her—as though she had forced him to stare. Those moments, though, were tolerable.

It was less tolerable when he moved her to the second row because a new girl had come in and he wanted to be able to help her easily. What was truly intolerable, though, was when he talked to the new girl, Louisa, in such an easy fashion that Emmeline was sure Louisa would believe that she was special to him. A wave of helpless anguish passed over Emmeline. It was only the way he was with everyone! And Louisa wasn't even pretty! Did the other girl know that he was a married man with a family? If she did, how could she be smiling at him in that way—as though there were some special connection between them? As Emmeline watched, her anger was at Louisa, but then for the rest of the afternoon she couldn't look at Mr. Maguire.

Later in the day she sensed that he was trying to get her attention, but she pretended to be more absorbed than ever in her work. Finally he came around, and, under pretense of examining her shuttle, told her that she must make believe she had left something behind in the evening, so that she would have an excuse to come back to talk to him. In spite of herself, her spirits rose; he might have contrived a meeting. On the second-floor landing that evening, she exclaimed that she had left her second shawl behind, and ran back up to the weaving room. He was putting out the last of the oil lamps.

"Tell me what's troubling you," he said.

"Nothing." But the picture of Louisa came back into her mind, and tears threatened.

"You're not ill. You're looking more beautiful than . . . You can't be ill."

"No I'm not ill. I feel fine."

"You're angry about something."

"No, I'm not. I'm not angry. You can do whatever you like and speak to whomever you like!"

He was puzzled. Then he began to laugh. "Oh, dear Lord!" He was still laughing. "Not even a woman yet, and already . . . " He became serious. "You know that I'm always nice to the girls, don't you, Miss Emmeline?"

She nodded, but she wouldn't look at him.

"Then stop this foolishness. Be jealous of my family, if you will, for they own me, and they make it impossible for me to be with you."

"But you said—"

"Or near impossible."

She raised her head.

"Look at you," he said. "So beautiful. The tears make your eyes shine more than ever. I'm too old for this nonsense. In another few years I'll be forty, Emmeline."

The tears fell, and he wiped them away; then he kissed her. She clung to him. Gently he disengaged her.

"Go now or the other girls will wonder."

"I don't care."

"You must."

"Well, then, I'll care on your account, but I don't care on my own."

"You will ruin your life if you don't care," he said darkly.

"Tell me that you will try to see me." She was

amazed at her own forwardness. It had something to do with Louisa; it was as though he would simply replace her if she didn't fight.

"Of course I shall try," he said. "Can you think I don't want to?"

He snuffed out the last light in the room, and she picked up her shawl and ran downstairs.

In this time her spirits never remained low for long. She had a sense of well-being unlike any she had ever experienced, even in Fayette. She was eager to spend time with Mr. Maguire but didn't feel that she had to do so immediately in order to get through the coming months in Lowell. In the weaving room, she befriended Louisa, quite a nice girl once one was certain Mr. Maguire didn't have a preference for her.

In the boardinghouse, she and Verna became inseperable. They spent every free moment together. Verna said that Emmeline was like a sister to her; she had never had a sister of her own, only five brothers. Emmeline's letters home, more frequent now, told her mother how neither had a sense of Verna's being the older, though she was in years. In their friendship they were equals.

Their color was high; their appetites were good. Sometimes men from the mill tried to talk to them as they walked hand in hand down Merrimack Street, but the men were never allowed to get very far. Emmeline had no interest in them, and Verna had a sweetheart in Chelmsford to whom she would have been married already, had his fortunes not taken a turn for the worse. The two girls appeared to have boundless energy. When they took walks with their four other friends, the others were always ready to turn back before they were. Often the two of them took the long walk to Pawtucket Street just to watch the thundering, foamy Falls in the moonlight. It was at these times, standing within view of the big house at the corner of School

Street, that Emmeline came closest to telling Verna the secret of Stephen Maguire; only the face that it was *his* secret prevented her. That and a certain uneasiness about whether Verna would understand. Once or twice she tried to create a character who was Mr. Maguire except that he wasn't married, and didn't live in Elijah Stone's house, and was not Irish, but the task boggled her imagination and she had to give it up.

The only small cloud on their horizon, these days, and at first it served to draw them closer together, was that Mrs. Bass had not only ceased to favor Emmeline, but appeared to have developed a suspicious dislike of her. Where she had once been concerned lest Emmeline inadvertently break the rules, she now seemed to be studying her, or both girls, for actions that were demonstrably outside them. Emmeline was never sure whether this new situation had begun with the advent of Verna or with Mrs. Bass's discovery that she had gone onto regular wages.

They were careful to be home within curfew time, for they both sensed that she would be quick to report them if they were not. Where once she'd pressed Emmeline to take more food, she would now see an empty platter near them and comment that she'd thought the meat would go farrrrrther than that. Emmeline had developed an aversion to salmon. The idea of not caring for any good food had always been foreign to Emmeline, but now the very odor of the fish bothered her, and the sight would have been enough to drive her from the room had she not been hungry for the other food. At meals where salmon was served, Emmeline heaped potatoes and bread and cabbage high on her plate.

"And since when do you not eat salmon, Miss?" Mrs. Bass questioned her, the second or third time this happened.

"It's never been one of my favorites," Emmeline lied—a phrase she had heard other girls use. Then she was confused by her own need to lie. She felt defensive all the time in Mrs. Bass's presence, so that a lie came more naturally than the truth.

Her friends began to make jokes about Mrs. Bass's "having it in for" her, and perhaps for Verna as well. They asked if Emmeline was quite certain she hadn't said or done something they didn't know about. She laughed, but was suddenly grateful that Mr. Maguire had forced her to be so careful. There was no way that Mrs. Bass could have seen them together without Emmeline's being aware of it.

Soon she would receive her third month's wages, and Verna her first. Verna didn't have to send money home, but had decided that she would wait until Emmeline could buy herself a bonnet, and do it at the same time.

They were walking toward the Falls. Spring wasn't yet in the air, but the cold was less bitter than it had been, and although they were later than usual, they decided to take a quick look at the Falls.

"You don't have to wait," Emmeline said gratefully.

"By rights," Verna said, "I should wait longer than you."

"No," Emmeline said. "Most of the girls buy them soon after they come. They're not very dear."

"Then I'll buy them for both of us and you can pay me back when you're able."

"Oh, no!" Emmeline said, "I could never do that!"

But the fact of Verna's wanting to do it made her feel so good that she grabbed her friend's hand and they ran the balance of the way to the Falls. There they stood on the bridge, as they always did, looking down over the foaming water, reluctant to leave right away even though they had the vague sense that curfew time was approaching.

"I wish we could have our own little cottage just down there," Emmeline said suddenly, pointing to the pastureland on the other side of the river, some yards down from the Falls. "We could work at the mill all day and then come home at night and have dinner by ourselves."

"We'd have to cook it for ourselves, then," Verna said.

"That would be more like home," Emmeline said gaily.

"I hate it at home," Verna said matter-of-factly.

Emmeline stared at her friend in astonishment.

"You don't mean it."

"'Course I do." Verna had thick brown hair and a ruddy complexion that turned radish-red in the cold. "At home you're never done. Here you work real hard all day, but then you come in and set down, and someone else's cooked your supper and washes the dishes when you're done. And the work ain't so boring, either, with all the others to look at and talk to. When you finish your work at the end of the day you go to another place, instead of spending the night looking at what you still need to do."

Emmeline was astonished. She could see that there was truth in what her friend was saying, yet none of it had ever occurred to her.

"Then you have your Sundays," Verna went on, as though Emmeline were arguing with her. "At home there's no such thing as a day without work."

"You sound as though you don't want to go home," Emmeline said.

"I'm not in a hurry, that's the truth of it. There's girls in the cloth room making three and four dollars a week. There's nothing I want that I can't have, if I stay long enough."

"What about your sweetheart?"

It was the first time during the conversation that Verna had paused.

"Well," she finally said, "I've been trying to think why he shouldn't come *here*. There's still jobs here for the men."

Emmeline wanted to know what Verna would do if

her sweetheart didn't want to come to Lowell, but couldn't think of a tactful way to ask. After a moment, though, the other girl turned to face her.

"If he wants me, he'll *have* to come here," Verna said with a force that was new to Emmeline. "Because I ain't going back *there*."

They'd become so absorbed in their conversation that they'd forgotten the time. Now they half-ran and half-walked back to the boardinghouse, but when they got there, out of breath and trying hard not to giggle, the door was locked. Emmeline knocked softly; there was no response. She knocked harder. Suddenly she was frightened. A month ago she might not have been, but now Mrs. Bass was against her. That lady now opened the door in a way that suggested to Emmeline that she might have been right on the other side of it all along.

"And where have you been?" she asked. "I have a mind to report you both!"

"We was just walking, Ma'am," Verna said. In the light from Mrs. Bass's lamp, Emmeline could see that the other girl's eyes were round with fear.

"We thought we were on time," Emmeline said. "We saw a clock on Merrimack Street, and we thought—"

"Are you telling me, then," Mrs. Bass demanded of Verna, "that you were together the whole time?"

"Yes, Ma'am, 'course," Verna said.

After berating them for a few minutes longer and telling them that their next lateness would be reported to the Corporation, she let them go upstairs. But then, as they were halfway up, she seemed to decide that she'd not been sufficiently severe, and called after them that for the remainder of February and the first half of March they would have to stay in after supper.

Verna seemed to feel that they had gotten off with a light punishment, but all Emmeline could think of was that she would not be able to see Stephen McGuire if, one evening, he were to find a way to make himself free. She lay awake in bed until early in the morning, her happy energy converted into a rage at Mrs. Bass, and an anxiety that he would be angry if she couldn't see him when he was ready. More than one voice within her responded to this concern. One said that it was less than a month, and Mr. Maguire might not have been able to see her anyway. Another said that it would serve him right if he couldn't, since until now he did not seem to have made any real effort in that direction. Beyond that, though, was another, stronger voice, saying that if he were to summon her, Mrs. Bass or no Mrs. Bass, she would find a way to go.

But when he summoned her, it was for another reason.

He had told her on this Saturday that he would like to speak to her at the end of the day, and she had noted with surprise that he made no particular effort to conceal what he was saying from the girl standing next to her. When the other girls had left, he told her that the dressing room was short of hands because three girls had left at once. He was going to let her go down there for a while. She would begin on Monday.

She stared at him blankly.

She was one of the quickest, he went on. She had already done drawing in and would pick up warping quickly. Not only that, it would be good for her to get away from the weaving room for a while.

"Get away from the weaving room?"

He nodded.

"I don't understand."

"Of course you do," he said, but he was uneasy. "You understand that they need warpers in the dressing room. They need dressers too, but you can't do that unless you've been in there a while. Listen to me, sweet Emmeline. From the day you walk in there you'll be earning fifty cents a week more than you earn now."

"And when will that be?"

"Monday," he said patiently. "I told you, Monday."

He paused. "Now, it's hard work, warping; I can't deny that. But you don't mind hard work. Isn't that true?"

She nodded, though she was barely listening. She would not be in the weaving room the next time she came to the mill.

"I've asked Whitehead to give you a chance at dressing in a few weeks. That's where you'll earn the money you need, Emmeline. There are girls in there earning five and six dollars a week."

Five and six dollars a week. Even in her dazed condition, this figure came through. It was more than twice what she'd been expecting to earn, and even dwarfed what Verna had told her the girls in the cloth room received. She would be able to go home much sooner if . . . But what was she doing, thinking of home, when for weeks she had dreamed only of a little cottage in Lowell, and a time when she would be able to see Mr. Maguire again?

"Are those girls not older?" she asked.

"Age doesn't matter," he said. "You're not that young."

"I'll be fourteen on March twelfth," she murmured. It was less than two weeks away.

"There's nothing you can't do with your hands," he said, a little impatient now. "I've seen you—don't you know? Don't you know I can tell the difference? You think that I'm blind because I . . ." He broke off the sentence and walked away from her. "Listen to me," he said after a while, still not looking at her. "You know as well as I that it's a good thing for you to go."

"No. I don't know that." She said it firmly, yet almost as though she were discussing a matter of principle.

"Mother of God!" he murmured. "What am I going to do with this child?"

"I'm not a child. You said I wasn't very young."

"No, of course not," he said. "If you were a child, I wouldn't have to—"

"Have to *what?*"

"Why are you being difficult? You haven't done that before."

"Difficult? I'm sorry, Mr. Maguire. I didn't mean to cause any difficulty." How could anything resembling a sentence issue from her lips when her mind was in a state of chaos? "Of course, I'll go wherever you tell me to go."

"I want you to see that it's best for you, Emmeline."

"Best not to see you?"

"You'll work better."

"Has my work been poor?"

"No, of course not. . . . Dammit!" This was a sudden shout. "Don't you see that it makes me a crazy man to have you here under my nose, and I can't speak to you, or touch you, and all the while I'm worrying that the others will see and start talking? Haven't you heard the talk in the mill? I've seen a girl ruined by it! More than one. It makes me crazy to sit here and look at you and think about what could happen."

"Oh, I see. *You'll* work better." She was groping for some explanation that would be bearable.

"You will too." He needed her to see, to feel, that he wasn't acting only in his own interest, but she didn't respond to *his* need now.

"No," she said carefully. "My work . . . is all right. I make a mistake if I'm not minding, but otherwise . . . When will I see you, then, if I'm in the dressing room? How long will I be there?"

"Emmeline," he said, pushing a stray wisp of hair from her forehead, "will you please not talk as though I'm sending you to jail?"

"Oh," she said matter-of-factly, "but it *will* be a jail, until I can see you again."

Tears came to his eyes, which only frightened her. She hadn't meant to make matters worse. Already, unknowingly, she had been giving him pain, when she had thought of herself as a source of pleasure in his life. He had told her more than once, in an unguarded moment, that she gave him his only pleasure, and that had been important. She stood on her toes to kiss him, to comfort him, very much as she would comfort one of her brothers who'd been hurt and was crying.

They were silent. Gradually the machinery around the mill had ground to a halt. The sounds on the stairs were finished. Everyone else was gone.

"I had better be going," she said.

"I'm going to try harder to find a way to see you," he said. But he was talking about being able to make love to her, and she was concerned with the need, much more real to her, to catalogue his features each morning. "Now I won't have to worry about you from morning till night."

She put her second shawl over her head, something she seldom bothered to do for the brief walk to Mrs. Bass's. She had the sense that it had grown quite cold outside while they were talking. She walked sedately to the door, pausing to turn and say good night.

"You're so beautiful," he said.

SHE had taken so long that Verna had returned without her. When she walked into Mrs. Bass's, the first thing she saw was Mrs. Bass talking to Verna, who had been on her way into the dining room with the other girls. Emmeline followed them, though for the first time in many days she had no appetite. She was very, very tired.

"I waited for you," Verna said.

"I know. I was late."

"What happened?"

"I'll tell you in the room." If she told anyone, even Verna, it would become more real than she could yet bear it to be. She scarcely touched her food.

"Is anything the matter?" Verna asked.

"I'm just very tired."

Verna grinned. "Just as well we can't walk to-night. . . . The Bass asked me where you was. I said I supposed you was still in the weaving room."

Emmeline nodded. It didn't matter. That was why he hadn't been careful about detaining her. Mrs. Bass was looking at her, and of course the old witch would be able to tell something was wrong, but that didn't matter either. What Emmeline needed to do was sleep. As soon as the first girls started leaving the dining room, she went upstairs, took off her boots, and got under the covers without changing. When she opened her eyes again, the church bells were ringing. It was Sunday morning.

At first she thought she was home. Not home, but someplace else. In her dream, spring had come. She was out in the pasture with someone—she couldn't tell who, except that it wasn't Mr. Maguire.

Only as his name came into her mind in this fashion did she remember his existence. And then she remembered where she was. And then she remembered about the dressing room. She sat up. Verna was already getting dressed. The other girls were doing their hair, except for Hilda, who sat on her bed, ready to go down but reading a book.

"There you are," Verna said. "I was beginning to think you was lost to us."

Emmeline heard Verna's country speech in a way that she had not since the day her friend had arrived, and had a momentary, irritable feeling of wanting to correct her—as Hilda had once done to her—but she stopped herself. The other girls went down, but Hilda remained, engrossed in her book. She had little to say to anyone these days, as she prepared to leave Lowell for her teaching duties. For a moment Emmeline found herself wishing that it were Hilda who was her close friend, rather than Verna. She needed someone older and wiser than Verna to confide in right now, though she didn't know precisely what she would be able to confide. She also wished that she and Verna were on their way to a different church, but she did not suggest this to Verna, because she still felt wicked having to admit that she disliked any minister of God's.

In church, though, she was glad that she had not suggested a change, for during the service, she ran over what she could remember of Stephen Maguire's words.

They were not quite so frightening now as they had been the day before. If she still heard that he was sending her away, she could now tell herself that he was not sending her very far—only to one floor below. If she still heard that she was making it difficult for him to work, she could remind herself that the reason had to do with his feelings for her. She considered, for the first time, what a great advantage it would be to earn higher wages. Perhaps she would get herself a bonnet *this* year. Or join the library in her own name. And then Stephen Maguire had said, after all, that he would try harder than before to find a way to be alone with her. She had to believe him. He had told her that he was a liar, but she knew that he wasn't. Liars did not announce themselves.

"I'm being transferred on Monday," she said to Verna as they walked back to Mrs. Bass's. "To the dressing room."

"Why is that?" Verna asked.

"They've lost three girls at once," Emmeline said. "I'll earn more down there right away."

"That's a piece of luck," Verna said. "I wish I could go with you."

"Perhaps I can ask after I'm down there," she told Verna.

She would manage. If a time of intense happiness had passed, that didn't mean she wouldn't be able to manage. She had nimble fingers. The other girls were full of congratulations when she told them. Susan said that while Emmeline was too young to be a dresser—a job requiring experience and great judgment—she would probably do well as a warper. Eventually she could hope to be a dresser, since she was already quite tall. Dressers were the taller girls, for they had to reach to the top of the high frames to make certain that the threads were being evenly sized. Emmeline, who had been as tall as her mother when she left home, was certain that she'd grown further since coming to Lowell. The waist of her old dress was quite high on her now, and the bodice was becoming skimpy. If her growth continued, she would have to take fabric from the hem of at least that one dress, perhaps the other as well, to set in at the side seams and the waist.

On Monday morning she awakened from a dream almost identical to the pasture dream of the night before, yet she knew where she was. She didn't feel very good, but she felt capable of going to work. She tried hard to hear every word of Verna's, and not to think about Mr. Maguire or wonder whether she might see him as he went up or down the stairs.

Fortunately, the new work was considerably more difficult than the old, and left her little time to think. She was one of seven girls whose job it was to watch the thread as it was warped off from large spools onto section beams and reconnect those threads which ran out or broke; it seemed they were always doing one or the other. Her arms were working at a different angle than before, so that a new set of muscles came into use, and there were fewer times to relax them. By the end of the day her arms ached as they had during her first week at the mill. On the other hand, she knew that her body would become accustomed to the new work as it had to the old. And Mr. Whitehead, who supervised the room, seemed extraordinarily kind.

But there was another problem about which the girls had said little in advance, for fear of alarming her.

Even on Monday morning, when the mill had been closed for two nights and a day, the sweet, unpleasant odor of the starch with which the thread was dressed had struck her as she entered the room. As the day wore on, and the heat and moisture from the steaming starch built up in the room, the fumes became overpowering. At noon, upon reaching the street, she gulped the fresh air, feeling that in two more minutes she would have suffocated indoors. She went back to the dressing room after lunch hoping that she would become accustomed to the fumes, but instead they became worse and worse. Her concentration was divided between handling the threads and trying to keep herself from becoming ill.

When Mr. Whitehead came by, he smiled in a kindly way and promised her that she would become accustomed to the sizing. Mr. Whitehead was tall and gray-haired and put her in mind of Pastor Evans much more than the Reverend Richards did. When he had walked on, Emmeline looked longingly toward the windows. They were nailed shut and would remain so until late spring. During her rare idle moments, she pressed her nose against the cold panes and breathed in the air that came through the cracks.

She awakened the next morning sick to her stomach, the sweet, starchy smell in her nose as strongly as though she had never left the dressing room. She prepared to go to the mill in spite of a conviction that she would not be able to cross the threshold of the dressing room without becoming violently ill, and forced herself to eat breakfast. She salted her pancakes as well as her bread; the smell of sweet cake or jam or syrup reminded her of the dressing room and made her nausea return. Afterward, she was surprised to find that she felt somewhat better.

But in the dressing room she fought again with nausea, and now sometimes dizziness as well. Mr. Whitehead was solicitous, but the greatest comfort she took from his noticing was in the possibility that he might mention her condition to Mr. Maguire, from whom she had had no word.

That night, Susan, hearing how badly the fumes were affecting Emmeline, lent her a treasured possession—a little phial she called her smelling bottle, which had in it vinegar as well as smelling salts and some herbs. Now Emmeline carried the bottle with her each day, inhaling from it whenever nausea threatened. It made a great difference in her ability to tolerate the fumes during the day, but they invaded her dreams at night.

Her best time of day was the evening, when the

exhaustion she had felt earlier in the day would
magically lift. She and Verna were not yet allowed out
to go to the library or play in the snow with Susan and
Dora and the others, but they would sit in the keeping
room and, when the others returned, exchange reminis-
cences and plans for the future. Because of her bad
dreams, Emmeline was never eager to go upstairs, and
would fight off sleep even when she became exhausted
again. Upstairs she would eventually fall into a restless
sleep. But then at some point during the night she
would dream that she was in the dressing room and
suffocating, and she would wake up gagging and
choking as though she were standing directly over the
steaming vats of starch. When she realized she was in
bed, the nausea would pass, but then she would lie
awake, vigilant against sleep, lest it return and bring
the dressing room with it.

One day she inadvertently left the smelling bottle on
the dining table. Mrs. Bass found it and, upon inquiry,
discovered it had been lent to Emmeline on account of
her transfer to the dressing room. She appeared to take
Emmeline's not having mentioned the transfer as a
direct affront, and questioned her at great length—
almost as though hoping to trap her in an admission
that the change had something to do with Mr. Maguire.

Now she seemed to be watching Emmeline more
closely than ever. Simple acts became burdened by the
possibility of misinterpretation. If Emmeline went to
the front door simply to stand on the landing and
breathe in cold air for a while, she felt the curtains in
the front room being parted behind her.

Often when she saw men at a distance she thought
they were Mr. Maguire. And occasionally, as she was
walking, she thought she heard him call her name, but
when she turned it was someone else. Or no one.

She tried to think of ways that she might cross his
path. She needed just a few words with him to know
that she was not in exile; that he was plotting to see her;
that he minded when he could not. It was almost the

middle of March; her birthday was coming. Did he remember the date? Probably not. He tended to forget what she told him about her age. Dates were both more and less important than they had been at home. At home there had been no presents in her family for some years, yet everyone knew when a birth date was coming. The day itself was the gift; a special deference was given to its owner. The others waited for you to sit down first at the table, and relieved you of some of your chores. Here she had seen the girls give each other gifts . . . a handkerchief, a box of sweets. But how did they know it was your birthday, unless you told them, and how could you tell them without appearing to be greedy? It wasn't even that she cared about the gift; she just wanted her day known.

On March 10 she dawdled after the others, waiting just inside the door until she heard what she thought might be Mr. Maguire's footsteps coming down the stairs. Then she left the dressing room. They came face to face as he reached the ground floor. He was startled, then furtive, then, when he was certain they were alone, affectionate.

"Ah, sweetheart, how're you doing in there? I think of you every time I pass this door."

Did he not ask Mr. Whitehead about her, then? She had assumed he was looking after her indirectly.

"I'm all right," she said. "The fumes made me ill . . ." He looked alarmed. ". . . at first. But now I'm all right."

"Ah, very good."

"I wondered . . ." she began lamely, put off by his abstracted manner, "if . . . Do you know me?" It wasn't at all what she'd meant to say; she had meant to ask if he knew that she would be fourteen in two days; but something about the way he was looking at her . . . or not looking at her . . .

Now he was seeing her. She blushed. He took hold of her shoulders.

"Do I know who you are, lovely Emmeline? What do you think?"

Tears came to her eyes. He kissed her.

"They're going to Boston at Easter time," he whispered in her ear. And that was enough. She could smile.

"There," he said. "I didn't mean to tell you, but you've gotten it out of me. Now run along before we make a display of ourselves right here on the steps."

She ran along. She didn't stop to ask why he hadn't meant to tell her; she was too happy to wonder when he would have gotten around to it if she hadn't asked. April seemed very close; her birthday had fallen through a crack in March, a month that no longer had any importance to her. She counted the days, and it was a triumph when April came, even though Easter was weeks away. She was in a perpetual state of excitement quite different from the one during those first weeks with him, which, even with their anxious edge, could have been described as happiness. This was only anticipation; she was living for the time when she would feel that happiness again. While she was expert at her work and highly valued by Mr. Whitehead, she had not yet become comfortable in the sweet, suffocatingly close air of the dressing room. The physical well-being that she appeared to have in spite of her discomfort—the rosy cheeks, the full figure—she could not enjoy until the day when he would enjoy it and make it real to her. The friends who, in their absence, had seemed a condition of happiness in Lowell in their presence offered only the barest kind of comfort, for she could not confide in them that which was always on her mind.

As a matter of fact, a strange new note had entered her conversations with the other girls, particularly Verna. Verna had drawn closer to Susan and the others, but somehow further from her—as though Mrs. Bass's suspicions had been contagious and she thought

Emmeline might not be a good friend after all. Since
Verna's manner had always been quite easy, it was hard
to say precisely what the difference was. But sometimes
when Emmeline came upon the others, she had the
feeling that she was interrupting a conversation. And in
bed at night, where she'd once often awakened to find
Verna curled up against her for warmth, the other girl
now seemed to make it a point to stay as far from her as
possible.

Still, the truth did not occur to Emmeline. In Fayette
she had thought of herself as almost a woman, but in
Lowell, for all her denials, she felt like a child.

On the day before Easter Sunday, still not having
seen or heard from Mr. Maguire, she again waited on
the landing at the end of the day—only to watch him
come down flanked by four of the girls from the
weaving room. They were laughing. When he saw her,
he stopped.

"How are you, Emmeline?" he asked in a terribly
hearty voice. "How are you finding the dressing
room?"

"It's all right," she said, trying to hold her voice
steady. She nodded to the other girls. "I've just . . .
I've left something behind."

"Ah, well . . ." He hesitated. He wanted to be kind
but could not be. "Good evening, then."

Desolate, she watched after them. She had no
strength in her body; certainly not enough strength to
walk back to Mrs. Bass's. She opened the door to the
dressing room. Mr. Whitehead was in the process of
checking the dials which measured how much work had
passed through each machine.

"Is there something wrong, Emmeline?" he asked.

His manner was so kind. She shook her head, but
then burst into tears.

He put down his journal and came over to her.

"Can I help you in some way?" he asked.

His voice was soothing, but she couldn't be soothed because she couldn't tell him what was troubling her.

"Is it possible you need . . . which boardinghouse are you in?"

"Mrs. Bass's." The very question alarmed her, and she would have lied if she'd thought it would serve any purpose.

"Mmmm. And she's not . . . she's not someone you can confide in."

"She doesn't like me."

"I hope that doesn't worry you, Emmeline. You're not the first, you know."

He was smiling at her. She could appreciate that he was trying to make her feel better, but she was beyond the pretense that he was succeeding.

"Is it possible . . . Would you like to speak with Mrs. Whitehead? We have daughters your age, or thereabouts, and perhaps . . . she's a mother. A mother may be the person you need."

What she needed was her *own* mother, to whom she could . . . but as that thought came into her mind, there came the other: *No, you could not even tell her about Mr. Maguire!* And with that thought came the most crushing sense of isolation she had yet experienced. If she could not tell her mother, she was alone in the world in both fact and feeling.

"Thank you," she said. Her lips were very dry. "You're very kind."

"I'll tell you what, Emmeline. I'm going to speak to Mrs. Whitehead. Tomorrow's Sunday. . . ." If he invited her to their home, she would go, anyway. Just being in the midst of a family would be pleasant. "I'll speak to Mrs. Whitehead, and on Monday . . . perhaps you'll have supper with us one evening, instead of at the boardinghouse."

She nodded politely. Her mind, which had once condensed much of March and April into a span of hours, perceived the time between Saturday evening and Monday morning as an infinity. Easter Sunday lay between the two.

Mr. Whitehead picked up his journal and finished his entries. She supposed that she should move to go, but the walk back to Mrs. Bass's loomed as large as the distance to Monday. He made his last entry and looked up at her.

"I think perhaps you'd better come home with me now," he said.

"Oh . . ." It was an acknowledgment. She wondered what Mrs. Bass would say if she didn't come home for supper.

He put away his books, turned out the lights, and picked up his coat.

"But what about Mrs.—"

"She won't mind. One more at the table hardly matters."

He closed the door and they left the mill. It had been Mrs. Bass, not his wife, who was on Emmeline's mind, but she was afraid to make him impatient by requesting that they stop at the boardinghouse. Almost everyone was gone, but here and there a dark figure moved through the night. As they passed Mrs. Bass's, she looked at him to see if it might occur to him that they should stop there. But he said nothing, and she was not certain that she could find his house if he were to go on before her. In her present mood, any new road was one on which she might get lost forever.

Mr. Whitehead's home was small and less majestic than Mr. Maguire's, being on the corner of a street of mill houses and being itself a simple square brick affair. But it was still of a good size and comfortable-looking, with a large plot of its own, surrounded by a neat picket fence. Mr. Whitehead led her around the back and into the kitchen, where a woman almost as tall as he stood at the cookstove, easily stirring in a pot so huge that Emmeline thought her own mother would not have been able to reach over the rim. Unlike Mrs. Bass, Mrs. Whitehead was robust rather than corpulent. She wore a dress which, if it was not homespun, was of some simple cloth.

"This is Emmeline Mosher, Philomena," Mr. Whitehead said. "She's been working in my room for some weeks, and she's feeling very poorly. A mite homesick, perhaps. I've invited her to take supper with us."

Mrs. Whitehead greeted her in a matter-of-fact fashion, which was more reassuring to Emmeline, at that point, than any concern would have been. Mr. Whitehead left them in the kitchen, along with two girls of about her own age who were assisting their mother, Gale and Amy. The girls were lovely and friendly, almost as tall as their mother and quite pretty. They asked her questions about her home, the boarding-house and the mill. Amy, the younger one, was a year older than Emmeline. She had finished school and wanted to work in the mill, but her parents would not let her. When she talked about being able to work, she sounded not entirely unlike Florina. It did not accord with Amy's vision to think of how it really felt to be shut up in a room from before it was light in the morning until after it was dark at night, standing on your feet the entire time, perhaps breathing sweet starchy air that made you ill. She could see only the excitement of activity away from home. Emmeline was fourteen years old; Amy was fifteen. She made Emmeline feel very old, and very tired.

Her mind kept returning to Florina, whom she'd forgotten for some time. What had happened to the other girl? she wondered, as Amy and Gale chattered on, trying to make her feel at home—when it was too late.

It was too late; her thoughts condensed around this idea, though she wasn't sure of its meaning. It was too late for Florina, wherever she was. What would that poor creature do—at her age the mother of three children? And how could Emmeline have forgotten her

until now? That was what was so frightening about
Lowell: Nobody had to take care of you. You were lost
among hundreds of people. The only person you
needed in the world spent his days a flight of stairs away
from you, not knowing—or worse, not caring! But that
thought was so frightening she could not contain it. She
pretended to need to go to the outbuilding, so that she
could conceal her panic, walking around to a side of the
house where she couldn't be seen, then leaning against
the brick wall, looking up at the sky. It was a cold night
for April, but she didn't mind; it was a long time since
any amount of cold had bothered her—before she'd
come to the dressing room. Here and there a patch of
snow still lay on the ground. Had it not been muddy,
she would have taken a handful of snow to press against
her cheeks. If she were in the Fayette woods, she would
have pulled off this dress by which she was so tightly
bound.

Something was nagging at the back of her mind.
Sometimes it took the form of Florina; sometimes it
appeared to be about her fears of Mrs. Bass; at other
moments she felt close to understanding some reason,
beyond his family obligations, that Mr. Maguire was
avoiding her.

For suddenly it was quite clear that this was what he
was doing.

He must be angry with her. If there had been some
change in his family's plans, so that they weren't going
to Boston, or if there were some other reason he could
not see her, then he would only have needed to explain
to her. After all, she'd lived on little more than hope
for many weeks now, and she'd been all right. She'd
been ill because of the dressing room, and she'd been
lonely because of her secret, but somehow she'd been
all right. Without hope . . . that was something else.

Wearily she made her way back to the house. Most of
the family were already seated at the big table in the
kitchen. The boys were there now. Not boys, really—
they were big, handsome young men; one was already

in charge of a machine shop on the Merrimack Corporation. Emmeline sat next to him, and more than once he tried to engage her in conversation, but she was shy of him. Increasingly, she experienced questions about herself as something to be fended off indiscriminately, yet she could not get far enough outside herself to ask about others.

She was barely surprised when, as the women sat before the keeping-room fire after supper—she herself having taken a chair at the back end of the room, as far as possible from the fire—there was a knock at the door. Mrs. Whitehead went to it, and almost immediately Mrs. Bass's shrill voice could be heard.

"I'm terrible sorry to trouble ye, Philomena," the voice shrilled, "but I'm concerned for one of my girls who works for Richard. She wasn't in for supper tonight, and it's not the first time."

A lie! Or was it the truth? She wasn't certain. Her heart fluttered violently. Gale and Amy looked at each other, then at Emmeline, and giggled, prepared to enjoy the joke on someone they didn't like.

Mrs. Whitehead invited Mrs. Bass into the keeping room. Perhaps she too would enjoy surprising the old monster. Mr. Whitehead and his two sons had gone out after supper; the girls were doing needlework. There were no tools for spinning or weaving in this home.

"I've already been to Maguire's, because I think that's who . . ." There was a significant pause; information was being passed by her silence. The two women were approaching the keeping-room entrance. "I spoke with Ivory. Stephen's at a wake over on the Acre. One of his brother's children has died. I didn't know. I don't keep up with any of those . . ."

So that was it! There was some good reason after all that she hadn't heard from him.

"It's Emmeline Mosher, who works for Richard now in the dressing room," Mrs. Bass continued. She and Mrs. Whitehead had come into the keeping room now, but Mrs. Bass's back was to Emmeline. There was a not particularly subtle difference between her boarding-house manner and the one in which she addressed Philomena Whitehead. Her desire to assert herself would always triumph, but here there was also an apology for it in her voice, an eagerness to please.

"Oh, yes," Mrs. Whitehead said. "Emmeline has had supper with us tonight. She should have stopped by to tell you."

There was a moment of silence. Then Mrs. Bass whipped around as though she had known all along that the enemy was present, but hadn't quite known where. Her face was red and contorted by pure hatred. Emmeline wanted to utter a polite apology, but she couldn't; the expression on the woman's face was too frightening. She was paralyzed.

"And what about the other times, then?"

It wasn't spoken so much as it was hissed. For a fleeting moment Mrs. Bass didn't look like a woman at all, but like a great black snake, darting its tongue at her in the vegetable garden in Fayette.

Mrs. Whitehead said something and her daughters left the room; she closed the doors behind them. Emmeline stood up. There was a fence around this garden and she was being locked in with the snake. Her eyes darted to the windows; they were too small, and the snake could coil around her before she reached them.

"And what about that?"

She was pointing at Emmeline, her arm outstretched, her finger aimed not at Emmeline's face, but at something lower down. Something that revealed guilt. Dress? Shoes? Emmeline looked down. She saw noth-ing unusual, except that her dress was tighter than it had ever been. Her bosom, instead of being held lightly by the bodice, was flattened severely by it, and beneath the waistline, her stomach swelled gently against the fabric. That was unusual too. Until recently her stom-ach had always been . . . Into her mind came another picture, also of the garden in Fayette. This time her mother was in it, looking tired but very beautiful. Her hair was braided to keep it off her neck, for it was summer. Her face was damp with perspiration, and her dress clung to her body, particularly around the large mound of her belly that would be Josiah, whom she was carrying. The picture disappeared. Emmeline stared at the mound of her own belly. It was small but growing larger, a truth she had not allowed to enter her mind until now. She couldn't pull her eyes away from it; she was transfixed. When she finally looked up, it was at the two faces at the other end of the room—Mrs. Bass's, raging and triumphant at the same time, and Mrs. Whitehead's, a mixture of astonishment, disapproval, and pain.

She lost consciousness and fell to the floor.

SHE awakened in a dark room that felt like the attic room in Fayette, but was larger. She guessed it to be the attic of the Whitehead home. She remembered everything that had happened as well as if it had been a moment before, and in fact she had not been unconscious very long. She had the sense that she must not get out of bed, or move around, until someone told her she could. Her whole body was alive with pain. She was on the verge of tears but could not cry—nor would she be able to cry for five months longer, until after her baby was born.

The baby had no reality to her yet, except as an intruder. The baby was proof that she had sinned; until there was proof, it had been possible to pretend that there had been no actual sin. After all, she had not hurt anyone, nor had she ever wished to.

A sudden image of Mrs. Bass made her sit up on the bed and think of where she could run, but she forced herself to lie down again. It was just as likely, more so, that she would see Mrs. Bass if she went downstairs. That she could not bear. She would die on the spot if she ever had to face Mrs. Bass again. Nor could she see—or be seen by—the others, with the possible exception of Mrs. Whitehead. That was why she was hidden away in the attic; she understood that without being told. The Whitehead daughters would have been told that she was ill and under some sort of quarantine. There had been a girl under such a quarantine in Fayette; Emmeline had heard whispers but had never understood them until now. The whole family had gone to live in Lewiston, and when they returned a year later, the girl's mother had a baby in addition to her brood of seven, most of whom had already come of age and left home.

Emmeline had no doubt that her life was over; only her body remained to be disposed of. She remembered her grandfather's body, laid out in the Moose Hill church before it was buried, and briefly— longingly—pictured her own in its place. But then she remembered that there was a body within her body, so that it could not be buried.

Someone was climbing the stairs. The door opened and Mrs. Whitehead came in, holding a lamp.

"Are you awake?" It was the same cool voice that it had been before everything else changed.

"Yes."

Mrs. Whitehead advanced into the room, stopping at the foot of the bed.

"Mrs. Bass tells me that you have an aunt in Lynn."

"Oh, no! Please! No!" But she knew even as she pleaded that it would happen.

"There isn't a choice. Unless . . . Is the man who did this to you someone who might marry you?"

"No." Mrs. Bass had as much as said it was Mr. Maguire. Was it possible Mrs. Whitehead had failed to understand?

"I think it is possible . . . I must tell you, it might be a little easier for you if that person is told. You will need money, unless your family can provide for you."

But I am providing for them!

It struck her for the first time that she would not be able to send money home anymore; her head spun with panic! She had just had another letter from home, written by Luke this time, saying that things were getting better because of the money she was sending! Not only would they lose the money now, but they would know! She sat up.

"Will I not be able to work at the mill awhile longer? No one need know."

"I'm sorry, Emmeline. If you think, you will see that . . . it's already known."

Of course. She was silent. She couldn't have faced them all anyway, for *she* knew.

"Your possessions will be brought here, until we can make arrangements for you to go to Lynn, or to your home."

Lynn or home. Lynn. She sank back on the bed. How could she face Hannah?

"Please ask my aunt not to write to my parents."

"I will tell her you have requested it." Mrs. Whitehead turned to leave.

"Please . . ." Mrs. Whitehead had said it would be easier if Emmeline told the responsible man, but did not seem concerned that she hadn't done so. Emmeline needed things to be easier. As they were, it seemed virtually impossible to go on. If a reason were required, she would die soon, for without even being able to send money to her family, she had not one. *She needed Mr. Maguire to know!* She did not want him to share her disgrace, but she needed him to know that she was doing this for him! If her own life was over, let him at least mourn her as he mourned his brother's child. It wasn't fair that he should be spared even that, when he must have known all along what could happen to her!

"Do you think I should tell him, then?"

There was a long silence. Then Mrs. Whitehead said, in a somewhat more strained voice, "I think . . . I think you have ruined your life, Emmeline. And you may have it in your power to ruin others'."

"I don't want to do that!" she protested.

"No."

"But you said it would be easier for me."

"If you were able to obtain some money."

Silence. She must listen carefully, try to understand exactly what Mrs. Whitehead was telling her.

"You know who it is?" Emmeline asked after a while.

"I know what Mrs. Bass thinks."

She nodded.

"I see."

Emmeline felt like one of the animals for whom her father set traps in the woods; what she wanted now was quite simple, but she did not know the hazards—or the possibilities—of obtaining it. She had best tell Mrs. Whitehead directly. Someone with a burden of shame was not allowed to lie in the small ways that other people did. If she said the wrong thing, the trap might close on her even more tightly. But what could happen that had not happened already?

"Will you tell him for me?"

"I will ask Mr. Whitehead to."

She felt her cheeks flush. She hadn't thought of Mr. Whitehead. If there was one man in Lowell she could have chosen not to know, it would have been Mr. Whitehead, who reminded her of Pastor Evans, in whom there seemed to reside those qualities she had not found in the pastor of the Baptist church in Lowell. It occurred to her now that if Pastor Evans had been in Lowell, all of this would not have happened to her.

She asked if she could have her Bible. There was no lamp here, and she wouldn't be able to read, but she could hold it during the night.

"Your belongings are to be brought over," Mrs. Whitehead said.

Of course. She had been told that already. She must not think of Mrs. Bass's touching her belongings, or she wouldn't be able to remain still. The thread on which hung Mrs. Whitehead's patience with her was both taut and flimsy. She mustn't make a single mistake now, or she would be thrown out into a world where there was no one. Nothing. She did not have a penny to her name.

"I hope your aunt will have you," Mrs. Whitehead told her. "You will have to remain in the attic until we hear from her. The girls have been told that you're quite ill. Do you understand me, Emmeline?"

"Yes, Ma'am."

Mrs. Whitehead turned away once again. What Emmeline wanted more than anything in the world at that moment was that Mrs. Whitehead leave the lamp, so she would not be alone in the darkness. The time that had to pass before the sun would come up was unthinkably long.

"Good night, Emmeline," Mrs. Whitehead said, opening the door.

"Good night, Ma'am."

The door closed on the light.

But she slept a great deal that night, as well as in the days and nights that followed. Often she had to be awakened when her meals were brought in. After Sunday she had her Bible. She kept it under the pillow, and often found her hand on it as she awakened, but if she tried to read in it her eyes would grow heavy and she would fall asleep, even if she'd only been awake a short while.

One day Mrs. Whitehead informed her that Mr. Maguire was so concerned for her plight that he was going to give her the money she would have earned had she worked in Lowell another full year. She asked if he had sent any other message for her. Mrs. Whitehead, her lips pursed in disapproval, said that he had not. The money would be ready by the time Emmeline's arrangements for leaving Lowell were made. At first, Emmeline didn't understand what this meant, beyond that she would not see him again, which she had begun to assume. After some days had passed, days in which this brief conversation worked at her mind like a grindstone sharpening the knife that was turning all the time in her brain, she came to understand that she would not get the money until it was guaranteed that they would be rid of her. As though she wanted to stay! There was nothing for her here but the streets!

After a considerable number of days had passed, Mr. Whitehead said that Emmeline's aunt had been heard from and that Emmeline was to take the coach to Lynn in two days. Other than an immediate sinking sensation at the thought of facing Hannah Watkins, she had little reaction to this news, and slept as much as ever until the morning Mrs. Whitehead awakened her and told her that she must prepare herself to travel. For the first time since Emmeline had been in the attic, Mrs. Whitehead had put warm wash water in her basin.

She avoided Mr. Whitehead's eyes until the coach had arrived and she was waiting to mount the steps. Then he pressed an envelope into her hand and told her that it contained a hundred and fifty dollars—even more than Mr. Maguire had promised.

"Did he say anything to me?" she asked.

"He cannot, Emmeline," Mr. Whitehead said gravely. Then, when he saw her expression, he explained. "He could not obtain this large amount of money without its being known to Mrs. Maguire. And then he could do nothing further."

That was painful, that Mrs. Maguire knew and would be angry with her. At that moment, she would gladly have exchanged the extra money for Mrs. Maguire not to know, and for herself to have a few words with him. A few words during which he looked at her face in the way he once had, and told her that if he had ruined her life, it was not without reason. That he loved her so much that were they thrown together once more, the very same thing might happen again.

IT was a moment before she recognized the stranger who was Hannah, and longer before Hannah recognized her. Then the woman burst into tears. Emmeline's own face was twisted with pain, but she didn't know that. She was full of wonder that someone she remembered with so little affection should be crying over her, when she couldn't cry for herself.

Hannah would not let her carry her own box, but walked with it in one hand, her free arm around Emmeline's shoulders. It was not a very long walk to her home. The streets looked not unlike those in Lowell as you got farther from the mills, except that sprinkled among the homes were smaller, narrow buildings which were the shops where most of the shoemaking work was done. Abner was nowhere to be seen. When she saw him later, he would be shy and uneasy, not able to meet her eyes.

If she was going to be confined here too, the confinement would be of a pleasanter nature. There was an extra room, which would be hers. Like the rest of the house, it was pretty and quite cozy, which made Emmeline feel different about Hannah. In general, Hannah seemed like a much nicer person than the one Emmeline remembered from Fayette and her journey. Emmeline drew close to her during

213

this time, and felt that if she could not be with her mother, she had the next-best person in the world. Together they made the plans by which money would be posted regularly to her home; her parents would never need to know that the coach had not brought it from Lowell. Mrs. Whitehead had promised to forward any mail that came to Emmeline at Mrs. Bass's.

Spring was really here now. The baby moved inside her. At first she refused to recognize the movements, believing they were a new kind of indigestion. After she understood, she made it a point to be busy when they began. For a long time, the baby meant nothing but pain to her.

Then in June, just as she was becoming used to it in spite of herself, just as she was beginning to look for signs from it to her, Hannah was able to arrange, as they had agreed earlier, for a couple to take the baby immediately after its birth, and then the pain turned into the pain of having a part of herself taken away.

She didn't think about this any more than she could help it, though. She kept very busy. She was such a help to Hannah that Hannah said, as her mother once had, that she didn't know how she had managed before she had Emmeline. She also worked on shoe uppers for Abner, who brought them into the house and left them in a basket near the front door, conveying the message, but only through Hannah, that Emmeline was doing excellent work. Hannah assured Emmeline that she was more than earning her keep by the shoes alone, and Emmeline was glad to hear this. She was extremely grateful to Hannah, and did not want to be a burden beyond what she already had been. They never quarreled, Emmeline doing whatever Hannah asked without question and without resentment. Hannah talked endlessly as they worked together, and Emmeline

valued every observation, scrap of gossip, and com-
plaint, for they took her mind from those events in
Lowell which otherwise repeated themselves endlessly
in her mind.

Spring turned into summer. She had never asked
Hannah to be let out of the house, but when it became
hot, Hannah said she might go out to the shade of the
yard if the house became too much for her. Once they
were out there, Hannah said it was foolish for her not
to go farther—to walk around the yard, and even work
in the small garden while she could. There was a high
picket fence around the yard, after all, and there were
no back windows in the shoemaking shop, so that the
men who worked for Abner would not be able to see
her.

In the privacy of her room, she lay down and cradled
the mass of her belly. She tried not to do this in
Hannah's presence, for then Hannah might guess that
most of her waking moments were devoted to schemes,
most wildly improbable, by which she might hold on to
her daughter, as she had come to think of the child. In
her dreams, she had lost the baby already and was
searching.

She and Hannah never talked about her situation,
though the midwife came in August to examine her and
make certain that things were proceeding as they
should. Mrs. Wedders was quite old, with thick gray
hair, lively eyes, and a caul on her lip. She was quite
obviously someone who could be trusted with one's life
and one's baby, nor did the circumstances of the baby's
existence seem to be of any concern to her. When
Hannah said, later on, that a man doctor had come to
Lynn whom it might be preferable to employ in the
event that the birth should be difficult, for the doctors
had instruments not known to the midwives, the terror
in Emmeline's face was so great that Hannah had

the good sense to drop the subject and not raise it again.

"Are they good people, who are taking my baby?" she asked Hannah in September, as she entered her ninth month. She hated them, but understood that this was unfair, since she knew nothing about them except that they wanted her child.

"Well, 'course they are," Hannah said. "I know them from church."

"Who are they?"

"We'll have none of that, Emmeline. You'll make yourself morbid if you think about that."

But she could think of nothing else.

"Have you never wanted a child, Aunt Hannah?" she asked, as the time drew near. Her strongest fantasy now was that she would persuade Hannah to raise the child as her own, except that Emmeline would stay there and work and see it every day.

"You are going to make me angry, Emmeline," Hannah said.

So that it was weeks—the end of September (Mrs. Wedders had guessed at the first week of October)— before she dared to refer to the baby again.

"Aunt Hannah," she said, her voice trembling, "will you only tell me the name of these people?"

"'Course not, child," Hannah said. She was not without pity, but she knew what had to be done and that sympathy would make it even harder.

"But it will be known anyway by many people," Emmeline argued, "when this lady appears suddenly with a baby."

"It won't be known where they're going," Hannah said.

Emmeline stared at her uncomprehendingly. "Where they're going?"

"They're leaving Lynn, once the baby's born. Starting a new life, where no one'll know."

"Where?" She was wild, now. *"Why won't you even tell me their name?"* Not to know their name, or where they lived! All hope was draining away! "I won't trouble them. I promise you!" She meant every word as she said it. She would make any promise she had to to keep her child from disappearing into total darkness! "Please!" Once she'd been frightened of the birth itself, of getting sick, of the pain, of dying. Now those fears were nothing, compared with the fear evoked by the image of a baby coming out of her only to disappear forever. She would prefer dying with the baby, if only the baby did not have to endure pain in the process!

Hannah stood up and said that she was going to bed.

Emmeline watched her, without moving. Hannah folded her work, took one of the two lighted lamps, and proceeded up the stairs. Abner was out somewhere, as he often was in the evening, a fact to which Hannah never alluded, except by referring, with apparent pride, to his importance in the community. The second lamp stood on the table near Emmeline's chair. The fire in it burned steadily. For one brief moment, she came very close to picking up the lamp and smashing it against a wall, not knowing which would be more satisfying—to see the glass shatter into countless bits, or to watch the fire catch onto something else, then slowly grow to devour the house and everyone in it.

E<small>MMELINE</small> stirred. Her hand reached out and found the pillow; she pulled it to herself. Her eyes opened and then immediately closed. When they opened again, the pillow was wet. Someone was trying to take it away, but she clutched it as firmly as she had . . .

"Emmeline?"

"She's awake."

"Emmeline? Can you hear me, child? You must try to take some water."

As she slept the sleep of childbed fever, which had lasted for three days, wet rags had been put in her mouth, so she would suck on them and not be consumed by the fever. She had not been conscious since shortly after the birth of her baby. She had watched, helpless, as the baby was severed from the cord, wrapped in a sheet, and taken from the room. Only when it was gone had she become aware again of physical pain. Then she had gone to sleep. The fever had built up during the night and was subsiding now.

Hannah held her up so she could sip at some water, but she didn't want it.

"You must, Emmeline," Hannah said.

She tried, but she gagged. Hannah gave her another wet rag to chew. With some effort she lifted her hand to her mouth and took out the rag.

"It's a girl, isn't it? Isn't she a girl?"

Hannah didn't reply, but Emmeline knew. She put the rag back in her mouth and lay back on the mattress. Her other hand had never let go of the pillow, nor would she let it be taken from her during her remaining months in Lynn.

It was her missing daughter.

For the first few days, whenever she was awake, she asked Hannah questions which were not answered.

Then one day Hannah said, "They've gone, Emmeline. They've left Lynn."

"No!" she cried out. "No! I don't believe it! You know where they are!"

"No," Hannah said. "I don't know. I told them not to tell me."

After that, for many weeks, Emmeline cried all the time—not bitterly, or passionately, but slowly and steadily. It seemed to have become part of her natural condition. The rest of her body healed, but her eyes did not.

Gradually she resumed helping Hannah in the household, although the easy feeling between them was gone; her daughter was always between them. At first she tried bringing her pillow when she came downstairs, but Hannah would not have it, so she took to interrupting her chores to go upstairs several times in the course of the day to sit on her bed, holding the pillow for a while.

She had given her daughter the name Maryanne, because she loved its sound. Maryanne never cried, although sometimes, when Emmeline was downstairs, she imagined that she heard her.

They increased the amount of money she was sending home each month to sixteen and later to twenty dollars. She wrote to her mother explaining that she was working in the cloth room now, and receiving higher wages than she'd expected. The reason for sending more money was to enable her to go home sooner than she'd once planned. Once she had dreaded seeing her family, but now that she and Hannah were less close than they had been, she was grow growing restive in Lynn. In the spring, when the money was almost gone, she would say that she had been ill and was recovered enough to come home, but could not work any longer.

At the end of February she wrote such a note. Her fifteenth birthday passed by without notice in March; Hannah had no reason to know it, and she herself had no reason to care. At the beginning of April, she made the journey home. Hannah gave her the pillow to take with her. She still had Ivory Maguire's thick black shawl in her box. She would never wear it again, but she would give it to her mother.

It was so quiet here. The noise in Lynn had been as nothing compared with that of Lowell, but she hadn't thought about noise when she was in Lynn, and now Lynn was absent from her mind. As the carriage moved down the Hallowell Road toward Fayette, the horses' hooves clamorous against the still countryside, it was almost as though she had never been at Hannah's house, but were coming directly from Lowell. It would not be difficult to avoid any reference to Lynn when she spoke to her mother.

The carriage stopped briefly to let out the last of the other passengers. In the moment of silence when the door had been closed and the driver had mounted to his seat, but not yet signaled the horses to move, the desire to see her mother welled up from wherever it had been sleeping and nearly overwhelmed her. The last hour of her journey passed more slowly than any of the others.

There was a picture in her mind—perhaps it had stemmed from Hannah's reaction upon seeing her when she arrived in Lynn—of herself walking into the house in Fayette. The house was empty, except for her mother, who stood at the table facing the door. Their eyes met; her mother, holding out her arms to Emmeline, began to cry. Emmeline entered her embrace and they cried together.

She did expect that if her mother did not sense the truth, Sarah would at least know that something terrible had befallen her. She knew that if her mother asked, she would tell the truth, and that she would be relieved. If she could share her secret with her mother, then she might feel like the Emmeline Mosher who had left Fayette only sixteen months earlier, and lose that sense she lived with all the time—that in Massachusetts she had lost not only her child, but the very core of her self.

Mrs. Bradley was sweeping the store porch. She looked up as the coachman helped Emmeline down, stared briefly as though trying to decide if the face looked familiar, and then went back to her sweeping. Emmeline's hand went to her head. The previous summer she had cut off most of her hair, and it had grown in now just enough to make a sparse coil at the nape of her neck. She was wearing the dress she and her mother had made just before she left Lowell. But there had not been a flicker of recognition in Mrs. Bradley's eyes.

Emmeline took her box from the coachman and walked to the other side of the road. Three horses were tethered in front of Judkins' Tavern, the only other building at the Corners. The sun was directly overhead; without it, she could not have sensed the time of day. The feeling of time, divided into minutes and hours, which she had acquired in Lowell, had disappeared after the birth of her baby. She began walking toward home. She had written them that she was coming soon, but had deliberately failed to tell them the day. She needed to get her bearings before anyone knew that she was there.

It was a beautiful day, the kind of day you could never have fully appreciated in Lowell without walking to the Falls. The ground was softening, and soon everything beneath their feet would be mud. But the sky was clear, the clouds white and fluffy, and the trees were taking on the green aura they had just before the leaves actually came in. She wedged her box against her

hip and walked slowly down the road. Nothing had
changed except the season. Why did she feel that it had
changed a great deal? The two other houses along the
road, the geese, the pond were like imitations of what
she had left behind. Around the last curve.

There was the house. If times had really improved,
an impression she had gotten from the last letter
forwarded to her, written by Luke, the house did not
yet reflect that improvement. It looked even shabbier
and less protected than it had before. Her body moved
toward it, but her mind kept its distance.

There were children playing outside. Someone was
swinging from the rope, and someone else was laughing
excitedly. All motion ceased when they saw that a
stranger was approaching. She smiled. It was Abraham and Josiah. . . . No, wait a minute, it couldn't
be . . . that was William she'd mistaken for Josiah,
and Josiah must be that sturdy-looking boy of . . .
he would be five before long! Time had passed in
Fayette as well. William was now two and a half.
His hair had been blond fuzz when she left; now it
was brown.

She walked up the slope toward them; they watched
her.

"Hello, Josiah," she said. "I'm your sister Emmeline."

His finger went to his mouth. William began to cry.

Luke appeared from around the back of the house.
He stopped short when he saw her.

"Em?" he said cautiously. "That you?"

She smiled, but his uncertainty was painful. He had
changed too; from being a little shorter than she, he
had grown to being considerably taller. His face had
lost some of its youthful softness, and his voice had
grown deep. But there was no question that she would
have known him no matter where they were.

"Yes," she said. "It's me."

"You all right?" he asked.

"Yes." She was about to move toward him and hug

him, but something stopped her as sharply as though a command had been uttered. She remembered that she was supposed to have been ill. "I'm all right now. I'm just tired."

He nodded. He too was at a loss to know what to do with himself—with his eyes, with his arms.

"Is Mama inside?" she asked.

He nodded. "Papa's got work at Fenton's sawmill."

"That's good," she said. "When?"

" 'Bout a month ago," he replied.

Their eyes met and then each looked away. Josiah whimpered softly. William had stopped crying. Emmeline opened the door to the house.

Her mother stood at the table, her back to the door, stirring batter in the biggest crockery bowl. At the far window, Harriet and Rosanna were spinning and carding; how strange it was to see someone doing the laborious task of carding by hand! Emmeline pushed aside a momentary disappointment that she could not immediately be alone with her mother.

The two girls looked up at the same moment. Rosanna, with a great smile, set down the cards and came running to hug Emmeline; Rosanna was nine years old and looked more like Emmeline than did any of the other girls. Now she looked more like the Emmeline of two years ago than Emmeline herself did. Harriet remained seated.

"She's here, Mama," Harriet announced flatly. Harriet was almost twelve. During Emmeline's absence she had been the oldest girl, and she was steeling herself against the prospect of having to relinquish any privileges that had accrued to her in that position.

Her mother turned. Emmeline released Rosanna and went eagerly to her mother. They embraced. Emmeline felt the soft skin of her mother's cheek against hers, felt her mother's bosom pressed against her own, which had been the flat chest of a girl when she left home. All the anguish of the past year welled up in her, threatening to break the dam she had erected to contain it. With a sense of impending relief, she waited to cry in her mother's arms. But the dam held.

Her mother held her at arm's length to look at her.

"Are you well now, Emmy?" she asked, searching Emmeline's face.

"Yes," Emmeline said. "Are you?"

Her mother nodded. There was a little more gray in her hair, but other than that, she seemed the same.

"You saved us, you know," her mother said.

Emmeline smiled; the tears that hadn't broken through the dam were there in her smile, but she didn't know that.

Her mother waved to the two other girls to leave them alone for a while, and the girls went out of the house.

"You're all growed up," her mother said after a while.

"A lot has happened to me," Emmeline said. She waited.

Her mother was waiting too.

"Come and set with me here and tell me," her mother finally said.

They went to the rocking chair, where Emmeline sat at her mother's feet as she had on that morning when she left for Lowell. Her mother stroked her head. She looked up at the loved face. If only her mother could guess just a piece of it! If only her mother would ask some question that would allow Emmeline to feel that she would not be astounded—revolted—*grief-stricken beyond the possibility of recovery*—were she to hear the truth. At this moment she felt that the greatest sin she had committed had been against her mother; she had done something the knowledge of which might be more than her mother could bear!

"Tell me," her mother said.

"I don't know where to begin," Emmeline said. "Ask me questions."

Her mother smiled. "I don't know what to ask."

She didn't know what to ask because the truth was unimaginable to her.

"It was very difficult at first," Emmeline said. "The work was hard. I was very lonely."

Her mother nodded. "I thought of you all the time, Emmy. All the time."

Emmeline laid her head down in her mother's lap and closed her eyes.

"The girls aren't friendly at first to a new girl."

"Mmmm," her mother said. "It takes time. Just like in Fayette, when new folks come."

But I was alone and I couldn't wait!

"More than that. They make fun of you. They call you 'country.' You look different and you sound different."

"Mmmm," her mother said. "You sound different now, Emmy."

"I do?" She was disconcerted.

"Yuh," her mother said.

"Well, I'm not," she said. "That is . . . I am, but . . ." She trailed off lamely.

They were silent for a while.

"You must've done good work," her mother finally said, "to earn such wages."

"Yes," Emmeline said after even longer. "I did well. It just took some time."

"'Course it did," her mother said.

Emmeline looked up at her with a sense of despair. *Please ask me. Please find some way to tell me that you would forgive me if I told you.* But after a moment, when her mother stroked her head, remaining silent, the despair eased. After all, she reminded herself, she had only just come home. There was no reason that her mother had to know immediately. They couldn't really expect to be so close—all at once—as they had been when every day of their lives had been spent together. She must be patient. She must settle in. She looked around her; every line of the room, every piece of furniture, each piece of crockery on the table was familiar to her. With her eyes closed, she could have put every object in the house where it belonged. *She* was back in her proper place.

"It's good to be home," Emmeline said.

And it *was* good, although other things had also changed.

While her father had always talked more to his sons than to his daughters, Emmeline had always felt that her presence was a pleasure to him, and he had clearly favored her over Harriet. Now, in her first months at home, he seemed to shy from her—as though he were ashamed that he had allowed her to go to Lowell. He never mentioned the money she had sent from Lowell or asked about her experiences there. In fact, for a long time the only matters he discussed in her presence were those connected with his work for old Levon Fenton at the mill.

Only Harriet and the two younger girls ever questioned her, the little ones with genuine curiosity, Harriet always with the intention of extracting from Emmeline some admission of the amount of money she had spent on herself, and the brilliant social events she had attended.

Luke was hurt by Emmeline's reserve with him, but she couldn't help herself. She loved him as much as ever, but she couldn't be free with him as she'd once been. Indeed, the reserve she felt with him she felt, to a lesser extent, with all of them except Rebekah, who was now seven, and the three youngest boys, none of whom remembered her from the time before she was sent to Lowell.

She could not fall asleep in the attic with the others. The first night she thought it was just the excitement of being home, but a second and third passed during which she was awake until dawn, her head on the pillow she had brought from Lynn, her mind uneasy with the thought that one of the others might awaken and see her cradling it, or even hear her murmuring in the darkness, as though to a child.

She asked her parents if she could sleep in the barn while the weather allowed. Her parents consented, but Harriet seemed to take her withdrawal as a personal affront.

"What will she do when the weather turns?" Emmeline heard Harriet demand of her mother.

"We'll think on that when it turns," her mother said calmly.

Emmeline brought out to the barn her pillow and her box, half of which was still taken up by Ivory Maguire's shawl. She was waiting for the right time to give it to her mother. Since she had no gifts for the others, it seemed better to wait until the following winter, when her mother, who was always cold, would really need it. They had been able to spare only one quilt from the house, and there were nights right through June when she could have used the warm weight of the shawl on top of the quilt, but she never took it out of the box.

(When winter approached, Luke built a wall across one end of the attic to make a tiny room for Emmeline. Harriet was enraged, although he promised he would do the same for her when the time came.)

By the time she went back to church, a week after her homecoming, she had abandoned the illusion that she would be able to confide in Pastor Evans, if not in her mother. Perhaps it was just as well, for he had been an old man when she left, and he seemed much much older now. Those members of the congregation who recognized her greeted her warmly, as did the others—once they found out who she was . . . the sad-eyed, slender young woman with her hair coiled in a tight bun at the nape of her neck who had come to services with the Mosher family.

Part Two

Time passed. The town began to prosper, as there had been signs, before those few bad years, that it would. The foundation for a new commercial building had been laid at the Corners in the early thirties, but a building had never been erected. Now another tavern went up on that spot to serve the increasingly large number of travelers passing through the Corners, which was on the mail route between the Kennebec and the Androscoggin, in addition to being a convenient stopping place on the route from Hallowell to the Coos Road into New Hampshire. The post office was in the store at the Corners too. In the ensuing years, more stores opened, and numerous craftsmen— a carriage maker, a shoemaker and a cabinetmaker among them—made their headquarters there.

Several times each year Emmeline wrote to Hannah, begging to know if her child was well. Hannah wrote back kindly but always told the truth: that she didn't know. Eventually Emmeline ceased to write. The Watkinses did not detour to Fayette during their rare journeys to Livermore Falls. For all she might argue with herself on this score, Hannah felt responsible for what had befallen Emmeline, and even as time went on it was difficult for her to think of facing Sarah and Henry Mosher.

Emmeline had two daydreams in which Mr. Maguire appeared at the door, magically unemcumbered by family. In the first, he saw Emmeline and then his eyes fell on Maryanne, his beautiful little girl. He wept for what he had done and vowed to spend the rest of his life making it up to them. In the second, he found Emmeline alone and wanted to make a new life in the West. She told him that there could be no new life until they found their child, and he gravely agreed. There was not a hint of romance in these daydreams; she didn't think of Mr. Maguire as a lover, only as the father of her child.

At seventeen Luke married a lively nineteen-year-old Fayette girl named Martha Green. They built a small house on Martha's father's land, just the other side of Fayette Corners, and within three years of their marriage they had their first two children.

Harriet married at the age of sixteen, only a year after Luke, without ever having reconciled herself to Emmeline's return. She had not actually become her mother's confidante in Emmeline's absence, but she felt that she had; she'd been eleven and twelve years old and had no sense of what was withheld. Now, though, she would come upon the two women talking and feel that Emmeline had again pushed her out into the cold. She married Winthrop Bradley, whose parents owned the store and who was precisely Emmeline's age, nineteen. Her mother feared that Bradley wasn't a man yet, and couldn't be relied upon, but she said this only to Emmeline, never to Harriet, and Harriet, on the day of her wedding, looked happier than Emmeline had ever seen her. This was more than tolerable to Emmeline, as it was more than tolerable to have the bleak cloud of Harriet's daily presence removed from the house. But it was almost unbearable to her when Harriet, who had visited infrequently since her marriage, became pregnant and started to come by the house nearly every day.

At such times, however Emmeline tried to gird herself to bear them, she would often have to leave the house, walking around the pond or in the woods. In poor weather, she sometimes went to visit with her friend Rachel Poole. Rachel was the only other girl of her own age in Fayette. They'd had no interest in each other when they were younger, but had become friendly at church after Emmeline's return. One of the reasons that it was pleasant to go to the Pooles' was that Rachel had her own room in the big house, as did her younger sister, Persis. A better reason for their friendship, though, was that none of the three intended to marry. Rachel's mother had died giving birth to Persis, and both girls had taken a vow, which they never told to anyone but Emmeline, that they would not marry and risk the same fate.

Rachel made fun of the boys who attempted to court them. She criticized the way they looked, their manners in church, and anything else she could think of. Persis and Emmeline would laugh obligingly at her jokes, but Persis was younger and softer and didn't yet need to push off the boys in this way, while for Emmeline they were of so little interest that she never thought about them if they weren't right there—and barely then. If they asked to walk home with her from church, she replied that she had her sisters and brothers to walk with—as though that were an answer. Harriet told her that she was getting the reputation of being more high-and-mighty than ever, and even Rachel occasionally became annoyed when Emmeline wouldn't go with her as far as a social in Livermore Falls. But Emmeline would not leave Fayette. She had the vague sense that she must be there in the event that someone came looking for her. After Rachel and Persis went to socials, they would compare the Livermore boys with those in Fayette—to the detriment, astonishingly, of both. But Emmeline never attended socials and never criticized.

She did attend church, though in a somewhat different spirit than she once had. Pastor Evans had died the year after her return. The new pastor was a nice enough man, though not someone in whom she would ever have confided, even when she was young. She also read the Bible a great deal, finding pleasure rather than comfort in it. It was seldom that she could obtain a novel in Fayette, and during this time she did not really care to read novels anyway. Their souls always lay in romance, and she had no interest in romance. She knew beyond a shadow of a doubt that she would never fall in love again.

As the others left home, there seemed to be a tacit understanding between Emmeline and her parents that she would stay with them.

Andrew married at twenty, in 1848; Rosanna at eighteen, in 1850; Rebekah at seventeen, in 1851. In that year, Emmeline was twenty-five years old. At home with her and her parents now there were only the three youngest boys.

Andrew built a house on the far side of the Mosher land, in a clearing at the top of the hill, and with his father's help was able to buy an additional two acres adjoining the farm. This gave them enough foraging land for several head of cattle, and her father talked with pleasure of the day when they might have still more land and more cattle. Her father was fifty-eight years old now, but had the vigor of a man twenty years younger. In addition to running the farm with Andrew, he was still working at the sawmill, where Simon Fenton, Levon's only son, had taken over upon the death of his father. Simon was a good fifteen or twenty years younger than Emmeline's father, but he was well liked by all the men. When Simon's wife died suddenly in 1852, and Simon, grief-stricken, stayed home with his children for an unusually long time, Henry Mosher took charge of the mill for him, and the two men became good friends in spite of the difference in their ages.

In that year, Abraham was sixteen; Josiah, Jr., was fourteen; and William, the baby, was thirteen years old. Sometimes the three youngest boys seemed almost like a separate family. They had always been closer to one another than to the two girls, Rosanna and Rebekah, who preceded them and who were close to each other. Aside from Harriet, whom they'd fled as she tried to establish hegemony over this second, younger family, the older children had seemed almost like adults to them.

They had no memory of the time when they had been close to starvation. They had grown up in relative comfort in a town that appeared to be expanding and flourishing without ever losing its rural character and scenic beauty. They had a sense of the world beyond Fayette that the others had gained later or not at all. They were obedient at home, and worked on the farm, but each one, as soon as he could, also found work away from home—Abraham at the gristmill, Josiah and, later, William assisting craftsmen with shops at the Corners. Each took any chance he was offered to go to another town, and Josiah, the most adventurous of the three, once went as far as Concord, New Hampshire, upon being offered the chance by the coachman who drove the Coos Road route.

In the years between 1849 and 1859, Andrew's wife, Jane Mosher, bore four children—a girl, then a boy, then another girl and another boy. Emmeline felt closer to Jane than to any of the other husbands and wives of her brothers and sisters, and in her loving care of Jane's children she came closer than she ever had to finding tolerable the loss of her own child. They spent almost as much time at Emmeline's home as in their own. Emmeline took great pleasure in teaching the children, as they grew old enough, not to simply listen to her stories, but to learn letters and numbers as well. In effect, she was their only teacher. Why would anyone bother about the clothing and notebooks required for school when the children could learn just as well by simply walking down the hill to Emmeline's?

Their grandmother, of course, was also in the house every day, but something was happening to Sarah Mosher over the years that made the children look elsewhere for attention.

In 1859, when Emmeline was thirty-three years old, her mother was only fifty years of age and her father was sixty-six. Yet seeing them together you might have thought that Sarah was the one who had reached that advanced age. It wasn't simply that her hair was white or her face deeply lined, for these things were true of her husband as well. It was more that something inside of her was gone. Not suddenly, but slowly, over the years, she'd lost that strong spirit which had once sustained them all. She had never been a great talker, but once you had felt that she was thinking about you and had strong ideas about what you should be doing. Now her thoughts—her very substance—were shadowy. Her only apparent pleasure in life lay in going to church—no matter who the minister, no matter how little he had to say. She came home from church suffused with a quiet radiance which each week seemed to last only until the sun went down on the Sabbath.

Henry Mosher, on the other hand, was more animated than he had ever been. As his three youngest boys reached manhood, he seemed to acquire a renewed vigor from them, and increasingly he talked about starting a family business for his sons—perhaps a cabinetmaking shop, in which they would utilize the lumber from Simon Fenton's sawmill. Or when a piece of land abutting Andrew's came up, he thought about buying it and growing a substantial herd of dairy cattle, instead of just keeping a few milk cows.

It was one of the great disappointments of his life, then, when in 1856, as they reached twenty-one, twenty, and eighteen, respectively, the boys announced to him that they planned to leave Fayette and strike out for the West.

The first Emmeline knew of their plans was when she heard a great shout from the barn and ran out, thinking her father was alone and in trouble.

The three boys stood facing their father, whose back was to her; their expressions made it clear that they were upset, or angry, or perhaps both. Chickens clucked at their feet. In the stalls were the two workhorses and the beautiful brown mare her father had bought for Emmeline two years earlier, when he saw that she had taken to riding for pleasure. Farther back were the cows; soon they would be going outdoors to graze.

"Who's to help me take care of them?" her father was shouting. "I'm getting on, you know!" Yet his voice had the power of a young man's.

"Well," said Abraham, the spokesman for the group, "we figured—"

"You figured!" her father roared.

"We all been workin' away from home anyhow," Abraham continued doggedly. "And there's still Andrew at the farm. And Emmeline, and Mama—"

"Women!" her father shouted. "You're leaving me with the women—is that what you're telling me?"

"Now, Dad, that ain't it at all. It's . . ."

But her father didn't want to hear any more. He stomped out of the barn, barely noticing Emmeline as he brushed against her on the path; changed his mind; walked around the house and down to the road. He would go to town. He would walk, just to show them that he was still strong and didn't really need them, if they were going to go in any event.

He wouldn't talk about it again, and rebuffed their attempts to do so. He could not win and he would not be consoled. He had to force himself to speak to them, to say goodbye when spring came and they left. He took on a bitter edge afterward, and when he stayed home with Emmeline and her mother, he was always restless and looking as though he wished he were out. When he did spend the evening away from home, more often than not he was under the influence of spirits when he returned.

After some months had passed, months in which he was sullen and withdrawn from his wife and daughter, he began to question Emmeline occasionally about men who had shown an interest in her at one time or another over the years. In the first of these conversations, he quite casually remarked one evening that he'd been surprised when young Winthrop asked for Harriet's hand, because it was Emmeline he'd always seemed to be mooning over.

"Oh, no, Papa," she said calmly. "I'm sure you're wrong."

Harriet and Winthrop Bradley had five children now. Old Mr. Bradley had died, and Winthrop ran the store for his mother, giving Harriet a position of power in town that put her in her element.

And truly, if her father was correct in what he was saying, Emmeline had been unaware of Winthrop's interest . . . as she had been deeply, determinedly unaware of the interest of the others. After her return from Lowell, it had taken months of daily life for her to become comfortable with the men in her own family, longer for her to tolerate so much as a brief conversation with a man outside it. In this year, when there was a new pastor at the church who spoke beautifully, she had once again begun to take pleasure in her attendance, and along with that pleasure had come the ability to see some of the men in town as individuals, one or two quite likable. Yet if one of those visited her, she did not miss him when he left, or concern herself with whether he would ever return. Most, discouraged by her kind indifference, simply stopped coming by.

Her father's employer, Simon Fenton, was one whose visits did not cease. Almost fifty years old now, and still a widower, Simon had three children, whom he took around with him when he traveled. In addition to owning the sawmill, he was the local agent for the road company, and so he had reason to travel frequently the roads between Fayette and Chesterville; Fayette and Livermore; Fayette and Hallowell; even Fayette and Norway and Lewiston. He had explained to them that after his wife's death he had made the decision not to search for another mother for his children, but to take them with him when he had to leave home. The oldest was now fifteen, and though she could easily have cared for the others in his absence, Simon still took them along, saying that he enjoyed their company too much to relinquish it on his journeys. This endeared him to Emmeline, who had not previously heard a man speak this way of his children.

By 1858 Simon had begun to weary of moving around. The year before, a railroad line through the valley had been completed, causing an immediate decline in the commercial fortunes of Fayette, the Corners now being bypassed by travelers. Most of the road crews were doing repairs on existing roads rather than creating new ones. Simon's mill was the oldest in Fayette and was not feeling the business decline; his intention was to spend more time in Fayette and less on the road.

More and more frequently, as 1858 gave way to 1859, then summer turned to fall, and then another winter, Simon came by in the evening to chat with Henry Mosher about business at the mill; the roads; the awesome spectacle of the new railroads; the tension between the states. Emmeline never thought of Simon as other than her father's friend, and she was astonished when one night her father suddenly demanded to know why she was not more encouraging to him.

"Encouraging?" she echoed uneasily. "I don't think he wants encouragement."

"'Course he does," her father said. "Can't you see what's in front of your eyes, Emmy?"

"He looks very contented as he is, Papa," she argued, dread building inside her. If her father's general mood was better than it had been after the boys' departure, it still often seemed that they had taken his even temper with them when they left. The boys had sent only three terse notes describing their whereabouts since they'd left, and sometimes, when her father talked about the roads, she had the feeling that he meant to find a way to go west and bring them back by force. "I don't think he's looking for a wife."

"He wasn't afore," her father said. "He is now."

She looked to her mother for help. In these increasingly frequent discussions about Emmeline's age and prospects, her mother was always on her side, but in a manner so remote and noncommittal as to provide no real support. Emmeline looked back to her father.

"Well," she said, "I'm sure he'll find one, then."

"Find one!" her father erupted, banging on the table with his fist. "Find one! He's found her, and she sits in that very seat night after night acting as if he don't exist!"

"I'm always nice to Simon," she protested.

"Nice," her father grumbled. "What a man wants . . . Every time he tries to talk to you alone, you find a way to—"

"But I don't see any reason to be alone with him!" she cried out.

"You're thirty-three years old!" he shouted. "That's enough reason! How'd'you expect to find yourself a husband if you're afraid to be alone with a man?"

"Henry," her mother said quietly.

"Never mind," her father said. "Never mind. It's not as though no one wanted her. If no one'd have her, I'd have to live with it. There's plenty as'd still have her, though, and Simon's the best of them."

"But I don't want to marry," Emmeline said.

He stared at her thunderstruck, as though in all the years of her adult life, this possibility had never occurred to him.

"I thought," he said after a long while, "you was just waiting for someone good enough."

The truth was that he'd never thought about it at all during those years when it had seemed better to have a second woman in the house than to gain a man in the family.

"No," she said, "Simon is good enough. But I don't want to marry."

"I don't want to hear that again," her father warned.

She closed her eyes. She wanted to run up to the attic room, which she had to herself now, but she was afraid that if she ran away he would become more agitated. She waited.

She could hear him push back his chair, stamp across the room, pause to get his coat from the hook, and open the door, then slam it behind him. She opened her eyes and looked at her mother again. This was the worst of the arguments of this nature, perhaps because until now, her father had been hopeful about Simon.

"Emmy," her mother said, "will you read to me?"

Emmeline took the Bible from the mantelpiece. She had a newer Bible upstairs now, for reading to herself at night. This one, its pages feeling so delicate that she was almost afraid to turn them—and indeed, a few had come out of the binding and been sewn by her to the following page—was the one she had taken with her to Lowell.

She read on and on, at first finding passages her mother particularly loved. But after a while she looked up and saw that her mother had fallen asleep. Then she continued reading, but she was no longer selective. She was enjoying the sound of her own voice in the quiet night. It was January of 1860. Outside, all was ice and snow, but there was no wind, and aside from her voice, the only sound in the world was the crackling of the fire.

She fell asleep and dreamed of Lowell. Everything was as it had been, except that it was silent. And motionless. There were the boardinghouse, the brick-paved street, the weaving room. Mr. Maguire stood looking out of the window in a waking sleep. The looms were there, but the girls were absent and the looms looked as though they were never used. The silence was beginning to frighten her when she awakened because there were men's voices outside. She opened the door to see Simon Fenton and another man from town supporting her father as they came toward the house. At first she thought her father was simply drunk, but then she saw that one of his legs was dragging along the snow and he was in pain. In his inebriated condition, he had slipped on the ice on the tavern steps, breaking his leg.

Simon helped to make him comfortable and then drove up to Livermore Falls to get the doctor, who set it and gave her father more whiskey to help him sleep. By the time the doctor left, the sun was coming up. Simon had fallen asleep with his head on the kitchen table. He awakened only to stretch out on the floor in front of the fire. She covered him with a quilt. He stirred.

"Emmeline," he murmured, more asleep than awake.

"Good night, Simon," she said.

"Emmeline?" His eyes were closed.

"Yes," she said. "I'm here."

"Will you do me the honor of marrying me?"

"No, Simon," she whispered, grateful for her father's loud snores. "I can't. I can't get married."

His eyes opened. He looked up at her. "Why not?"

"I just can't." She couldn't tell him the truth, but she never lied. The one lie she had to maintain, the center of her life, was so great a burden as to make it unbearable for her to tell the small lies other people sometimes used to get by. "I'm too set in my ways, Simon." She smiled. "I'm an old maid, and meant to be."

He continued to look at her gravely. He would not be put off by such silliness.

"It's true," she said. "I've lived here all my life, except for—"

"I'm not asking you to leave Fayette."

"I can't leave *here*. Especially now. I have to take care of my father."

"I'll take care of both of them," Simon said. "They can come live with us at my house. There's enough room."

It was a much better house, too, one of the largest and most beautiful in Fayette, though he was too tactful to point this out to her.

She shook her head. "They wouldn't want that."

"Do you?"

She didn't answer.

"I'm not a youngster," Simon said after a while. "But I'm in good health."

She smiled. "You're not too old, Simon," she said. "*I'm* too old."

"There's something you're not telling me," he said.

She could not look at him.

"Is there someone else?" he asked.

"Someone else?"

"Someone else you want to marry."

"Oh, no," she said. "On my word, Simon, there's no one."

"I'm not in any hurry," Simon said.

Simon could not afford to pay her father his full wages, but he got a young boy to do the job while the leg was healing, and then gave her father the difference between his usual wages and the boy's. He also had an idea for another source of income for the Moshers. In the spring, the road between Wayne and Livermore Falls, which cut through the Corners, was to be widened and repaired. Soon the surveyor and the head of the road gang would be coming in. They would need a place to stay; they earned good wages and could be charged well for room and board.

"What would we do without you, Simon?" Emmeline asked.

Indeed, her gratitude toward him had a measure of love in it.

"We don't need to know that," he grumbled, irritated because the words did not mean what he wanted them to mean.

She was full of energy, and happier than she had been since she was a child. There was a general sense of anticipation which was particularly unusual for those dreary winter months. Everyone looked forward to the company of the men who were coming to work on the road. Her father had not asked for whiskey, nor did he seem to miss it. He was philosophical about the accident and said that as long as he was laid up, he was glad to have good company. Perhaps he had resigned himself to the inevitable; more likely, he was optimistic about Emmeline and Simon. Simon was at the house whenever he was needed and often when he wasn't. After a trip to Lewiston, Simon brought him a bunch of maps showing the railroad and the turnpike road systems, as well as the plank roads laid in the past ten years or so. Her father pored over these maps for long hours. He began to mention the three boys regularly and without rancor for the first time since they'd left home, pointing out to Emmeline and her mother places where they'd once been or might go next. The fact that he could trace their movements seemed to have made the departure itself bearable to him.

Sometimes he and Simon pored over the maps together. The maps brought close to home the disputes and battles that were leading to the War Between the States. They were all abolitionists, of course, like everyone in Fayette, having no doubt whatever that if they had to farm their own lands or pay for help, the gentlemen of the South should be obliged to do the same. Her father's attitude on the issue of the South's sovereignty had hardened in recent times as well.

Where she'd once heard him claim that the Southern states should be allowed to form their own union, if that was what they wanted, he was now fond of pointing out on Simon's maps the railroad routes that already linked the North and the South indissolubly.

"Look here, now," he might say to some new visitor, having already exhausted Simon's ability to listen to this particular argument. "You can get on the railroad in Savannah, Georgia, and never get off of the tracks till you reach Augusta, Maine. Lookee here. Savannah, Macon, Atlanta; Chattanooga, Tennessee . . . Knoxville . . . Abingdon, Virginia; Lynchburg; Washington, D.C.; Baltimore, Maryland . . ." He savored the names, giving the impression that each city had some distinct meaning for him which the rest of them didn't know. Maryland was Mary Land, the land of a beautiful woman he remembered from his youth, before he had settled down. "Phila . . . delphia, Penn-n-n-sylvania; . . . Trenton, New Jersey; New York; New Haven, and Providence, Rhode Island; . . . Boston; Portland; Augusta"—and there you were! Now, what were those tomfool cotton planters talking about with their separate union? It was clear as the nose on your face that it was all the same country!

It was only when Simon told them the men would arrive any day that Emmeline began to feel qualms about being at such close quarters with two strangers. She decided that even with a wall between her and them, she didn't wish to remain in the attic. She set up a sort of room for herself downstairs, at the opposite end of the room from her parents' curtained-off bed, bringing down a mattress from the attic. On a rope hung across the width of the room, she strung two quilts which could be drawn closed during the night. Still, she found herself looking up the ladder to the attic and thinking that she would have been happier if they had been able to put up the men in the barn.

She was too nervous to remain around the house for any length of time. She walked up the hill one evening to pass some time with Andrew and Jane, but all the children had gone to sleep, and the tired parents were eager to do the same, so she said good night and walked back, deciding on the way to visit Rachel and Persis.

She rode her horse, having told her parents that if the weather took a turn for the worse she would stay over at Rachel's. It was the end of March, but the winter snow was still packed down on the roads, and it felt as though more snow was coming.

Rachel and Persis were delighted to see her, but after a while she grew restless there too. Rachel teased her a great deal about Simon, saying she heard that he spent more time at the Moshers' now than at his own home. She was certain that Emmeline was going to break their vow. This wasn't the first time Rachel had gone on at great length about Simon, and it was getting more difficult for Emmeline to respond with humor. Sometimes she wondered if Rachel really saw something in her friendship with Simon that she herself didn't see. Was it possible that this easy fondness she felt for Simon was what some people called love? Perhaps she would have thought so too, if she had not once experienced a love so intense as to negate her separate existence.

"Have you ever loved someone?" she turned from the window to ask Rachel and Persis.

"Aha!" said Rachel to Persis. "You see where our friend's mind is dwelling!"

Emmeline laughed without amusement. "You will take anything I say to mean that it's true."

"If I were a man," Rachel said, "I would make you a wager—that you'll be married before the year is out."

It was so unlikely that Emmeline didn't bother to respond. A short while later, though, she decided to head for home. Persis giggled, and Rachel said that she must not dare to miss one of Mr. Fenton's visits.

The road was icy under the fresh snow. The horse moved slowly, sometimes raising a hoof and lowering it without advancing, then trying again and moving forward by inches along the road. Her shawl and skirt were coated with snow, but the air was cold enough to keep it from melting and chilling her through. It took her so long to reach home that she was surprised to find Simon's wagon in front of the house. Only when she saw two strange horses in the barn did she remember that the men were due to arrive.

Fully awake now, she moved toward the house. She would be sleeping downstairs, and above her would be two strangers with freedom to walk through the house. Simon's intentions had been good, but why had they consented to this invasion? Surely if her father had been talking of setting up the boys in business only a few years before, the money that would have gone to that business had not been spent. They could have managed with a bit of that—although she had already observed her father's reluctance to touch those savings.

Cautiously she opened the door to the house. Her father sat at the head of the table, his back to her, his leg up on the bench in front of him. The crutches Simon had made for him at the mill rested upright against the table, where he could reach them easily. Simon sat at his left hand, a portly gray-haired man at his right. At the far end of the long table, beyond the oil lamp, at once a part of the group and quite removed from it, was a much younger man. He was tall and broad-shouldered, but she couldn't see his face clearly, for it was in the shadows. He was the only one who had seen her come in, and she could feel him watching her.

Simon turned as she closed the door behind her.

"Look at you," he said. "You're going to be soaked right through."

It had a fatherly sound. Was it that he always sounded that way and she hadn't noticed before? She took off her shawl and hung it at the fireplace, then shook out her skirts. Her mother was already in bed, the curtains drawn across the big bed.

"Here are your boarders, Emmeline," Simon said. "Thomas Flint and Matthew Gurney, Miss Emmeline Mosher."

"How de do, Ma'am?" Tom Flint said. He was the older one, the surveyor. He lived in Augusta. Together he and Matthew Gurney would recruit the remaining men for the road crew; then Tom Flint would return to Augusta and Matthew Gurney would lead the crew. Matthew Gurney was leaning forward, closer to the oil lamp. She could see his face more clearly now. He had light brown hair and light eyes—blue or gray, she couldn't see for sure. A lock of hair tumbled down his forehead into one eye. Emmeline nodded shyly without looking too long at either of them, then turned back to the fire. The flakes that had clung to her uncovered hair melted and ran down her forehead and her neck. She closed her eyes.

"Have you seen the room?" she asked.

"Yes, Ma'am," Flint said. "It's just fine."

"You can't stand up, except in the middle," she said.

"That's all right," Flint said. "By the end of the day, these lads don't have the energy to stand."

"Good," she said.

There was silence. Each of the men had a cup of something, and her father drained his; then Simon did the same.

"I suppose I should be getting on," Simon said. "I'm realizing this is your room now, Emmeline." Then he was embarrassed. He put on his coat and asked if she would mind coming outside with him for just a moment. But when they were outside, he didn't seem to know what it was he wanted to say. He stared at her as

though he were sure there was something she wasn't
telling him. He kicked at the snow with his boot. He
looked at the sky and said he couldn't remember that in
his entire lifetime they'd had a snow quite like this so
late in the year. Then he laughed and said he supposed
she knew his entire lifetime was a very long time.

She smiled.

He said he hoped his horse would be able to keep the
wagon on the road, and then waited, perhaps hoping
she would tell him he could sleep in front of the fire
again. Finally he said good night and trudged down the
slope to his wagon.

She went back inside. The atmosphere had changed.
At first there was silence. But then her father spoke,
and even without understanding the words, she could
have heard the challenge in his voice.

"Now, you can't tell me," he said, "that right out
there in the middle of Kansas there's no such issue as
slavery."

Matthew Gurney shrugged. It seemed as though he
wouldn't bother to reply.

"What do you take us for, lad?" her father demanded.

She came in and closed the door. Thomas Flint
mirrored her uneasiness.

"I'm not taking you for anything," Matthew Gurney
said. "I'm just telling you how it was with us."

His speech was accented in a way that was foreign to
all of them; it was a medley, really, of the East, where
his parents had been born and raised; of the Kansas
Territory, where they had lived when he was growing
up and where his parents lived still; and of the various
towns along the railroad lines throughout the Midwest
and then the Northeast where he'd worked and lived
and sometimes even meant to stay, as he made his way
toward the East Coast.

"How it was with you," her father mimicked irritably.

"How *what* was?" Emmeline asked, hoping to avert unpleasantness, and curious as well.

Gurney looked at her over the oil lamp; the flickering light lent his eyes an eerie, almost transparent quality. She felt profoundly uneasy. She shook her head without knowing precisely why—unless it was because she had just become absolutely certain that it would not be an easy matter to fall asleep at night with two strangers in the house.

Without looking away from her, Gurney reached for his cup, drained what was left in it, licked his lips, and set down the cup.

"We never did care for the slaves, one way or the other," he said. "We only wanted the land we been farming right along."

She waited for more, but it didn't come. When her father saw that Gurney was contented with what he'd said, he began spluttering again. She had never seen him get angry so easily at anyone outside the family; he liked people or didn't bother about them at all.

Tom Flint rose from the bench.

"Well," he said, "there's another day coming, and we've been on the road this entire one. How 'bout some sleep, Matt?"

Matthew rose readily; it was a matter of indifference to him whether he convinced her father. He went up the ladder without saying good night to any of them.

"He's a good boy, Mr. Mosher," Tom Flint said. If Tom had more education than most people in Fayette, he wasn't a man who was strange to them by his very nature. "You'll see. He takes a while, that's all."

Her father muttered, but he allowed himself to be helped back to the bed by Flint and Emmeline. Then Tom Flint went up to the attic, and Emmeline sat down in the rocker. After a while, she could hear her father breathing regularly.

She turned the rocker so that it faced the fire and sat again. Above her head, she could hear the two men moving around, then settling down, then talking. She thought it was mostly Tom Flint's voice she heard, and only an occasional brief response from the other one. Matthew Gurney. She could tell herself that she was remaining awake in front of the fire because there were strangers in the house, but it was Matthew Gurney's face that she saw when she closed her eyes, his gray eyes staring at her intently over the oil lamp, without shyness or apology. He frightened her as she hadn't been frightened by any man she'd known before, certainly not by any of the Fayette boys who'd courted her, whose faces she had never seen after they left the room.

The fire died down to glowing embers. Someone was moving around upstairs. Quickly she got up and went to her makeshift room, pulling the quilts across the rope. Someone came down the ladder and stopped for a moment, then walked across the room so softly she might not have heard him if she hadn't known he was there. The door opened and closed again.

She lay down on her mattress and drew up the covers, knowing that she wouldn't sleep. The room grew colder. The hem of her skirt was wet from melted snow, but she hadn't wanted to change into her nightgown. She had the sense that she needed to be prepared to get out of her bed. Even to run.

She assured herself that she was being foolish. Like herself, Matthew Gurney had been awake and restless. So he had taken a walk—without bothering her or bothering *about* her. Furthermore, he wasn't a stranger they knew nothing about, but the carefully chosen head of the road crew, well known to Thomas Flint, who was obviously a good man.

She turned over on her side, wrapped the quilt more tightly around herself, and closed her eyes so tightly as to make it clear that there was no chance at all of her falling asleep. If only he would come in and settle down in his place, perhaps she would feel easy enough to sleep! But the very thought of his sleeping just over her head in the attic made her entire body tense until it was stiff as a board.

Somewhere outside, a mouth organ was being played. Only the high notes reached her, and at first she thought they might be in her imagination. But the music stopped for a while, then began again, and this time she was sure it was real. Telling herself that she could not be any more frightened than she was now, she wrapped the quilt around herself and tiptoed to the door.

The snowflakes were bigger and heavier than they'd been before; soon they would turn to rain. The music was coming from across the road. She walked down toward the pond.

He was leaning against the mica rock, facing away from the pond, up toward the house. His eyes were closed. She leaned against a big elm tree a few yards away from him, listening, watching. He finished one slow, sad tune that was unfamiliar to her, then, with scarcely a pause, moved to a series of sounds which were less a song than a succession of birdcalls and forest sounds . . . wind rustling the tree leaves . . . the soft, eerie sound of the mourning doves . . . When she looked at him, and listened to him, it was as though her eyes and ears were not separate but were one organ, taking him in. In fact, her whole body was taking him in, as it took in the first warm sunlit day of spring. She was crying, although she didn't know it.

After a while, he stopped playing and opened his eyes, looking straight at her. She smiled and only then realized that she was crying. He watched her gravely, not smiling back.

"I could hear you from the house," she said.

"Did I wake you?" he asked.

"No," she said. "I wasn't sleeping."

He nodded. "The chair was still rockin' when I come down." He had been testing her and didn't mind if she knew it.

"I sit on that rock often," she said. "But I always face out to the pond."

"Pond?"

She laughed. "In back of you." It was still mostly ice, and now it was covered with snow, but to her it seemed that it was clearly a pond.

He turned to see, then looked back at her.

"I thought it was a field."

She shook her head.

"I barely looked at it," he said. "That's the truth of it."

"In the summer it's beautiful," she said. "You'll see." Suddenly it occurred to her that no one had told her how long he would be there. "Will you be here this summer? How long will the road take?"

He shrugged. It was the gesture with which Matthew always denied the possibility that life would push him someplace he wasn't ready to go.

"Ain't seen the north side from town yet. But I'll be where I want to be, come summer, just like I always am."

If it had a great deal of the swagger of youth to it, there was also considerable authority.

The snow had turned to rain. Their hair and their faces were wet, and the quilt she'd wrapped around herself was soaked. She began to shiver, but she didn't want to be in the house any more than he did. In unspoken agreement they walked back across the road, up the path around the house, and to the barn. He pulled open the barn doors; a horse whinnied. It was very dark, and she was afraid to go in there with him.

"It's colder in there than out here," she said.

"It's dry," he told her. "We can build a fire."

"Here? In the barn?"

"Just inside the door where the rain won't put it out."

"What if it catches?"

"Won't. There's plenty of ways. Wet stuff on the

bottom, then half dry . . . If it looks about to catch, I'll shovel the whole thing out the door."

"No," she said after a moment. "I'm afraid."

He waited silently. She couldn't see him in the darkness.

"Let's go in the house and build up the fire."

He came forward so that she could see him better.

"Won't your pa mind if he wakes?"

"He doesn't wake in the night."

Matthew pulled out his mouth organ, wiped it off on the inside of his jacket, and began playing again, disappearing into the barn as he did so, walking so far back that she thought he would surely stumble on something in the darkness. But he didn't. The songs he played were faster and lighter than before; on another instrument they might have sounded harsh, but the mouth organ had a way of muting everything that came through it but sadness. Finally he returned to her side and said, "Okay."

"Okay?" She had never heard it before and had no idea what it meant.

This brought forth a small laugh. His language was sprinkled with words from the Plains and other parts of the country whose meanings she could at best only guess. From that moment on he would enjoy mystifying her with them.

They returned to the house and he was easily able to get the fire started again, though there was no kindling. They spread out the quilt and his wet jacket on the floor behind them, and sitting so close to the fire that they were nearly in it, they talked until the sky began to lighten and they were afraid that the others would waken.

As they would every night in the weeks that followed. Not because they were doing anything wrong, but because the two of them talking—really Matthew talking, and Emmeline listening, nodding to show that she understood, that she was listening, that she remem-

bered something he'd said before—was simply too
precious to be shared.

Tom Flint returned to Augusta, and three other men
arrived to work with Matthew. Instead of sharing the
attic room with one of them, Matthew delegated all
three to Andrew and Jane's, telling Henry Mosher that
he would pay double to have the room to himself. Her
father was irritated, but there was nothing he could
really complain about; Andrew picked up an extra
boarder, while he himself lost nothing. In general, her
father withdrew into himself and his maps when
Matthew was around. Matthew stayed out of the house
as much as possible after dinner, and Emmeline would
find him as soon as her chores were done.

Sometimes he talked about the work on the road.
Other times she asked about his life before he'd come
to Fayette; if he elaborated on his simple answers, it
was usually to make some specific point, such as how
little her father and his kind knew about the realities of
life in the Plains and farther West.

She dreaded the time when he would ask her about
Lowell, but he never did. As much as she wanted to
know about his life before she'd met him, he wanted
not to know about hers.

Something he said made her suspect that he'd been
married and had a child. For days she made up dreadful
stories about his attempts to save them from massacre
by Indians. Then she finally found the courage to ask
him if they existed. He told her, in a manner so casual
that she was totally unprepared for what he was going
to say, that he had a child, but not a wife, for he had
never married the mother. Seeing the expression on
Emmeline's face, he became defiant.

"She come after me," he said. "Not the other way
round." He defied Emmeline, furthermore, to waste
any pity on the woman, who had a hundred and sixty
acres she would never have been able to claim without
him and the baby. She had probably, Matthew said,

found herself a husband within a few days of his departure.

Emmeline didn't respond. She felt a sadness so heavy as to weigh down her entire body. What she was thinking of—seeing—more clearly than she had in many years, was Mrs. Whitehead telling her that she was fortunate that Mr. Maguire was giving her so much money. And Mr. Whitehead explaining that because of the amount, Mr. Maguire would not be able to see her.

Why didn't you tell me at the beginning? she wanted to cry out to Matthew, but she knew at the same time that this was not an honest question. There had been no beginning in that sense; from the moment her eyes had met his, it had been too late.

At a time when most emigrants from the East were moving no farther west than Iowa, Matthew Gurney's parents had pushed on to the westernmost area of the Kansas Territory. They might have gone farther, but it was planting time and the mountains were ahead of them.

Matthew was his parents' only child until he was eleven years old, when his mother had another boy and then, shortly after, a girl. Their way of life then changed considerably. Where once the three of them together, for example, had always taken the day's journey to town, his mother keeping a watchful eye on Matthew at every moment, as though if she looked away he would disappear forever, his mother now stayed home while Matthew accompanied his father. Or if his mother went, he stayed home with the children, which irritated him enormously. He had always been a restless boy, and nothing was harder for him than to spend two or three days confined to home because his horse had been hitched to the wagon for his parents' trip and he couldn't walk a few yards before one child or the other would be calling after him.

One day in town, he took advantage of his father's absorption in an argument over the price of his cattle to get on his horse and follow a group of men who were passing through town, working on a road that would connect to the Santa Fe Trail, thus creating a direct route to Lawrence. Matthew was big for his age, and capable, and didn't talk too much. Within a short time he had been accepted as a member of the group. He worked with these men all that year, 1854, and into the next, eventually falling in, as he put it, with a family that headed up one of the claims clubs. This was the difficult time when so much of the land in eastern Kansas was disputed, and that dispute was feeding into the battle between the North and the South. Matthew told Emmeline that he didn't like to talk of that time, when he and the men he was with had done many things she wouldn't want to know about. At some point in 1856 he had left Lawrence with a different road crew, heading into Missouri, where in Jefferson City he had seen his first railroad and fallen in love.

From that point on, Matthew had never taken a road job when he could get work on the railroad. St. Louis, Cincinnati, Columbus, Pittsburgh. He reeled off the names as her father had, but Matthew's hand-drawn maps had no names on them because he couldn't read or write. He had been unable to sit still for what little schooling he'd had. His mother had tried to teach him during the winters before the other children were born, but it hadn't "taken." He loved to hear Emmeline read aloud, but if there were other people in the room, as when she read the Bible at night, he would pretend not to be listening.

The railroad ended abruptly just east of Pittsburgh, which was at this ink dot, and didn't pick up again until Harrisburg, so he'd taken some time going through there. Coal country. He'd worked for a while in the tavern of an inn, where his size was a great asset. On payday the men got rough, and the owner was a woman, recently widowed, who couldn't handle them. Yes, he had stayed with her for a while, the first one he'd been with for any length of time since Lawrence, Kansas. Emmeline pried these details out of him and then he grinned at her defiantly, waiting for her to dare to criticize when his past existed now only because she was asking questions about it. A woman in St. Louis had told him the railroads were in his fate because of the tracklike cross-hatching on the three major lines of each of his palms. He thought that was stupid, as he thought it was stupid for her to say that no two people had palms or fingerprints exactly alike. If you knew enough people, you were bound to find some whose marks were identical to your own.

She needed to hear all this, no matter how little it pleased her, no matter how it maddened her to think of another woman's holding his hand. Georgina had the tavern; Hildreth had told his fortune; Betsy was the mother of his child, a boy, in Kansas. By naming them, he in some way shared them with her, which made them less dangerous. Georgina and Hildreth had asked him to write, and he had promised that he would; Emmeline was the first to know that he could not.

The railroad ended at the Delaware River, on the Pennsylvania border. In New York State he'd gone back to the roads. Plank roads now, rather than macadam. Hemlock, mostly. Sometimes the organization of the work was so poor that they ran out of lumber and had to stop for a few weeks. He would work in the local sawmill then, cutting planks. Planks used that fast were green, of course, but it wasn't like building a house with them. When they dried out, the moisture in the roadbed would swell them again. By the time that process had ended, they'd probably be worn through or sunk into the roadbed anyway. Plank roads were half as dear to build as paved ones were, but they didn't last half as long, so there was no advantage. No two ways about it, Matthew said—another of his favorite expressions—railroad tracks were the best "roads" of all.

At the town of Hudson, New York, he'd gone back to the railroads, working on repairs to the old line that went from Hudson clear across Massachusetts to Boston, zigzagging to work on some short lines around Lynn, where there was a strike going on in the big shoe factories; then into New Hampshire and up to Maine. Portland.

Her heart missed a beat when he named Lynn.

"My aunt who took me to Lowell when I was a girl lives in Lynn," she said. "It was a long time ago, of course; there were only the small shoe shops then. I can't imagine great factories there." It was the first time she'd ever told anybody she had once seen Lynn. She was about to caution Matthew not to mention this, then realized it was unnecessary, for he never mentioned *anything* to her family.

He yawned.

"Don't you want to know, Matthew," she asked, "what I was doing in all those years before you came?"

"Nothing," he said. "You weren't alive. You come to life overnight, just before I got here. Like a boom town."

She smiled sadly. "When you leave I will be a ghost town."

He had told her about coming on a ghost town once, northeast of Colorado City. It was midday. There were a few buildings but no sign of life. It crossed his mind that there had been a massacre, but when he walked through, it was almost worse than if there *had* been. At least then you would have *seen* the bodies; here you just *felt* them all around you. He'd learned later that the town had been inhabited for only a year or two. There had been word of a gold strike on the south face of the foothills a little farther up. Twenty or thirty men, some with families, had come back over the mountains, where they'd been panning with no success. They'd put up these few buildings and roamed the foothills. Then one day there'd been word of a big strike deeper into the mountains. Those without families had picked up and left in an hour; the others had followed within days. In one building, there was not only furniture but dishes and pots on the table. The picture had haunted him until the day he left home, though he hadn't thought about it often since.

He looked at Emmeline.

"I ain't leaving," he said.

Tears came to her eyes.

"You aren't?"

He shook his head. He was watching her.

"What will you do when the road is finished?"

He shrugged. "I can always find something."

"It's different here than where you've been," she said. "They have to know you." Times were changing for the worse again. One of the cabinetmakers at the Corners had left. When Simon Fenton was looking for a boy to replace her father, more than a dozen had applied, some from as far away as Hallowell.

If Matthew had to leave, she wanted to go with him, but she kept remembering the other women and she was afraid to say that.

"You might have to go to Lewiston to find work," she said. "Or Portland."

"Don't like Portland," he said. "It's on the water."

She smiled. "I've heard the ocean is very beautiful."

"No more'n the Plains."

"Have you seen the ocean?" she asked.

"Don't need to," he said. "I seen the Plains."

Something had been settled between them. He wouldn't simply pick up and leave, though she didn't know whether this meant that he loved her, or that if he *did* go he would take her with him. Even if he loved her, he might not want to marry her because of the difference in their ages.

"Are you thirty, Mr. Gurney?" she asked teasingly.

"Nope." He wasn't twenty-five either, but he didn't tell her that. He had not yet understood the unconditional nature of her love, or seen that nothing he told her could change it.

She would marry him without hesitation if he asked her. And she liked to believe that when she talked about going with him, she meant as his wife. But since the night he'd first come, her only bad dreams had been of the day when he would leave, and the dread inspired by these dreams was so great as to make her uncertain what she would do if he was willing to take her but not to marry. She couldn't picture herself standing at the door to wave goodbye; in any picture she conjured up, she always ran to catch up with him.

It was out of fear alone that she had kept him at arm's length until this time; discretion alone would have been no match for her feelings. Maguire had taken a near-child who didn't know what he was taking and barely felt what he was giving. Only now did she experience the undertow he'd been struggling against. Only now was her soul's craving for a mate matched by her body's desire. With Maguire she had never understood the possibility of becoming pregnant. Now she thought about it constantly, her dread that it might happen too soon in direct proportion to her longing for it to happen at any cost. She seldom thought of her lost child now, but somewhere inside was the hope that Matthew would make up to her for that loss. She kept that hope at bay, along with her desire to touch him. Once they came together, there would be no coming apart without the destruction of her very self.

She let him take her hand the next Sunday as they walked home from church through the woods. But then the very feeling of it frightened her—its strength, its enveloping warmth—and she shook free and ran ahead of him. He caught up with her and took both her hands, making her look at him. Her body grew weak.

"No," she said. "No. Please."

He shrugged and released her, looking stung.

"Matthew," she said, "I . . ."

"What?" He was sullen.

"I'm frightened."

"Of what?"

"I don't know." She couldn't tell him less than the truth. He began walking ahead of her. It was a beautiful day in May, the sun shining, the sky cloudless, the leaves filling in the trees.

"Matthew!"

He turned.

"You've never asked my age. Do you know that I'm thirty-four years old?"

He shrugged again. He had finally, reluctantly, confessed to being twenty-six, but *her* age didn't concern him, because he wanted her; only his own might be wrong.

"Why do you want to stay in Fayette?" she asked.

He squinted at her. "That ain't the smartest question I ever heard."

"Soon you'll want to move on," she said. "Go back to the railroads. You're accustomed to moving." He had told her he never promised the others he would stay, and she believed that he meant to stay now, but one long winter would doubtless destroy his resolution. "You don't know how it is in Fayette in the winter."

"I come in the winter," he pointed out.

"But that was the end of it! You just don't know. Nothing happens in Fayette in the winter!"

Matthew! If you're going to leave me, leave me now before I ever touch your hand again!

"I know," he said. "It don't matter. I'm staying here with you."

She stood watching him for a while, trying to believe him utterly or not at all. Then she ran to him; kissed his cheek lightly and so quickly that he had not realized what she was going to do; and ran the short remaining distance to the house. She had opened the door before he caught up with her.

She was flushed and happy as she entered, then felt a twinge when she saw that Simon was there. He had stopped coming by in the evenings, although this could have been because the outdoor work at this time of year left everyone too tired to visit. Her father still invited him for Sunday dinners.

She felt bad about Simon, who looked at her mournfully when he thought she could not see him. When he was there, she tried not to stare at Matthew, as she was prone to do at other times.

Simon hadn't brought his children, but Andrew was there with his two younger ones. Andrew and Matthew had taken to each other. The questions her father asked Matthew to challenge him had answers that really interested her brother, who had never left home and never would. Her father was angry with Andrew over his betrayal, though not so angry as he was with Emmeline. Sometimes he talked about buying a piece of land nearby for Luke and his children, as though Andrew weren't there with him and Luke weren't quite contented over on the other side of the Corners.

"Where were you?" her father asked her irritably. He didn't look at Matthew, who had come in and was standing behind her. "Do you know how long we been waiting?"

This was clearly untrue. Emmeline herself had put up the hen to stew before leaving for church, but the potatoes baking on the cookstove had just begun to turn dark, and Andrew's children were setting out the plates.

"We were walking," she said.

"Don't know what's gotten into you," he grumbled. "Never think about your mother anymore."

Her mother never noticed what was going on between the men. She thought Matthew was a fine young man and couldn't understand her husband's effort to draw out of her some negative opinion of him.

"Do you need help, Mama?"

"You can put the greens in the pot, Emmy."

At dinner Simon said that he saw in the Boston paper that some of the Southern states were talking about leaving the Union if Mr. Lincoln were elected.

"Now, let's see," her father said, "if Mr. Gurney

don't know something more about that than anyone else."

Matthew didn't look up from his plate. He was accustomed to being set up against Simon, which made Simon much more uncomfortable than it made him. If the subject engaged Matthew, he argued; if not, he shrugged.

There was silence at the table.

"We're waiting to hear you, Mr. Gurney," her father said. The tone of mockery was strong now. Emmeline held her breath.

"Don't wait," Matthew said after what seemed like hours. "Your chow'll get cold."

Her father's face grew bright red. He reached for one of the crutches that rested beside him, and for a moment it was uncertain whether he had in mind to leave the table or to strike Matthew with it.

"Chow," Simon said quietly. "Now, that's a real interesting word, Matt. It seems to me I heard you use it before now."

They all waited to see whether her father would be willing to let Simon take them past the difficult moment. As they watched, his color subsided and he lowered his arm. Finally he picked up his fork and began eating again. Everyone else followed except Matthew, who sat looking at his plate awhile longer, then got up from the bench and walked out of the house.

Emmeline was about to follow him when her father told her to stay where she was, and she obeyed because if she did not, he might become even angrier at Matthew.

"Don't know what's wrong with that boy," her father muttered. "There's no way to get on with him."

"You don't try to get on with him," she said softly.

"What are you talking about, daughter?" her father asked.

"Maybe," Andrew said, "it would be a good idea for Matt to exchange with one of the men at our place."

Emmeline's father looked at her. If she approved of the idea, he would fight it; if she didn't, he would accept it. She said nothing. If she didn't like the idea of Matthew's being elsewhere, she didn't see how they could all remain under the same roof much longer.

"What that boy needs," her father said with great deliberation, "is a civilizing influence. He needs to find hisself a nice young girl and settle down and raise a family."

A flush of humiliation rose in her cheeks. She stared at her father, who refused to look back at her, and at her mother, who was eating with a placidity that suggested she was hearing nothing of all this. Emmeline swung around on the bench so suddenly that her plate, with most of the food still on it, was overturned. Without stopping to fix the plate or pick up the food, she got up and ran out of the house.

Matthew was nowhere in sight. She went down to the pond; he knew that she would come here if she left after him. But perhaps he'd wanted to be by himself. Or perhaps he was angry at her because of her father. She walked around and around Mica Island, going over in her mind the names of all the wives she knew who were older than their husbands, beginning with Hannah and Abner, ending with Martha and Luke. In most cases the difference was smaller than that between her and Matthew, but why should that matter? Her father had had nothing but good things to say about Martha and Luke! What was important was that Matthew was a man. He'd been taking care of himself for years in circumstances where someone less than a man would surely have failed. He was the *leader* of the road crew and was treated with deference by the other men because of his greater experience in the world. That very respect of the men—and even of Simon Fenton—seemed to act as a goad on her father. He kept trying to demonstrate Matthew's unworthiness, which was ridiculous in more ways than one—like trying to prove that spring wasn't here when every morning she went out to warmer air and more green around her.

She heard the mouth organ and looked around her. He was sitting in the crook of the lowest branch of a gnarled old apple tree about twenty yards away, watching her. She ran to the tree and looked up. "If you go, I'll go with you," she called up to him over the music, forgetting for the first time to make any conditions. "I'll go wherever you go."

The music stopped.

"He's not driving me out of here," Matthew said, so fiercely that even having expected anger, she was startled. Her own anger with her father never went as deep as Matthew's did, because she knew that however he might behave, he loved her.

"I don't think he wants to drive you out," she protested.

"He does. They all do. Fenton."

"I'm sure you're wrong," she said. "Simon has been so fair, so . . ."

But he didn't want to hear it; he was off in his own thoughts, sitting on the apple-tree branch, staring out at the distance as he talked.

"He's like my old man. I been thinking that since I come. The way he talks. They're the only ones know anything."

"Matthew, please come down."

Instead he told a story about being out on the trail with his father. His voice shook with feeling, and most of the time he didn't look down at her, but seemed almost to be talking to the woods.

He'd heard at the market that some hungry prospectors had come down from the mountains and were laying ambush to small groups going home with their earnings. He had told his father that they should take a different trail. His father had laughed and said that while only the boys were hearing those stories, the trails were safe. Halfway home they'd been robbed of everything they had and beaten when they fought for it.

His father had been like a wild man—yelling, cursing, calling out the vigilance committee. But never had his father let on that he'd been warned, or said a word about it to Matthew or anyone else! Even now, when Matthew thought about it, he got mad all over again.

"Come on up here," he said after a pause.

"I can't."

"You can. Just start up and I'll pull you the rest of the way."

"I'm afraid."

He muttered something, but he came down and took her hand, pulling her toward the road. For a moment she thought he might be taking her back to the house, but they continued walking past it, and eventually they came to the foot of Moose Hill and began climbing it, Matthew moving so fast that she was out of breath trying to keep up with him. Finally they reached the clearing at the top.

She hadn't been up here since she was a child, and she had forgotten how high it was, how grand the view. Looking down and around them they could count a dozen ponds and almost as many villages. Halfway down the side of the hill a herd of fine Jerseys grazed. With a glass, you could see Portland Harbor from here.

"Look at the mountains," she said.

"Those ain't mountains," Matthew said scornfully. "Just bigger hills."

It was the kind of statement that drove her father wild, yet she herself loved to hear him talk that way. Except that his descriptions of the West always made her feel that he could not long be happy in the East.

"Whose is that?" Matthew asked, looking at the hill closest to them.

"That's the Chases'," she said. "They say it's one of the highest pieces of cultivated land in Kennebec County. It's surely the most beautiful."

"I'll buy it for you," he said.

She laughed. "I doubt they mean to sell it."

"Then I'll buy another piece of high land and I'll build you a house."

"Have you so much money as that?" she asked.

"I saved some without even trying," he said. "I didn't care to afore now or I could've had much more." He squinted at her in the sunlight. "You believe me?"

"Of course," she said. "I always believe you."

He dropped to the ground on his knees and pulled her down so that she knelt facing him. He searched her face—to see if she meant it; to see if she was being foolish because she loved him; to see if that love could change.

"You think I never lie?"

"To me?"

"No," he said, looking out over the precipice. "I reckon I pretty much tell you the truth." His eyes came back to hers. "Why you looking at me that way?"

"I can't help but look at you."

He moved forward to kiss her, his eyes locked with hers. Her breath caught; she was fading, sinking. She closed her eyes and fell back to the grass, Matthew coming with her.

He wanted to make love to her, but for all his aggression, he never tried to force himself upon her, and when he said, now—"Okay?"—and she said, after a long time, "No," he immediately sat up and looked away from her.

"I think we had better go back," she said.

"You go," he told her. "I ain't ready."

But it was hard for her to walk away from him.

"Andrew said maybe you could exchange with one of the men at his place, so my father would still have the board. . . ."

"Andrew said that?"

"Because you and he get on so well," she explained.

"We'll build our own house," he said.

"But in the meantime . . ."

He didn't reply. He didn't mind moving over to

Andrew's so much as he minded having one of the other men sleep under the same roof as Emmeline.

When she returned, Simon was waiting outside the house.

"Emmeline," he asked, "can you still tell me that you don't mean to marry?"

"Simon," she said helplessly, "you're such a fine man."

"That's not what I need to hear," he said angrily. "I need you to answer my question."

"No," she said. "It was true when I told it to you. It's not true anymore."

Matthew began investigating land and found it to be more expensive than he'd anticipated. He had it in his mind that he wanted to approach her father about marrying her after he was a landowner, since she said that the approach must be made. But while land prices had peaked a few years earlier, they had not fallen off sufficiently so that he could pay for a good piece of land in addition to buying the materials to build a house. He had his eye on a piece of land about a mile up one of the hills out of Fayette Corners, but if he bought that piece, he would have to work months longer to earn the money for the materials to begin building. By then winter would have returned, and that would mean that another year, at least, would pass before they could be together in their own home. It was unthinkable to him that they should live with any of her family, even Jane and Andrew, of whom he was very fond.

The solution was obvious. Her father owned the narrow strip of land across the road which bordered the pond and was as long as the piece where his own house and barn were. If he could be persuaded to give them this land, Matthew would have enough money to begin building the house now. He had the time, too, for the roadwork was almost completed.

It seemed to her that such an arrangement would also

be good for her father. Even without his mending leg to think about, he was past the time when he could do all the farm work himself, except in the winter, when there were only the animals to be tended. Andrew was the only one working with her father now. With Matthew's help they could cultivate more of their land in the summer and possibly take on more cattle as well. Life would be better for all of them.

Matthew's first reactions ranged from incredulity to a forced amusement to fury that she should broach the idea. He railed against her father in terms so strong as to force Emmeline to defend him, which angered Matthew further.

"You think I come more'n halfway across the country," he asked, "to get away from my old man, and now I'm going to set with yours?"

"It is a separate piece of land," she pointed out. "It's been separate since the road was made. The only reason he owns it is that my grandpa built the house before there was a road." Grandpa Mosher had picked a point close enough to draw water from the pond, but high enough so that he never had to worry about spring flooding. In all the time Emmeline had been alive, however, the pond had never gone more than a foot or two past its natural boundaries.

Matthew brought up dozens of other objections, but they really came down to the same one: that all those qualities in her father which she lovingly explained away by the difficulties of his life and age, Matthew took as signs of evil—and an evil directed at him!

She waited. Sometimes she thought Matthew would suggest moving to a nearby town, but he never did. To him that would have represented a defeat.

"Simon's courting Persis," her father said to her one night. "If you ask me, you're going to lose him if you don't do something pretty quick."

"They make a nice couple," Emmeline said.

"What? What are you saying?" It was obvious that he had barely believed what he was telling her. "It's you Simon wants."

"Not anymore," she told him.

"That's nonsense, Emmy."

Matthew and Andrew came in together from the barn, where they had been attending to a sick horse.

"Why d'you think he keeps me on his books?" her father demanded. "Why d'you think he brings me the paper? And spirits, once in a while?"

"Because he's a good man and he values you," she said. Her heart was beating very rapidly, but her demeanor remained calm. She looked at Matthew out of the corner of her eye. She wanted to tell him to stay back, to stay out of this, matters would only be worse; even Andrew seemed to be motioning to Matthew that they should leave. But Matthew was ignoring both of them, watching her father carefully.

"He's a good man," Emmeline repeated. "He won't stop doing those things just because he isn't courting me anymore."

He squinted at her. "Did you refuse him?"

"Yes."

"What do you think of your sister, Andrew?" he asked after a while, "turning down a man like Simon?"

Andrew, of course, was silent.

"What d'you think of a thirty-four-year-old spinster refusing Simon Fenton?"

Matthew said, "Don't talk about her like that."

Emmeline's heart sank.

Her father turned around slowly, as though he were aware of Matthew's presence only now, for the first time.

"Now, what do we have here?" her father asked. "A thirty-four-year-old spinster who refuses Simon Fenton and an uppity lad who tells her own father how to talk to her!"

Andrew ran out of the house before his father could think to order him to stay. Her father advanced toward

Matthew. She had never seen him look like this before; through all his recent bad tempers she'd never seen him look like this. It was as though Matthew's view of him as malignant had called a new malignant person into existence! He advanced on Matthew, leaning on one crutch, his other arm raised, as though he were going to strike.

"Don't think 'cause you're her father I won't knock you down," Matthew said.

Her father stopped cold in his tracks. Even her mother looked up from her sewing and watched, her work resting in her lap. It was so quiet that they could hear the wind outside.

Then, without actually moving, her father's entire body altered—collapsed into itself—as though the wind itself had passed through him and blown away the starch that had let him believe he could win over a strong young man. This was a young man who would not give him leeway simply because he was sixty-seven years old and leaning on a crutch to walk.

"All right," he said. "Knock me down, if that's what you want." But there was no challenge in it.

"I don't want," Matthew said. "Just keep your distance."

"Okay, okay," her father said. Emmeline glanced at Matthew to see if he noticed her father's use of his word. There was no recognition on Matthew's face, but to her astonishment, her father suddenly looked amused! He threw his crutch on the floor between himself and Matthew—as though it were a weapon he was surrendering—and threw up both hands.

"What else, son?"

Matthew was not amused.

"I mean to marry Emmy."

This took a while longer but did not visibly shake her father.

"Oh? Emmy know this?"

"Ask her."

Her father looked at her without moving his body.

"Emmy?"

"I love him, Papa."

"Oh-ho," he said, "Love, is it?" As though the possibility hadn't occurred to him. "Well, now . . ." With an uncertain step, because he hadn't been walking without the crutch until now, he made his way to the table and sat down.

"Hear that, Sarah?" he asked her mother. "Our oldest daughter says she's in love with Mr. Gurney, here."

"That's nice," her mother said tranquilly. "He's a fine young man."

It was the kind of remote, unsatisfactory reply he always got from her these days, which was why he'd mostly stopped trying to evoke responses from his wife of thirty-five years.

Emmeline looked at Matthew; he still had the air of an animal about to be pounced upon. She smiled, but he didn't see her because he was watching her father. He did not seem to have any sense of having won a battle.

"Well, now," her father said, "it looks to me as if your minds are made up already. Is that right, Emmy?"

"Yes, Papa." She was acutely uncomfortable and could barely summon her voice.

"Well, then, Mr. Gurney," her father said after a long pause, "I think we ought to drink on that together." Matthew exhaled audibly, but Emmeline still wasn't comfortable. That was because Matthew cared for nothing but her father's immediate intentions, while Emmeline required some deeper reassurance. "D'you happen to have any spirits?"

"Up at Andrew's." Matthew glanced at Emmeline. "I'll go get 'em."

Her father smiled at him encouragingly. At that instant Emmeline had the feeling that his whole performance had been aimed toward getting a glass of whiskey! She sat across the table from him, waiting. The mask of joviality disappeared as soon as Matthew went out the door. Her father sat there, sad and tired, the man she'd always known. Suddenly she was fearful in a way that was unfamiliar to her. Her father's face blurred in front of her.

"What is it?" she asked, although she didn't know why she was asking or have any sense that he could answer. "What is it, Papa?"

"What is *what*, Emmy?"

"He's more than you think he is," she said, holding her head, blinking her eyes hard to clear her vision.

"He's a boy. I don't care how much he's traveled. He's a boy." The manner was matter-of-fact—much more frightening than his previous hostility.

"He's been on his own for six years," she said. "Working. On the road. He wants to settle down."

"He won't stay. The boys like him that come from Fayette, they're gone. There's not enough here for 'em."

She pressed her fingers against her temples; the dizziness was consolidating into an ache that threatened to pound her head to nothingness. She looked to her mother for moral support. Her mother had fallen asleep, sitting in the rocker. There was an utter stillness about her; it crossed Emmeline's mind that her mother was not going to live a very long time.

"Mama?"

Her mother opened her eyes, smiling. "Yes, dear?"

"No, it's not . . ." She was about to ask if her mother didn't think Matthew would settle down in Fayette, but before she could do so, her mother's eyes closed again.

"We'll have children," she said to her father.

"That don't mean he'll stay," her father said.

She stared at him helplessly. He didn't even know about the woman and child in Kansas! But Matthew had never promised that woman anything, never told her anything but that he was passing through! Matthew came in with the bottle, but she barely noticed as he got the cups and poured for her father and himself. He sat down at the end of the table, facing her father. She wished he would look at her; when her eyes met his, other matters didn't have the same power to affect her.

For a while the two men passed the bottle between them. The pounding in her head subsided to a steady, bone-squeezing ache.

"So," her father finally said, "you're not moving on with the road crew."

"That's right."

"How d'you plan to make your living?"

"I never had trouble finding work."

"Uh-yuh. But it's different out there. Out there everything's expanding. Here, it's . . ." He finished the sentence with his hands, drawing them together in a cupped position, until they were against each other.

"Don't worry about it," Matthew said irritably. The whiskey had not mellowed him as it had her father.

"Not worried, son. Just asking."

"We want to build a house before next winter," Emmeline ventured. "Matthew has been looking at land."

"Looking at land?" Her father took another drink. "Well, now, that's plain foolish. Why don't you build right down across the road and save your money?"

"Oh, Papa!" She ran around to the other side and gave him a joyous hug. "You're so good!" She looked at Matthew, who was watching her father speculatively.

"Matthew," she said, "my father wants to give us the land!" Why wasn't her headache going away?

"He didn't say nothing about giving it to us," Matthew pointed out. "He said I could put up a house on *his* land."

Her father laughed. "I'll deed it over to you, son, if you want it that way. It don't do me any good, just lying out there." He took a swig, directly from the bottle this time.

"What do you want from *me?*" Matthew asked.

"Well," her father said, "there's not enough cleared land down there for more'n a small vegetable patch. I s'pose I'd want for you to work this place with Andrew and me, when you're able. And then take your share of the food, too."

"How much time you talking about?"

Her father shrugged. "Well . . . if you have yourself other work, it's going to be less time . . . and when you don't, it's going to be more time."

It was so reasonable that even Matthew could find no objection.

"Why?"

"You mean why am I giving you the land when I wanted Emmy to take Simon Fenton?"

"He's too old for her," Matthew said. "He's nearly as old as you are."

Her father squinted at Matthew, and for a moment it was touch-and-go whether he was going to explode like a pot with its lid on too close. Matthew watched him calmly, but Emmeline couldn't. She got up and turned her back on them, looking at her sleeping mother.

The room was quiet. In the dim light, her head resting on the back of the rocking chair, Sarah Mosher's face looked unlined and peaceful. Emmeline felt a surge of overwhelming love such as she had not felt in years—since before she'd left for Lowell. But as she stood looking down at the loved face, the love was washed away by a rage that flooded her without warning and left her weak and dizzy.

She sank to the floor. Exhausted, she let her head rest on the folds of her mother's skirt, at the edge of the seat, and wept. Her mother, without waking, moved a hand so that it rested on Emmeline's head. It was almost weightless. Emmeline shivered.

The two men were talking quietly. They had reached some sort of peace, though Emmeline hadn't heard the words it was made of and didn't hear them now. She was too absorbed in some grief that had little to do with them, but was about her and her mother and the way it had once been between them. Once she had required little more than her mother's understanding to be comfortable. She had learned to do without it; to require it now would be like seeking comfort in one of the shadows she made as she walked along the road in late afternoon.

If only the hand resting on her head had a little more weight to it! With more weight it might have pressed away the terrible ache that threatened to crush her head from within! Before her mother had become a shadow, the assurance that Matthew was a fine young man would easily have outweighed her father's pessimistic view; now she needed something more. She was so tired.

She pulled herself up and went to Matthew. He was looking at a crude map her father had drawn of the piece of land on the other side of the road. The plot began at the path, just after the mica rock, which it did not encompass, and continued for perhaps a hundred and fifty yards. At most points it was so narrow that a house could not be built that wouldn't be dangerously close to the water. But at a point perhaps twenty yards up the road from the Mosher home, the road curved away from the pond, creating a broad patch that was at least twice as deep as what was required.

Her father was going to make over the land to Matthew, and Matthew would immediately begin to buy the materials. He claimed that within a few weeks of the time that the foundation was dry, he would have the floor, the outside walls, and the roof on the house. Then they could get married and move in and finish the remainder while they lived there. Her father professed great admiration for Matthew's ambitious project.

Her father put his head down on the table and was snoring a minute later. On the map of the land, Matthew began to draw a house. It had a pitched roof and an attic window. The drawing was so adept that it was hard to believe that the hand which had drawn it could not make the letters that constituted its owner's name. He turned over the paper and began sketching the interior.

Emmeline closed her eyes. She was half asleep. She could see the house, all built and painted white. There were two small children playing outside. Suddenly one of them ran toward the pond. She called to it to stop, but it wouldn't listen. When she opened her eyes, she was crying.

"We have to build a fence," she said.

"A fence?"

"I mean," she said, as reality began to compete with the dream, "later. . . ." But she was still crying.

"What is it?" he asked.

"My head hurts," she said.

He put the pen back in the well.

"Come on outside with me."

It was a warm, clear night in June. They walked along the road to the place where they would build. Blackberry bushes bordered the road, but there were few trees here, and the work of clearing wouldn't be bad. In the light of the moon and the millions of stars that filled the sky they could see clear across the pond—the outlined trees, the sawmill with its stacks of lumber piled higher than the building itself. Much closer to them, the light glinted off the mica rock. It all seemed unreal. She might have been looking at the machines in a Lowell mill, for all the pleasure she felt in the night or in Matthew.

"Why do you want to marry me?" she asked.

"Ain't that what people do?" he asked, without humor.

"But I'm too old for you," she said. "And I've never been anyplace except . . . You don't even know me!"

He took her in his arms and tried to kiss her, but she screamed; for a moment it seemed that he was a part of the vise that was holding her head. She broke from him and ran to the pond's edge, kneeling in the mud to splash cold water on her face, screaming again into the palms of her hands because in the second that she had been doing it before, her headache had been almost bearable. What she really wanted to do was to run into the cold water and let herself sink to the bottom.

"Come back here!" Matthew called.

"You don't know me," she said to the water, telling herself that she should say it louder so Matthew would hear. "You don't know that I've belonged to someone else, that I have a child." He wouldn't want her if he knew. She must tell him now or keep him from ever knowing!

He came up behind her and lifted her up and turned her around to face him.

"You don't know me," she said desperately. "You've never let me tell you about my life!"

"One person's life ain't that different from the next."

"That's not true!" she cried. "There are things that have happened to me—"

He pressed his lips down on hers, and finally she gave in and allowed herself to melt into him. She had been holding at bay some unknown enemy; she had no strength left to fight off Matthew as well. Nor could she force him to hear what he did not want to know. She let him lead her back to the clearing where their house would be, and she let him into her, and they lost themselves. And for a while it was possible to feel that he had drawn the unknown enemy away from her. To believe that she herself did not know the things she had tried to tell him.

IN the weeks that followed she was in a state of perpetual excitement. She was happier than she had ever been, yet anxiety never deserted her. The passion she was knowing with him for the first time in her life served only to make that anxiety more intense.

Now that he was her lover he became more loving, more temperamental, more demanding. He told her that she was more beautiful than any woman he had ever seen; that he had never loved anyone before; that with her, he felt he had "come home." And then the next day, as they ate lunch under the trees to shield themselves from the midday sun, or she brought a pail of water from the pond to where he was measuring for beams in the twilight, she would find him looking at her with what appeared to be anger, or maybe it was suspicion—as though she had gotten him to say those things against his will. Her very success at finding what would please him seemed to frighten him, while she worried only about the day when she would not be able to please him anymore.

Being with other people was torture, even when it was Andrew and Jane, who were their only close friends. Not that others were unfriendly. With the exception of Harriet and her husband, that was not the case, though Matthew often claimed it was.

Harriet made no bones about her disapproval of

Matthew, who appeared to represent, in her mind, the last of a series of outrages perpetrated by her older sister since their childhood. It sometimes seemed that Harriet had taken on for their father all those objections that Henry Mosher himself had abandoned after Matthew's show of strength. Harriet didn't like his looks. He was sneaky-looking. Shifty-eyed. (Emmeline had to repress a smile at the thought.) How could Emmeline have refused a man like Simon, whom she didn't deserve in the first place? It must have been purely out of spite for her family. (Business at the store had fallen off a bit, which worried Harriet, although she and Winthrop still made a good living. They had been looking to Simon for financing of a venture in carriage making, and lately Simon had lost interest, but Emmeline didn't know about any of that.)

"Come, now, Harriet," Emmeline said mildly.

"'Come, now, come, now,'" Harriet mimicked. She was in a fury such as Emmeline hadn't seen since Harriet had begun her own family and she herself had appeared to settle into a spinster's life. "You're so cool, Emmeline Mosher! You don't care for anyone! You never did! I'll never forget the day you went off to Lowell!"

Emmeline stared at her in astonishment. It had come out without hesitation, as though Lowell were an incident of twenty-one days ago, instead of twenty-one years.

"You were just as cool as a piece of ice on the pond! Everyone else was worried sick about you, but all you could think of was a chance to go to the city and get two new dresses!"

One, Emmeline corrected in her mind, but did not say, for it was clear that reminding Harriet of this fact would add a grievance to her ancient list, rather than redressing any of the old ones. Her mind couldn't even stay with Harriet's insane complaints. At the first excuse she ran across the road to the "new house." The foundation had been laid and the lumber for the floor ordered.

A festive atmosphere had come over the enterprise. No new home had gone up in about three years. Matthew's choosing to build in Fayette was taken as a hopeful sign even by those who were not particularly taken with him, or with the idea of Emmeline's marrying a boy who was not only young, but very much the outsider. The men, in particular, tended to get caught up in the details of planning and construction, often staying to lend a hand when they had only come by to observe. (Simon Fenton did not come by. It was rumored that he and Persis would marry, and that she had pressed for an early date but he was delaying.) The women kept a greater distance. Emmeline was somewhat estranged from her former close friends Rachel and Persis—from Rachel because she had broken her vow not to marry, from Persis because of the latter's jealousy over Simon. Once in a while Emmeline wondered how the two of them managed to stay so close in their anger against her, when the same contradictions existed between them.

But the truth was that she didn't give it a great deal of thought, because it was not about Matthew and therefore not truly compelling. If Rachel complained that *she* hadn't deserted *Emmeline*, it was rather that Emmeline had no time for *her*, there was some truth in this. For while Rachel didn't seek out Emmeline, or wait for her and Matthew after church, she might have been quite happy to have the lovers invite her to accompany them at some time.

This, of course, it did not occur to them to do. Their entire energies were directed toward each other. Everyone else was virtually an inanimate object— worse, an obstacle. When other people were around they couldn't touch each other constantly, as they needed to. They had to pretend to be listening to what was said, even when it wasn't said by him or by her and could not, therefore, be of any serious interest. Those who most earnestly wished them well also wished that they would get married and have children and be done with that intensity which made it so uncomfortable to be around them.

The floor went down, and the lumber for the frames was delivered. Matthew worked on the farm with Andrew and her father for half the day, then came back to work on the house. Tom Clarke was going to build them a chimney when he finished the one he was working on. The frames for the windows were set in, and they ordered the lumber for the exterior walls.

They set the second Sunday in August for the wedding. She dreamed that on the night before the wedding, her daughter, who had been in the West, returned and told Matthew who she was. Then Matthew and her daughter ran away together. Emmeline awakened sobbing, nor did being awake help very much, because it was dark, and she was alone in her bed, and the waking reality was that her child could indeed find her and destroy her happiness. Until now there had been no difficulty or disgrace she would not readily have endured in exchange for having her child return.

It had grown harder rather than easier to contemplate telling him. Where he had once been indifferent to Simon Fenton or any other man who might be interested in her, he now bristled at so much as the mention of their names. When Eben Varnum stopped by and, seeing their plans, suggested they buy lumber from Simon because the Fenton lumber was seasoned longer than that from the other mills, Matthew muttered something which Emmeline didn't hear, but which made Eben turn pale and walk away. She thought it was Eben's praise of Simon that had upset Matthew, but one night shortly thereafter, her father, in order to set a point in time, referred to the period when Elias Small had been courting Emmeline. Matthew grew rigid and wouldn't speak for the rest of the evening. A few days later something similar happened, except that this time the man in question hadn't been a suitor, but simply Isaac Davis, with whom she'd gone through several winters of school.

"What is it?" she asked as they walked to the new house a while later. The third wall was up. It was one of their standard excuses for getting away in the evening that Matthew had to show her what had been done at their house since she'd eaten lunch with him there. She expected him to tell her that his ill humor had nothing to do with her father's mentioning Isaac Davis.

Instead, he kicked a stick along the edge of the path and said, "He does that all the time."

"Does what?"

"Talks about them," Matthew said. "He don't miss a chance to—"

"Talks about who? Isaac Davis is someone who was in sch—"

"He does it to get me."

"Oh, Matthew," she said softly, "that's not true. He doesn't. He wouldn't. . . . I think he's come to be fond of you." Certainly her father had behaved well toward him since that night.

"That's a damned lie," Matthew said. Her heart skipped a beat; she had heard him use profane language with the men when he didn't know she could hear. This was directly to her and had the force of a curse. "If he had any way to do it, he'd get me out of here faster'n . . . You don't ever see what he's doing! You don't hear what he's saying when he talks to me! Fond of me! He'd be fonder of a rattlesnake he found in his bed in the morning!"

In spite of herself, she laughed.

"Nothing to laugh at," he said. "You coming?"

Slowly she moved to him on the path.

"I love you so much, Matthew," she said, "and I

cannot understand what it means to you for my father to mention a boy who was behind me in school, whose mother—"

"I don't want to hear about him!" Matthew shouted. "How come you don't understand that? I don't want to know about anyone you ever knew!"

*D*EAR *friends, we have gathered
here this afternoon to unite this man and this
woman in holy matrimony. This is an institution
ordained by God in the very laws of our being, for
the happiness and welfare of mankind. To be
true, this outward ceremony must be but a symbol
of that which is inner and real—a sacred union
of hearts that the Church may bless and the State
make legal, but that neither can create or annul.
To be happy, there must be a consecration of
each to the other, and of both to the noblest ends
of life.*

*Believing that in such a spirit as this and with
such a purpose you have now come, you may join
your right hands.*

They faced Pastor Avery at the altar. Emmeline
wore Jane's grandmother's wedding dress, which Jane's
mother and Jane herself had worn at their weddings.
Jane's grandfather had been a sea captain who brought
the material home from either Asia or Africa—no one
remembered any longer which—but it was a cotton so
smooth and shiny that it might have passed for silk, and
had lace trim of such an intricacy that none of the
women who had seen it thought she would be able to
duplicate the pattern. Matthew had bought his own

suit, though several men had offered him theirs.
Emmeline glanced at him and trembled, so beautiful
was he to her and so precious, with his unruly hair
wetted down and slicked away from his forehead, and
his gray eyes looking at Pastor Avery so that only the
dark lashes were visible to her.

Pastor Avery was a slender, handsome young man
with the look of a fawn in a clearing who has just sensed
that it is being watched. Yet on this day he seemed to
Emmeline to be endowed with a sacred majesty.
Adored by the Fayette matrons, he was said to
have been disowned by his father, an Episcopalian
minister in Boston, when he became a Baptist. In
his everyday speech he had a mild stammer, but there
was no sign of it now, beyond an occasional hesitation as he led them through the marriage vows and
Matthew placed the gold band on her finger. He pronounced them man and wife. Again they joined right
hands.

*Our Heavenly Father, who hast set the human race
in families, binding us together by these sacred and
tender ties, these, Thy children, have now, with
clasped hands and mutual pledges, taken upon
themselves these lifelong obligations. We trust that it
is indeed true that these outward acts only symbol-
ize a union of hearts already made sacred by the
love with which Thou hast bound them together.
From out of the innumerable multitudes of earth
these two have come, looked in each other's
faces, and are made one. Their converging path-
ways have united and henceforth are to be the
same.*

*If it be possible, may their pathway be ever easy
and pleasant beneath their feet. May the skies be
ever sunny over their heads. But if sorrow must
come—as it comes to all—let the pressure of trial
only bind them closer together. Let the experiences*

*through which they pass only make them more and
more completely one. . . .*

It was over. Her fears were gone—or at least they
had been relegated to her dreams. The author of those
words had understood how it was between her and
Matthew, which meant that people had had such
feelings before. This was reassuring, because she
sometimes felt as though she were adrift in waters that
were uncharted—or worse, unreal.

She looked at Matthew. He was staring at her as
though he'd never seen her before. He bent down to
kiss her and then yanked himself back upright—as
though until that moment he had forgotten that there
were other people in the church. Many were standing,
waiting for them to walk back up the aisle. There was a
low murmuring amongst the congregation. Her parents
were somewhere close by, as were her brothers and
sisters, but she couldn't see their faces or hear their
words.

They walked up the aisle and out of the church,
blinking at the bright sunlight as though they were
coming from darkness.

The grass in front of the church had been cut low,
and over to one side, several tables had been lined up.
All the Mosher women had been preparing food for
days, and covered pots and dishes were set out on
the tables, waiting until the crowd had worked up
an appetite by dancing. Matthew was leading her to
the path away from the church. The others were following, but he was walking too quickly for them—and for
her.

"Matthew," she laughed, "where are you taking
me?"

"Home," he said.

She stopped walking.

"You know we can't do that yet," she said, looking
up at him in wonder, aching with her love for him,

thinking, *What will I do if he insists?* She was sure that her will was no match for his.

"When can we?"

"There's dancing," she said, "and then supper. And then more dancing, but by then—"

People were pressing around them now, and for a while they were separated. The first cider of the year was broken out—too early, but it didn't really matter. Harriet moved through the gathering like a black cloud without ever managing to dim the sunshine, and Simon Fenton was considerate and pensive without being able to bring himself to directly congratulate the bride and groom. But it was a wonderful party.

After supper, Matthew was persuaded to take out his mouth organ, which had been in his back pocket all along, and with the two local boys who had been fiddling for the dancers before supper, he began playing again. Slowly the younger people, who had digested their food more rapidly, began dancing again. Shyly, Luke came up to her and asked her to dance. Happily, she kissed his cheek, and they began, but a moment later Matthew was next to them, taking her by the hand and pulling her away from Luke and the party.

Luke looked dazed. The people nearby were staring, but the others hadn't noticed.

"It's very early," she whispered as he pulled her along.

"We been there all day."

She laughed. "Not really."

He led her off the path into a small grassy area. They were less than a hundred yards from the festivities and could hear voices clearly, though she knew they could not be seen.

"This is wrong," she said.

He grinned at her.

She had no will. Once, after making love to her, he had told her that she could do anything to him that she wanted to do, but it was clear to her that *she* was the powerless one. He pulled her down on the grass, and she didn't bother to try to resist him for she was flooded—weakened—by the desire that she had never known before she knew him. When he began to make love to her, she protested, but her no's sounded like yeses to both of them.

They were happiest when they were alone, and as summer turned into fall, there was so much work that they seldom had reason, or energy, to be with others, except in the farm work with her family. Often they tumbled into bed before it was dark.

It was clear by now to everyone that her mother was not well, though Sarah Mosher never complained. Slowly her strength had left her. She seldom went outdoors and couldn't work in the garden, though she would still sit in her chair for hours, shelling peas, trimming beans, or cutting the stems and bad parts out of tomatoes to be put up for winter. Her husband's leg had healed but still gave him discomfort, and it was apparent that he would always have a limp. The heavy work of the farm was left to Andrew and Matthew, though her father still fed the animals, milked the cows, and did other simple tasks.

By the end of September the interior walls of the house had been finished. Like her parents', though smaller, the house had one large room downstairs, and an attic. Unlike theirs, it had a proper set of steps. The mattress brought over from the Mosher attic had been their only furniture. Now Matthew began building a table and benches. They argued about the size. He built a small table, saying that it would be more than sufficient for a while. She had wanted it to be the same size as her parents' because in her mind it was already filled with children. Once the first month of her marriage had passed, the dread of being pregnant had turned to eagerness that it would happen soon.

Matthew also bought—using up virtually all of his small remaining amount of money—a stove that burned both wood and oil. He was enormously pleased with the stove and said that if Tom Clarke didn't start their chimney soon, they would forget it. They weren't going to have him hanging around all winter. The way he said it made it sound as though Tom Clarke were arranging life so that he could spend the winter with them, but Emmeline didn't think much about it at the time. She pointed out to Matthew that a stove would not provide the light of a fireplace; he went out and spent the last of his money on four lamps and an additional keg of oil to keep them burning through the winter.

Then he began to worry about not having any money. He was accustomed, as he said, to having "some change in my pocket." One of the three taverns at the Corners had closed for want of sufficient traffic through Fayette since the advent of the Androscoggin Railroad. The owner of the second tavern was said to be considering going West, and Mr. Judkins had told Matthew that if that happened, he would need some help at his place. There was apparently some resentment that it was an outsider like Matthew who was being considered for the job, but the fact was that only a big strong young man could do the job—someone who could handle the men when they got rowdy from drinking—and Matthew was the best person around for that. In the meantime, he built a coop so they could keep their own chickens, because he didn't like the idea of having to go across the road every time they needed some eggs. He said that next spring he would build a barn onto the house as well. This didn't make sense, but she didn't argue with him, because there would be time enough to argue in the spring. Nothing ever seemed important enough to argue about now; their quiet times together still had the precious quality of those moments stolen from the others when she lived in her father's house. He built a cupboard, though they barely had the possessions to require one—a few pieces of clothing, some quilts, two pots, a kettle and some dishes. He and Andrew went hunting and killed four deer between them. Andrew and Jane got two of the deer, because of the children; Henry and Sarah got one, though Sarah never touched meat anymore; Emmeline and Matthew took the last. With the skin she made him a self-lined vest, which she interlined with a disintegrating quilt. She told him that the following year, when she got more hide, she would make sleeves for it and he would have a coat. He told her he wasn't accustomed to sleeves and wasn't sure he could work in a coat.

Tom Clarke showed up one day in November and said that he was ready to start the chimney. Matthew told him that he had no money left, clearly expecting that Tom would then refuse to work. Instead Tom said he'd just as leave work while the weather allowed, since he had nothing else to do. Tom was an old bachelor, in his late sixties, or perhaps seventies. He had lived in his parents' home all their lives and was there still, though they were dead. He had always been tall and wiry, but since their deaths he had gradually gained a considerable girth and was ruddy with drink, the veins in his nose as clear as the routes on Matthew's maps.

Emmeline and Tom were having midday dinner when Matthew came in from the farm. Matthew sat down with them but did not speak during the meal. He ate quickly, pushed away the dishes, got up and walked out of the house without a word. She followed him out.

"Is something wrong?" she asked. She thought maybe her mother was worse and he hadn't wanted to tell her.

"Why is he in the house?" Matthew demanded.

"Tom? He's just been hauling up stones and setting up to do the chimney."

"Why does he have to come in to eat? I don't want to come home and find you settin' with a stranger."

"I've known him all my life!"

"He's a stranger to *me*," Matthew said. "And I don't like the way he looks at you."

"Looks at me?"

"Never mind," Matthew said. "Forget it."

But he told Tom Clarke that he didn't want a chimney started until spring. His tone was defiant when he told Emmeline; he was sure she'd be angry, but she was only puzzled, and disappointed.

"I love to look at a fire," she said.

He promised that he would let Clarke . . . "or someone" . . . do the chimney in the spring.

Increasingly, Sarah Mosher spent her days, as well as her nights, in bed. She had little interest in food, grew thinner and thinner, but was peaceful. In the evenings, Emmeline went to sit with her for a while, so that Henry Mosher could get away, usually to the tavern, where Matthew was now working. It was easier for Emmeline than for any of the women who had children at home to spend the evenings with Sarah, and she readily took the greatest share of these watches, using some of the time to prepare the food her father would eat (her mother lived on milk and broth, now) and do the other household chores. It was when there were no chores left, or when she had only sewing, that the hours passed badly for her. Sitting in the rocker, which, no matter how many people used it over the years, had been and would always be her mother's chair, she felt a sadness so deep that she could not cry to ease it. More than she ever had in her adult life, she wanted to confide in her mother. More than ever, she wished that she had not made the terrible mistake of keeping secret what had happened to her in Lowell. The secret had put a barrier between them, and now that barrier would never be crossed. But night after night, as she waited for some sign that her mother was responsive to her, Emmeline, rather than simply to the fact of her presence, she felt instead that she was looking at the shell of a person who had already left for the other life.

She had been isolated from female companionship for most of the winter. Jane was limited as a confidante by her age and narrow experience. Emmeline had once tried to broach to Jane her anxiety about failing to become pregnant, and Jane had blushed and made some excuse to get away—as though she were not herself a married woman with four children! If only Emmeline could have one more chance with her mother!

As April began, the end seemed near. Her father wrote to the three boys in Nevada, as well as to any other living relatives on either side whose whereabouts he knew, including the Watkinses. Most were too distant to make the trip to Fayette, but the Watkinses wrote and said that they were planning to come.

Emmeline had not seen them in all the years since her return from Lynn, nor had she written since Hannah had convinced her that she did not know where the couple had taken the baby. At least once, her parents had gone up to Livermore to visit because the Watkinses were there, but Emmeline hadn't joined them. What would have been the point? They could only relive that painful time together. It was safer not to see Hannah; safer not to worry about concealing their secret from others.

Now, from the moment her father told her the Watkinses were coming, Emmeline was in a state of panic. She had arguments with herself in which she gave herself assurances which she never believed: it was Hannah's secret as much as her own; Hannah had not been without culpability; she had seen nothing in Hannah that would lead her to believe that her aunt would not want her to be happy. But the doubts remained: Hannah might think it was wrong of Emmeline to have married at all, after what had happened;

Hannah, in her surprise, might make a slip that would reveal all. Emmeline told herself that if the worst happened and Matthew learned the truth, he still would not leave her. He had told her, when she complained that he worked too late at the tavern, that she shouldn't be jealous, for he was someone else at the tavern and himself only when he was with her. If that was true, how could he leave? On the other hand, maybe he would stay on indefinitely without ever forgiving her!

That night she dreamed that a witchlike Hannah told Matthew before she herself even knew the Watkinses had arrived, and Matthew ran away before she could talk to him. She would never see him again.

She awakened, freezing and perspiring at the same time, terrified, groping for him in the darkness, but then not contented with only touching him. She got out of bed and lighted a lamp, then sat on the side of the bed, holding the light up to his face, taking it in. Not to *see* him again! She pulled in his features with her eyes as though the threat were real. She would have counted his lashes if only she'd been able to move the lamp close enough.

There was a smudge of dirt on his cheek; she wiped it away. He stirred but didn't waken. She touched his lips. When he was awake, his mouth revealed little, but it had an expression when he slept—almost, but not quite, a pout—which she liked to believe that no one else had ever seen. Now, as he slept, his lips parted so that her finger was between them. She let her other hand, holding the lamp, rest on her lap. She wanted to move, but she was afraid of disturbing him; her finger in his mouth made her feel safe. She closed her eyes, telling herself that she would only rest, not fall asleep, but after a while she drifted into a light sleep. The lamp fell to the floor at her feet.

The glass shattered, and both she and Matthew were startled awake. There had been little oil left, but what there was caught fire as it touched the floor at the

bottom of her nightgown. As she stared at it, dazed, he
scrambled out of bed and smothered the fire with his
pillow.

She began to cry. One of her feet had been burned,
but that wasn't why she was crying; she didn't even feel
it yet.

He raised the nightgown and peered at her foot in the
darkness.

"Wait here. I'm going to get cold water from the
pond."

"Don't go," she wept.

"Wait here," he repeated.

She crossed her leg, trying to see the burned foot in
the darkness. It was beginning to hurt. Where was he?
Surely he could have gone to the pond and back several
times by now. *Where was he?* Maybe he was angry with
her over this stupid accident and had run away altogether. She began to cry again and didn't stop until he
came in—a matter of minutes that could have been
days. He was dripping wet, because he had seen some
fragments of ice still floating on top of the water a few
yards from the shore and had waded out to fetch them.
Only she could know what it had meant for him to do
that; he couldn't swim, her strong husband who was
afraid of no one, and was so frightened of the water
that he never went more than a couple of feet deep into
it to bathe. He gently put her foot into the bucket,
pressing the ice gently against the burned skin. The
pain was getting worse, but she didn't cry anymore.

He lighted another lamp and placed it a few feet
away, where neither of them could knock it over, then
he wiped up the small amount of oil that had spilled on
the floor. He held her foot on the rim of the bucket and
examined it; the skin had not yet begun to disintegrate,
and it looked no worse than the smudge on Matthew's
cheek, though the area was considerably larger. He
cradled it in his hands and then, before plunging it back
into the icy water, he kissed the toes, the instep, the

skin around the burn. The pain was excruciating now, and even the gentle pressure of his breath near the skin made it worse, but she wouldn't tell him that for fear that he would stop.

When the ice had melted and the water grown almost tepid, he dried the rest of her foot and gently smeared butter over the burned area. Then he stacked their extra quilts and clothing, and his pillow, at the bottom of the bed for her foot to rest on. When her foot was still lower than her head, he put a log under the pile of soft things. The pain was somewhat diminished when her foot was that high; still, it was too great for sleep, and she remained awake for all of that night, and the next.

She was thirsty all the time. Matthew built a small table that was the same height as the bed so that she could reach the pitcher of water at any time of day or night. He brought her meals and changed the dressing on her foot twice a day, boiling water to wash the rag strips as he removed them. When it was necessary for her to get out of bed, he carried her. He wouldn't go to work, but told Mr. Judkins he would have to be out for a few weeks.

She was concerned about her mother. Matthew said that Harriet and the others, who'd done so little until now, could relieve her father at night. He was going to stay here with her until she could walk.

The skin had come off, and the foot was raw and ugly. He washed it several times each day so it would not "go bad." She must not go out of doors until the scab was formed, because she couldn't risk getting dirt in the open wound. She slept for short periods of time, mostly during the daylight hours. He tried to stay awake with her, and when he finally dropped off, she looked at him until her own eyes closed.

He talked to her more than he ever had. She had told him that she'd never seen a man care for anyone so

tenderly, and this evoked a series of memories. He told
her now that Kansas wasn't the earliest home he could
remember, but that he had been born in Ohio, whence
his parents had continued zigzagging generally west-
ward until they landed in the Kansas Territory. His
mother found the northern winters too hard to bear,
and Matthew had been a sickly child, plagued from
birth by a series of respiratory ailments. His mother
had feared for his life during the Plains winters, and she
was always pressing to head south, while his father was
convinced that the great opportunities lay in the
northwest territories. They'd always ended by compro-
mising—moving west; then north into Michigan; then
south into Indiana; then to Illinois. His mother had
never heard the end of it from his father. His illnesses
had cost his father untold opportunities to make a fortune, or so they both kept hearing.

Once, when he was five or six years old, Matthew
had awakened during the night, burning with fever and
so heavily congested that he could barely breathe, even
through his mouth. His mother had collected snow to
melt in the kettle for steam which would help him
breathe, and had awakened his father as she moved
around the cabin. His father had yelled and cursed and
then gotten dressed and stormed out of the cabin,
shouting that he was never coming back. For three days
Matthew and his mother had been marooned in that
cabin, believing him, watching the snow fall over land
that was known to be roamed still by the Black Hawk
Indians. By the fourth day, when his father stomped
back into the house, any feeling Matthew had ever had
for him was dead.

The scab formed slowly because there was so little
flesh on her foot. The pain went away, but Matthew
didn't want her to put pressure on it by walking,
because then the scab might break. She used her
father's crutches to move around. She wanted to see
her mother, but Matthew delayed her going up across

the road. He said that it wasn't as though she could do anything for her mother, who was in a coma, now.

On a Sunday when most of the family had assembled at the Moshers', Emmeline and Matthew finally made their way across the road and up the slope. The older children were kept outdoors until dinner time, but at the foot of her mother's bed Rebekah sat nursing her new baby, a sight that sent a pang through Emmeline. She looked at Matthew, but he had gathered into himself, as he always did in the midst of her family.

In general, there was a strange mood in the house. Sarah Mosher lay dying peacefully, and the men talked of nothing but the war. The news of Fort Sumter had reached them only a week earlier. President Lincoln had asked for seventy-five thousand Union volunteers, but most of those first troops would be from states closer to the conflict than Maine. On the other hand, it was only a matter of time.

Her father looked, with briefly unconcealed longing, at his wife, dying on the bed they'd shared for thirty-six years, and said that if he were ten years younger he'd join the first company that marched out of Livermore. Talk like that was in the air, and the younger men could not meet their wives' eyes when the women looked for the promise that they wouldn't go. When Emmeline heard about the volunteer call, she had asked Matthew if he would consider going, and he had laughed. His father was a strong abolitionist, ready to destroy the Southern states before he'd let them go their own way. He himself believed that they should have the right to secede if they wanted to; certainly he would not fight to hold them.

Between her father and Matthew there had been a cooperation perhaps no deeper or more genuine than the peace between the North and the South prior to Lincoln's nomination. With Andrew, Matthew worked the farm, and held his comments to himself when her father made too many suggestions because he could no longer actively participate. Then they met at the tavern, where the sentiment was overwhelmingly abolitionist and Matthew never took part in the discussions. Emmeline had chosen to believe that they had become fond of each other, but Matthew had gotten angry with her the one time she expressed this belief to him.

Now her father, who had been staring at Sarah almost as though he were in a trance, wrenched his gaze from his wife and said, with a sudden, forced jocularity, that he supposed Matthew would have to be the one to uphold the family's military honor, since he was the only one without a large family to support.

Emmeline stared at her father, stricken. His eyes went back to the figure on the bed. It was almost as though he had stirred up this tension to divert himself! She looked at Matthew, praying that he would be able to understand at least well enough to ignore the remark.

"Don't suppose I could do that," Matthew drawled, his speech closer to what it had been when he first came to Fayette than to what it had become a year later. "I might kill one of my wife's kin."

Her father, his pathetic offensive turned back, lapsed into silence. Everyone else was quiet for a moment too, and then there was a sudden burst of activity. Rebekah walked around with her baby, patting it on the back as though it had been crying. The other women checked to see if Harriet needed help, put out dishes, discussed bits of news that hadn't been interesting enough to remember until now.

But the day had been ruined. It was no longer possible to feel that it was all right for Sarah Mosher to die simply because she herself did not mind.

It was a beautiful day, but the clouds were moving rapidly and it felt as though there would be rain by night. After dinner, the men decided that with all of them there and rain coming, they should sow the first corn. Winthrop asked to be excused because he hadn't changed out of his church clothes, but they all knew that he considered it beneath his dignity to work in the dirt, and that Harriet did their vegetables with whatever help she could get from the children. There were knowing winks between the other men, and it seemed, as they went out, that they might be able to recover their good feelings at Winthrop's expense, but when the kitchen chores had been done, and Emmeline limped out to find Matthew, the men had finished planting the corn and were sitting in the back pasture, gloomily passing the pail of cold water among them.

Not too far back in the pasture stood a cow that had birthed less than two weeks before, and her calf. There had been two calves. This one had come out readily, while the second had been a terrible struggle to deliver because it was dead and had no force of its own. Matthew and Andrew had pulled it out of the suffering mother. Then, after they'd disposed of it, Matthew had come home and gone to sleep, not telling Emmeline about the calf for several days.

Now her father was talking about selling all the livestock and buying their milk from the Cranes. He said he had a mind to slaughter them all for the meat. The others paid him little mind, knowing that he was melancholy about Sarah.

They could hear but not see a wagon coming down the road, and then Judkins' new wagon appeared at the front of the house. Next to Ephraim Judkins in the front seat sat an elderly couple. Children materialized around the wagon from wherever they'd been—the barn, the pond, the house—curious to see who the strangers were, but Emmeline knew that it must be the Watkinses.

She had managed to push them so far to the back of her mind that it was almost as though they weren't really going to come, but now they were here. In fact, they seemed more real than everything around them; the house, the farm, the sky, her family had taken on a dreamlike quality. Hannah was sixty-two now, and Abner fifty-six. He had become round with age and was no longer dwarfed by his wife. They moved in an identical manner, getting down from the wagon with some difficulty, then picking their way up the slope through the dirt and rocks in a way that made it clear they'd spent their lives in the city.

Emmeline couldn't breathe.

"What is it?" Matthew asked, seeing that the color had drained from her face.

"It's the Watkinses," she said—almost deliberately misunderstanding. "My aunt and uncle from Massachusetts."

"So?"

"Nothing."

Her father had risen and was moving slowly down the hill. They would see that her father had a limp now; what would they see in Emmeline? Her heart was beating furiously. Had her father even mentioned in his letter that she had married? She'd meant to ask him, but she'd barely seen him since the accident to her foot. The truth was that before then she had considered writing to Hannah to tell her, but that same fear had always stopped her: Hannah would believe that it wasn't fitting for her to have married. Now Emmeline became frightened, then angry—ready to argue with Hannah for her right to Matthew, for the idea that she had done penance for long enough! As a matter of fact, she had wondered more than once whether, in her inability to conceive Matthew's child, she was not still doing that penance.

The adults moved toward the house, which her father and the Watkinses had entered. The children were being kept out while the Watkinses paid their respects to Sarah. Matthew was watching her.

"What is it?" he asked again.

"I love you more than I love my life," she said. "I love you more than I love heaven and earth and everyone on it. May He forgive me . . . I love you

more than I love God." She wanted to cry, but she
could no more cry than she could easily breathe. He
drew her to him and kissed her, but she had to pull back
from him because she was suffocating. She clutched his
hand and pulled him toward the house.

It was quiet inside. Hannah sat on the side of the
bed, holding Sarah's hand, speaking almost in a
whisper. Abner stood at her side, and beyond him
stood Emmeline's father, holding Rebekah's second
girl, who was four. Rebekah's baby slept on a folded
quilt on the long table, watched over by Harriet's oldest
daughter, a sweet, shy girl who was now ten.

Emmeline had almost asked Matthew to wait outside
so that she would have a chance to tell Hannah before
she saw him, but then something had made her afraid
to walk into that room without him beside her.

After a while, Hannah stood up and turned around.
She saw Emmeline and for a moment stared hard at
her. She had been crying, but now she smiled.

"Is it you, child? Emmeline?"

Emmeline smiled back tremulously. Of course Hannah would understand that this was another time;
nothing here had anything to do with what had
happened in Lowell.

"It's me, Hannah," she said. "But I'm hardly a child
anymore."

Hannah came toward her, arms outstretched, and
they embraced.

It's going to be all right, Emmeline thought. *She feels
warmly toward me.*

"I think about you every day of my life, Emmeline,"
Hannah whispered in her ear. "I'm sorry that it had to
come to this afore I saw you."

She released Emmeline and appeared to notice
Matthew for the first time.

Emmeline smiled. She was encouraged by Hannah's
warmth, but her fears had not yet been laid to rest.

"I'm married, Hannah," she said shyly.

"Well, for goodness' sake!" Hannah said. She was surprised but not displeased.

"We married last year," Emmeline said. "I meant to write you, but . . ."

"Well," Hannah repeated. "Well, congratulations, young man. You have yourself a fine . . ." She put her hand on Matthew's shoulder.

It was going to be all right.

"But I don't even know his name," Hannah said, turning to Emmeline.

"Matthew," Emmeline said happily. "Matthew Gurney."

Hannah's hand didn't move from Matthew's shoulder. Nor did her expression immediately change. The meaning simply went out of it, so that without any physical change, it went from being a smile to being a grimace. Then, after an eternity, it faded away.

What was happening?

The color had drained from Hannah's face. Emmeline could feel the others watching them; thank God they couldn't see Hannah's face. Even Harriet was quiet; something terrible was happening.

"Hannah," Emmeline said weakly. "Please . . ." Her head swam. Her worst fears were being confirmed and denied at the same time.

"Come outside with me," Hannah said. Her voice was shaking, and she hadn't regained her color.

Obediently, almost as though she were sleepwalking, Emmeline walked out of the house, pulling along Matthew. Hannah followed them, closing the door behind her. Without speaking, they walked down the slope, Matthew and Emmeline first, Emmeline clutching Matthew's hand as though for life, stumbling on ruts she'd known since she was a child. When they reached the road, Hannah turned to face them. But then her attention was caught by their clasped hands, at which she stared as though they represented a horror greater than anything Emmeline had been through or any of them could imagine. Finally the sheer force of that stare made them drop their hands.

"I can't make out what's happening," Matthew said.

"Who are you, Matthew?" Hannah asked.

"What d'you mean?" He was curious. If a man had challenged him this way he would have known how to react, but this was a chubby, gray-haired woman who'd been smiling at him warmly a few minutes before.

"Who're your folks?"

He shrugged. "That's who they are. My folks."

"What is it, Hannah?" Emmeline asked. "What are you doing?"

"Where're you from?" Hannah asked him, ignoring her.

"Kansas." He was still only curious, but Emmeline was growing distraught. The only thing that prevented her from being more angry was that Hannah herself was so horribly upset.

"Kansas?" Hannah repeated. "Just Kansas?"

"They moved around," he said. "Iowa before that. Ohio."

Hannah closed her eyes. "Before that?"

"Not sure. Pennsylvania. I think they started out from around Boston someplace, but they never told me. I just saw some papers in a book once . . . someplace in Massachusetts."

Hannah's eyes remained closed.

Very soon, Emmeline thought, her head would stop swimming and she would grow collected enough to be angry with Hannah over what she was doing. This was worse than anything she'd imagined might happen!

"How old are you?" Hannah asked. Her voice cracked as she spoke. Her eyes were still closed.

"Twenty-six."

Her eyes opened. "Is that true?"

He was silent.

Emmeline looked at him. His arms were crossed in front of him. He was defiant now, but no more than might have been expected.

"What is it, Hannah?" Emmeline pleaded.

"Are you twenty-six? Or are you younger than that?"

Matthew still didn't speak.

"Twenty-six?" Hannah repeated. "Or twenty-one. Almost twenty-one."

"Hannah! What are you doing?" It was a scream, but Emmeline didn't yet know why she was screaming.

Still Matthew said nothing.

Hannah's eyes were closed again. Her whole body was shaking. "October seventeenth," she said.

"NO!" Emmeline screamed. "NO! NO! NO! NO! NO!"

Hannah opened her eyes.

People appeared on the slope outside the house, but Hannah waved them away without turning.

"NO!" Emmeline screamed. "Tell her she's wrong, Matthew!"

"Why does it make such a difference?" Matthew asked. "Why do you care? Everyone thought I was too young. Everyone acted like . . . Your father said . . . I'm not too young! I've been on my own for seven years!"

"NO!"

"You know my folks?" he asked Hannah.

Emmeline looked at him one last time, then turned and ran down the dirt path to the pond.

"You'll hurt your foot!" Matthew called after her, but he was too uncertain to move after her. Hannah's eyes were closed; her body was swaying. He was still trying to understand what had happened. It didn't occur to him, until he heard Emmeline splashing in the water, that she had been heading into the pond, and by that time she was swimming.

He ran down to the shore, calling her, and when he saw that she was swimming out toward the middle, barely able to move her legs for the heavy skirts that swathed them, he waded in after her, shouting her name, yelling at her to come back. When she contin-

ued, he actually kicked off from the ground and swam
after her. But he had never swum before, and the best
he could do was to flail around in his heavy clothing and
shoes. When he gave up and let his legs stretch out, he
could still touch the bottom.

"Get help!" he shouted to Hannah. "Get someone
who can swim!" Emmeline was almost at the middle of
the pond by now.

"Emmeline!" he shouted desperately, "come back! I
can't swim after you! COME BACK!"

She couldn't hear him, nor would she have stopped if
she could. She was looking for the center of the pond,
that cool dark spot where, if your line was sunk deep
enough, you could pull up a few fish even in the hottest
days of summer. When she thought she had reached it,
she stopped swimming and let herself rest for a
moment, her arms and head above the water, her dress
pulling the rest of her down. She had worn no shoes
since her accident. She tried to tear at the skirts, but
couldn't get a strong enough hold on the fabric. Finally
she took a deep breath and plunged down into the
depths of the pond.

Her head was clear. She was looking for the bottom,
but her skirts billowed around her head and she had to
keep pushing them away. She pictured her mother and
father, Luke, Matthew . . . No. Not Matthew. . . .
Luke, Andrew . . . She saw her parents' house; she
saw the bedroom in the Watkinses' house where she'd
lived for more than a year and where she del . . . No!
. . . She saw her room at Mrs. Bass's; she saw her
young self, looking in the mirror at Mrs. Bass's, and
lying on her bed. She saw herself lying on the bed in
Lynn, her hands on her great warm belly with the baby
inside it, except that her face was not the face of her
young self—she looked the way she looked now, and
that was Matthew inside of her!

The skirts were winding around her head and she was
fighting them off, rising toward the surface at the same
time. She got clear of the skirts and tried to force

herself down again, but her lungs were near bursting, and against her will, her body was forcing her up. At the surface, she was still thrashing wildly, trying to plunge down, but with almost equal force, trying to reach the air. Her skirts fell away from her head and she was still thrashing, now without any aim, but the thrashing motions were carrying her closer to the far side of the pond. When her stomach and feet scratched along rocks on the bottom, she stopped moving her arms, and she floated, her head sometimes below the water, sometimes above it, to the shore.

She lay there for a considerable length of time, fully awake. She was cold, but she didn't care. Her foot hurt badly. It had scraped against the rocks on the pond's bottom and then along the dirt and pebbles at the edge. She didn't mind the pain. She had dragged herself onto the land not because she minded the cold water but because it was the natural end of her journey through the pond.

Her recent uncertainty was gone. She could see her life clearly, but the vision did not upset her; her brain was connected only to her eyes. She could see her mother braiding her hair twenty-five years earlier with the same clarity as she could see Matthew undoing the braids and spreading the hair over her shoulders—as though one had led directly to the other. She could see Harriet, ten years old, refusing to move over on the mattress so Luke and Emmeline could carry on the conversation they'd been having, and then she could see that same expression on the face of her grown sister Harriet, arguing that Emmeline should not embarrass the family by marrying the young drifter Matthew Gurney. Harriet fought for everything as though she expected to get nothing, and at thirty she had a permanent expression of outrage around her mouth.

Harriet will be bad to me now, Emmeline thought idly.

She saw Luke, who would never be bad to her,

though his wife had not been warm to Emmeline and she seldom saw them now. Then she saw Andrew and Jane. Jane was never unfriendly, but there was in her sweetness a childlike quality that might not stand testing. Emmeline wasn't certain of Jane.

Of course, she had not yet asked herself how *she* might be tested. Nor had she allowed herself to think of Matthew. That might force together her body and mind, and then she would go mad with grief.

It was Matthew who found her. The men had tried to make him leave, and he had said he would leave after they found her. Her father had told him Emmeline was drowned in the pond and taken down his gun from the wall. Matthew had said that her father could shoot if he wanted to, but that otherwise he would leave after he found Emmeline. Then he had begun walking around the pond, calling her name, sometimes looking out to the water, where the three men—Andrew and Luke and their father—were rowing around, looking for signs of her, sometimes moving away from the pond to look in the brush, where he was certain he would find her.

She heard him calling her name for some time before he reached her. She was lying on her side and she looked in the direction of the sound, but she didn't move or respond. He appeared between the trees; their eyes met first, as though these had been the magnets that pulled them together. He came to her side and knelt in the mud beside her. It was almost dark. Insects hovered around them.

One of the men had seen them, and now he called from the boat; it was the first she knew of their being there. Matthew didn't call back to them or look away from her.

"Was she saying the truth?" he asked.

She nodded.

"You lied to me," he said.

She had no desire to point out to him that he had not

let her tell him the truth—or even that he had lied to
her as well. For a moment she had the uncanny
sensation that he wasn't even talking about her own
past but about his, that he was accusing her of not
telling him when he was a child that he'd been adopted.

The men called again.

"Yes," Matthew called back. "She's here!"

He still hadn't looked away from her, but now a
gunshot sounded from close by on the water.

"I trusted you," he said. Then he stood up and he
was gone.

She could hear the oars creaking in the locks, the oar
tips swishing through the water. Then Luke pushed the
boat onto the shore while her father and Andrew came
to see what they still thought would be her body.
Andrew started violently when he saw her looking
directly at him.

"She's alive!" he called as though she weren't.
"She's . . . You awake?"

She couldn't speak, but she slowly pushed herself up
so that she was sitting. He drew back. She never looked
at him, or at the others, though she could see that her
father was still holding his rifle ready to use, if not on
Matthew then perhaps on the ghost of his daughter.
She looked down. Her dress was caked with mud and
with blood from the torn scab on her foot. With some
difficulty, she stood up. She faltered and expected that
Luke would reach out to steady her, but he didn't, and
then she realized that he didn't want to touch her. She
made her way to the boat. There were two benches in
it; she took the smaller one, sitting so that she would
face out to the pond, rather than in toward the men.

The water shone in the near-darkness. There were
one or two lights on the opposite shore, but she
couldn't make out the people holding them. She
thought perhaps someone was standing on the mica
rock, but she couldn't be sure. The trees were just

behind them. As the boat drew closer to the shore, she could see others.

"Dear God," said a woman's voice, "she's alive!"

There was no relief in it.

Someone stood at the shore with a lamp, but moved away as they came in with the boat. Emmeline was the first out of the boat. She climbed over the side and into the water without waiting for Luke to pull it onto dry land. Then she walked past the others and went to her house without looking to see exactly who they were, those people who had been waiting so eagerly to learn whether the men had been able to find her body.

SHE couldn't rest on the bed that was hers and Matthew's. She lay on the floor through the night, her sleep, if you could call it that, being little more than an extension of her waking memories, her life still passing before her eyes as though she were drowning. Her dress had never dried. By the following afternoon, when Andrew came to see how she was, it had dried some and stuck to the sore part of her foot, which hurt almost as badly as it had when it was first burned. Why hadn't Luke come? It was Luke who had been closer to her than anyone in the world until . . .

"You all right?"

He couldn't say her name or meet her eyes, but he could see her condition. Various thoughts went through her mind, some of which would have been answers if she had been able to connect her brain to her tongue. The second time he came—it must have been the next day—he asked her if she'd eaten, though it was obvious that she hadn't. He found the bread that was in the cupboard and then went to the spring, returning with a pail of fresh water. When he saw that she hadn't touched the bread, he told her that she should eat some. With some difficulty she broke off a piece, chewed it, drank cold water to help get it down. He saw that her filthy dress had fresh blood and pus on it wherever it had touched her foot, and told her that she must wash the foot, and that she must change her clothes and clean herself. Then he left. She went to the pond and waded into it, standing still until she could feel her dress come loose from the sore. Then she took it off and rinsed it out, using a clean part to wipe off her infected foot. She touched her hair and realized that it too was caked with dirt where she had lain in the mud, so she went into the water above her head, washed it, and came out, shivering. Back at the house she dried herself and put on her other dress, then carefully hung the old one on the line outside, thinking that the sky looked as though it would be months before it rained again.

At night Andrew brought her a bowl of stew.

"You understand everything?" he asked.

She nodded.

"Should I light a lamp?"

She shrugged—and was briefly confused, for it was Matthew's gesture, not her own.

Andrew set the lamp on the floor, where she still ate and slept. Her dress was raised so that it wouldn't touch the festering sore.

"Do you need something for that?"

She shook her head.

He paused. There was something he wanted to say, but it was difficult—even more difficult than coming here and talking to her, which until now had been the most difficult task in his life.

"They asked me to find out what you mean to do," he finally said.

She looked at him directly for the first time. He was standing just beyond the ring of light, and in the near-darkness his face seemed contorted beyond recognition—as though he were watching a hideous death.

"Do?" she repeated blankly, her voice coming out in a whisper because she hadn't used it in so long.

He looked toward her at the sound of it, then quickly away.

"What is there to do?"

"Good Lord, Emmy!" he exploded. "I don't know what you want from me! I'm just the one they—"

"They?"

"Papa. Everyone."

"They made you be the one to talk to me."

He was silent.

"Is there something they want me to do?" she asked, thinking that she must talk to Pastor Avery. She needed to be able to pray, if not for herself then for Matthew.

"They figured you'd want to go someplace."

"Go? Where would I go?"

"Don't know." His head was bowed and she could barely make out his words. "Somewhere where you're not . . . where they don't know."

"But I'll always know."

He was silent. He had no vocation as an advocate, and he was, of course, particularly miserable with this mission, which had fallen to him because in the entire family, he was the only one who could conceive of speaking to Emmeline. Their father, since the moment when Hannah, pale and trembling, had told him in halting language what had happened in Lowell, had been behaving like a madman. After bringing Emmeline back in the boat, he had gotten his axe, gone back to his barn, and begun to systematically chop down its walls without regard for the animals inside. There was no question of stopping him; he swung the axe when anyone came near. Within hours the front end and one side of the building were down, and the roof collapsed with them.

"Where's Luke?" she asked. "Does he want me to go too?"

"With his family."

As though she were no longer his family. On the contrary, his family was a fortress to protect him from her.

"Does he blame me too, then?"

"There's no one else to blame."

"But I didn't know! Neither of us knew! Doesn't that make a difference?"

"'Course it makes a difference. But it still happened."

Not only had it happened, but something else had happened years ago and she had lied to them about it, keeping up the lie for all these years. Andrew was being decent, but there was no softness in his decency, nor could there be, because it had happened. She had shamed the entire family, even though they'd had nothing to do with any of it.

"I'll be back one more time, anyhow," Andrew said when he left.

She ate the stew, sitting on the floor, looking at her surroundings for the first time since it had happened. It was as though she'd been away; everything was a little smaller and sparer than she'd have thought it. On the cold stove was a pot containing the beans she'd set to soak before going to her parents' for Sunday dinner—how many days ago? On one of the benches was a shirt of Matthew's, waiting to be washed. Ahead of her were the stairs, which stretched to the hemlock crossbeams upon which the attic floor would be laid. Would have been laid. The first pine boards were stacked under the stairs. On hooks next to the front door were his deerskin vest and her woolen shawl. She took them from their hooks, carefully folded the vest, wrapped it in her shawl, and put the bundle in the cupboard. Then she blew out the light so that she was in darkness again.

Through the window she could see a full moon over the pond. She went outdoors, hearing the frogs and crickets as though they were making new sounds. She walked to the mica rock and climbed onto it, looking up toward her parents' house, thinking of her mother for the first time. Thinking, *Thank God she doesn't have to know!*

There was a lighted lamp flickering somewhere

inside. What was happening up there? She hadn't thought to ask Andrew about her mother's condition. Would he have told her if it was worse? If her mother had died? Without hesitation, she climbed off the rock and walked across the road. If her father was inside she would turn and run. But there was a light in front of what had been the barn, and that was a hopeful sign. It could only be her father or Andrew.

In fact, it was both of them, sitting on chairs near the wrecked building. They could not bear to be in the house all the time and could no longer show their faces at the tavern. The whole town knew. Each of the women had told her family and one close friend. If they carried such a burden in silence, it might appear that they were sympathetic to Emmeline. If only they had known, they said to each other. All these years she had hidden the truth from them. There was a devil in her, and a power to deceive that was a gift of the devil. They drew close to each other, many closer than they had ever been. Harriet became their temporary leader because she alone had never trusted Emmeline, although others could summon up times when they had been angry with her. None of them could bear to be alone at night, and if one of the men went out, he had to first fetch another woman to stay with his wife.

Jane was alone in the house with Sarah Mosher, but she knew that Andrew and his father were close by. Jane sat in Sarah Mosher's rocking chair, awake, though her eyes were closed. On another such quiet night, she might have drifted into sleep, but no one of them drifted easily into sleep these days. Wakefulness had spread through the town as though they must all be on guard for other crimes. Nightmares hovered over family and friends alike, waiting for them to lose the strength they had when they were awake.

Emmeline walked to the far side of the house so the men wouldn't see her and climbed the steep dirt bank without regard for her clothing or for her foot. But when she reached the top, she brushed off her dress and smoothed away the hair from her face. Then she peered in. Her mother's hands rested one upon the other, looking arranged. Was she alive? Her body was so still that it was impossible to tell, yet Emmeline thought that she was. Jane appeared to be sound asleep in the rocking chair.

If she opened the door with extreme caution, and tiptoed through the room . . . she might be able to kiss her mother and leave without awakening Jane. Even if she did awaken her . . . the worst that could happen would be that she would be forced to leave without the kiss. She could almost feel the soft skin of her mother's forehead on her lips.

Slowly and carefully she opened the front door and set one bare foot inside the room. Jane's eyes opened and she screamed. Emmeline turned and ran down the bank and across the road, reaching it before the men had gotten to Jane. In her house, she bolted the door, which was difficult, for the bolt had never been used and was stiff and unyielding. Then she sank to the floor and cried. She was still there when Andrew knocked at the door.

"Who is it?"

"Me. Andrew."

With some difficulty she rose, unbolted the door and set it ajar. Then she went to the window and looked out, her arms resting on the sill. The moon was still there, as though nothing had happened.

"You scared her," Andrew said.

"I saw that," Emmeline said. "I'm sorry. I wanted to see Mama."

He was silent for a moment. Then he said, "Papa says to tell you he'll kill you if you go there again."

She turned to peer at his face in the darkness because she couldn't believe that he meant it. Then she turned back to the window, understanding that he did.

"How's Mama?" she asked.

"She's going," Andrew said.

Emmeline began to cry again.

In fact, her mother had died, though no one yet realized it. Perhaps Jane's scream had snapped the fragile chain of heartbeats. Jane and the two men had left the house briefly to talk outside, and then Andrew had come down to speak to Emmeline. No one yet knew.

"You'd best go," Andrew said.

"I don't know if I can." Where would she go? How would she know where to go so that she would not stumble onto Matthew before either of them could bear it? *Where would she go?* "I don't know . . ." She started to say that she didn't think she could leave while her mother was dying, but at that moment there were loud shouts from the other side of the road—her father calling Andrew.

He left her house and didn't return until the following day, when he told her that their mother had died. She sat down and closed her eyes. He waited. She said that she supposed that if her father wanted to kill her, she would not be permitted to go to the funeral, and he said that was so. She asked if she could talk to the Pastor, and he said that the Pastor would speak to her after the funeral, but not before.

"Oh? Who made that decision?" Probably Harriet. "Never mind," Emmeline said wearily. "Never mind. I won't go."

"Have you thought any more on what we talked about?" he asked after a while.

"About leaving? No. I haven't thought about it. I've been thinking about Mama."

"Do you have money?"

She shrugged. She didn't know whether Matthew had had his earnings in his pocket when he left, or whether there was something in the cupboard.

"We're not telling you to leave without a cent," he said. "We'll put together what we can to give you a start in a city."

"That's very kind of you," she said.

He had no use for her irony. Jane had taken the children and gone to stay with her parents on the other side of Fayette, saying that she would not come back while Emmeline was there. Jane had burned her wedding dress, telling him that she felt ill when she thought of Emmeline's wearing it. Rosanna and Rebekah had retreated to their homes in Livermore and would return for their mother's funeral, but not after that. Luke and his wife were considering a move to Chesterville, and Harriet and Winthrop were talking about Portland or Boston. Uncertainty about the war kept them from making more concrete plans. In their daily lives there was little sense of change, but men passing through town talked about nothing else, and you could hear a rumor to support any suspicion you might have. Some said the fighting would never come farther north than Virginia, while others were convinced that the Confederate troops were already making their way up the coast toward New York. In Livermore a company was being raised for the Eighth Infantry, and men were being recruited from Fayette as well as the other neighboring towns. Between themselves, Andrew and Luke talked about joining to defend the Union, but felt they couldn't leave because their wives had a claim beyond that of other wives, having married into a family with a name that now shamed them. Of them all, of course, it was Harriet who was most actively at him to get Emmeline to leave, and most hysterical in her insistence that she could not herself speak to her sister. Born between Luke and Harriet, Andrew had never been fond of his younger sister and had spent much of his life as a child dodging her to tag after Luke and Emmeline. If circumstances had brought him closer to Harriet now, that only increased his anger at Emmeline. Why could she not spare them a small part of the misery she had created?

The funeral would be the next day. She asked Andrew to tell Reverend Avery that she accepted his offer to speak to her at a later time, and to ask him also whether she should come to the church or he would come to her house.

"You can't . . ." Andrew started to say, but changed his mind. "All right," he said. "I'll ask."

She found her Bible and sat with it under the window, meaning to read in it the psalms that her mother had loved. But the very act of opening the book, of touching its pages, knowing that her mother was gone, created a groundswell of grief which threatened to dissolve the very boundaries of her being. Quickly she stood up and put aside the Bible, looking around the room.

Why hadn't she told her mother?

If she had told her mother . . . long ago . . . upon first returning from Lowell, not only would she have had the comfort of her mother's confidence, but then perhaps Hannah would have been willing to let her mother know the last name of the couple who had taken the baby, and then . . . But she could think no further than that. It was easier to contemplate living what was left of her life without being spoken to by any member of her family than to imagine not having known her son.

She straightened up the house, getting water from the pond to do the dishes in the sink and to wash Matthew's shirt. The spring water on her father's land would no longer be available to her. She would have to walk through the woods to the next stream she knew to find drinking water.

There were comings and goings on the road. At one point she looked out the window and saw her father's wagon leave. Later it returned. The next time it left she saw Andrew and Luke sitting in the back, and something about their positions made her realize that their arms were resting on her mother's coffin.

She couldn't stay here. Not now. Suddenly the house was a prison rather than a refuge. She went to the door

and looked out across the pond. It was a warm day near
the end of May . . . or perhaps it was June. Time had
gone back to the condition, endless and unmarked, that
it had held for her when she was very young. Perhaps
when she saw Andrew again he would be willing to tell
her which day it was and she could keep track from
there. Not because it mattered, but because there was
something frightening about not being able to know.
The thought of having to find her own food didn't
dismay her, and she could tolerate the lack of
companionship . . . she had been lonely for so many
years . . . but the absence of a way to measure time
made her future seem like a massive black cloud that
would never break for rain or let the sun shine through.

Why shouldn't she leave? Not just for a while, but
really leave? If she could leave for an hour, why not a
week? A year? Longer! She would make her family a
little less miserable and herself probably no more so.

She would leave immediately and spare herself the
grief of sitting in this house alone while the rest of
Fayette mourned for her mother.

It wasn't going to rain for at least a few hours. From
the cupboard she took the satchel in which Matthew
had carried his goods. It crossed her mind that she
should leave a note so that if he returned, looking for
his possessions, he wouldn't be angry with her. Then
she smiled, remembering that he couldn't read, though
in recent months he had begun to distinguish some
letters. (If he became aware that she was watching him
do it, he pretended to be absorbed in something else.)

Into the satchel she put her clothing, the loaf of
bread Andrew had just left, the vest wrapped in her
shawl, Matthew's maps and pens and knife, and the
Bible. There was almost ten dollars in bills in the
cupboard, and she took that along with the change,
because somewhere she really knew that if Matthew
came back, it would be after a very long time.

She looked around the room once more. On the wall
over their bed Matthew had drawn a map whose center

was Fayette, and which went east just as far as the
Kennebec. It showed little directly north of Fayette,
but the southern area was filled in, and off to the west it
traced both the Androscoggin and the Little Androscoggin rivers to their final points in Maine. She had
written in the river names, as well as those of the towns
she could identify, and it was on this wall that Matthew
had begun to make out letters. Her father had been
impressed in spite of himself with the accuracy of the
map, which he compared to ones he had from Simon
Fenton. The rivers were blue, the town names red.
Matthew had even drawn the neat bridge over the
Androscoggin that made it possible to go from East
Livermore to Livermore Falls.

She would not head in that direction. The road was
full of the homes of people she knew. Lewiston, which
had become a mill town, would be a natural destination, but she couldn't really think yet in terms of a
destination, or what she would do when she reached
one. She only knew that she was going to leave Fayette.
The road to Lewiston was long and forbidding, and she
would have to cross a railroad line to get there. It didn't
occur to her that she could get on a railroad train; it was
the process of leaving Fayette that absorbed her. She
finally decided to head directly south to Wayne and
then on to Litchfield, which was little more than a name
to her. Then, without thinking any longer, she left the
house.

When she found herself on the road outside of
Fayette, she was surprised to realize that the sun had
already gone down. She stopped to rest for a while. She
had no sense of urgency, because she had no destination, and no sense of danger along the way. As she
began walking again, a man came by on a wagon and
offered her a ride. He was unsavory-looking, with few
teeth left and a scarred cheek on a rough, young face.
When she refused his offer, he asked if her satchel
wasn't too heavy. She said that it was not. He was

reluctant to start up his horses again, eyeing her as though there were some particular orneriness in her refusal to ride with him, but she just looked back at him without moving or speaking, and after a short while he moved on.

Here and there she passed a house, sometimes two or three together. As it grew darker there were lighted lamps visible in some of them. She found herself wondering who lived in them—whether there were people inside she had known, or who knew her. She didn't know how it would feel to be with people who did not know what had happened to her, although it seemed that it would be different in some way. What Andrew had said to her had made her think for the first time of what the rest of the town must be saying.

Occasionally, where there was a stream lighted by the moon, she took some water and a piece of bread. Sometimes she dropped off for a short while into something that was not sleep, for she was aware of every sound around her, but was more restful than being awake. Then she continued on, through Wayne and into unknown territory, well into the night, until, when she passed houses, there were no longer any lights.

While it was still dark, she passed a house where there were lights and activity in both the house and the barn. A woman appeared at the barn door, holding a lantern, and made her way around to the front of the house, pausing on the doorstep.

"Someone there?"

It was a deep, strong voice, close to a man's.

"Yes," Emmeline said, stopping only a few yards away. "I'm going to Litchfield."

"Litchfield? At this hour?" The woman held her light higher. "Come here, child."

"I'm not a child," Emmeline said, coming forward. "It's only the light." *I'm not a child. I have a son who's a man.* She stumbled, and the woman reached out to keep her from falling.

"Yes. 'Course. Do y'know how far you are from Litchfield?"

Emmeline shook her head.

"Do you want to tell me where you're from?"

"Fayette."

"Well," the woman said brusquely, "come in, if you want. Take some food. Rest."

"You're very kind," Emmeline said. "Will I be keeping you?"

"No," the woman said. "You'll be keeping no one. There's sickness in the house and there's sickness in the barn. I've had all the sleep I'm going to have, one way or the other."

Her name was Frances Turner. She lived with her sister and their father, all the brothers having left over the years, the youngest having recently joined the First Maine Cavalry. They'd always kept a few horses, but sheep was where they made their living, and the reason Emmeline had found her awake at this hour was that some malady had brought down about half their flock and she was scared to death of losing all the sheep. This at a time when her father was old and ailing and her sister, who was only a couple of years older than she, had been running a debilitating fever for weeks. As she spoke she moved her hand in front of her face, as though she were brushing cotton from her eyes.

They had tea together, and corn pudding, which was a favorite of Matthew's.

Why did every word, every object, evoke some memory of him? It was far worse than when she'd been at the house!

"If you want to stay awhile," Frances Turner said, "there's plenty of work here."

"You're very kind," Emmeline said.

"Not being kind. I can use the help."

Emmeline hesitated. It was tempting. She had been walking since the previous afternoon, and she had gained a reasonable distance from Fayette.

"You're not in trouble?" Frances Turner asked. "Don't mean to pry," she added quickly. "You can stay, no matter."

Emmeline looked at her closely for the first time. She had a strong, kind face, with keen blue eyes and the kind of deep brownish-red complexion you saw on men who worked outdoors the year round.

"I've been married," Emmeline said. "I have a child."

Frances waited.

The man I married was . . . She rose from her seat, as frightened as though it had tumbled out of her lips.

"I think I'd better go."

Frances was startled. She looked up at Emmeline with a combination of curiosity, concern, and disappointment, but she said nothing.

When I was still a child who had never slept a night away from my brothers and sisters, I was sent to make a living in Lowell, where my employer was kind to me and I did not understand why he was being kind. . . . No . . . that isn't true. It was Mr. Maguire's nature to be kind, but it was not his nature to take sufficient care of me, and . . .

Her mind snapped closed. She could not bear the look of compassion in the other woman's eyes. If she stayed here, she would melt under it.

"I'm sorry," she whispered. "I have to go." And she took her satchel and fled from the house, in her confusion taking a few strides north toward Fayette before she realized that she was walking in the wrong direction.

The sun was rising. The sky was clear. It would be another sunny day. She found herself dreading the light, wishing that she could travel a little farther under cover of darkness. She was badly shaken, for it hadn't occurred to her that she would have to deal with strangers and that she would have difficulty in knowing how. Worse, that she would have an overwhelming desire to confide in a woman she hadn't known for half an hour. Was it to be that way with every stranger, or was it only the newness of the journey and the sympathetic quality of Frances Turner?

As the sun rose higher she left the road and walked on the far side of the bordering bushes where she was partly shaded by trees. Wagons and mounted riders were passing now; when she heard them coming, she sank to the ground so they would not see her. She needed to rest but was afraid if she did she would fall asleep. She realized that she would have to go farther away than she had anticipated, far enough from home so that she wouldn't worry all the time about being discovered.

The sun was almost overhead when she succumbed to exhaustion and went deeper into the woods to find a resting place.

Not far ahead of her there was a low stone wall behind which the forest became an orchard. On the far side of the road a large herd of Holsteins grazed on a piece of land so immense that it had been some time since she had passed the house and farm buildings of its owner. Both the farm and the orchard were well tended, like the big farms in Fayette. The apple trees were in full leaf here; it seemed to her that they'd not yet come into their leaves at home, but then, she'd been unaware of her surroundings for a number of days. Suddenly she saw herself standing on Moose Hill with Matthew, looking out over the neighboring farmlands and talking about where they would build their home. With a scream, she dropped the satchel and whirled around, her palms pressing into her eyes as though she could push away forever the pictures she could not bear. Instead she became dizzy and fell to the ground.

When her head had cleared somewhat, she looked around her. She wasn't where she'd meant to be when she stopped. The stone wall was a few yards away, and she'd intended to lean her satchel against the wall, then

use the satchel as a pillow. But when she looked at the
distance between her and the wall it might have been
miles, for all the chance there was that she could get up
and cross it. Her body ached all over, and her feet were
cut and bleeding because she'd been walking barefoot.
There had been no way to get on her boot over the
swollen, infected foot. She reached for the satchel and
pulled it toward her, meaning to place her shawl on top
of it, but before she could get open the leather ties, her
head was on the satchel, and almost instantly she was
asleep.

The sun moved across the sky. In the afternoon it
was covered by clouds for a while, and the air became
cool, but Emmeline, sleeping deeply, never noticed.
The clouds moved on and the air became warm again.
The sun went down.

She was in a forest like this one except that the trees
were pine instead of birch and hemlock. She was with
someone, though she couldn't tell who it was, and they
had some task to perform which was important without
being unpleasant. They were near water—a pond, but
narrower, and the water moved rapidly. Strange objects floated in its stream—not strange, but objects one
didn't see floating on water: a bed, a basket; a map; a
clock. The man beside her—was it her father or was it
Luke?—used a long stick, trying to tow in some of the
objects for her, but every time he was close to success,
he had to move along to another place on the pond.
The chickens were clucking to be fed. Harriet, wearing
her mother's dress, was yelling at her because she'd
neglected them. Harriet held up one of them to show
Emmeline that it had starved to death. It was stiff and
hideous, and when Emmeline did not respond properly, Harriet threw it at her. Emmeline saw her
mother's empty rocking chair and began to cry. The
man picked her up as though she were a child and
brought her to another place, where she stopped

crying. She *was* a child. She was cold. He covered her so that she couldn't see his face, and she began to cry because she couldn't breathe. Someone was singing, but it wasn't her mother . . . or any person, actually. It was a ghostly sound . . . as though the wind were whistling through a mouth organ. Now she was in another bed, lying on her side, curled around her baby. The sheets were made of some extraordinarily soft material, perhaps percale, like the Maguires' sheets. The pillowcases were embroidered. At the foot of the bed there was a soft blanket, but she didn't need it because she was very warm, although she was naked. Her long hair was draped over her shoulder and covered the baby. She touched the soft spot at the top of his head, kissed his downy hair, then the indented place in the back of his neck. It was soft beyond any softness she had ever felt. Gently she turned him in the bed so she could see his face. He was Matthew. She began to cry, and this time there was no stopping.

When she awakened she was still crying. She looked around her, but before she knew where she was, she had grabbed her satchel and made her way back to the road. Her head throbbed. The dream still had the force of reality in her mind; the real world was muted. Without hesitation she began walking back toward Fayette. She accepted each time a ride was offered to her, and then walked the last mile into Fayette and around the pond. She was in her home by late that afternoon.

THE next morning she began breaking up the earth on the south side of the house for a garden. None of the chickens had died, though they were wildly agitated and had broken several eggs in their excitement. She could be grateful now that Matthew had insisted upon building their own hen house. There were three roosters, twenty hens, and more than a dozen chicks. As she broke up the sod, she shook loose as much earth as she could, then piled the rest on the spot beyond the coop where they had been dumping the chicken manure for use the following year. There would be no fertilizer this year, but it probably wouldn't matter because it was the first time anyone had planted there. She was thinking that Andrew could not refuse to bring her seeds, if they were all she asked for, when she saw Pastor Avery coming down the road on his horse.

He hadn't yet seen her. He dismounted and looked around as though trying to decide from which tree he and the horse would be able to make the fastest retreat, settling on a cluster of birches, around which he tied the rope. She set the shovel against the house and wiped her face on her skirt. He hadn't seen her yet, and she was glad of the chance to observe him first; it was helpful to her to see how nervous he was, because it reminded her that it was another human she had to deal with.

"Good morning, Reverend Avery," she said.

He looked up, startled.

"Good morning, uh, Sister Mosher."

"Is my marriage dissolved, then?" she asked.

"Yes," he said. "Yes, of course."

Her hand went to the neck of her dress, under which her ring hung from a strip of cloth.

"Yes," she said. "Of course."

They were silent. He looked at the ground. Something about the way he clutched his Bible made her remember the thirteen-year-old Emmeline, clutching her piece of mica as she left for Lowell.

"Would you like to come in?"

"No," he said quickly. "No, thank you."

She waited.

"Do you know why I've come?"

"Because I requested it?"

"No," he said, obviously surprised. "I didn't know that you requested it."

"Oh. Well, then, I imagine you've come because you know I need spiritual guidance."

He said nothing.

". . . Or on my family's behalf."

"I didn't know," he repeated. "I had no reason to believe that you would want me to come."

"You have no reason to believe I'm Godless," she said.

"You have committed two grave sins," he said.

"I didn't know!" she cried out. "The first time I was a child! I didn't even know it was *possible* for me to sin! I thought only evil people sinned. I was never even on guard!"

He took a deep breath, and she was relieved to see that his face was moving through various expressions, even though she couldn't decipher them. It meant that he was hearing what she was saying, rather than listening without hearing, as Andrew had.

"I had seen the word adultery in my Bible," she

continued, pausing as he blushed deeply. "When I asked my mother what it meant, she told me I would know when I needed to know."

His hands were at his chest, the Bible clutched between them. She pitied him, but she had determined that she would never again say less than the truth.

"I was thirteen when I went to Lowell," she said. "I had no friends. My employer was kind to me. It never occurred to me that he would let me do anything wrong. He was like a father to me."

"He was a married man?"

"He was a married man. More than twice my age. I didn't know what I was doing. I loved him, but I was without passion."

He closed his eyes. *"If a soul sin, and commit any of these things which are forbidden to be done by the commandments of the Lord; though he wist it not, yet he is guilty, and shall bear his iniquity."*

"I do bear it," she said after some time. "I bore the loss of my child. Twice I have borne that loss. I vowed to deny myself a husband and other children. For years I lived and worked for my parents."

"Why didn't you tell your mother when you returned? Why didn't you confess to your pastor?"

"When I returned, the Pastor kept changing," she cried. "And I wanted to tell my mother; I gave her opportunities to ask me what had happened. But when she failed to . . . I thought she couldn't bear the truth. I'm not lying," she said steadily. "It was more for her sake than for mine."

He walked away from her, down to the edge of the pond. She herself walked to the mica rock and sat on it, waiting for him to speak to her again. Finally he turned to face her, his legs apart, his hands, holding the Bible, behind his back.

"Your sister believes," he said slowly, "that you knew when he came here that Matthew Gurney was your son, and conspired with him—"

"You needn't tell me which sister," she interrupted with unconcealed bitterness. "Only one could have dreamed of such a thing."

But she had dreamed she saw her baby's face and it was Matthew! She looked away.

"Do you want to save your soul?" he asked after a long time.

"Yes," she said. "Of course. But I do not believe that I will save it by leaving Fayette."

"Because he hath despised the word of the Lord, and hath broken his commandment, that soul shall utterly be cut off; his iniquity shall be upon him."

"Will that not be true if I remain here?"

"Yes," he said. "The Church has already voted to exclude you."

"Then my penance is served if I stay here."

"Yes, but—"

"But that does not satisfy my family. They think they will manage to forget me if I go. Perhaps they'll pretend that I don't exist, that I succeeded in drowning myself in the pond. Isn't that a sin? It's a lie, certainly."

"You have given them great pain."

"I have lost everything in my life that I held dear."

"You could begin a new life. Nowhere in the Bible is it written that you must suffer eternally. *'The Lord is generous and full of compassion; slow to anger and of great mercy.'"*

She smiled. *"How shall we sing the Lord's song in a strange land?"*

"You are clever, Sister Mosher," he said. "But you must not use the Lord's word to justify that which you have decided to do for your own purposes."

She was ashamed and was silent for a while. Then she said, "If I go to a strange city, I will have to lie. If I tell the truth, I will always be sent away."

He came and sat down on the rock, facing out to the pond, as she did. The sun sparkled off the water. It was so beautiful and she loved it so much, that at that moment she was not certain that anything was a punishment that allowed her to stay.

He said, "Let us pray." There were tears in his eyes. They knelt on the ground.

Have mercy upon me, O God, according to thy loving kindness; according unto the multitude of thy tender mercies blot out my transgressions.

Wash me thoroughly from mine iniquity, and cleanse me from my sin.

For I acknowledge my transgressions: and my sin is ever before me.

Against thee, thee only, have I sinned, and done this evil in thy sight: that thou mightest be justified when thou speakest, and be clear when thou judgest.

Behold, I was shapen in iniquity; and in sin did my mother conceive me. . . .

My soul melteth for heaviness: strengthen thou me according unto thy word.

Remove from me the way of lying: and grant me thy law graciously. . . .

Make me to go in the path of thy commandments; for therein do I delight. . . .

Let my soul live, and it shall praise thee; and let thy judgments help me.

I have gone astray like a lost sheep; seek thy servant; for I do not forget thy commandments. . . .

When he finished, she was crying. He arose.
"I wish you well, Sister Mosher."
She remained on the ground, weeping.

She was still there, though she was calm, when Harriet, having heard from Pastor Avery the results of their meeting, finally came to speak to her in a cold rage.

At the sight of her sister, Emmeline's peace vanished. She tried to remember the words of the Pastor's prayer, but her mind was blank. She wanted to stand, but her legs were cramped and she was afraid she would be unsteady. She had seen Harriet aspire to majestic fury before, but not achieve it; some childish pettiness had always taken away its power.

"I didn't come because I wanted to."

Emmeline nodded.

"No one else would do it. They're afraid of you." Harriet was trembling. She was afraid, too. "You're like a witch. Worse. You've ruined my whole life. Everyone's."

Of course. When she remembered the list of complaints Harriet had had about her even before this . . . By her very existence, by having been born first, by being so close to her mother, she had always spoiled things for Harriet. And now her sister, who wanted so badly to hold herself above her neighbors, could not face them at all.

"I'm sorry, Harriet."

"Sorry!" She spat it away. "Sorry . . . You're not even sorry. You're lying. All you do is lie. You lied to the Pastor, but I know you better than he does. Everyone else could tell . . . anyone could see Matthew Gurney was no good from the minute he walked into this town. A no-good—"

"You're talking about my child," Emmeline said. "I love him."

Harriet stopped and stared at her, open-mouthed.

Emmeline went to the mica rock and leaned against it. The sun, at her back, shone in Harriet's eyes, adding a squint to the face that was already shot through with rage.

"I thought you could never say another thing I wouldn't believe I was hearing."

"If I'm to be cut off from everyone," Emmeline said, "then why are you here?"

"We'll pay you to go." Harriet managed the words with some difficulty, as though there were hands around her neck.

"Pay me?"

"We'll all put money together. As much as we can. And we'll send you more when we're able. That must be what you want, unless it's purely to drive us mad."

"No."

"No what?"

"No, I don't want to cause you any more suffering, and I don't want money."

"Then what do you want?" It wasn't a question but a scream of desperation which traveled across the pond and echoed back through the moist June air. *"What do you want?"*

Emmeline thought carefully. She had to tell the precise truth.

"There's nothing I want," she finally said. "Everything I want is gone."

"Then why won't you go?"

"I can't."

"Yes, you can!" Screamed so loudly that several swallows took flight from a branch that was more than a hundred yards along the pond. *"You can! All you have to do is collect your things and go!"*

All she'd had to do to drown was swim out to the middle of the pond with her clothes on and let go of life, but she hadn't been able to do that either.

"I'm sorry," Emmeline said. "I can't."

With both hands Harriet grabbed hold of her own hair, pulling with all her might so that the skin on the sides of her forehead, just beneath the hair, turned dead white, though the rest of her face was flushed. Her eyelids began to twitch. She stood there pulling, the rest of her body motionless, for a time that seemed as long as all the time they'd known each other, which was the thirty-one years of Harriet's life. Then, slowly, Harriet let go. Her arms dropped. Her color became even. Her mouth returned to its usual set.

"You'll be sorry," she said. "You think that if you stay long enough, and behave, we'll forgive you, and everyone will start speaking to you again. But that won't happen. None of us will ever forgive you, and none of us will ever speak to you again. Ever."

Harriet turned and walked back across the road.

Eᴍᴍᴇʟɪɴᴇ lived in Fayette, in the house Matthew had built, until her death thirty-nine years later, but that was the last time she ever heard the sound of another woman's voice.

For some time she heard no voices at all. Yet survival was relatively easy. There was her garden. There were fish in the pond; chickens which gave eggs and more chickens; apple trees; more maples than she had buckets to tap. Men from the sawmill across the pond began to leave wood for her when her supply ran out, a kindness that continued over the years even when the men themselves changed.

If she was lonely, she preferred loneliness to the other possibilities. Just as the burn on her foot had healed, leaving a smooth white scar that could not tolerate exposure to the sun, so, under the smooth routine of her daily life, the events of the past repeatedly acted themselves out in her mind with a power that suggested it was just as well that she not be exposed to the loving concern of others.

Every few years she received in the mail a newspaper from some town . . . at first, during the years when the Civil War raged, from the deep South . . . then, after the War, New Orleans . . . then farther across the Southwest . . . in 1874, from California . . . and she was sure this was Matthew's way of telling her where he was.

She had little sense of passing time and no regret about aging; but once she found a small mirror in a packet of goods left for her in exchange for rag rugs she'd braided to be sold in the general store, and when she looked in the mirror, she saw that her hair was turning gray. She had a moment of panic—he wouldn't know her if he returned! She buried the mirror in a corner of her garden.

By this time it had become customary for one or two men from town to come by to see what she needed, and as she grew older, an increasing number of children were allowed to visit, perhaps to pass on a packet of tea from their parents. If there were women in town who forgave her, none ever risked her reputation by saying so, no matter how many years had gone by. Ten years ... twenty ... thirty ... thirty-five ... thirty-eight. ...

The winter of 1899 was a particularly severe one. Snowfall piled upon snowfall at the end of the dirt road where, by this time, only Emmeline was living. The men, absorbed in their own winter problems and family illnesses, didn't stop to think that if horses couldn't get down the road, neither could Emmeline get out of the house. She died of cold and starvation during a period when, for six or seven weeks, no one happened to come by.

Feelings so powerful that they could have come only from God lead some to those acts most strongly condemned by His word. It is useless to tell others that the Commandments are simple only for those who fail to see why they had to be set down.

**For the nearly
1 million readers who
read and loved MAGGIE—**

**LENA KENNEDY'S
heart-winning
wonder of a novel**

Kitty

**The enthralling
tale of an unde-
featable woman
who survived the
worst of times in London's slums
to win life's greatest treasures:
Love and a happy heart.**

**Look for KITTY—
Coming in November from
POCKET BOOKS
Wherever paperbacks are sold!**

184

Fine Fiction By
TOP WOMEN WRITERS

Novels that speak to women's needs,
desires, problems.
Novels about women who are sensitive,
talented, demanding and ready for anything.
Great new novels <u>by</u> women <u>for</u> women
who are not afraid to ask for what they want.

_____ 83531 WIFEY Judy Blume $2.75

_____ 44221 LOOKING FOR MR. GOODBAR
Judith Rossner $3.50

_____ 44100 ATTACHMENTS Judith Rossner $2.95

_____ 42169 BOOK OF COMMON PRAYER
Joan Didion $2.95

_____ 82147 THE GRAB Maria Katzenbach $2.25

_____ 82677 TIME IN ITS FLIGHT Susan Schaeffer $2.95

_____ 82814 PRAXIS Fay Weldon $2.50

_____ 43119 LOOSE CHANGE Sara Davidson $3.50

_____ 83019 LYING LOW Diane Johnson $2.95

_____ 83370 THE SHADOW KNOWS Diane Johnson $2.75

_____ 82834 SOME DO Jane DeLynn $2.50

POCKET BOOKS Department WFF
1230 Avenue of the Americas · New York, N.Y. 10020

Please send me the books I have checked above. I am enclosing $_____
(please add 50¢ to cover postage and handling for each order, N.Y.S. and N.Y.C.
residents please add appropriate sales tax). Send check or money order—no
cash or C.O.D.s please. Allow up to six weeks for delivery.

NAME_____

ADDRESS_____

CITY_____STATE/ZIP_____

Discover the writer women everywhere are talking about—

Janet Dailey

whose contemporary romances win millions of new readers every day.

_____	43668	TOUCH THE WIND	$2.95
_____	43665	THE ROGUE	$2.95
_____	43667	RIDE THE THUNDER	$2.95
_____	43666	NIGHTWAY	$2.95
_____	97634	JANET DAILEY BOX SET	$11.80

Janet Dailey—
She'll make you
believe in love again.

POCKET BOOKS
Department JDT
1230 Avenue of the Americas
New York, N.Y. 10020

Please send me the books I have checked above. I am enclosing $_____ (please add 50¢ to cover postage and handling, N.Y.S. and N.Y.C. residents please add appropriate sales tax). Send check or money order—no cash or C.O.D.s please. Allow six weeks for delivery.

NAME_____

ADDRESS_____

CITY_____STATE/ZIP_____

143